For God & Gold

Front cover image of Saint Peter's Basilica, Vatican City courtesy of Shutterstock.

Back cover image aerial view of Vatican City courtesy of Shutterstock.

Vatican City Map insert image courtesy of Wikimedia Commons licensed under the Creative Commons Attribution-Share Alike 4.0 International license.

This is a work of fiction. The characters, places, events, and dialog portrayed in this novel are the product of the author's imagination and are either fictitious or used factiously. Any resemblance to actual people living or dead, events, or locales is entirely coincidental.

"For God & Gold," by Douglas Clark. ISBN 978-1-63868-196-0 (softcover); 978-1-63868-197-7 (hardcover); 978-1-63868-198-4 (electronic).

Published 2025 by Virtualbookworm.com Publishing Inc., P.O. Box 9949, College Station, TX 77842, US.

BY DOUGLAS CLARK

BELFAST
TAKE FIVE
SHELL GAME
EVERMORE
CRITICAL MASS
FAULT LINES
PROVOKE THE DEVIL
THE IRISH SPY
ENDGAME
HUNTING ODESSA
THE AMERICAN SPY
HAVANA
MOSCOW WINTER
SOUTHLAND NOIR
FIRE IN THE HOLE
FOR GOD & GOLD

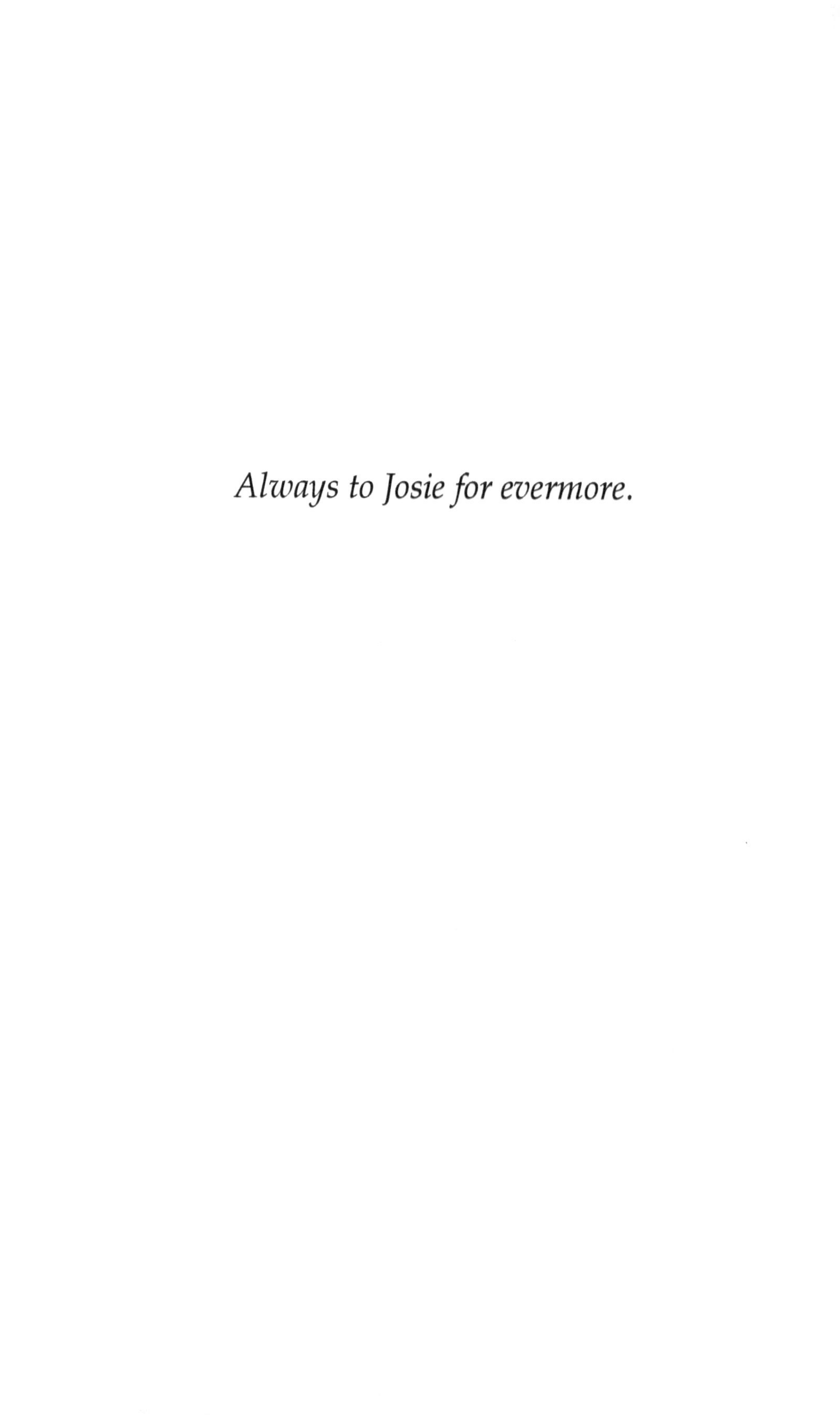

Always to Josie for evermore.

For God & Gold

A Novel

Douglas Clark

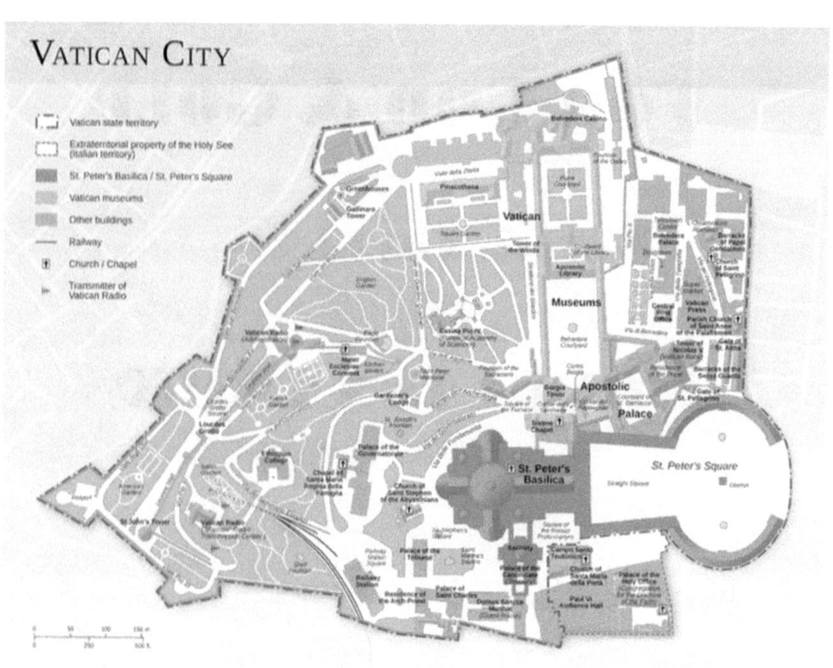
VATICAN CITY
Vatican state territory
Extraterritorial property of the Holy See (Italian territory)
St. Peter's Basilica / St. Peter's Square
Vatican museums
Other buildings
Railway
Church / Chapel
Transmitter of Vatican Radio
Vatican
Museums
Apostolic
Palace
St. Peter's Basilica
St. Peter's Square
Pinacotheca

CHAPTER 1

Bevagna, Umbria, Italy | December 1978

On a sunny day in mid-December, the small medieval Umbrian town of Bevagna was quiet as usual. Situated at the top of the highest point within the walls surrounding the village stood the 13th century church of Church of San Francesco assessable by a flight of stairs. The church bells tolled at midday. Inside a priest celebrated a requiem mass. The modest casket resting on a catafalque before the altar held the remains of an elderly Roman Catholic priest. A former resident of Bevagna, Monsignor Vittorio Scarpelli left over fifty years ago to attend seminary then to spend his life in service at the Vatican in Rome.

The elderly local priest conducting the mass was assisted by two altar boys. The pews were entirely empty of congregants. The priest and altar boys represented the only attendees to the service. Monsignor Scarpelli had no living relatives. Scarpelli having served his entire career in Rome, the elderly priest saying mass constituted Scarpelli's only personal relationship with Bevagna. The final stages of cancer brought Scarpelli back for interment in his place of birth. The older priest knew Scarpelli from a young age when attending seminary together before pursuing different ecclesiastical careers.

They remained in touch over the years largely through correspondence. The last time seeing each other was when Scarpelli visited Bavagna a month before his death. A profoundly sad time. Not only did Scarpelli share his medical condition and provide funds to arrange for returning his remains for burial in Bevagna, but he also requested something his old friend would find uncomfortable. Scarpelli asked him to hear his final confession.

Not a confession to unburden a reciting of typical transgressions. This was about a disturbing act of moral complexity that was to be fulfilled following his death. Yet Scarpelli would not burden his friend by equally embroiling him in this dilemma of conscience. His friend would undoubtedly advise a course of repentance that Scarpelli had already rejected. The seal of the confessional bound a priest to absolute confidentiality. What Scarpelli had to confess would create in his friend the same conflict of conscience that Scarpelli was suffering. Acting on a matter of conscience would commit a conflicting grave sin with whichever course of action he chose. He therefore made his confession purposely vague. Hardly a proper confession of the whole truth but a form of contrition that might allow him to die with a measure of peace.

Scarpelli began his confession, "Bless me, Father, for I have sinned. My last confession was three months ago. Yet I have never related the circumstances of a particularly grave sin until today. Facing my imminent death, I must expunge a terrible burden that I have concealed for years. I have set in motion the revelation of certain information that I swore to conceal upon the threat of excommunication. Yet I contrived to commit this act to address what I determined as a higher spiritual responsibility. A responsibility to call out a conspiracy of evil that is coursing through the Vatican. An evil that has dire implications for the Holy See.

"I choose not to be more specific to avoid encumbering you as my confessor with a similar intractable conflict of conscience. What I have done defies a sworn oath affecting the Holy See. However, I firmly believe that in the eyes of God, He will look on my behavior with understanding and compassion. My actions will revealing certain knowledge by the Vatican of illicit activities that run counter to the fundamental mission of the Church. My death will serve to bring a merciful end to the torment of possessing information with which I must remain silent."

His friend listened without interruption for several moments before responding. "You understand, Father, that I cannot grant absolution by the Sacrament of Penance without understanding the nature of the sin."

Scarpelli replied, "Of course. I understand completely, my old friend. Yet my conscience still feels strangely at ease by at least relating to you my inner conflict. Perhaps through telling you of my distress God will hear me and either grant His absolution or deliver what He deems as appropriate judgement upon my soul. You may never know what I have set in motion. Better that way. Thank you for hearing my imperfect confession, Father." Scarpelli made the sign of the cross. "Nothing more I can say. God bless you for being my friend, Edgardo."

Monsignor Scarpelli returned by train to his spartan apartment in Rome. With instructions prepared and devoting his remaining days to prayer, he died peacefully in his sleep within a few weeks.

†

Monsignor Vittorio Scarpelli resigned his position as Assistant Archivist of the Vatican Secret Archive just a few months prior to his death. He spent three decades in the ultra-secure recesses of what amounts to a concrete bunker within the Vatican at the Cortile del Belvedere adjacent to the Vatican Library. The material contained within the Vatican Secret Archive are the holdings of documents deemed the pope's personal property, not those of any department of the Roman Curia, the governing body of the Holy See.

The Curia consists of administrative departments by which the pontiff governs with absolute authority the Holy See representing the ecclesiastical jurisdiction over the Roman Catholic Church. That authority also includes sovereignty over the city-state known as Vatican City. The Holy See, as the supreme governing body of the Roman Catholic Church worldwide, is considered a sovereign entity under international law.

The Vatican Secret Archive contains classified materials not available to outsiders or even Vatican ecclesiastical staff without specific authorization of the reigning pontiff. Furthermore, access to material from any former pontificate is denied for 75 years after the close of a pope's reign.

In his final days, Scarpelli contemplated the meaning of his imminent death in this year of so much turmoil and tragedy for the Roman Catholic Church. Pope Paul VI died on 6 August after a pontificate stretching fifteen years. Then the unexpected election of the Patriarch of Venice Cardinal Albino Luciani, was followed by his death just thirty-three days under circumstances surrounded by misinformation, mystery, and conspiracy rumors of foul play. 1978 became the year of three popes with the death of two popes followed by the election of Polish Cardinal Karol Józef Wojtyła taking the name John Paul II. John Paul's election as the first non-Italian pope since the 16th century only added to the unprecedented circumstances within the Vatican.

The secrets Scarpelli intended to release perhaps could be beneficial in cleansing the Vatican of unholy corruption. At least Pope Paul VI who suffered so greatly in the last months of his papacy would not have to face increased personal attacks. Many of Pope Paul's failures during his fifteen-year pontificate contributed to embroiling the Vatican bank in an international financial scandal that continued growing.

†

Emma Nicoletti was at heart an investigative journalist. Someone not satisfied with merely reporting news but seeking to discover in-depth details sufficient to form a larger picture of newsworthy events. Nicoletti's parents were academics prior to WWII. The family survived by fighting with Italian partisans against the invading Nazis after Mussolini was deposed in 1943. That year she was just sixteen. Armed with a revolver, she carried messages for the Italian Resistance. Her father was killed by the retreating

Nazis in late 1944. Her mother survived the war and returned to teaching at the University of Bologna. Only eighteen when the war ended, Emma wanted desperately to leave the chaos of post-war Italy. Instead of becoming a student at the University of Bologna, her mother arranged for her to study in New York.

Her parents became close with an American OSS agent that worked closely with their partisan group during the war. The American was a New Yorker. Emma already spoke passable English because of her parents' insistence that it was necessary for a professional career. With her mother's and the American's help, she secured admission to the Columbia School of Journalism. The American and his wife sponsored her to live with them while attending Columbia until her graduation in 1950.

Returning to Italy, she secured a position with Italy's largest newspaper *Corriere della Sera* headquartered in Milan. A representative newspaper of the moderate bourgeoisie, *Corriere della Sera* was considered politically center-right-leaning. It took ten years of toiling at conventional reporting before she was able to convince the editor to allow her to pursue more complex stories with broader interest.

Investigative journalism required skills in research. How to draw information from interviewing people. How to connect a piece of information to a new line of inquiry? What sources to use? How to take vast amounts of information and begin shaping a larger picture? How best to obtain corroboration? A willingness to delve into complex subjects to accurately understand in sufficient depth to communicate with readers. It took diligence, concentration, patience, and most of all an intellect, challenged by the hunt for truth. She served enough time on reporting events to add editorial conclusions to her pieces that clearly demonstrated exceptional skills. Eventually her editor selected her to cover stories requiring deeper serialized treatment in successive articles as the story broadened.

Her current position was as a senior reporter with *Il Sole 24 Ore*, a daily broadsheet newspaper also headquartered in Milan. Established in 1965, by 1978 *Il Sole 24 Ore* was regarded as the leading financial newspaper in Italy for its objective reporting.

She came to *Il Sole 24 Ore* in 1975 as the disintegrating financial empire of Italian financier Michele Sindona began making headlines in Italy and the United States. While financial affairs were not Nicoletti's specialty, her articles covering Sindona while at *Corriere della Sera* brought her to the attention of the managing editor of *Il Sole 24 Ore.* Nicoletti's writing explained obscure financial business terms in concise language understandable to the average reader. Her pieces therefore created greater interest than otherwise dry business reporting. Events surrounding Michele Sindona engendered wider interest beyond reporting of financial wrongdoing. Nicoletti's reporting delving into the complexities of Sindona's international business enterprises showed a remarkable talent for explaining complex international finance using offshore tax havens.

Within the breaking scandal of Michele Sindona there surfaced unexplained financial involvement of the Vatican's *Istituto per le Opere di Religione,* in English the *Institute for the Works of Religion,* or simply the IOR. Popularly called the Vatican Bank, the IOR did not operate as a conventional bank, neither retail, commercial, nor investment. It was a hybrid creation that reported directly to the pontiff in a closed environment of secrecy that went beyond the inherent general secrecy of the Vatican.

Nicoletti identified Sindona's strong personal ties to Pope Paul VI. Her sources also uncovered business associations between Sindona and Banco Ambrosiano Chairman Roberto Calvi. Those sources further revealed extensive business connections between the Vatican Bank and Banco Ambrosiano. That association would play prominently in extending the financial scandal of Italian banking by several years.

Ownership of *Corriere della Sera* had recently been acquired by Angelo Rizzoli, founder of the largest publishing empire in Italy. The investment became an immediate financial disaster. Substantial loans were necessary to sustain *Corriere della Sera.* The large state-owned banks refused to loan money resulting from lack of support by *Corriere* for the governing Christian Democrat coalition of Italy. Rizzoli was saved by loans provided by Banco Ambrosiano, a prominent private bank.

At the time, Nicoletti knew nothing of the connection between her employer *Corriere della Sera* and Banco Ambrosiano. She knew only that Ambrosiano was identified with both Michele Sindona and the Vatican Bank thereby it became a line of inquiry she began developing. Later she would find out more about Banco Ambrosiano's bailout. That would prove another subset of the widening financial scandal in which Banco Ambrosiano would figure prominently. For the new owner of *Corriere della Sera,* Nicoletti's reporting critical of the Vatican ran counter to the business interests of the newspaper. Attempts by the managing editor for her to avoid reporting on the newspaper's own financial difficulties further aggravated her sense of journalistic freedom.

Nicoletti's incisive reporting on the implications of the Sindona financial empire collapse impacting the economy of Italy however was enough to impress the managing editor of *Il Sole 24 Ore.* Accusing *Corriere* of practicing self-censorship she readily accepted a job offer from *Il Sole 24 Ore* to jump ship.

As a coauthor of a well-researched exposé on the Vatican Ratlines published in 1962, she had firmly established her investigative journalistic credentials. Her work did not reflect any political bias. Nor was any subject out of bounds. That included the Vatican. Her book viciously savaged Pope Pius XII for condoning Roman Catholic priests actively assisting World War Two war criminals by facilitating their escape to South America. Emma Nicoletti followed the facts wherever they led. Vatican silence and absurd justifications by apologists about the despicable episode incensed her sense of injustice. She was raised Catholic however this was not a matter of religion. Her condemnation was toward the Vatican. A tiny sovereign state ruled by an absolute monarch that had no business in interfering with secular events. Priests were not entitled to give absolution for mass murderers by aiding in avoidance of justice.

Nicoletti was at her office desk when the mailroom cart attendant deposited several pieces of mail in her inbox. One envelope caught her attention. The return address read from a law firm in Lugano, Switzerland. She did not recognize the name of the firm. Inside were two letters. She read the one from the lawyer first.

Heffelfinger Mischler & Andrist
Lugano, Switzerland

27 February1979
To: Signora Emma Nicoletti:
Subject: Estate of the late Monsignor Vittorio Scarpelli

Dear Signora Nicoletti:

As estate executor, I wish to inform you of the passing of Monsignor Vittorio Scarpelli in December of last year. Father Scarpelli was interred in his place of birth in the town of Bavagna, Umbria. Father Scarpelli spent his entire life in service to the Holy See and with no living family he engaged our law firm to administer his modest estate. I understand he did not know you personally but wished to bequeath to you a body of materials that he believed you would find useful in your professional work. I am not familiar with the nature of these materials, however Father Scarpelli felt them of sufficient value that he sequestered them in the custody of the private Swiss bank Societe Generale located here in Lugano on Viale Stefano Franscini 11.

The documents are held at the bank under your name. Attached is a sealed letter from Father Scarpelli that will provide you with the necessary instructions and account number to retrieve those materials held within the bank's vault. I have also included a letter of introduction to the bank should any issue arise with respect to the disposition of said materials in their custody.

Should you require further assistance in this matter, please do not hesitate to contact me.

Yours sincerely,

Gianantonio Volpi

Gianantonio Volpi
Attorney at Law

For an investigative journalist the lawyer's letter was mysteriously intriguing. Reading the first paragraph of Monsignor Scarpelli's letter, her jaw dropped.

Dear Signora Nicoletti,

I am sure you are wondering what this is about. I chose to bequeath to you my only possessions of value. Perhaps tainted possessions that were not mine to give away, yet nonetheless of value to expose truth in the pursuit of justice. That it involves the Holy See of the Roman Catholic Church the material I am providing carries much greater moral meaning than the secular misdeeds that it exposes. Misdeeds by the Vatican Institute for the Works of Religion, the IOR, commonly known as the Vatican Bank. Yet as you will find within this store of documents, the misdeeds go beyond those administering the Vatican Bank. Misdeeds suggesting a more pervasive cancer permeating the Holy See for at least a decade.

As you probably know the Institute for the Works of Religion functions apart from governance by the Roman Curia as does the other major financial institution of the Holy See, the Administration of the Patrimony of the Apostolic See. The APSA is governed under the dicastery of the Secretariat of the Economy and serves as the treasury and central bank of Vatican City and the Holy See. The APSA is the successor dicastery of the Roman Curia created by Pope Pius XI in 1929 to manage the £750 million lire in cash and £1,000 million lire in 5% Italian government bonds transferred to the Holy See as financial compensation for the loss of Papal States sixty years earlier with the unification of Italy. This windfall salvaged the Holy See from near poverty status by providing funds sufficient to embark on investment with sustaining revenue.

Pope Pius XII chose to remain in close control of secular affairs with the establishment of the Vatican as a sovereign city state. Before becoming pontiff, Eugenio Pacelli was Cardinal Secretary of State to Pope Pius XI. As Pius XII, he chose to act as his own secretary of state. With respect to financial affairs, he chose to exert increased control by creating the IOR in 1942 as the principal financial institution responsible to the pontiff directly. The IOR is not subject to oversight or even audit by the Curia as the administrative body of the Holy See. It produces no financial reports even for internal distribution. While the Vatican operates with unusual secrecy in every respect, the IOR added another layer of impenetrable secrecy. The IOR is therefore more comparable to what are considered tax havens such as those that exist in the Bahamas, Cayman Islands, Lichtenstein, Luxemburg, and even Swiss banking. Locations that levy no taxes on profits from outside their sovereignty, while providing comprehensive secrecy from reporting of corporate ownership or financial transactions.

I fear I am preaching to the choir. You undoubtedly possess a broad working knowledge of international finance given your journalistic reporting. Forgive the ramblings of a dying old man.

It is worth noting that I spent the last thirty years of my ecclesiastical career as the assistant director of the Vatican Secret Archive. Some confuse this with the Vatican Library. As with the financial institutions of the Vatican, there again exists the same critical distinction between the Vatican Library and the Vatican Secret Archive.

The holdings in the Secret Archive are considered the pope's personal property, distinct from the Roman Curia or the Holy See. Access to the Vatican Secret Archive is controlled directly by the sitting pontiff. Furthermore, requests for access to materials even with papal consent are predominantly declined until after 75 years of the reign of a prior pontiff. I cite this only to explain just how documents relegated to the Secret Archive become inaccessible even to ecclesiastical princes of the Church. This is the exclusive repository of documents that the pope alone deems necessary to bury.

Those documents secured in the Swiss bank vault were stolen by me over the last decade. A violation punishable by excommunication. However, I embarked on this because I could not remain a willing participant in such a vast crime committed not only by an institution within the Holy See, but with the knowledge of two of the recent Vicars of Christ. Namely Pope Paul VI and Pope John Paul II. Within the Roman Catholic Church, the pope is considered the

Vicar of Christ and speaks for Jesus Christ and represents God on Earth. To engage in such base acts of sin resulting in untold damage to perhaps millions of people is an affront to every Catholic and to those that have dedicated their lives in the service of the Lord.

Which sacred oath do I honor? Uncertainty as to what to do in my position with exposure to incriminating evidence drove me to remove incriminating documents as my way of searching for truth. Was there substance to allegations of the IOR partnering with those named in the international scandal? Why does the Holy See choose to remain largely silent? I prayed for divine guidance. My diagnosis with terminal cancer I believe to be God's answer to my moral dilemma. I shall expose the evil lurking within the Vatican and death shall save me from excommunication and the denial of the sacraments. Please forgive my philosophizing rationalizations.

I chose you as my instrument because of your objective journalistic efforts to pursue the truth. The documents relate to how the Vatican in the form of the IOR became a willing participant in financial crimes including outright theft, bribery, tax evasion, currency manipulation, and money laundering of illicit funds from organized criminal activity. It does not paint a comprehensive picture. It instead provides critical pieces of information to add to the body of work of those in journalism and law enforcement investigating these crimes with tenacles spreading across the globe.

You came to mind as someone to entrust with my trove of documents for another reason.

Your earlier published book condemning of the Vatican Ratline for aiding in the escape of war criminals from justice following World War Two made you a voice for truth. That era of grave moral error by Pope Pius XII and other clergy held a special interest for me as it did for you. Like you, I was a researcher. The archetypical archivist. Assisting mass murderers to avoid justice profoundly troubled me. It did so since in my professional capacity my superior, the Archivist of the Vatican Secret Archive, played an instrumental role in facilitating the ratlines in the years following the war.

I speak of Archbishop Marcello Tagliente. His name appears in certain documents included in the documents cache. Unfortunately, how he might be related to the functioning of the IOR is not clear. Yet I will provide you with information that is likely not known beyond the walls of the Vatican and only whispered by a few within its walls. Archbishop Tagliente as the Archivist of the Vatican Secret Archive is largely a cover. His principal function is directing the Vatican secret services. The secret intelligence service known as Santa Alleanza was created five centuries ago and the more modern creation of the counterintelligence service Sodalitium Pianum in 1913 before the Great War.

Tagliente was ordained in 1939. Pope Pius XII personally installed Tagliente into the Vatican Secretariat of State. Here Tagliente worked closely with Monsignor Giovanni Montini, the future Pope Paul VI. It is from this early start that Father Tagliente became indoctrinated into the Vatican intelligence service. Scant records existing as to Tagliente's professional history is a tribute to his ability to remain in the shadows for decades.

To add a further layer of secrecy to these unspoken Vatican intelligence organizations, Pope Pius XII installed Cardinal Gideon Fumasoni-Biondi as head of Santa Alleanza. However, the conspiratorial Pius XII made Monsignor Tagliente the functional chief while serving as assistant director of the Vatican Secret Archive as cover in 1956. The Vatican secret services suspended operations under John XXIII's short five-year pontificate. Paul VI resurrected Tagliente's clandestine role while the Pope's secretary served the official role as head of Santa Alleanza. With Pope John Paul II, Archbishop Tagliente continues to direct the Vatican intelligence services, with the visible recognized head currently being Archbishop Luigi Poggi.

Why is this of importance? It is my belief that there is far more to the Vatican's participation in these financial misadventures than just independent actions of the president of the IOR, Bishop Paul Marcinkus. That Marcinkus remains in place is inexplicable except as perhaps cover. As for Archbishop Tagliente, his elevation to archbishop occurred only after my leaving the Vatican and part of the new pontiff's important appointments. That means that Pope John Paul II recognizes the value of Archbishop Tagliente and his likely continuing role heading the Vatican secret services. You will find in your research of Archbishop Tagliente that he holds a degree in economics and a doctorate in international law. Bishop Marcinkus curiously has no background in banking or even finance.

Perhaps the new pope wants Tagliente to expand his scope of secret activities.

I have insufficient time remaining to pursue these mysteries further. I hope my contributions will be of use. Good hunting, Signora Nicolette. May God be with you.

Monsignor Vittorio Scarpelli
Fr V Scarpelli

Emma Nicoletti leaned back in her office chair absorbing what she had just read. She knew full well the function of Vatican Secret Archive. This was the repository of the holiest of holies. More accurately the darkest secrets that the Roman Catholic Church wished to conceal indefinitely. If this priest was truly the assistant archivist, what he stole might be a journalistic treasure trove.

From her desk, she extracted a map of Italy. Lugano, Switzerland was right on the border with Italy fifty kilometers northwest of Como, only eighty kilometers from Milan.

To her editor, she pleaded the need to take a couple of days off for personal reasons. Nothing on her desk that could not wait. She telephoned the Swiss lawyer and arranged a morning appointment for the next day. Enough time to meet with the lawyer then pay a visit to the Swiss bank. Anticipation demanded examining the documents immediately. Should the documents live up to Scarpelli's hype, she needed to assess the quality of the material. Best to do that in the security of the Swiss bank.

CHAPTER 2

Lugano, Switzerland & Milan, Italy | February 1979

Nicoletti presented herself at the Societe Generale bank on Viale Stefano Franscini. Housed in a nondescript building with a tiled roof that looked nothing like a bank, the only identification was a brass nameplate next to large double wooden doors.

Access proved an efficient process. After being situated in a small room, an attendant delivered a large safety deposit box on a wheeled cart.

"You will not be disturbed until you are finished, Signora. Take as long as necessary. When you are done, simply lift the telephone receiver and you will be connected with a bank employee."

Nicoletti lifted back the lid of the metal box. Inside was a stack of papers several inches deep. She lifted out a handful, laying them on the conference table. She sat down and began examining each document for subject, recipient, and author.

Two hours passed. She abandoned her cursory manner of review after looking at the first couple of documents. Each document rivetted her complete attention, even rereading to grasp how this secret information fit within the known contours of continuing public reporting on the Italian Banking Scandal. This was not just a wholesale cache of unrelated documents. By the nature of the content she was reading, Father Scarpelli was judicious in his editing. Each document conveyed substantive information of specific interest. Obviously Scarpelli followed the public revelations as the international financial scandal first broke years earlier in 1974 with the spectacular failure of Franklin National Bank of Long Island, New York. Italian banker Michele Sindona purchased the U.S. bank just two years earlier. From that beginning the scandal would eventually expand to envelop another Italian banker Roberto Calvi and his prominent Italian private bank Banco Ambrosiano. Like a serialized disaster, the scandal grew as holdings within the troubled financial empires of first Sindona then Calvi repeatedly made the news involving some questionable revelation of mismanagement involving great sums of money.

Drained by the intensity of her reading, Nicoletti sat back from the stack of documents before her. By now she could gauge something of Scarpelli's methodology as he followed the breaking news stories spanning years. The stack of papers in the bank vault appeared organized by date starting with the oldest on top to the latest at the bottom. The secret documents he chose to remove from the Vatican Archive provided details previous unpublished. Each document Scarpelli selected revealed information implicating Vatican culpability. Nicoletti understood that was the principal reason for Scarpelli to commit such an extreme act of sacred transgression. This was not to explain an economic disaster facing Italy but to expose the misdeeds of those within the Vatican.

Having only examined a portion of the documents, Nicoletti already found enough information to begin several new avenues of investigation. Scarpelli's material provided a rare glimpse inside the Vatican. Not only within the unknowns of the Vatican Bank, but the nature of the materials relegated to the Vatican Secret Archive. Sensitive enough to remain forever buried. With just the oldest documents reviewed, Pope Paul VI is exposed as personally responsible for promoting Italian banker Michele Sindona to become a trusted consultant into the financial affairs of the Vatican Bank.

Nicoletti needed time to review the material. Unlimited time. Time to fit this newly discovered information into the reported arch of the continuing story spanning years. She could also use some expert help. That meant Gabriel Eisenberg. The Jewish French American fellow journalist with whom she collaborated in writing their acclaimed book *Ratlines* published in 1963. They regularly kept in touch. Both were presently reporting on this persistent international financial scandal. The scandal continued to grow with new revelations coming out of the seemingly dysfunctional Italian banking system.

Researching and writing *Ratlines* profoundly affected both of them. Eisenberg lost family in the Holocaust. For Nicoletti, raised Catholic, discovery of priests and even prelates expending considerable efforts to aid escaping mass murderers was unconscionable. With the Vatican exposed as a party to financial crimes involving millions, it became just another corrupt secular institution. As to the Vatican's spiritual importance, that no longer held for her any personal relevance.

Nicoletti called for the attendant. "I am through for the day. However, I expect to return tomorrow. Will that be satisfactory?"

The young man replied, "Most certainly, Signora."

With that she left the bank in a taxi to return to the law office to consult with Signore Volpi.

"I just left Societe Generale after examining the documents Father Scarpelli bequeathed to me. I now understand why he chose me as the beneficiary. He must have discovered that I am researching a particular period in the history of the Roman Catholic Church. Before coming to Lugano, I researched Father Scarpelli's background. Decades of service in the Vatican Library. Apparently an historian in his own right. Something of an expert on the period I am researching according to an academic colleague of mine that knew of him.

"The materials Father Scarpelli left for me is his life's research work. His life cut short before he could proceed further. In his letter he was kind enough to explain that he respected my scholarship. Felt his life's work would continue as opposed to becoming just archival material within a library.

"I explain all this to you, Signore Volpi only to convey the historical value of these documents. Some are quite old. Obviously acquired by Father Scarpelli with great effort over many years. It will take extensive study to make use of so much material. The originals must remain in a secure location. Specifically, the bank vault. Therefore, to begin further research work I need to make copies from which to work from or make duplicates for other scholars' opinion."

Volpi asked, "How many documents are involved?"

"A great many. Probably hundreds. A stack about this high," she said indicating with her hand the height of the stack.

The surprised Volpi said, "Good heavens. A task of considerable proportions, Signora Nicoletti."

"Would the bank have a xerographic copier that I could use?"

"I can certainly inquiry."

"If they could place a copier at my disposal, I will do the copying myself."

Volpi nodded and placed a call. Holding his hand over the receiver, he said to Nicoletti, "The bank can provide you access to such a copying machine. When may I say you will arrive?"

"Tomorrow morning when they first open."

Returning to her hotel, Nicoletti placed a call to Brooklyn, New York. With the six-hour time difference, it was midday in New York.

The call to the *New York Times* was directed to the desk of Gabriel Eisenberg. "Gabe, this is Emma," she said in accented yet fluent English.

"Hello, Emma. How are things in Milan?"

"Most interesting. I'm calling from Lugano, Switzerland."

Like her, Eisenberg followed and wrote about the Italian financial scandal starting from the headline-making failure of Franklin National Bank, at the time the largest bank failure in the history of the United States. After telling him of the events that led to Father Scarpelli's stash of secret Vatican documents, she read Scarpelli's letter to Eisenberg.

"This Archbishop Tagliente sounds like a person of interest."

Nicoletti said. "Someone to research when I get back to Milan. Right now, it's about the documents. I began examining them today at a Swiss private bank, Societe Generale. This is extraordinary material, Gabe. Directly exposes complicity of the Vatican Bank in relationship with Michele Sindona and Roberto Calvi's Banco Ambrosiano from what I already looked at."

"New material you say? This priest stole them from the Vatican Secret Archive?"

"That's right. Not only that but he was also judicious in what he stole. Looks as if every document holds some piece of relevant information associated with Vatican Bank involvement. Haven't yet examined every one of the hundreds of pages. Returning to the bank tomorrow to begin making photocopies. We can then work from these while the originals remain secure in the bank's vault."

"We?"

"Of course, Gabe. I need your help. We're both working on the same storyline. Need your advice on how we should use this information. Too much for me to tackle alone so I'm willing to share with someone I completely trust. I need you to come to Milan for a week or two, Gabe. This is explosive material. Enough that it could carry some risk."

"Risk? You mean personal risk?"

"Yes. Physical risk, Gabe. Italy has become a violent place. Not just the terrorist attacks by the *Red Brigades*, but killings associated with this banking scandals. A crime reporter murdered in Palermo. Probably his reporting on the Sicilian Mafia struggle but there are accusations that Michele Sindona may have been laundering money for the Sicilian Mafia. Sindona is Sicilian with a colorful checkered past that even includes known connections with the Mafia during the war years.

"Then the murder of Milan prosecuting magistrate Emilio Alessandrini just weeks ago who was investigating Roberto Calvi and Banco Ambrosiano. We need to proceed cautiously."

"Okay. I understand. How are you going to secretly get copies made?"

"They are still in the Swiss bank vault under an account in my name. Tomorrow I will begin making copies with a xerox copy machine provided by the bank. We can work with these photocopies while the originals remain secure in the bank vault. We need to map out how to proceed. Make additional photocopies so you can have a set to take back to New York. This will take time to integrate the material into what is already known. Opens all sorts of new lines of investigation. We can attack this story from both sides of the Atlantic. Can you come to Milan, Gabe?"

"Let me check my schedule and get back to you tomorrow."

"Okay. Call me at the Hotel International au Lac in Lugano tomorrow night no matter how late. Please come, Gabe. This is too big to tackle by myself. Perhaps when the story concludes we can write another book."

Eisenberg replied, "Vatican doings always make for good copy. They certainly dominated international headlines last year with the deaths of two popes. The lingering mystery of the death of John Paul I after only a month as pope is fostering all sorts of conspiracy theories. Comingled now with the allegations of financial misdeeds of the Vatican Bank. The name of the American Bishop Paul Marcinkus as the head of the IOR is suddenly added to the mix of colorful characters."

Nicoletti said, "And to that the election of the first pope in hundreds of years that is not Italian. The new Polish Pope John Paul II however is reverting in kind to his predecessor Italian pontiffs. Evoking the typical Vatican response to bad publicity by remaining silent. Surviving for two millennia reinforces the strategy of keeping silent indefinitely until scandal passes into history."

†

Eisenberg telephoned her the next evening. "I have made arrangements to join in your new project, Emma. But the best I can arrange for coming to Milan is not until April. Too many irons in the fire with staff shortages of those taking spring vacations to avoid the summer heat. I've already put in for four weeks of vacation. Spending it in Italy and seeing you sounds wonderful? I've booked tickets to arrive in Milan Thursday April 5 on American flight 198 arriving 9:05am."

Nicoletti became acquainted with Gabriel Eisenberg's wife who was a fellow journalism student at Columbia and Nicoletti's best friend before meeting Eisenberg. Regrettably, she died prematurely of a brain tumor in 1960 leaving two children Joshua and Sarah. Adults now call Nicoletti Auntie Emma. Nicoletti remained close to the family which led to collaboration with Eisenberg on their coauthored book *Ratlines* published in 1963.

"That's great, Gabe. I'm returning to Milan tomorrow morning. I made copies today of the entire cache of almost 400 documents. This is rich material, Gabe. Couldn't be timelier. The demise of Michele Sindona might be history but the uncertainty surrounding Banco Ambrosiano is not over. Roberto Calvi and Bishop Paul Marcinkus still have a final act to play out. With this new material the Vatican will have as you say in English, a *shit fit.*

"Over the weeks until you arrive, I'll try to catalog the documents to give us a start on how this works into the larger narrative. I'm taking the copies back to Milan. The originals remain in the Swiss bank."

"Good thinking, Emma. What do you make of Monsignor Scarpelli's reference to this Archbishop Tagliente going back to the Vatican ratline years? I don't recall his name coming up in any context. Do you?"

"No. Never even heard his name before Scarpelli's reference. Archivist of the Vatican Secret Archive is an obscure position. If Scarpelli is correct and Tagliente functionally heads the Vatican secret services going back to Pius XII, an official position as Archivist of the Vatican Secret Archive makes a perfect cover."

Eisenberg said, "What do you know about the Vatican secret services? And for that matter the Vatican Secret Archive? How is that different from the Vatican Library?"

"I know very little about the Vatican secret service. Not something that is spoken about openly. Most prelates even deny that such an institution exists. Yet periodically the references to Santa Alleanza, Holy Alliance in English, appears in the historical record. All I know is that it originated in the 16th century. Pius V created a group of spies to kill Elizabeth I of England and bring Scottish Catholic Mary Stuart to the throne. I know nothing about it surviving for centuries into the 20th century."

Eisenberg said, "If Monsignor Scarpelli is correct about this prelate Tagliente's involvement in the ratlines, it explains a lot. Neither of us could explain how German Bishop Hudal and the Bosnian Croat Croatian priest Draganović managed the complex logistics necessary to get so many war criminals to South America. That Tagliente continues to secretly run a Vatican spy service is a remarkable revelation."

Nicoletti added, "Archivist of the Vatican Secret Archive is a seemingly obscure position. The Archive is distinct from the Vatican Library. The materials held there are considered the personal property of the pontiff. Not subject to the administrative body of the Vatican the Roman Curia. If the Holy Alliance continues to this day as a secret service, it undoubtedly must report directly to the pope. That also holds true for the Vatican Bank. It reports only to the pontiff not through the Curia."

Eisenberg said, "The Vatican Bank also reports only to the pontiff. What if all three of these Vatican institutions are connected in some way? Seems we might consider a second line of research."

"What do you mean?"

"We of course began by integrating the Scarpelli material with the published material on the financial scandal to help uncover the extent of Vatican involvement. Not as a victim but as a willing coconspirator of the illicit activities of Sindona and Calvi. But we should also begin investigating whether the Holy Alliance functions as an intelligence agency to this day. Were they instrumental in the ratlines? What about other secret involvements during the 20th century?"

Nicoletti replied, "I agree. I will start by researching Archbishop Tagliente in greater depth. If Scarpelli is correct and Tagliente heads the Vatican secret service, then it means that the new pontiff perhaps embraces its use as did Pius XII and Paul VI. What about during the short reign of John XXIII? Then along comes

John Paul II who elevates Bishop Tagliente to archbishop. Perhaps that holds greater significance to current events."

†

Nicoletti greeted Gabriel Eisenberg's arrival at Milan Airport. Although they spoke and wrote regularly, they had not seen each other since Nicoletti visited New York three years ago.

As he stepped into the terminal at his arrival gate, Nicoletti rushed to embrace him. "So good to see you, Gabe. Thank you for coming."

"Wonderful seeing you, Emma. Excited about this find of yours. Do you still feel the documents are everything you thought?"

"Absolutely. Much of the information uncovered by Father Scarpelli needs further research to gain corroboration where possible but clearly condemning of the Vatican Bank when put together. I'll let you judge for yourself."

Once in Nicoletti's car and leaving the airport, she said, "On another note, I've spent considerable effort on researching Archbishop Marcello Tagliente. Interesting background. His family is among those considered the *Black Nobility*. Lay persons of influence that closely support the Roman Catholic Church. Generations that go back to the times of the Papal States. The Tagliente family were close to the family of Pope Pius XII. The pope actually attended Tagliente's ordination. This followed with Tagliente's immediate appointment to serve in the Vatican Secretariat of State office."

"Good career move. Who you know counts."

"No doubt. Tagliente became an assistant to Monsignor Giovanni Montini, the future Pope Paul VI. Here's another interesting aspect of Tagliente's background. He holds a degree in economics and a doctorate in international law. Academic credentials useful for someone close to the pope that understands the complexities of what is being reported in this never-ending banking scandal."

Eisenberg added. "An equally important background if in fact he really directs a modern incarnation of the Vatican's Holy

Alliance. Could explain how the post-war Vatican ratlines logistics functioned so successfully. If the Vatican was operating a secret intelligence service, they would have the resources to secretly move war criminals escaping justice when agencies of western governments like the U.S. Army's CIC were seeking to arrest them. The Holy Alliance could secretly even have offered help to the Americans as part of their *Operation Paper Clip* to bring Nazis to the West with the new adversary now the Soviet Union. If things had publicly gone wrong, the U.S. could shift blame to the Vatican. Perhaps there's another story there if we could prove involvement of the Vatican secret service. By extension that might lead directly to Pius XII refuting Vatican claims that the ratlines were the work solely of rogue clerics."

Nicoletti said, "Here's another observation. An early mentor to Tagliente was a politically far-right Portuguese cardinal named Manuel Gonçalves. Gonçalves embraced the Portuguese *Ditadura Nacional,* the National Dictatorship, formed after the coup d'état of 1926 against the unstable First Republic. Equally outspoken in support of Mussolini's fascist movement and Hitler's National Socialists in Germany. Created cardinal by Pope Pius XI in 1929. A real political far-right cold war warrior until his death just a couple of years ago."

"And how's this relevant to Tagliente?" Eisenberg asked.

Nicoletti said, "Communism and the immediate threat of the Soviet Union remain at the forefront of Western international relations. For Italy, the PCI communists are a major political party. Terrorist attacks by the *Red Brigades* are part of Italian life. Pope Pius XII held a deep personal hatred toward communism. The new Polish Pope John Paul II is decidedly anti-communist having lived under the thumb of the Soviet Union. In the secular world of today, an intelligence service becomes a vital necessity for a sovereign state. Is Tagliente's elevation to archbishop a signal from the pontiff?"

Eisenberg commented "Let's not get too deep into conspiracy speculations. We've enough to digest. From what you received from Father Scarpelli the Vatican will come under increased public pressure for participation in financial misdeeds. As a sovereign state, the Vatican is not subject to Italian judicial pressure. Threatening its public image however becomes a serious matter."

"No doubt about that, Gabe. Let's keep mindful of the risk I spoke about. We're about to make powerful enemies. Just two days ago a lawyer and sensationist journalist for *Osservatore Politico* named Carmine Pecorelli, a weekly magazine specializing in political scandals, was murdered in Rome. All the earmarks of a Maffia assassination. Possibly political. He undoubtedly made many powerful enemies. Yet so are we. I mention this because in Scarpelli's stolen documents there are references to the Sicilian Maffia. Money laundering."

CHAPTER 3

Rome, Italy | March 1979

Archbishop Marcello Tagliente looked out the window of his third-floor office window in the building housing the Vatican Secret Archive. A sunny afternoon in early March. The view from window behind his looked over the courtyard of the Vatican Museum to the entrance of the Braccio Nuovo, or the new wing, of the Chiaramonti Museum. His official title was Archivist of the Vatican Secret Archive. The repository of documents considered the pontiff's personal property. The most secret place in the obsessively secret Vatican City State.

Tagliente's office reflected refined elegance. A massive 19th century ornate desk. Bookshelves lined with leather-bound volumes occupied one wall. Two original paintings by Canaletto hung on the opposite wall. A tall 16th century crucifix by German sculptor Hans Leinberger dominated the wall opposite his desk. Below the crucifix a richly engraved 16th century Latin bible by Dutch printer Christopher Plantin lay open on a carved antique lectern.

Tagliente came from a wealthy family. The Canaletto paintings and the Leinberger crucifix were his personal property. A wealthy multi-generational family venerated as among the Black

Nobility. Influential lay individuals close to the Holy See. In the one thousand years of the existence of the Papal States prior to the unification of Italy in 1870, the Black Nobility represented the administrative aristocracy of the secular holdings of the Holy See of central Italy. Yet Tagliente also numbered several close relatives among the Roman Catholic clergy. A deceased great uncle was an archbishop in the Vatican under Pope Pius XI. An uncle served Pope Pius XII in the Vatican Secretariate of State. It was this uncle that was instrumental in encouraging Tagliente to enter priesthood. Historically politically conservative, other family members held ties to the Mussolini government and various Vatican institutions in a lay capacity before WWII.

After a subtle knock, the heavy oak door opened as Tagliente's secretary Father Stadler stepped in. "Your Excellency, Father Alberti would like to speak with you. Says it concerns a matter of importance."

"Of course. Send him in."

A middle-aged priest stepped into the room as Stadler left closing the door.

"Good afternoon, Father Alberti. How can I help you?"

"I believe documents are missing from the Archive, Your Excellency."

The alarming statement got Tagliente's attention. "What documents?"

Father Alberti remained standing. Clearly uncomfortable when in the presence of Archbishop Tagliente who seemed to invoke a sense of unease among many of the Vatican clergy, even those wearing the red zucchetto of a cardinal.

"I cannot identify by name only the catalog number given. I have found a dozen missing so far. It will take more time to go through the records in question."

"What type of records?" Tagliente asked sharply.

"Documents. All of recent vintage spanning the last decade."

"How is it that you discovered documents missing?"

"Monsignor Scarpelli assigned me the project to categorize and cross-references boxes of uncatalogued documents spanning the last several years."

"Using what markers?"

"Subject, author, date, cross-reference by key words."

"Did these missing documents relate to a specific subject?"

"Yes, Your Excellency. All concerned some reference related to the *Istituto per le Opere di Religione,* including key names of individuals, banks, investments, and such that have appeared in the public media."

The Institute for the Works of Religion, the IOR, was commonly referred to as the Vatican Bank. Tagliente absorbed the disturbing information for a moment before asking, "Who developed the cross-reference criteria?"

"Monsignor Scarpelli."

"How long have you been working on this project, Father?"

"For over a year, Your Excellency. However, it has only been since Monsignor Scarpelli left that I have taken it upon myself to put some order into these files until someone is appointed to replace Monsignor Scarpelli."

"Does anyone else know that documents are missing?"

"No, Your Excellency. I felt it of such importance that I should report this only to you directly?"

Tagliente nodded. "You have done correctly, Father. This must be kept absolutely secret. To ensure that, I want you only to resume a thorough search. Determine which documents are missing. Report your progress daily to my office. Provide Father Stadler with a sealed envelope advising only how many new missing documents you have discovered. Include no details. If you find something you deem of special importance, request a meeting with me. To anyone asking what you are about, say only you are following my direct instructions that are to remain confidential."

Tagliente rose from his chair and came around the desk to stand close to the standing priest. Slim at six feet tall with regal good looks and a full head of gray hair suggested Tagliente was younger than his age of sixty-five. His dark gray eyes exhibited unusual intensity. He wore a tailored black clerical suit of fine fabric with an amaranth red zucchetto.

"This is a disturbing violation of the sanctity of the Archive. You have done us great service, Father Alberti. May God be with you."

The priest knelt and kissed Tagliente's offered ecclesiastical ring.

After Father Alberti left, Tagliente returned to his desk. What was Monsignor Scarpelli doing? Even organizing files that related to events still developing was an unusual practice. Did he alone remove documents or was another priest involved? For what purpose would a priest risk excommunication for violating a scared vow made to the Holy Father?

He raised the receiver on his desk phone connecting him with his secretary. "Father, please locate Monsignor Donaggio and request he come to my office as soon as possible. I have a matter of urgency requiring his council."

✝

The Vatican secret services comprised not only *Santa Alleanza,* in English the Holy Alliance, but also a counterintelligence service known as *Sodalitium Pianum* or simply S.P. Archbishop Tagliente headed both functions. Forty-one-year-old Monsignor Ettore Donaggio was his principal subordinate, a protégé and former secretary with a background in the Secretariat of State office. Donaggio headed the counterintelligence unit Sodalitium Pianum consisting of select agents willing to engage in covert missions that might include unsavory undertakings deemed necessary to protect the Holy See. Donaggio possessed a distorted interpretation of the priesthood. His devotion to Tagliente as protector of the Holy Father bordered on psychological obsession. Having begun his ecclesiastical career as secretary to the conspiratorial Tagliente transformed the young Father Donaggio into a holy warrior. From his first appointment in the Secretariat of State, he became ardently devoted to the charismatic Tagliente.

Recognizing Donaggio's unique talents, Tagliente assigned him to the counterintelligence unit Sodalitium Pianum. Learning the tradecraft of covert intelligence operations, he eventually rose to command S.P. Within its network of agents are ordained priests, lay brothers, and various paid or simply devoted Catholics that found reward in rendering service by passing information. Sodalitium Pianum functioned no differently from any operational unit of an intelligence service. Ostensibly created to provide counterintelligence to safeguard the Vatican from foreign intelligence penetration, the skills of its agents applied equally to other covert activities.

Monsignor Donaggio viewed his role in the secular context of a soldier protecting the Holy See as a sovereign entity. Behaviorally, Donaggio relished his life in the shadows. His service to Archbishop Tagliente provided him with a sense of elevated importance.

Donaggio appeared at Tagliente's office within thirty minutes. Although dressed in an ecclesiastical black suit and collar as any priest, outside the walls of the Vatican Donaggio always wore conventional clothing to avoid identification as clergy.

"We have discovered something of concern, Ettore. Confidential documents are missing from the Secret Archive. It appears that the late Monsignor Scarpelli likely committed a most grievous sacrilege. What happened to those documents must be determined. Use whatever resources necessary. Urgency is paramount. Keep me informed of progress."

Donaggio nodded, "Yes, Your Excellency."

The following day Donaggio reported to Tagliente by a secure line connected to a concealed telephone in Tagliente's desk drawer. The number available only to the pope, the pope's secretary, Monsignor Donaggio, and a very small select number of others.

"Scarpelli's apartment is now occupied by a new tenant. I approached the building superintendent dressed as a priest and asked what happened to his belongings. I represented myself as from the Vatican Library where I said Scarpelli worked up to his death. Explained that I was looking for notes that Father Scarpelli may have made that may be crucial for adding to the historical record of something of great importance. The man said that

Scarpelli provided instructions for his belongings to be shipped to a priest in the town of Bevagna in Umbria.

"Two S.P. agents discretely entered the apartment of the Bevagna priest. A thorough search revealed a box of papers and other items labelled as belonging to Monsignor Vittorio Scarpelli. Among the papers was an address book and several papers mentioning Lugano, Switzerland.

Tagliente said, "Lugano? What sort of papers?

"Hotel receipts for stays on two different occasions a month apart. A typed list of legal firms and banks in Lugano. A search of his address book revealed entries for the legal firm of Heffelfinger Mischler & Andrist and the private bank Societe Generale in Lugano."

"Excellent. Your conclusion, Ettore?" Tagliente asked.

"Scarpelli had no monetary estate of any consequence. If he stole confidential material, the only reason for engaging a lawyer and bank outside of Italy suggests the documents are being held at a bank. Realizing his imminent death from cancer, the lawyer might be necessary to arrange for conveying the documents to a beneficiary in the event of his death."

"A logical possibility, Ettore. Therein lies your next mission. Find that person before these documents become used to harm the Holy See. Bear in mind these documents are the personal property of the Holy Father."

Donaggio replied, "I understand, Your Excellency. Without relatives that leaves only the priest in Bevagna that might know something, but more likely Scarpelli made specific arrangements using the Swiss law firm. It may be necessary to take extreme action since everything ends with the law firm."

"Leave the Bevagna priest out of this for the time being. With respect to the law firm, if you must resort to crude methods make sure it is explainable without any association to Scarpelli's position in the Vatican. However, we must learn who has access to those documents."

"Yes, Your Excellency."

†

Within a week, Donaggio found what he was looking for in Lugano. Supervising a team of four agents, they began an intense surveillance and investigation of the lawyer mentioned in Scarpelli's address book. The lawyer was in his late thirties. Married with two teenage children. Observed together entering a Protestant church suggested a typical family within this conservative Swiss community. Sharpley in contrast, they discovered discovery that Gianantonio Volpi had a mistress. Not surprisingly, a secretary at his law firm.

Donaggio's agents amassed a collection of compromising photographs of Volpi and his younger vivacious mistress. Volpi was then served with an envelope found on the driver's seat inside his car one morning. Among enlargements were not only photographs of Volpi kissing the woman, but something more jarring. Several photos using a telephoto camera into her second-floor bedroom window revealed the woman in various stages of undress with Volpi clearly identifiable next to her. A note inside the envelope told Volpi to go immediately to his favorite rendezvous restaurant.

Dressed in a cheap suit, Donaggio approached Volpi's table and sat down. "Did you enjoy the photos? Your mistress has exceptional breasts."

"How much money is this going to cost?" Volpi replied, assuming this was blackmail.

"Not money, Signore Volpi. Information."

"What information?"

"You had a client by the name of Vittorio Scarpelli that met with you on two different occasions last year. A Roman Catholic priest now deceased. I assumed you drafted a will and managed the distribution of his modest estate. Among Monsignor Scarpelli's possessions were a cache of documents. Those documents were stolen from the Vatican. My firm has been hired to recover those papers."

"Who are you working for?"

Donaggio smiled menacingly, "Well that would be unethical for me to reveal the name of my client. As it is for you. However,

I believe you must make a difficult decision to compromise your professional ethics or suffer a greater loss both professionally as well as personally. I need to recover these stolen documents. In exchange you can continue your life as before."

Volpi remained silent for several moments as Donaggio stared at him. "What's it to be, Signore Volpi?"

"If I tell you what you want to know, how can I be sure you will not continue blackmailing me?"

Donaggio turned aggressive. "My client has no interest in blackmailing you. However, I'm prepared to ruin your life if I cannot resolve this matter. Where are these documents?"

Truly frightened since the documents were out of reach, Volpi said, "I'm willing to help you, but the documents are held in a bank vault. A local bank located here in Lugano. Societe Generale."

"The number and name of the account?"

"I do not have that information."

Donaggio slammed his palm on the table. In a quiet threatening voice, "You will tell me who has access to these documents, or you cease to be of value. You then become expendable. I'll see to your destruction."

Volpi took a deep breath, "If I tell you all I know, will you return these photographs?"

"Only if it leads me to the documents."

"Very well. Monsignor Scarpelli bequeathed these documents to a newspaper reporter named Emma Nicoletti. I mailed her a letter and a sealed envelope from Father Scarpelli to her office at the Milan offices of *Il Sole 24 Ore*."

"Did Nicoletti pay a visit to the bank?"

Volpi hesitated but then answered, "Yes."

"Well? What did she do? Did she have any discussion with you after obviously examining the documents?"

Volpi nodded. "She asked about how to make photocopies of the documents. Said there were hundreds of documents. Asked if the bank might be able to provide a photocopier. I do not know if that happened. I had no further communications with Signora Nicolette other than that one visit to my office."

Donaggio felt that Volpi was not holding back information. His description of the scenario of Nicolette's actions made sense. Archbishop Tagliente's worse fears therefore realized with confidential Vatican Secret Archive materials now in the hands of a journalist for many weeks.

"For your sake, I will assume you have told me everything. You shall never hear from me again unless I find you have withheld anything." With that, Donaggio stood up to leave."

"What about the negatives to the pictures?" Volpi asked desperately.

"They remain as insurance for your continued silence that our meeting never happened."

†

Donaggio returned to Rome in the evening after confronting the Swiss lawyer. Tagliente had already left his Vatican office. Telephoning his residence, Tagliente's housekeeper answered the telephone. Donaggio was among callers that the housekeeper was instructed to pass the call through to Tagliente.

"Your Excellency. I discovered who has Scarpelli's stolen documents. Unfortunately, it is a newspaper reporter for *Il Sole 24 Ore*. A woman by the name of Emma Nicoletti. A known critic of the Vatican."

Tagliente knew of Nicoletti from her reporting on the banking scandal. The discovery could not have been worse. *Il Sole 24 Ore* was the leading financial publication in Italy. Since he dispatched Donaggio to investigate, Father Alberti had made further progress on determining what documents were missing. He confirmed that all related in some manner to the Vatican Bank. The missing documents dated from 1971 to 1978. Most either addressed to the pope with his initials or in some cases including handwritten comments by the pope. The pope's secretary was responsible for gathering papers the pope wished to be delivered to the Secret Archive. As the Archivist since the pontificate of Paul VI, Tagliente reviewed each document before passing on his assistant Monsignor Scarpelli. Among the authors of the most telling documents were Father Pasquale Macchi, Pope Paul VI's secretary, Paul Marcinkus, president of the Vatican Bank, Cardinal Jean-Marie Villot, Cardinal Eugène Tesserant, Cardinal Giovanni Benelli, Fathers Diego Lorenzi and John Magee, secretaries to Pope John Paul I. Tagliente knew the nature of every document. Every secret destined for burial within the Secret Archive

Remaining calm, Tagliente said, "Excellent work, Ettore. No time to waste, however. Please join me at my residence. We must develop a plan of action to recover the documents or at the least, institute damage control."

Tagliente occupied a villa in the heart of Rome just across the Tiber River from the Castel Saint Angelo in the Piazza Fiammetta. A 600 square meter villa of several stories tucked among taller buildings. A luxury residence close enough to permit walking to the Vatican as a daily exercise regimen. Tagliente came from old money. Personally wealthy, he enjoyed the finer material benefits of wealth along with his stature as a prince of the Church.

Seated in Tagliente's fourth floor study and library, Donaggio recounted details of his Bevagna and Lugano investigations. Listening with only an occasional question, Tagliente said, "We must assume that Nicoletti made photocopies to work from while the originals remained safe in the Swiss bank vault. Place her under constant surveillance. Is it possible to electronically monitor her telephone?"

"At her residence yes, Your Excellency. Not sure if there is a way to monitor calls from her office since calls go through an internal central switching system. Access to install a listening device directly on her desk telephone would be especially difficult. Possibly only after hours with someone posing as maintenance or housekeeping."

"Get a wiretap on her residence telephone then. Of more immediate concern is understanding everything possible about her personal habits. Where she goes. Who she meets. Friends, family. Professional associations."

Three days later, Donaggio reported to Tagliente's office at the Vatican. "We've been monitoring Nicoletti's telephone calls from her residence for the last forty-eight hours. An hour ago, she placed an overseas call to New York. Spoke to a Gabriel Eisenberg at his office with the *New York Times* newspaper. This is the same American journalist she collaborated with in writing a book critical of the Vatican and Pius XII."

"Yes, I know the book, *Ratlines*. What did they discuss?"

"Eisenberg's trip to Milan in early May. They discussed the documents. You were correct, Your Excellency. She made copies, leaving the originals in Switzerland at the bank."

Tagliente simply nodded in understanding. Stealing Nicoletti's copies accomplishes nothing. It would simply forewarn her causing her to rethink how to make use of the material. The only solution required drastic action. Destroy not only the copies but Nicoletti and Eisenberg.

"Introducing the American journalist into the mix changes everything. It requires recovering the copies of the stolen documents immediately. Regrettably that also could mean eliminating these two journalists. The original documents obviously then become abandoned at the Swiss bank. God only knows how many terrible secrets remain forever hidden within the Swiss banking system. They rival the Vatican in maintaining secrecy. That works in our favor. Your suggestions as to how to go about this task, Ettore?"

Donaggio responded without hesitation. "Expecting that might become necessary. I already gave that some thought. Our Sicilian proxies have enough incentive to discharge what seems to come easily for them. This is no different than the assassination of Mario Francese the crime reporter of the *Giornale di Sicilia* in January. His anti-Mafia articles undoubtedly proved the reporter's undoing. Then the Milan criminal prosecuting magistrate Emilio Alesandrini just days later gunned down in Milan by the Marxist-Leninist extremists of *Prima Linea*. Another terrorist attack on two more journalists, especially one being American will get lost in all the background violence. Nothing will connect to the Vatican."

The thought occurred to Tagliente that Ettore Donaggio may not have a soul. Why he became a priest remained a mystery to Tagliente who nonetheless recognized the usefulness of someone devoid of conscience. Someone highly valued for performing unpleasant dark duties perhaps shaped Donaggio's identity. That Donaggio was supremely faithful to whomever ruled as pope dictated every element of his life. His usefulness came from discharging his duty as though Archbishop Tagliente directly spoke for the Holy Father.

"Who do you suggest using for this task?"

"Stefano Bontade. He has sufficient financial incentive to assist in eliminating an enemy of the Vatican. Bontade has been Sondona's closest connection within the Sicilian Mafia. He's also a staunch Catholic. I communicate with Bontade through a trusted S.P. agent, a fellow Jesuit priest serving at the Church of the Gesù in Palermo in the district controlled by Bontade's Santa Maria di Gesù Mafia Family.

"Very well. I see no alternative but the removal of these journalists. However, of equal importance is recovering the copies of the documents. A delicate matter of timing. Whether before or after their deaths must be thought out carefully. Can the deaths of these journalists be accomplished in such a way as to blend into the background of this period of violence in Italy?"

"I believe so, Your Excellency. I suggest their deaths should result from a bombing. Better to mimic leftist terrorists attacking a reporter from the country's leading financial publication. A symbol of capitalism. A destabilizing event directed at the Christian Democratic Party dominating the government. Something like the kidnapping and murder of Aldo Moro.

"As to the copies of the documents, we must trust that for practical reasons Nicoletti probably keeps them at her residence. My own agents shall maintain round-the-clock surveillance. We look for the first opportunity when she and the American leave the apartment vacant. My agents will then make covert entry. Either we find and seize the documents or learn they must be hidden elsewhere. In that event we wait until Nicoletti and the American return. At that point we turn them over to our Sicilian associates. The Sicilians will apply their brutal methods to extract the information."

"Then what?" Tagliente asked.

"We have the Mafia kill them using a car bomb after placing the unconscious victims in the woman's car."

Tagliente absorbed Donaggio's plan for a moment before responding. "For the time being say nothing to our Sicilian underworld associates. Keep Nicoletti and this American under constant surveillance. How much notice do you require if I determine we must resort to this more extreme solution?"

Donaggio replied, "Perhaps a couple of weeks, Your Excellency. I can reduce that lead time if you permit me to make advance preparations without revealing any specifics. A three-man team of Sicilians will be sufficient. A bomb maker and two others to subdue the victims. I bring them to Milan and have them ready to move within a few hours' notice."

"Very well, Ettore. Have your conversation with the Sicilians but without witnesses or identifying the targets. You may tell them they share a direct interest in this mission to impede further investigation into laundering Mafia money. Proceed immediately to learn everything about Nicolette and her American associate. Report to me daily by telephone.

After Ettore Donaggio left, Tagliente poured himself a cognac and placed a record on a phonograph. The strains of Bach's energetic violin concerto in A minor fit appropriately with his mood. Although the theft by Monsignor Scarpelli left him little choice but to resort to extreme measures, this continual threat to the Vatican imposed by the financial scandal must also be dealt with more forcefully. He alone possessed the only resources within the Vatican with the ability to deal decisively with these secular issues. The Holy Father cannot become involved. Plausible deniability is essential. That is Tagliente's value. That the pontiff Pope John Paul II has continued to entrust him with the most secretive of Vatican offices set Tagliente's unique responsibilities apart from the ecclesiastical roles of other princes of the church. Tagliente believes his use of unsavory methods lay outside conventional morality. The phrase *necessary evil* aptly applicable. His duties indirectly authorized unknowingly by the Holy Father so secretive they cannot be revealed even in the confessional.

Once having neutralized the threat of the stolen secret archive documents is resolved, time to direct his attention toward containing the damage to the Vatican associated with the banking scandal. The paramount objective being to preserve the Vatican Bank's continued function as a principal source of funding the Holy See. Since the establishment of Vatican sovereignty in 1929, the Holy See rose from near financial oblivion to wealth comparable to other much larger sovereign states. The mismanagement of the last decade must be corrected while ensuring the continued financial functioning of the Vatican as a modern city state.

Listening to Bach, Tagliente contemplated a radical strategy. Secrecy is his greatest weapon. The secrecy of the Vatican affords the means of protecting itself by cloaking itself as a religious institution. The internal organizations under Tagliente's influence function outside the authority of the governing Roman Curia provide a layer of internal secrecy. Tagliente's strategic objective is to sacrifice the Italian banker, Michele Sindona. Make him the villain of this fiasco. Portray the Vatican as yet another victim in this brilliant criminal's duping of influential business and officials not only in Italy but even the United States. The beginning of this was the unexpected failure of a prominent American bank. Tagliente will begin a campaign to expose Sindona as the clever confidence man behind the financial misdeeds. Regardless of Bishop Marcinkus' complicit venality, Tagliente would use all means to portray the Vatican Bank as victim while judiciously counseling to ignore attacks from outside by employing silence.

Pope Paul VI mistakenly brought Sindona into Vatican financial affairs. Perhaps the banker Roberto Calvi is next to fall unless he can become useful in stemming further losses of his financial empire. Bishop Paul Marcinkus unwisely entangled the Vatican Bank with Calvi's reckless debt-driven growth.

Marcinkus was yet again another mistake of Pope Paul VI. Installing the financially inexperienced Marcinkus to direct the Vatican Bank was unconscionable. Unfortunately, Marcinkus must be protected at all costs. He is a Vatican prelate held in high regard by John Paul II. The arrogant Marcinkus knows too much to be reassigned. Better for Tagliente to become collegial by offering

Marcinkus clandestine advice. Act as a supporter to Marcinkus. Given Tagliente's most secret position of functionally heading the Vatican secret services and as the archivist of the Vatican Secret Archive, he also reported directly to the pontiff as did Marcinkus. Like Marcinkus, Tagliente shared a close relationship with former Pope Paul VI and now with John Paul II. While Marcinkus was a liability, the only option for Tagliente was to coach him in mitigating the damage of the continuing financial crisis threatening the Vatican.

With Sindona relegated to exile in the United States after conviction in absentia in Italy for bank fraud, the public focus now shifted to Roberto Calvi and Banco Ambrosiano. Tagliente understood that Banco Ambrosiano represented an even greater threat for the Vatican. The largest private bank in Italy with an eighty-year history of strong ties to the Vatican that now had at risk hundreds of millions invested with Ambrosiano.

CHAPTER 4

Milan, Italy | April 1979

Emma Nicolette was there to greet Gabriel Eisenburg as he stepped out of the jetway into the terminal of Milan Malpensa Airport. Eisenberg was ten years older than her. Having not seen him for several years, she thought he looked older than his sixty-two years. Still had his bookish look with unmanageable thinning hair and rimless glasses. An incomparable researcher, colleague, and personal mentor. The brother she never had and the husband of her best friend when she came to New York to attend Columbia University.

Her girlfriend died unexpectedly of a brain tumor in 1960. Emma believed that working with Eisenberg on their book *Ratline* following his wife's death contributed to his recovery.

He smiled broadly as they embraced. "You look marvelous, Emma!"

"So wonderful to see you, Gabe. Thank you for coming to Italy. I've been working diligently for these last weeks. The acquired material is everything I thought it was. You won't be disappointed. This'll be a great project. Need your help though. This scandal spreads across the globe. The Vatican's involved up to their clerical collars."

"Can't wait to see what you've discovered. This must certainly make your transition to Italy's foremost financial publication more journalistically stimulating."

She replied "Reporting on Italy's public and private financial institutions is never as dull as covering Wall Street. Italian economics is like America in the early decades of the century. But with this mess implicating the Vatican Bank, the continuing saga of financial misdeeds takes on greater significance for heavily Catholic Italy."

Nicoletti drove them to her Milan apartment in her old Fiat. "How are Joshua and Sarah?"

"Doing well. They send their love. Unfortunately, neither of them could make the trip with me. Josha's completing his first year of cardiology residency at Massachusetts General in a couple of months, then immediately begins his surgical fellowship program. Sarah hopes to complete her doctoral work at Columbia this year."

"Understandable. They're both brilliant like their parents. You've done a remarkable job raising them as a single parent after Miriam died when they were both so young. Being so busy launching their careers, it should be me visiting them in America. Maybe after we get further along with this project."

Eisenberg smiled. "Thanks, Emma. You have always been such a great friend. A real aunt to Joshua and Sarah."

After opening the entry gate, she drove through the driveway into the interior courtyard surrounded by apartment buildings. "Here we are. Nothing fancy but comfortable and a good place to work."

Although Nicoletti kept her modest third floor apartment neat, the worn furniture left her slightly embarrassed. Stepping through the front door, "Not much to look at but it's good sized. Spare bedroom that I fixed up a little. Well stocked kitchen. Plenty of coffee."

"No apologies necessary, Emma. You have a fine-looking place. Good functional work area over there. Is that second typewriter on that folding table for me?"

"All yours. Let me show you why I chose this place."

She stepped out a door from the kitchen onto a balcony. Two chairs with a small round table looked over the interior courtyard where she parked. Several tall trees gave some feeling of nature. "I get the sun in the morning. Quiet. Good place to enjoy my coffee or a glass of wine in the evening. I have a good Borolo for this evening. Cooking spaghetti carbonara for dinner. How about some coffee right now? Feeling some jetlag?"

"A little. Coffee sounds good. Anxious to see these documents."

"Excited to show you what I've been up too. I need your expertise to put this material into a larger context. Every new revelation adds more complexity to the growing story of this international financial scandal, Gabe."

"Still convinced that the Vatican Bank is culpable?"

"Oh yes. Although often by indirect reference, the material paints the Vatican Bank as a willing participating partner with fraudulent Italian bankers in bed with the Sicilian Mafia. Hard to tell the extent of the repercussions. Clearly implicates the IOR at least circumstantially. Can you imagine a department within the Vatican known as *Istituto per le Opere di Religione,* in English, the Institute for the Works of Religion becoming engaged in things like bank fraud, illegal currency transactions, and money laundering for organized crime? This material shows just how deeply the Vatican has strayed into the secular world of criminal financial activity. Some of the material even implicates Pope Paul. It was Giovanni Montini's friendship with Michele Sindona who is at the heart of these remarkable financial crimes. The amounts of money involved are staggering."

"I know enough to appreciate the magnitude, Emma. The failure of the American bank Franklin National Bank years ago alone was spectacular. Opened the public's eyes to how much banking has become international. Is there anything in your cache of documents that deals with some scheme involving Vatican Bank with counterfeit stock certificates being floated by the American Mafia?"

"As a matter of fact, yes. That was in 1973 before the collapse of Franklin National. I'll show you a cryptic memo Marcinkus drafted to the Pope Paul. Doesn't specifically state knowledge of counterfeit certificates in major American corporations totaling almost a billion U.S. dollars, but it shows Pope Paul's knowledge of the opportunity."

"What do you mean cryptic?"

"Marcinkus never alludes to the questionable origin of the certificates. Reading other documents that Father Scarpelli stole from the archive portrays Marcinkus as a willing conspirator. Perhaps financially unqualified but he's mastered the art of Vatican obscure communication. Avoiding being explicit provides cover for both parties in a communication. Pope Paul was even less conversant in financial matters than Marcinkus. Marcinkus' memo is couched in language that is intentionally misleading. Pope Paul likely had no idea or interest in understanding details. He simply acknowledged the memo by signature which therefore ended up in the Pope's Secret Archive. Several of Scarpelli's documents reflect the same remoteness of Pope Paul's interest in details involving the IOR. Details of which he likely would not fully understand."

"You believe Marcinkus was playing on the pope's lack of interest in the IOR?"

"Not sure I would characterize it that way. Perhaps just typical vague *Vatican-speak.* Pope Paul was deeply concerned about Vatican finances. He was just not technically knowledgeable. Trusting by nature, he left the functional details to trusted subordinates. That is how Michele Sindona became so deeply involved with the IOR."

Nicoletti poured coffee for each of them. "Let's go out on the balcony. Keep your jacket on but the sun is out and it's warming up."

Seated outside, Eisenberg said, "Seems you believe Michele Sindona to be the beginning character of this long-running serial financial crisis. Last I checked he is reported living in luxurious exile in the Pierre Hotel overlooking Central Park in New York. Convicted and sentenced in absentia but inexplicably never extradited back to Italy."

Nicoletti commented, "Not only that, but he's on the lecture circuit. Imagine a bankrupt convicted financial criminal getting paid to speak about banking and investment. Can't say why he's not been extradited yet I can speculate that it's because of his powerful connections in Italy. Michele Sindona is a worthy villain to pursue. No one can dispute his brilliance. Evident even from an early age."

Eisenberg smiled. "While I enjoy my coffee and relish being in Italy, tell me about Signore Sindona."

"An amazing story. Born in 1920 in a small town in northeast Sicily to a poor family. Father made a living as a florist specializing in funeral wreaths. Educated at a Jesuit Catholic school where he showed an aptitude for mathematics. Attended the University of Messina, earning a law degree in 1942.

"The following year, the Allies invaded Sicily. This became the first opportunity for Sindona to embark on a remarkable career. Ambitious and not troubled by scruples, he aligned himself with the Sicilian Mafia. Mussolini's Fascist government having failed in its attempt to eradicate the Mafia's stranglehold in Sicily made them naturally supportive to the Allied invasion. Sindona found a place working with the Mafia and Allied Expeditionary forces to distribute food to the welcoming Sicilian population. In the process, Sindona successfully profited from black market enterprises using his close ties to the Sicilian Mafia and American occupation officials.

"Following the war, Sindona became recognized for his abilities to transfer money to Switzerland and Liechtenstein to avoid Italian taxation. In 1950 he founded Fasco AG where he originated the system of back-to-back financing. A loan agreement between entities in two countries in which the currencies remain separate, but the maturity dates remain fixed. The gross interest rates of the loan are separate as well and are set on the basis of the commercial rates in place when the agreement is signed. Initiated as a way of avoiding currency regulations it also afforded arbitrage opportunities that Sindona exploited.

"Sindona's associates in the Sicilian Mafia took notice. He began laundering heroin trafficking proceeds for the Bontade, Spatola, and Inzerillo Sicilian Mafia families."

Eisenberg interjected, "You have source material to support this?"

"Some. Other material remains confidential in police files. Material I gathered from various sources I have in the Guardia di Finanza, the Italian financial police, provided material that fits together like a giant puzzle to form a picture. The Guardia's jurisdiction also includes organized crime. According to them, the Sicilian families are involved in narcotics trafficking with the Gambino crime family in America. Perhaps Sindona's money laundering services are international in scope."

"Interesting. Maybe we can expand our sources internationally. I know someone personally at Interpol. My younger brother Michael's closest friend when they attended NYU together. Italian American. Haven't seen him for many years. I believe Michael told me Frank Amatrano has been living and working in Europe. I'll place a call to Michael. Might be helpful to get a read on how other jurisdictions besides Italy are looking into criminal activities of Sindona's collapsed financial empire. Maybe get more on this other character Roberto Calvi you say is another banker involved with Sondona."

Nicoletti added, "And involved with the Vatican Bank. You might say that Michele Sindona mentored Roberto Calvi. Odd bedfellows. Sindona is personable and engaging. Calvi is known as cold and introspective. Their commonality is brilliance in international finance fueled by greed."

†

The following morning, Nicoletti and Eisenberg got down to work.

Nicoletti began by saying, "Yesterday, you asked about the counterfeit U.S. corporate stock certificates scandal that implicated the Vatican IOR. It's a good place to start to give you a sense of what these documents stolen by Monsignor Scarpelli provide in the way of evidence. Remember these are documents considered the personal property of the pontiff, not the Vatican City State or even the Holy See. That can mean material either drafted by a pontiff or otherwise dictated as his personal property. Unclear who decides what goes into the Vatican Secret Archive, but safe to presume it is virtually anything the pope touches if acknowledged by signature or initial.

"Remember what I said about Vatican communications being indirect to the point of offering alternative meaning to both parties. Take a look at this. It clearly points to Pope Paul's awareness of authorizing the IOR to participate in a questionable scheme to enrich the Vatican. Marcinkus worded his proposal carefully. Here is the memo IOR President Bishop Marcinkus presented to Pope Paul VI."

ISTITUTO PER LE OPERE DI RELIGIONE
VATICANO

10 May 1971

Greetings Most Holy Father,

A significant financial opportunity has been presented to the IOR in the form of facilitating a very large financial transaction. It involves triple-A rated corporate bonds and stocks in several major American corporations while incurring no investment risk to the IOR. The process requires the IOR to purchase these financial instruments for a discounted investment of $650 million dollars. The IOR will then hold $950 million U.S. dollars' worth of bonds and stock certificates in escrow as collateral thereby allowing the IOR to underwrite bank loans to fund our close friend and financial advisor Signore Sindona in his efforts to acquire controlling interest in Bastogi S.p.A., Italy's largest holding company managing Italian real estate investment companies. His Eminence Cardinal Tisserant spoke to me about this matter just before his untimely passing last year. For its services, the Vatican shall receive a profit of $150 million U.S. dollars for underwriting the funding.

I recommend that we proceed, however considering the magnitude of the venture, I felt it required approval by Your Holiness.

Sincerely, Your Faithful Servant in Christ,

P. C. Marcinkus

Bishop Paul Marcinkus

Paulus PP VI

Nicoletti handed Eisenberg another document. "Then there is this letter. All the other documents are original, except this is a poor-quality carbon copy. The heading in Latin translates as the *sacred congregation of the religious.* That and the symbol are meaningless. There is no institution by that name in the Vatican. No typed name identifies the author, and the signature is entirely illegible. Created intentionally for some unknown purpose but without acknowledgement by Pope Paul. Regardless, this copy ended up in the Vatican Secret Archive for some reason."

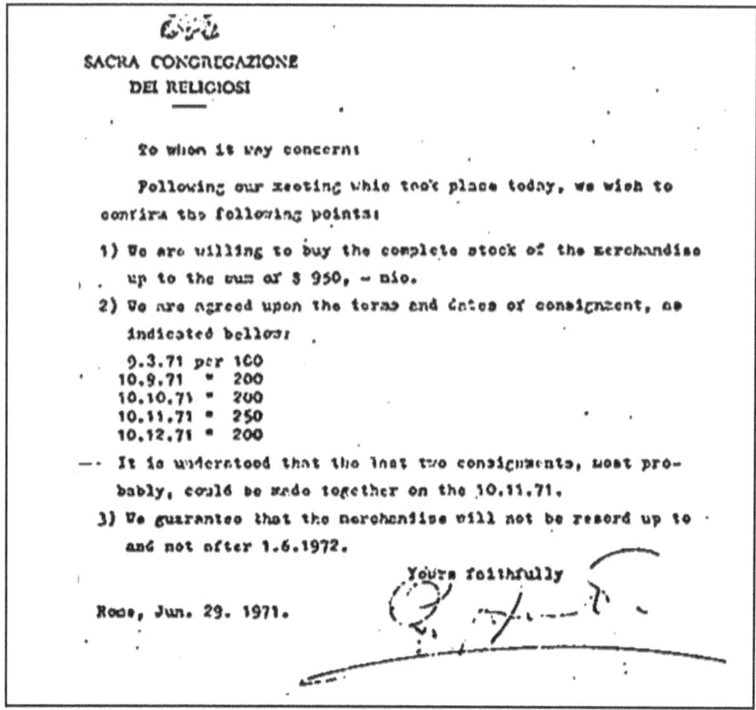

SACRA CONGREGAZIONE
DEI RELIGIOSI

To whom it may concern:

Following our meeting which took place today, we wish to confirm the following points:

1) We are willing to buy the complete stock of the merchandise up to the sum of $ 950, - mio.

2) We are agreed upon the terms and dates of consignment, as indicated bellow:

9.3.71 per 100
10.9.71 " 200
10.10.71 " 200
10.11.71 " 250
10.12.71 " 200

-- It is understood that the last two consignments, most probably, could be made together on the 10.11.71.

3) We guarantee that the merchandise will not be resold up to and not after 1.6.1972.

Yours faithfully

Rome, Jun. 29. 1971.

Eisenberg said, "I recall vaguely that the Justice Department was unable to make a criminal case involving counterfeit corporate certificates after uncovering the scheme before it materialized. The bonds and stock certificates were near-perfect counterfeits. Rumored as an American Mafia creation by some involved European conspirators. I assume after given immunity for their cooperation. Somewhere in the mix the Vatican Bank was implicated as an integral element in the subterfuge. That allegation apparently came to nothing for lack of evidence.

"Yet as Marcinkus' memo states, the idea that these financial instruments could somehow be offered at a 30% discount is absurd. Marcinkus must have known something illicit was involved."

Nicoletti said, "Seems obvious, doesn't it? The whole scheme never materialized, eventually becoming yet another unexplained event in the subsequent international banking scandal. I learned from other Vatican sources that American officials spoke with Marcinkus about the fraudulent stock certificates. Undoubtedly, Marcinkus gave them nothing. He did not have to. The Vatican is a sovereign state not subject to U.S. or even Italian law. Stay silent. Eventually the storm will exhaust itself. Take a long view. The Vatican way.

"Here is what I think went down. The Vatican bank expected to profit by more than the $150 million *commission*. The IOR by now is heavily involved with Roberto Calvi and the esteemed Banco Ambrosiano. Calvi plans to make loans totaling $950 million using its several offshore banks with the IOR acting as underwriter using the counterfeit bonds and stocks as collateral. Calvi intends to use the $950 million to fund a major expansion. The IOR then shares in a windfall of fees and interest. If the counterfeits are never discovered the American Mafia gets away with a $500 million profit."

"I'm impressed, Emma. I see what you mean by the inner workings of the Vatican. Impossible to tell what Marcinkus actually knew. That Pope Paul signed off on a deal of this size based on such scant information shows his confidence in Marcinkus perhaps combined with his inadequacies for understanding finance. Deniability for both parties."

She replied, "All that was years ago. A sidebar to the Italian Banking Scandal but illustrative of just how corrupt the Vatican Bank has become. With Sindona in exile in New York and convicted in absentia in Italy for bank fraud, the key figures in the crisis now become Bishop Marcinkus and Italian banker Roberto Calvi."

Eisenberg said, "You used the term corrupt. Did you mean Marcinkus or others at the Vatican?"

"Hard to say about Marcinkus. He's somewhat of a flamboyant figure, atypical of most Vatican churchmen. A brash American from Chicago. If he's corrupted it is not in the conventional sense for personal financial gain. Lives in a modest apartment outside the Vatican in a building owned by the Vatican. An avid golfer rumored to have a five-handicap. Known more for overseeing papal foreign trips and acting as unofficial pontifical bodyguard. For Popes Paul VI and now John Paul II. Marcinkus is a muscular fellow with a height of almost two meters."

"What about Marcinkus' relationship with John Paul I?'

"That certainly remains a mystery, just like the pope's unexpected death. His pontificate lasted only thirty-three days. As for Bishop Marcinkus, Vatican sources paint to his circumstances as highly problematic with the election of John Paul I last year. Their troubled relationship started years earlier in 1972 with the IOR sale of controlling interest in Banco Cattolica del Veneto to Roberto Calvi's Banco Ambrosiano."

Nicoletti pulled out a stack of papers stapled together. "This is a list of Monsignor Scarpelli's documents stolen from the Vatican Secret Archive. I've made a short summary of the content of each document and how it relates to the Italian Banking Scandal saga. There's one related to the sale of Banca Cattolica del Veneto. A venerable bank that catered to the Catholic clergy with the Vatican IOR having a controlling stockholder interest. Known as the *priest's bank,* small shareholders constituted the remainder of the ownership holdings. A source of income for many with consistent payment of dividends by the bank. Banca Cattolica del Veneto was one of the wealthiest banks in Italy. The majority shareholding of the Vatican IOR was touted as a means to ward off any hostile takeover by *secular* banking interests."

Nicoletti consulted her stapled list of Scarpelli's documents then retrieved a photocopy from the file. "This is another of the Monsignor's documents. It is clear that Scarpelli was judicious in his selection of documents to remove from the Vatican Secret Archive. He chose only those documents that implicated the Vatican in financial misdeeds. Documents that added to the continuing narrative appearing in the news media.

"This memo from Marcinkus to Pope Paul speaks to the secret sale of a 37.5% shareholder stake in Banca Cattolica del Veneto to Calvi's Banco Ambrosiano. Done in secret without the knowledge of Venice patriarch Archbishop Albino Luciani, the future Pope

John Paul I. Judge for yourself the complicity of both Marcinkus and Pope Paul.

"Luciani found out about the sale only after the fact. Unconfirmed reports says that Luciani was so upset that he came to the Vatican requesting an audience with Pope Paul, but the pope dodged the confrontation and sent Luciani to Marcinkus. You can imagine that probably did not go well. It must have seemed a personal crisis for Marcinkus following the death of his benefactor Pope Paul VI followed by the unexpected election of Luciani as pope. Unsubstantiated accusations of foul play appear in sensationist publications with Bishop Marcinkus mentioned as possibly complicit because of animosity over the sale of Banca Cattolica del Veneto."

Eisenberg commented, "You make Marcinkus out to be inexperienced in banking and finance. He must therefore rely on subordinates with technical proficiency. Do you know who those might be?"

Nicoletti smiled. Eisenberg could have been a successful detective. "My thoughts too. Best guess is Luigi Mennini his chief deputy and chief accountant Pellegrino de Strobel. Both have a long history of service in the Vatican Bank. Mennini was brought into the Vatican Bank by Bernardino Nogara, the financial architect that founded the modern workings of the Vatican Bank going back to Pope Pius XI before World War Two.

ISTITUTO PER LE OPERE DI RELIGIONE
VATICANO

15 July 1971
Most Holy Father,

I have been approached by our good friends and most respected men of confidence Signori Michele Sindona and Massimo Spada. They have spoken before of another banking associate and someone close to the Church, Signore Roberto Calvi. Signore Calvi represents Banco

Ambrosiano, a Milan private bank very close to the Catholic Church. It was founded in 1896 by Monsignor Giuseppe Tovini to counter the influence of lay banks at the time. Father Tovini required the bank's work to be moral and pious with profits used for charitable purposes and Catholic schools. I have recently met with Signore Calvi resulting in a most favorable impression regarding his international financial knowledge.

Times have changed with banks like any other enterprise needing to adjust their operations to modern financial realities. In today's world, profitable businesses become targets for acquisition that see an opportunity for increasing profits by realizing a return on such an investment. The IOR currently has a controlling shareholder interest in a sister bank close to the Catholic ideals of Banco Ambrosiano. I speak of Banca Cattolica del Veneto, known as the priests' bank, so named because of the large number of minor shareholders among the clergy. We have maintained shareholder control to prevent any unwarranted takeover bid by outside interests.

These respected gentlemen are recommending the IOR sell that controlling interest to Banco Ambrosiano. Banca Cattolica is a wealthy bank and therefore an attractive takeover target. Merging with Banco Ambrosiano will institute more progressive banking methods to increase investment profits that will provide greater shareholder dividends to the many small shareholders. The sale to Banco Ambrosiano becomes a defensive move to place Banca Cattolica in the hands of a sister bank that embraces its already close ties with the IOR. Banco Ambrosiano is offering an attractive share price over market price that will immediately benefit all shareholders, including the IOR.

Due to the especially close Catholic relationships of both these banks, I wanted to seek the blessing of Your Holiness before proceeding with what I believe to be of benefit to all parties concerned.

Sincerely, Your Faithful Servant in Christ,

P. C. Marcinkus

Bishop Paul Marcinkus

Paulus PP VI

After Eisenberg set down the photocopy of the memo, Nicoletti said, "And now Banco Ambrosiano is at the center of scandal. Tens of millions of dollars unaccounted for and assumed stolen. I have credible sources that point to Banco Ambrosiano and its collection of offshore foreign holding companies complicit in laundering Mafia drug trafficking money with the help of the Vatican IOR.

Eisenberg nodded and commented, "Bishop Marcinkus is a real piece of work. What's your take on why he became entangled with these crooked bankers?"

Shaking her head, "Haven't figured that out. He's not stupid. Must have suspicioned that whatever Sindona and Calvi have been doing for years was likely illegal. Just too many unnecessarily complex financial transactions involving foreign subsidiaries in tax haven countries. All he needs to do is read the newspapers. Maybe became too deeply involved to feel he could back away. Could be just a craving for power. Maybe a warped sense of self. Doesn't much matter. He is the pivotal figure that makes the Vatican's Bank's conduct criminal."

"This scandal started years ago. Why didn't Pope Paul VI remove Marcinkus from running the Vatican Bank?" Eisenberg asked.

"Good question. No one knows the answer. Several influential cardinals suggested just that to Pope Paul. I'll show you several documents from Scarpelli's trove counselling that. Perhaps it was just in Pope Paul's makeup. He liked and trusted Marcinkus. Then again Paul suffered serious health issues in the months preceding his death. Many reports point to his deteriorating depressive state of mind. The kidnapping and murder of Pope Paul's close friend former Prime Minister Aldo Moro just three months before his own death weighed heavily.

"Then there is the question of why Pope John Paul I did not remove Marcinkus after election as Pope Paul's successor. After all, Luciani had his own reason for disparaging Marcinkus's actions at the IOR. The sale of IOR controlling shareholder interest in venerable Banca Cattolica del Veneto within Luciani's diocese to Banco Ambrosiano disturbed John Paul I profoundly."

"What's your read on that?"

Nicoletti shook her head. "Like everyone, I don't know. Possibly nothing more than dealing with more pressing matters before his death after only thirty-three days. I'm not interested in the swirl of conspiracy speculations. Was John Paul I murdered? Possibly, but there is nothing except questionable circumstantial circumstances. No question that his death was grossly mishandled. The Vatican's obsessive secrecy breeds conspiracy conjecture. That Marcinkus is mentioned as a suspect seems too obvious and therefore not credible. However, considering John Paul I's exceptionally brief pontificate, nothing can be entirely ruled out. Like so much within the Vatican, it may remain forever a mystery."

Eisenberg said, "What about the shadowy Vatican secret service? Its existence never publicly acknowledged by the Vatican. Father Scarpelli's letter to you indicates this ancient Holy Alliance exists to this day. Headed by Scarpelli's boss Archbishop

Tagliente using the position of Archivist of the Vatican Secret Archive as official cover."

Nicoletti shrugged and raised her eyebrows, "Nobody within the Vatican openly admits to the existence of the Holy Alliance today. Yet it does continue to function. Its existence is commonly known but never openly acknowledged. You and I wondered if it was involved in facilitating he post-war Vatican ratlines. I've been doing some research on Archbishop Marcello Tagliente. A most interesting prince of the Church. Discovered his early work in the Vatican Secretariat of State office. He was actually involved in working within the Holy Alliance as Father Robert Leiber's principal assistant. The mysterious Father Leiber was Pius XII's closest advisor for years and speculated as being associated with the Holy Alliance. We'll get into that tomorrow. "

"How about we take a walk before dinner? When we return, I'll open the wine and make dinner. Only have to heat the noodles. Already prepared the sauce. We'll stop on the way back and get fresh bread."

"Sounds great. Perfectly Italian. Good to relax a little before getting down to real work tomorrow. To appreciate how these confidential documents implicating the Vatican Bank in criminal activity might become important, I need to know more about this Italian Banking Scandal. I confess in not being that conversant with all the details. Working for an Italian financial newspaper, you've been immersed in this professionally for several years."

Nicoletti said, "It's an ever-expanding story. Carried along each month with new revelations. Because these documents clearly involve the Vatican, once we publish them it will raise the scandal to a whole new level."

CHAPTER 5

Milan, Italy | April 1979

The following morning, Nicoletti began giving Eisenberg an introduction to how Monsignor Scarpelli's stolen documents contributed to the currently known elements of the Italian Banking Scandal. "Let me try to give you a sense of where the Vatican first entered the domain of secular financial investment. Without making this sound like a history lecture, it began in 1929. That of course is when the Holy See became a sovereign state within Italy."

"Yes, the signing of the Lateran Treaty," Eisenberg said. "Benito Mussolini having come to power wanted to use relations with the Catholic Church for his own political interests in dominantly Catholic Italy."

Nicoletti replied, "Precisely. But within the terms of the treaty, Mussolini offered financial compensation for the loss of revenue since the unification of Italy in 1870 and the loss of the church's secular revenues from the Papal States. For a bankrupt Vatican at the time, the money was a windfall. Article 1 of the Lateran Treaty financial convention stated: *Italy, on the exchange of ratifications of the Treaty, shall pay to the Holy See the sum of 750,000,000 in Italian lire and at the same time consign Italian 5 per cent bonds with the nominal value of 1,000,000 Italian lire.*

"Pope Pius XI saw this as a means for resurrecting the stature of sovereignty of the Vatican City State, essentially the name for the location which serves as the seat of the Holy See which is the governing body of the worldwide Roman Catholic Church.

"The funds could free the Vatican from financial reliance on the inadequate revenues derived from diocesan contributions from around the world in the form of Peter's Pence donations of the faithful. The Italian infusion of money could provide sustaining revenues derived from capital investment. Provided the willingness of Pope Pius XI to abandon age old Church prohibitions regarding money. Secular mechanisms of capital appreciation and profiting from interest prohibited by Church dogma since medieval times.

"Pope Pius XI wasted no time in changing the course of Vatican financial management. He brought in the brilliant Benardino Nogara, a lay person, to invest the Lateran Treaty funds, unencumbered by any dogmatic restrictions. Until his retirement in 1954, Nogara achieved spectacular results serving Pope Pius XI and his successor Pius XII.

"In 1942, Pius XII created the *Istituto per le Opere di Religione*. Pius XII liked to run things himself. He even continued serving as his own secretary of state after elected pope. The IOR would be outside the oversight of the Roman Curia. No required reporting. No shareholders. It could operate anywhere in the world from within a neutral sovereign state during this time of war. It paid no taxes nor was it required to show a profit. Signore Nogara could continue managing Vatican finances without bureaucratic interference housed from within the Torrione di Nicolò V, a 15th century former dungeon within the walls of the Vatican.

"At the time, the Vatican was virtually bankrupt. Depending on donations of the faithful from around the world. Under Nogara's financial leadership that all changed. Fast forward to 1968. Vatican Incorporated was functioning like any major international corporation. You might say that was also the beginning of what is currently labelled the Italian Banking Scandal. Since

Nogara's creation of what can accurately be labelled the Vatican financial empire, the Vatican adopted 20th century financial practices. Foreign banks, holding companies, and shell companies in tax haven countries that operated under complete secrecy. Secrecy was something the Vatican understood very well."

"Nogara's creation of a modern international financial institution funding the Vatican became essential in 1968. The Italian government removed the longstanding Vatican's tax exemption on dividend taxes of the Vatican's extensive Italian holdings thereby making foreign investment more attractive. This promoted increasing investment outside Italy accomplished by moving profits outside the country using offshore foreign corporations. Add to this that the Vatican investments in Italy were not doing so well. Profits in the international property group *Società Generale Immobiliare* in which the Vatican owned 33 percent declined in the last few years with the cooling of the post war Italian real estate boom. The Vatican holdings in SGI were in the Vatican's other banking institution, the Administration of the Patrimony of the Apostolic See functioned as the Vatican's treasury and central bank under direction of the Curia."

Eisenberg asked, "What exactly is the ASPA? That's different than the IOR, what we call the Vatican Bank?"

Nicoletti said, "Most definitely. The ASPA operates as the treasury and the central bank of the Vatican City State, a sovereign independent state. It comes under the control of the Roman Curia, the administrative body of the Holy See. The ASPA has two separate sections. The Ordinary Section manages the assets of the various Vatican congregations and real estate holdings. Some of these holdings are legacies of the former Papal States lost in 1870 with the unification of Italy. For example, the Vatican owns thousands of apartments just in Rome. Holdings exist everywhere throughout Italy. The Extraordinary Section began as the department charged with managing the original financial funds given the Vatican by Italy in 1929 as compensation for the loss of the Papal States in 1870 with the unification of Italy. This is what Bernardino Nogara used as seed money to grow Vatican, Inc. Which he did successfully. Those methods became more aggressively applied by the IOR following its creation in 1942. Particularly useful during the years of World War Two. The IOR enjoyed far greater secrecy than the ASPA."

Eisenberg asked, "Yet reports are published about large operating deficits of the Vatican. Is the Vatican in financial difficulties?"

"Depends on how you look at it," Nicoletti answered. "If a deficit truly exists, it's a matter of cashflow or flagrant spending. Let me show you a document. Written by Cardinal Secretary of State Jean Villot to Pope John Paul I within a week of his elevation to the papacy.

CARDINALE SEGRETARIO DI STATO
JEAN-MARIE VILLOT

3 September 1978
Greetings, Your Holiness,

It is with much love that I congratulate you on your elevation to the throne of Peter. Many of your brethren feel the hand of God in your election.

Although you must feel overwhelmed, it is important that I provide you with certain information bearing on the financial health of the Holy See with so much public misinformation. Particularly with rumors that our finances are in disarray. That we have experienced troubling operating deficits running into the millions of lire in the last several years in no way points to a desperate situation. It does point to the need for more disciplined management of spending to live within our revenues. That will fall largely to those you appoint to various financial roles.

To assist you, I have taken the liberty of providing you with an asset evaluation. These figures include investments and cash reserves but do not include objects of art. The Administration of the Patrimony of the Apostolic See Ordinary Section has assets of £800B Italian lire. The Extraordinary Section 960B Italian lire in assets. The assets of the Institute for the Works of Religion amount to approximately £800B Italian lire. IOR investments currently yield profits exceeding £96B Italian lire for the IOR. Vatican operating expenses are paid entirely by the ASPA from proceeds of investments and worldwide diocesan contributions. It is in this area of controlling rising expenses that improvements should be made. However, public allegations that the Vatican is responsible for massive losses in international financial transactions has no merit.

These numbers should remain confidential, Your Holiness. Only certain members of the Curia with a need to know are privy to these evaluations. I offer this information only so that you may have a broad picture of the financial health of the Holy See for making informed decisions in the early weeks of your pontificate. As you can see, the Holy See is far from being bankrupt.

Your devoted and faithful servant in Christ,

Ioannes Paulus PP. I

Jean-Marie Villot
Cardinal Secretary of State

Eisenberg said, "This letter states the ASPA has total assets valued at over $2B USD in 1978 at the current exchange rate. And the IOR with assets over $1B USD. Yet the Vatican claims an operating deficit? How's that make sense?"

"It doesn't. But remember, the Vatican never publishes financial statements. Even the Curia is limited only to a brief sanitized income statement of the ASPA. The deficit would involve only a shortfall in ASPA revenues to meet operating expenses. Even the ASPA does not release financial reports. Nothing is ever published even internally by the Vatican Bank, the IOR. That remains the private domain of the pontiff. Not even the Curia has access to IOR financial information. That Cardinal Villot even drafted this letter to the new pope came from his standing as the *Camerlengo,* or designation as the temporary head of the church following the death of a pontiff. In this case the death of John Paul I.

"All these public allegations of questionable activities relate to the Vatican Bank, not the ASPA. The deficit relates only to operating costs coming under the purview of the Curia. It is the IOR under Bishop Marcinkus that is involved with the Italian bankers Sindona and Calvi at the center of the financial scandal. The ASPA deals more heavily with currency markets and conservative financial instruments mostly with major Swiss banks. The IOR's alleged involvement comes in the form of loans, corporate shares purchases, bond investment, and other unspecified financial transactions. Most of which involve offshore incorporated companies and banks in tax haven countries. The ASPA is not what you would call transparent, however the IOR is perhaps the most secretive department within the Holy See. Equivalent at least to the Vatican intelligence service.

"By the era of Sindona, Calvi, and Bishop Marcinkus, under the pontificate of Paul VI, the far more secretive Vatican Bank operated as its own tax haven. It shared the same secrecy as other tax havens like the Bahamas, Luxemburg, and Lichtenstein in which to establish a network of offshore legal entities. It started when Sindona stepped in to liquidate the Vatican stake in SGI for double the market price in exchange for an option to purchase the Vatican's premier bank Banca Cattolica del Veneto. He exercised that option in 1972 as we discussed yesterday in an arrangement involving Calvi and Banco Ambrosiano. The entire sale of SGI and later the sale of Banca Cattolica of course were conducted through the IOR thereby in secrecy without oversight by the Vatican Curia.

"Enough time spent on background. I'm anxious to show you why I brought you to Italy, Gabe. I'll walk you through some additional Scarpelli documents that implicate the Vatican Bank. Show you how the information ties into the larger narrative."

Eisenberg said, "Okay. The most incriminating allegation against the Vatican Bank is money laundering for the Sicilian Mafia. Unlike other financial crimes that speaks to something completely condemning to the Vatican as the spiritual center of the Roman Catholic Church. I'm dying to see what documents you have that support that accusation."

"Then I'll begin there," Nicoletti replied. She pulled a folder from the stack of documents. "I've sorted Scarpelli's documents into categories." Opening the folder labelled *Mafia,* she extracted a photocopy and handed it to Eisenberg.

"This is a letter written by Cardinal Giovanni Benelli to Pope Paul dated 1977. At the time Benelli was Vatican deputy secretary of state. Benelli is comparatively young, aggressive and some say authoritarian during his ten years in the Secretariat of State. With Cardinal Secretary of State Cicognani too old to fulfil many of the duties as the number two person in the Vatican behind the pope, Benelli effectively ran the Secretariat of State. A dominate figure in the Curia, he was considered a front runner as the next pontiff following the death of Pope Paul VI. The second letter with the same date is from another cardinal that brought documented details setting this in motion.

ARCIVESCOVO GIOVANNI BENELLI

12 May 1977
Most Holy Father,

It is with heavy heart that I must be the bearer of distressing news. Within the international news media, there appear constant accusations that the Vatican Institute for the Works of Religion has been complicit in what is referred to as the Italian Banking Scandal. Unfortunately, the financial affairs of Michele Sindona and Roberto Calvi have at times involved using the IOR for various international financial transactions. Some of those banking details are well known, others only speculated without firm basis in fact. Bishop Marcinkus as president of the IOR has therefore been named repeatedly in this banking scandal that remains a continuing distraction now for years and with seemingly no end in sight.

In my position in the Secretariat of State, many within the Curia are deeply troubled about the wider implications of this secular scandal casting harm upon our Holy Mother Church. That concern becomes elevated with certain information recently coming to my attention. The seriousness dictates that I bring his matter to your attention, Your Holiness.

The information I refer to originates from several parish priests in northeast Sicily. Over time these priests presented troubling information provided by many parishioners of the Diocese of Monreale, a part of the Metropolitan Archdiocese of Palermo. I believe these faithful parishioners have without question risked their lives and the lives of their families by passing on what they know to their trusted parish priests. Those priests in turn have risked passing that information to their bishop who personally held an audience with Cardinal Salvatore Pappalardo, Archbishop of Palermo.

Cardinal Pappalardo and I have spent considerable time reviewing this material together. I have included his own personal letter to Your Holiness. The material coming from Sicily mentions several known senior Mafia according to sources in Italian law enforcement. Certain references specifically reveal statements made by those individuals bragging about their connections with certain Italian bankers that 'export their profits to safe havens in foreign countries'. That language can be interpreted as 'money laundering', a recurring allegation appearing in newspapers.

Cardinal Pappalardo and I both counsel that it is imperative that we discontinue any activity that connects the IOR in any manner with organized criminal figures. Given modern international financial transactions involving foreign holding companies and shell companies, identifying the threads of illicit money laundering activities is a difficult undertaking that works to the advantage of those engaged in illicit activities.

To maintain absolute secrecy, Cardinal Pappalardo and I recommend that it becomes necessary to immediately replace Bishop Marcinkus as president of the IOR. This in no way casts blame on Bishop Marcinkus but becomes essential for severing any transactional links believed to be associated with organized crime. In that task, we propose using only clergy trained in finance, accounting, or banking, including existing lay IOR staff, remaining ever mindful that we must maintain secrecy to preserve the trust in Vatican financial institutions.

Your Faithful Servant in Christ,

Arcivescovo Giovanni Benelli

Paulus PP VI.

12 May 1977
Greetings, Holy Father,

I have read Archbishop Benelli's letter to Your Holiness and concur with his recommendations. This terrible blight on the Holy See must be exorcized and set right. The Sicilian Mafia has plagued my beloved providence for over a hundred years starting before the unification of Italy. A shadow government that bleeds the wealth and dignity from a devotedly Catholic population. The whole island lives in fear, nowhere worse than in the northwestern region centered around Palermo.

Palermo Police Chief Inspector Giorgio Boris Giuliano personally provided me with information directly implicating someone connected with the transactions within the IOR disguised as legitimate business transactions. Giuliano's officers also discovered cheques and other documents in a raid of a senior Mafia figure implicating Michele Sindona personally. Documents showing Sindona recycling proceeds from heroin sales by the Mafia through the Vatican Bank to his Amincor Bank in Switzerland in which he has controlling ownership. Guiliano unfortunately has only a code name obtained through a wiretap. He has withheld that information from the Guardia di Finanza national police fearing possible Mafia infiltration has perhaps reached that high.

Every person knows those individuals who are part of the Mafia families. Even those public officials and police that are corruptly aligned with the Mafia. I have taken the liberty of attaching summaries to illustrate the scope and substance of the allegations. The names of the priests that brought forth these allegations from their parishioners represents an act of faith on their part given the associated risk. No names of individual parishioners making these statements are shown to protect their identities from Mafia retribution. Yet these ordinary people did not shy away from identifying specific Mafia individuals and their illicit activities to their trusted parish priests.

The Holy See cannot remain being even indirectly associated with these immoral activities. Archbishop Benelli and I beseech Your Holiness to remedy this clear sacrilege of our holy church.

With your humble servant in Christ,

C. Salvatore Pappalardo

Cardinal Salvatore Pappalardo

Paulus PP VI

"Obviously Benelli is no friend to Bishop Marcinkus," Eisenberg remarked.

Nicoletti said, "Yet Pope Paul did not act on Benelli's accusations. Note the date on the memo. A month later Pope Paul elevated Benelli to cardinal and named him Patriarch of Florence. Benelli then left the Curia and Rome. Did Pope Paul find reason to remove the convenient Benelli? Pope Paul was not in the best of health. The obligations as pope also weighed heavily on his emotional health. Bishop Marcinkus was one of his favorites. Did Pope Paul's notorious indecisiveness result in promoting Benelli to a position away from Rome to avoid dealing with the accusations?"

"Looks like Benelli has an ally in this other cardinal that also wrote to the pope. Who is Cardinal Pappalardo?"

"Cardinal Salvatore Pappalardo is Archbishop of Palermo. A native-born Sicilian. Known as a rigorous opponent of the Mafia. His memo to Pope John Paul points to priests within his archdiocese uncovering incriminating details of possible Vatican Bank involvement in Mafia money laundering."

Nicoletti then handed Eisenberg another photocopy. "Pope Paul VI died in August of last year. Note this letter Benelli gave to newly elected Pope John Paul I is dated only a week following John Paul's elevation to pontiff. Benelli was part of the conclave that elected Cardinal Albino Luciani of Venice as pope. Benelli likely knew of Luciani's dismay over the earlier sale of Banca Cattolica. Benelli would therefore reasonably suspect that Marcinkus already coming under public pressure might now be vulnerable from the new pontiff with personal reason to remove him from the IOR."

ARCIVESCOVO GIOVANNI BENELLI

2 September 1978
Greetings Holy Father,

My heartfelt congratulations on your election, Your Holiness. You shall have my best wishes and faithful support in God's selection as his voice to the faithful of the world.

Undoubtedly you must feel overwhelmed with the demands of your exalted office. I pray for God to bestow wisdom and strength upon you. I regret that I must burden you with what appears to be a worsening crisis. The never-ending financial scandal of which there are frequent allegations increasingly threatening to the Vatican Institute of the Works of Religion. New information provided from diligent parish priests in Sicily gathered information that confirms the IOR may has been complicit in laundering money for the Sicilian Mafia in its association with Italian bankers Michele Sindona and Roberto Calvi, prominently named in the public banking scandal.

It is no secret that the IOR has for many years engaged in financial transactions with Sindona and Calvi. Both bankers had been held in high regard as respected gentlemen by your predecessor Pope Paul VI. Regrettably, both these bankers have betrayed our trust. Through them, the IOR has unwittingly become involved with thieves and murders of the foulest order.

I have attached copies of a letters I addressed to Pope Paul. Unfortunately, health issues and other intervening crisis such as the kidnapping and murder of Pope Paul's friend Aldo Moro accelerated Pope Paul's declining health. His physical and mental resources in his final months likely made tackling this sensitive task impossible.

Cardinal Pappalardo and I implore Your Holiness to act decisively as we previously recommended.

Your Faithful Servant in Christ,

Cardinal Giovanni Benelli

Eisenberg said, "Benelli did not drop his attack on Marcinkus. What's your take on what happened, Emma?"

"Don't have a theory. Pope John Paul I would die in less than four weeks. By his signature on this letter, he saw Benelli's and Pappalardo's earlier letters and backup material. There is no question that Albino Luciani was ill-suited to the papacy. Maye just overwhelmed like Benelli said. Maybe uncertain. Perhaps intimidated by Marcinkus' earlier rebuff over the Banca Cattolica del Veneto incident. Unlike the conspiracy seekers, I still don't believe it adds any credence of a murder plot because Marcinkus feared the loss of his position. More likely some underlying medical condition cut short the new pope's life."

CHAPTER 6

Milan, Italy | June 1979

The year 1979 began with the murder of another public official in January. Five men dragged Milan criminal prosecuting magistrate Emilio Alesandrini from his car as it was stopped at a traffic light. Forced to his knees on the street and executed him with witnesses looking on in horror. Alesandrini's death became immediately connected to Roberto Calvi and Banco Ambrosiano. A scathing report issued by the Bank of Italy in November devoted twenty-five pages detailing legally questionable activities between Ambrosiano and the Vatican Bank. The central bank was stymied with proceeding against Banco Ambrosiano because of the transactions conducted with foreign shell companies that remained beyond the reach of investigators. The Vatican Bank fell within the definition of a foreign legal entity.

Alesandrini was involved with other investigations. His murder would later be attributed to an ultra-violent offshoot group of the *Red Brigades* known as *Prima Linea*. However, at the time it appeared as the beginning of a string of murders related to the Italian Banking Scandal. For Tagliente it provided ample evidence of the ability for the Vatican Bank to conceal its financial misdeeds by remaining silent and uncooperative with Italian authorities.

All the more reason to keep Nicoletti's stolen documents from offering new evidence not otherwise available within international banking transactions.

On 20 March, ambitious journalist Carmine "Mino" Pecorelli specializing in political scandals was shot dead by two Mafia gunmen in Rome's Prati district with three shots to the mouth as a warning. While having nothing to do with the banking scandal it added to the growing list of victims of premeditated public murders by Italian organized crime.

On 13 June 1979, two men machine gunned down head of security for Rome, Carabinieri Lieutenant Colonel Antonio Varisco while his car was stopped at a traffic light. The murders were blamed as a *Red Brigade* terrorist incident. Tagliente would seize the opportunity to use the excessive background of violence to impede the investigation of the Italian Banking Scandal.

Speaking to Monsignor Donaggio, "We need our Sicilian associates to do something they do best. Is it possible to communicate with them directly? Do we know how Sindona communicates with them?"

Donaggio nodded, "Yes, Your Excellency. A trusted Palermo lawyer."

"Excellent. Tell his lawyer that you have received a communication from Sindona through a priest in the confessional that he believes his case in the American court might be irreparably damaged by potential testimony and evidence of the appointed liquidator of Sindona's Banca Privata Italiana. You know what evidence I mean?"

"Yes, Your Excellency. The payment of $5.6 million American dollars to the American bishop at the IOR and a Milanese banker." Tagliente and Donaggio knew this was Bishop Paul Marcinkus and Roberto Calvi.

"Have our Sicilian associates immediately eliminate Giorgio Ambrosoli. Do so quickly. In dramatic fashion to make headlines." Tagliente understood that Ambrosoli may have already provided the Americans with the evidence, but that was not Tagliente's purpose. Put a nail in Sindona's coffin while sending him a message to remain silent about the Vatican and his relationship with the Mafia. Sindona laundered proceeds from heroin trafficking for the Bontade-Spatola-Inzerillo Sicilian Mafia and the American Gambino Mafia Family. Speaking to U.S. prosecutors to negotiate a deal would mean his death sentence.

"Yes, Your Excellency."

"However, there is more. The same fate needs to be arranged perhaps for the Palermo police chief we spoke about. This will reinforce the message to Signore Sindona to maintain his silence.

"Have your intermediary explain to the Sicilian bosses this is intended to assist Michele Sindona in his legal difficulties in the United States. They should expect public backlash. That will blow over. This is about business. Offer appropriate financial remuneration."

"I understand, Your Excellency."

Donaggio's sources previously uncovered information that Palermo Police Chief Boris Giuliano informed Ambrosoli about discovering incriminating documented evidence involving Sindona. Documentation supporting Sindona's routing of Mafia funds through transactions using the Vatican Bank to move laundered funds to Sindona's Amincor Bank in Switzerland.

The Mafia murders generated headlines not only in Italy but in the international press since the victims were government officials. Since the beginning of 1979, Italy was awash in violence. A mix of terrorist attacks by the Marxist-Leninist *Red Brigades* and Italian organized crime. The public conflated all these attacks on Italian officials or institutions as part of a broader attack on Italian society. That suited Tagliente's purpose of disguising his specifically targeted violence.

†

In Milan on 11 July 1979, three Mafia gunmen murdered Giorgio Ambrosoli, the lawyer commissioned as liquidator for Michele Sindona's banks. Monsignor Donaggio's agents spread the rumor that the assassination was ordered by Michele Sindona. A desperate reaction of a banker out of his element. Although the two recent murders were unrelated, it provided Tagliente with a basis to move against the two journalists that possess the confidential documents stolen by Monsignor Scarpelli. Tagliente of course read the letters addressed to Popes Paul VI and John Paul I when first delivered to the Vatican Secret Archive. Another bombing as suggested by Monsignor Donaggio would be lost among the background of violence sweeping Italy.

Summoned to Tagliente's office at the Vatican, "It is time to act, Ettore. Arrange for the demise of Chief Inspector Giorgio Boris Giuliano of the Palermo police department. Tell our associate Bontade that Inspector Guiliano has information we do not want passed to officials in Rome. Giuliano is a crusading enemy to the Sicilian Mafia. His death as obvious Mafia retaliation becomes just another statistic of war in that violently backward province."

Donaggio did not know what Tagliente discovered about the Palermo police inspector but knew better than to ask. Donaggio would again use Bontade's Gesù Mafia family responsible for the murder of Giorgio Ambrosoli.

On 21 July, Palermo Deputy Police Chief Boris Giuliano was brazenly murdered in the Lux Bar in Palermo. The aggressive police officer was shot three times in the neck by a lone Mafia gunman as he was enjoying a morning cappuccino while waiting for his car to arrive to drive him to his office.

Days after Giuliano's murder, Tagliente gave Donaggio new instructions. "With these Mafia assassinations as a backdrop, it is time to eliminate the journalists Nicoletti and her American collaborator. As you suggested, by using a bomb. The newspapers will speculate their deaths as either Mafia or leftist terrorists. The *Red Brigades* might even claim credit. You have kept the journalists under continual surveillance?"

"Yes, Your Excellency. Except for the woman spending the day at her newspaper office, they are mostly stay in her apartment. The American takes a walk each morning for an hour then stays the remainder of the day inside the apartment. On both of the last two weekends the woman drove them to a restaurant where they spent a couple of hours."

Tagliente nodded. "You suggested previously using a bomb. How and where?"

"Rigged in Nicoletti's car. Need to catch them both in the car together. May mean waiting until the weekend. However, we can rig the car in advance and wait for the opportunity to catch them together."

"Detonated outside the woman's residence?"

"Yes, Your Excellency. She parks her car within an interior courtyard enclosed by other apartment buildings. The explosion will blow out most of the buildings' windows but will not otherwise compromise the structures. Collateral injuries are possible but should be minimal."

"Bear in mind that it is essential that the photocopies of the stolen documents be recovered before the deaths of the journalists. Do you have someone you can trust to activate the bomb when presented with the opportunity for eliminating both targets?"

"Yes, Your Excellency."

"Then proceed. For you and those you command, remember these unpleasant undertakings involving casualties are for the greater good of the Holy See. Necessary for sustaining the primacy of the worldwide Roman Catholic Church, the only true church of Jesus Christ. Your work must remain forever unheralded. For five centuries the Holy Alliance has protected the Church. Our mission has never changed. God be with you, Ettore."

What Tagliente set in motion began the next phase of his strategy. Sindona was among the expendable. Attention must focus on shoring up the disaster created by Marcinkus' mismanagement. That meant retreating from providing any assistance to Roberto Calvi. If Calvi proved able to survive the many forces aligned against him, so much the better as long as it puts the IOR in a more favorable position. However, Calvi's financial survival seemed unlikely without assistance by the IOR. Therefore, Calvi must also go the way of Sindona. What Nogara created decades ago before Sindona and Marcinkus entered the picture, still remained in place. Fundamentally sound. Just in need of overhaul. The failure that became the Italian Banking Scandal came about from the excessive self-confidence and naked greed of Sindona and Calvi.

Coupled with Pope Paul's naiveté and Marcinkus' inexperience. Unwittingly the IOR became drawn into the bankers' highly leveraged growth schemes now suffering heavy losses. Dragging with them unwitting investors like the IOR and the Sicilian Mafia.

Perhaps with this new Pope John Paul II, the Vatican Bank can be secured and set on a truer course. The Vatican Bank provides the economic underpinning that allows the Holy See to engage with secular influence among the family of larger nations. Wealth equated to power even in organized religion. Tagliente and like-minded prelates sought to rebuild the power of the Holy See. Reestablish the influence of the Roman Catholic Church as the moral bastion against Communism. A secular mission requiring using unpleasant methods. Methods that fell outside the spiritual embodiment of the Church. A delicate mission requiring absolute secrecy.

The Vatican must take steps of damage control. That is what he and Secretary of State Cardinal Casaroli will counsel the new pope. Cardinal Villot who served as secretary of state for both Paul VI and John Paul II died in March of this year. As *Camerlengo,* Villot also acted as the interim administrator of the Holy See during the two papal election conclaves of 1978. It was Villot that sequestered both Paul VI's and John Paul I's papers in the Vatican Secret Archive. Neither Cardinal Casaroli, Villot's successor as secretary of state, or Pope John Paul II saw the letters drafted by Benelli and Pappalardo. They likely knew only the public face of the financial scandal not the details incriminating the Vatican Bank as a willing accomplice.

Tagliente's immediate task was to save the Vatican Bank from further structural damage. That meant salvaging Archbishop Marcinkus. Working with the American CIA's overtures to fund the Solidarity Movement in Poland to destabilize the Polish communism government puppet regime. Tagliente agreed with Pope John Paul II in that mission as offering a means of doing something constructive against the Soviet Union. Promoting that course of covert participation with the assistance of Archbishop Marcinkus should please Polish Pope John Paul II.

†

Over coffee, Nicoletti read the headline in the Sunday addition of the *Corriere della Sera, PALERMO POLICE CHIEF MURDERED*. The column read: *Palermo Chief Inspector Giorgio Boris Giuliano was shot dead yesterday while seated in the Lux Bar on Via di Blasi in Palermo, Sicily, having a cappuccino as he waited for his car to drive him to work. The assailant shot Giuliano in the neck three times then fired four more bullets into Giuliano's back before walking away. The vicious public execution-style murder is typical of Mafia assassinations intended to send a warning message to others. Guiliano pursued a relentless campaign against the Sicilian Mafia centered in northwestern Sicily.*

"Gabe, this headline announces that Palermo Chief Inspector Giorgio Boris Giuliano has been murdered in Palermo. He's the police official that provided Cardinal Pappalardo with the documented evidence linking the Vatican Bank to illegal Mafia activities in connection with Sindona and Calvi. Could this be somehow related to these missing documents?"

Eisenberg replied. "No way to know. However, there is no question that possessing these documents is dangerous. Has the theft from the Vatican Secret Archive by this priest been detected? The priest's letter to you mentions his superior was Archbishop Tagliente who is also the head of the Vatican secret service."

"I have been researching Tagliente. A shadowy figure that appears only infrequently in brief anecdotal references without detail. My Vatican sources say only that insiders are unwilling to even repeat rumors about Tagliente. Unusual for an institution that is consumed by rumors. I got the distinct impression that Tagliente is feared. Clearly a senior prelate entrusted with extraordinary Vatican secrets by successive pontiffs from Pius XII to John Paul II might breed a sense of sinister mystery among his peers.

"All I know for certain are the known available facts about his life. Born here in Milan in 1914. Third son of a wealthy Milanese business family. His paternal family heritage places him among what were known as the Black Nobility, lay persons close to the Vatican going back to the time of papal States before Italian unification in 1870. As a younger son with older siblings, he chose a career in the priesthood. A typical career path probably influenced by relatives having risen to prelates within the Vatican. Attended the Jesuit Pontifical Gregorian University, from age 16 graduating in 1939 with degrees in history and theology. Ordained a priest in 1939 into the Jesuit Order soon after the election of Eugenio Pacelli as Pope Pius XII. Pope Pius even attended his ordination since their families were close.

"Pius XII immediately brought Tagliente into the Vatican Secretariat of State office. There Tagliente worked closely under Monsignor Giovanni Montini, the future Pope Paul VI. Simultaneously with his Vatican duties, Tagliente attended Sapienza University of Rome, acquiring a degree in economics and a doctorate in international law in 1943."

Eisenberg interjected, "Tagliente then has an academic background related to banking and international law. Now he holds positions in the Vatican Secret Archive and Vatican intelligence, both reporting directly to the pontiff the same as the Vatican Bank. Archbishop Tagliente certainly occupies a unique position. Maybe there is good reason why some of his fellow churchmen view him with a degree of fear."

Nicoletti added, "Well, I'm not going to become paranoid about Tagliente. Lots of strange personalities exist within the walls of the Vatican.

Two days later, Nicoletti answered the telephone. Speaking in Italian for a few moments with the caller, she switched to English, "It's for you, Gabe. Someone named Frank Amatrano."

Eisenberg took the phone. "Frank, good to hear from you. Where are you calling from?"

Amatrano said, "Paris. Interpol headquarters. Still living and working in Europe. Been over 20 years now. Joined Interpol in 1960 after leaving the State Department Bureau of Diplomatic Security. Michael phoned me. Asked if I would call you at this number in Milan. Are you working on a story?"

"You might say that. Came to Milan to investigate some material that came into the possession of a close friend and professional colleague. Emma Nicoletti. She was the one that answered the telephone."

"I recall her name. Your coauthor of *Ratlines*. A great book. Fascinating work you both did on acquiring so much material about the Vatican aiding the escape of World War Two war criminals to South American. Always bothered me that Interpol never become involved. Article 3 of Interpol's Charter, prohibits intervention in political or religious matters. I disagree that tracking down mass murderers should be considered political or religious."

Eisenberg said, "The reason for my call is Emma and I are pursuing another story related to the Vatican. Not political or related to religion for that matter. It involves the Vatican Bank. In short, the Italian Banking Scandal that became public years ago and continues to have legs. Because of the ultra-secrecy of the Vatican and its stature as a sovereign country, so far there have only been unconvincing allegations as to Vatican Bank violations of international laws and laws of other counties."

"I'm aware of these allegations. Especially where it concerns money laundering."

"Money laundering is something of which we have, let's say for the moment, relevant information. Specifically, money laundering for Italian organized crime. The Vatican Bank acts no differently than any other tax haven that functions without oversight or reporting obligations as to origin of funds, stockholders of foreign legal entities, etcetera."

"Okay. What is it that I can help you sort out, Gabe? I can't provide any confidential information from either Interpol or law enforcement agencies from our nearly 200 member countries. Interpol is just an investigative body, not itself a law enforcement agency. I don't even carry a firearm."

"We're not looking for you as a source for confidential information. What we're looking for is how you might recommend we proceed with newly acquired material already within our possession.. This international financial crisis started with Italian banker Michele Sindona. Already discredited, he is at the source of this complex international scandal involving the disappearance of hundreds of millions of dollars. Sindona now lives in exile in New York after convicted in absentia in Italy for bank fraud. The U.S. Department is investing his activities. However, the crisis goes much deeper than Sindona's activities in the failure of Franklin National Bank years ago. Sindona is likely guilty of much great bank fraud theft than charged in his Italian conviction. Currency manipulation, equities market manipulation, and money laundering for the Sicilian Mafia.

"Let me be blunt about our dilemma. There exists a pervasively corrupted public sector in Italy. Includes law enforcement and even some elements of the judiciary. The U.S. DOJ is moving at a snail's pace. These international financial transactions involve numerous tax haven counties in Europe, the Caribbean, and Central America. Switzerland itself a tax haven is notoriously complicit in aiding sovereign countries without regard for the origin of money. Banking for the Nazis and stolen Jewish Holocaust wealth being prime examples. Then you have the seemingly impenetrable paranoidal secrecy-obsessed Holy See of the Roman Catholic Church sticking their unholy fingers into the mix. How can journalists be expected to expose the truth with all officialdom abetting the bad actors?"

"Christ, Gabe. Enough. I get your point. At the risk of sounding insensitive, isn't that the challenge you investigative journalists always face?"

"Sorry for getting off on a rant, Frank. Just been reading some of Emma's material and the venality of the Vatican as a spiritual institution is profoundly troubling. Even Interpol is circumspect about political and religious implications as you say. That's where we could use your professional advice. You know European law enforcement. Who might be sympathetic? Who might be compromised? Where to avoid the minefields?"

"What if I came to Milan in an unofficial capacity? I have extended family in Genoa where I was born. An aunt and uncle and a few cousins. Don't get to see them as often as I should. Good excuse to pay a visit. I get to Rome a couple of times a year on official Interpol business to liaison with the *Guard di Finanza*, the Italian financial police. Lots of turmoil going on in Italy. *Red*

Brigade terrorist attacks, a seemingly emboldened Mafia, and of course this banking scandal with international scope. I have enough official reason to warrant making another trip to Rome.

"Reviewing your material should not violate Interpol policy. I might be compelled to report certain evidence of crimes that comes to my attention though. Can't do much along those lines if you redact sensitive details that reveal names of your sources. Learning more about the nature of what you have, I can be better able to advise how you might proceed in furthering your research.

"What if I schedule an indirect trip to stop off in Switzerland then see you in Milan before continuing to Rome? Sometime within the next week if that works for you. Give me the address, I'll be coming in by train from Zurich after attending a meeting in Bern."

"Emma and I greatly appreciate you taking time to assist us, Frank."

"Not at all, Gabe. Investigative journalists like you and Signora Nicoletti serve the cause of justice in important ways. A free press is what separates democratic institutions from totalitarianism. Evidenced by the violence plaguing Italy for those going after criminals your profession can be dangerous. Keep your incriminating evidence secret until safeguarding your personal security."

CHAPTER 7

Milan, Italy | June 1979

Two men in the employ of Monsignor Donaggio waited in a service van parked on Via Maddalena south of the Plazza Duomo in central Milan. An upscale district, the tenants of the apartments enjoyed added security by the ability to drive into an interior courtyard through a barred gate with designated parking.

Dressed in uniform overalls with the name of a plumbing service displayed on the side of the service van provided cover for their presence parked on the narrow street. Their orders were to report when both subjects were observed leaving the building and to notify others in a car parked a short distance away on the same street by two-way radio.

One man walked to the gate with a clipboard waiting for a car to depart leaving the gate open allowing his colleague to drive the van inside. Their instructions were to wait until observing Nicoletti and Eisenberg both driving away together before making entry into the apartment.

This being a Saturday morning, Nicoletti and Eisenberg left the apartment together as they did on previous weekends. Donaggio's agents observed both targets carrying suitcases. Regardless of what that signified, their orders were clear. Make entry into

Nicoletti's apartment. Seize the documents if found then proceed with the plan for eliminating the targets. If the documents cannot be recovered they were to abduct both targets and hold them in a secure location. That would be most regrettable. It would require forcing the journalists to reveal the location of the documents. Obviously by using physical means of coercion. Killing to protect the Holy See was a regrettable act, however even someone with as twisted a sense of morality as Donaggio found the idea of torture objectionable. He did not abide the historical application of torture by the medieval Inquisition, nor death by burning at the stake. If necessary to take life for the greater good of the Church, it should be swift.

Donaggio simplified the plan in order to take control. Instead of employing Mafias to perform the execution, he would only require their assembling of a bomb. If the copies of the stolen documents were not found in the woman's apartment, he would determine the next course of action that would require using Mafia thugs.

A week ago, Donaggio's most trusted agent, a lay Jesuit by the name of Brother Gideon, who possessed a military background, picked up a lone Mafioso at Milano Centrale railway station. The Mafioso delivered a prepared bomb consisting of four sticks of 40% nitroglycerin dynamite taped together.

Seated in a car in the train station parking lot, the Mafioso handed Brother Gideon the prepared bomb. Four sticks of dynamite eight inches long bound together by layers of tape with two insulated wires protruding. "No need to worry about it going off. Just don't let the dynamite get too hot making it unstable. Four sticks of 40% straight dynamite should destroy the car and kill the occupants. Inside two of the sticks of dynamite are blasting caps to make sure of detonation. You'll connect these wires to the car's ignition system. I'll show you how. Important to place the bomb where it'll do the most damage. What kind of car?"

"A 1971 Fiat 128. That's why I'm here today with a later model 128 so you can show me where to place the charge," Brother Gideon replied.

"Good. Fiat didn't change the 128 much over the years. Four sticks will do the job. It will cause a lot of surrounding damage."

"That will not be a problem."

"Okay. Then I'll show you where to place the bomb and how to wire it."

Both men exited the vehicle. Brother Gideon raised the hood of the rented Fiat.

The Mafioso looked down into the engine compartment. "Enough room here right up against the firewall," he said after unwrapping the insulated wire. Setting the dynamite into place, he said. "All you need to do is attach each of these wires to the terminals on top of the ignition coil here and here," the Mafioso said pointing to the terminals. "I provided alligator clips to make that quick and easy. That's all there is to it. When the victim engages the ignition, the battery current detonates the imbedded blasting caps which then detonates the dynamite. It'll take out everybody inside. Just make damn sure the engine is off before you attach the wires. Anything else?"

Brother Gideon said, "No." Then reaching into his suit jacket pocket, he extracted an envelope. "As agreed, twenty-five hundred lire. Have a good trip back to Sicily."

The Mafioso disappeared back into the train station.

One of the men in the plumbing service uniform approached the gate that Saturday morning with clipboard in hand. Through the bars of the gate, he observed Nicoletti and Eisenberg exiting the building walking toward Nicoletti's Fiat. Nicoletti stopped to unlock the gate to the street. As she drove out, the man said to her, "*Buongiorno.* I will lock the gate when we complete a plumbing repair, Signora."

Nicoletti drove away with Eisenberg in the passenger seat. The dummy plumbing service van entered the courtyard.

Brother Gideon sat in a car parked behind the service van. From a two-way radio in his lap came a voice saying, "Both targets drove off together in the Fiat." Brother Gideon switched the radio to transmit, "Enter the apartment. Find the papers and radio immediately when you locate them. Make a thorough search. You need not be delicate about creating disorder but do not arouse attention from neighbors. Time is critical." Turning to the driver of the car, "Follow that Fiat."

After a short drive lasting only twenty minutes, Brother Gideon recognized Nicoletti's destination. Milano Centrale railway station. To his driver, "Follow until she parks then find a spot close enough to observe them."

From the trunk of the Fiat, Nicoletti and Eisenberg removed two small suitcases. To the driver, Brother Gideon said, "Follow them on foot. They have suitcases likely meaning boarding a train. You are to board the same train. Stay close to them and report to me by telephone when they disembark at their destination." Reaching for his wallet, Brother Gideon extracted cash handing it to the driver. "For expenses."

†

Donaggio's entry person easily picked the lock to Nicoletti's apartment. Dressed in a plumber's uniform other residents had no reason to question his activities. Once inside he went to the office area occupying half of the living area. Opening the top drawer of a two-drawer file cabinet he thumbed through folders full of various papers and handwritten notes. Moving to the bottom drawer he found what he was looking for. Told to look for a large quantity of photocopied documents on Vatican stationary or with ecclesiastical seals. Sworn by an oath not to read details or scrutinize the signatures. The man loaded the documents and file folders into cardboard boxes brought along for the purpose.

Withdrawing a two-way radio from his belt he pressed *transmit.* "I have the material. I repeat. I have the material. Leaving the location immediately."

Brother Gideon acknowledged the transmission as he sat alone in the car parked at Milano Centrale. His next step was clear now with recovery of the photocopied documents. Set the bomb into place. As for the originals, they would forever languish in the secrecy of a Swiss bank vault.

From the trunk he extracted the dynamite device concealed in a paper bag. Walking to Nicoletti's old Fiat, he laid the bomb on the ground. Opening the hood, he looked down into essentially the same engine compartment configuration as the later model Fiat in which the Mafioso showed him where to position the bomb.

Connecting the wires took only a few minutes. Closing the hood, the thought crossed his mind that this was July. The Mafioso cautioned about excessive heat making the dynamite unstable. That depended on how hot the next few days became and how long before Nicoletti and the American returned. Then again, every plan contended with variables outside of one's control. So far, everything has moved in his favor.

Contrary to suffering feelings of guilt for killing these people, Brother Gideon experienced only a sense of relief. Their deaths would be swift enough as to be painless. No need to resort to barbaric methods to inflict pain, ultimately ending far from a merciful death.

Brother Gideon walked into the cavernous Milano Centrale building and found a payphone. "Your Excellency, we have the stolen documents. I shall deliver them to your Vatican office within the hour."

†

Eisenberg said. "When we first discussed these Vatican confidential documents the archive priest went to lengths to call attention to Archbishop Tagliente in his letter to you. The priest was dying when he wrote that letter. Undoubtedly, he would have liked to pass on more information about Tagliente but was too ill to continue his surreptitious investigations. He pointedly directed you to pursue Tagliente as a person of interest."

Nicoletti said, "I have devoted some preliminary efforts to that but have been more focused on studying how these documents fit into the known aspects of the Italian Banking Scandal. Frankly, there is very little about Archbishop Tagliente in the public domain other than basic background facts."

Nicoletti paused for a moment in thought. "I know someone that might be of assistance in learning more about the elusive

Archbishop Tagliente. A colleague from my earliest days in journalism when I worked for *Corriere della Sera* in their Rome bureau. Carlo Langella is now the Rome bureau chief. More than that, he is an authoritative Vatican watcher. I stay in touch with Carlo. See him occasionally when I'm in Rome."

Eisenberg said, "Maybe we should pay him a visit. Tagliente is a mystery and therefore intriguing. A gut instinct says he may be part of our larger story."

"Good idea. You will like Carlo. We can train to Rome and return the following day. Can't spend all our time sequestered in the apartment. You're in Italy, Gabe. You are like visiting family to me so we should devote some downtime."

After receiving her degree in New York from Columbia, Nicoletti returned to Italy. That first job was an entry reporting position with the Rome bureau of Italy's largest newspaper *Corriere della Sera*. A representative newspaper of the moderate bourgeoisie, *Corriere della Sera* was considered center-right-leaning, supportive of the Christian Democratic Party and friendly to the Vatican. Carlo Langella became her mentor eventually lobbied for her promotion to a position at the newspaper's headquarters in Milan.

Now the Rome bureau chief for *Corriere della Sera,* Carlo Langella was known as a veteran Vatican watcher. A softspoken social individual, his many sources within the Vatican felt comfortable in sharing sometimes sensitive information. Privy to the stream of insider rumor, Carlo was careful to avoid conjecture, preferring to report only information accompanied by reliable corroboration.

As a Catholic, Langella was deeply dismayed by the conduct of the Vatican in assisting the escape of war criminals to South America following World War Two. He applauded Nicoletti's ground-breaking investigative work revealing details and names in her book *Ratlines*. He shared Nicoletti's critical view of Pope Pius XII. Allowing mass murderers to escape justice with the active support of clerics close to the Vatican was unconscionable for someone professing to speak for God. Providing for spiritual rehabilitation with mercy rather than harsh uneven justice by execution by the Soviets proved an unsatisfactory argument professed by Vatican apologists. Pius XII's silence on the subject further added to the Germanophile Pius XII's label as Hitler's pope with his equal silence to criticism that he did not sufficiently speak out against the Nazi perpetrated Holocaust.

Like Eisenberg, Nicoletti was anxious to learn more about secretive Archbishop Tagliente. Monsignor Scarpelli was clearly not a fan of his boss. That Tagliente controls the most secretive functions with the Vatican under direct control of the pontiff needs further exploration.

Langella was delighted when she telephoned about visiting him. He would free up the afternoon for her followed by drinks and dinner. She booked rooms for the night at a hotel near the railway station to take an early train back to Milan the following afternoon.

†

Nicoletti and Eisenberg arrived at Rome's Termini railway station where Carlo Langella was waiting on the platform. After exchanging pleasantries, Langella drove them the short distance to the *Corriere della Sera* office on Via Campania.

Seated in a small conference room, Nicoletti said, "So good to see you, Carlo. I appreciate you taking time to meet with Gabriel and I."

"Not at all, Emma. I always enjoy seeing you. You need to get to Rome more often. Tell me about this new project you're working on."

Nicoletti replied with the cover story she and Eisenberg settled on. They were not yet prepared to candidly discuss the stolen documents that narrowed the project to a story exposing the Vatican's participation in financial misdeeds. The most condemning aspect of which was knowingly participating in money laundering of illicit drugs profits for organized crime as a source of income for the Vatican. A sequel exposé to their *Ratlines* book, with the working title of this new project titled *For God & Gold.*

Nicoletti said, "The project is about the tumultuous Vatican period from 1963 and Pope Paul VI to the new Pope John Paul II.

The origins of the Italian Banking Scandal implicating the Vatican Bank, the death of two popes, one lasting only thirty-three days, to the election of the first non-Italian as pontiff in hundreds of years. Gabriel wonders if there is more to Archbishop Tagliente during this period that we are studying."

Eisenberg interrupted saying, "I confess that I am obsessed with exploring mysteries. Tagliente is a mystery."

Nicoletti continued, "Archbishop Tagliente appears as some indistinct prelate that came to the Vatican Secretariat of State office upon ordination with his family's close association with the family of Pope Pius XII. Presently he occupies the role of Archivist of the Vatican Secret Archive, a seemingly non-mainstream office but remote from the public eye. Fragmented references of his association with the historical Vatican Holy Alliance may just be rumor. Does a Vatican secret service still exist? Does Archbishop Tagliente unofficially run the Vatican's secret service? Who is the best historical authority on the Holy Alliance? Does Tagliente have any role in managing damage control to counter the allegations against Vatican Bank involvement with Sindona and Calvi and therefore possibly indirectly to the Sicilian Mafia?"

Langella said, "Archbishop Tagliente is very much a mystery. An elusive creature within the Vatican menagerie. Does he run the Vatican secret services? Does the Holy Alliance, or as existing rumor refers to as the *Entity*, actually exist today? The answer to each of those questions is yes. As to its function, that remains sheer speculation. Beyond ancient history, everything currently known about *Santa Alleanza,* the Holy Alliance in English, comes largely from rumor, the staple of Vatican internal discourse. Catholic prelates are like Italian washerwomen gossiping while communally washing clothes in the nearby river. Holy Alliance may not be a well-kept secret, yet its activities remain shrouded in secrecy more absolute than most other areas within the Vatican."

Eisenberg added, "And Archbishop Tagliente seems to be integral to those most secret areas. Those that report directly to the pope, bypassing the Curia."

Langella replied, "I've had the same thoughts. But from a journalistic perspective, there is no story centering on Tagliente. No reason to investigate him outside of curiosity."

Nicoletti said, "Well, we may have found some reason, Carlo. Just a thread that Gabriel and I are pursuing in this banking scandal implicating the Vatican Bank. Might Tagliente have any involvement with the Vatican IOR? He has an academic background in economics and international law."

Langella said, "Not that I have heard about. Or even speculated by rumor. Of course, IOR President Bishop Marcinkus is a much different cleric. Well known and highly visible, Marcinkus is nonetheless publicly very uncommunicative about IOR involvement in the banking scandal."

"How well we know," Nicoletti commented.

Eisenberg said, "Who is the best historical authority on the Vatican secret service? That alone is a mystery that we cannot ignore in our project. We need to learn more to see if it has relevance to events surrounding this banking scandal since 1963."

"Not sure who I can recommend. At least anyone I know willing to speak from actual knowledge. Let me give that some thought."

Carlo Langella did know someone. An older priest. Consulted regularly by Langella about the Vatican secret service. Under sworn agreement, Langella never identified Monsignor Guido Orsini as a source. Langella doubted that Orsini would consent to speak with Nicoletti or Eisenberg, however he would leave that decision to Orsini.

After Nicoletti recited what they knew of Tagliente's background, Langella said, "You know as much as I do about the factual background of Archbishop Tagliente. Let me offer some insights I have gleaned from various sources within the Vatican. Bear in mind these are gossipy old men living in an insular environment. Although men of God, they still severely suffer from the sins of pride and jealousy. Men with political ambitions in their chosen profession as priests. Little different from those in corporations or governmental institutions. With that preamble, let me give you my opinion of Archbishop Tagliente, but only from secondhand opinions. I've never met him personally.

"Vatican consensus portrays Tagliente as you describe him, Signore Eisenberg, as somewhat of a mystery. Respected as exceptionally intelligent. Remote and even aloof in his interactions with others. His title as Archivist of the Vatican Secret Archive, places him outside the Vatican organizational mainstream. Not to be confused with the Vatican Library, the Vatican Secret Archive operates independently from the Curia. For an otherwise talented bishop, his elevation by the new Pope John Paul II to archbishop while publicly retaining only his appointment as archivist of the obscure Vatican Secret Archive seemed inexplicable. It may signal John Paul's regard for Tagliente's covert services requiring elevation in rank.

"Therefore, as I said, it is common knowledge that the Vatican secret services exist to this day. Plural. That includes the normal intelligence gathering of papal nuncios situated in countries throughout the world as well as priests of different Catholic orders. As a Jesuit, Tagliente has access to perhaps the most educated and secularly involved of all the ecclesiastical orders. This is the Santa Alleanza originating in the 16th century by Pope Pius V. Its mission at that time was to end the life of Elizabeth I of England and install Catholic Mary Queen of Scots on the throne.

"There also exists another secret service known as *Sodalitium Pianum*, S.P., established by Pius X in 1913 as a counterintelligence service to combat infiltration from the many intelligence services operating throughout Europe during the years prior to the Great War. Nothing is known or even rarely rumored about its current function.

"It is commonly understood that Archbishop Tagliente is the operational head of the Vatican Secret Services. The archivist position is not a particularly subtle cover. Adding to the obfuscation is the officially accepted, but never formally acknowledged head of Santa Alleanza, sometimes referred to as the *Entity,* as being Archbishop Luigi Poggi, a long-serving member of the Vatican Secretariat."

Eisenberg added, "Does it seem coincidental to you, Signore Langella, that if Tagliente is in fact the actual head of Vatican intelligence and officially supervises the Vatican Secret Archive, that both offices report directly to the pontiff instead of the Curia? Would it be a stretch given Tagliente's background to speculate about his possible involvement with the Vatican Bank? Operating covertly while reporting directly to the pontiff might be useful in countering attacks on the Vatican related to the banking scandal?"

Langella gave the question a moment's thought. With a smile, he said, "I see your point. Not at all farfetched."

†

After their late dinner with Carlo Langella, Nicoletti and Eisenberg spent the night at a hotel close to Rome Termini train station. They would catch an early train the next morning to return to Milan.

"Didn't learn much of anything new about Tagliente, or for that matter anything definitive about Vatican intelligence," Nicoletti said as they rode on the return train trip to Milan.

"Oh, I don't know. What Carlo related reinforces my instinct that somehow Tagliente plays a larger part in our project than we think. Anyway, I enjoyed meeting Carlo. Stimulating company for a wonderful evening over a three-hour dinner. Drank too much wine and grappa. Like you, I don't get away from work enough to smell the flowers. What's on the agenda when we get back?"

"I've chronicled the sequence of what is known since this scandal broke. Beginning in 1974 when Michele Sindona's financial empire started unraveling. The insolvency of the American bank Franklin National. Sindona's forty-million-dollar loss then precipitated the downfall of his other banks like a house of cards. Simultaneously, public scrutiny in Italy turned toward Banco Ambrosiano in Milan and Roberto Calvi. The spotlight on Calvi brought forth accusations of Vatican Bank involvement and its president Bishop Marcinkus. We need to fit our newfound information provided by Father Scarpelli's documents into the known elements of the scandal to build a clearer picture."

Eisenberg said, "The unknown with the greatest potential to harm the Vatican comes from allegations of laundering money for the Mafia. Apart from questionable business financial transactions to enrich the coffers of the Vatican, association with international drug traffickers and murderers becomes morally indefensible to the world, especially to the Catholic faithful."

Nicoletti said, "Not so sure. The world never sanctioned the Vatican for helping Nazi and Croatian Ustaše mass murderers to escape to South America. Our book did not cause worldwide condemnation. Most people today probably do not even know that happened."

Eisenberg replied, "Our book came out in 1963. The Vatican ratlines operated many years earlier. Pius XII was dead. Those events were already history. Giovanni Montini became Paul VI but chose to remain silent about Nazi war criminals during his fifteen years as pope. Not unusual because Montini occupied a prominent position in Pius XII's pontificate. Perhaps he knew too much from his service to Pius XII during the years of the ratlines. Other world events dominated world attention in 1963. The Second Vatican Council. The Cuban Missile Crisis in the autumn of the prior year left lingering fears of the Soviet Union. The assassination of American President John F. Kennedy. The beginning of the catastrophe that would become the Vietnam War.

"This financial crisis is currently newsworthy. It continues. Its conclusion remains uncertain, not yet history. The Vatican in bed with the Sicilian Mafia if proven true will shake St. Peters Basilica to its foundation."

Nicoletti said, "Well, we still must prove that connection. My review of Scarpelli's documents only makes the Mafia connection through a web of foreign shell companies involving the Vatican Bank indirectly through Sindona and Calvi."

Their train pulled into Milano Centrale station in the early afternoon. Walking through the massive station, Nicoletti said, "I'm famished. Let's get some sandwiches to take back to the apartment."

"Sounds good," Eisenberg said.

At a delicatessen stand, they ordered sandwiches and coffees in paper cups.

"You take the food and coffee, I'll manage the bags," Eisenberg said.

"Very good. Here's the car keys," Nicoletti replied reaching into her purse and handing Eisenberg the keys.

Exiting the train station they began walking across the parking lot.

The same man that boarded the same train as Nicoletti and Eisenberg the previous day exited behind them maintaining a discreet distance. He had spent a long sleepless thirty hours observing their movements in Rome. Back in Milan, he knew what came next.

As Eisenberg reached the Fiat, he opened the trunk placing the suitcases inside. Nicoletti approached more slowly balancing the cardboard tray so as not to spill the coffees.

"Eisenberg turned toward her. "I'll drive. We'll see if I can still master a standard transmission. You can hold our coffee and lunch on your lap. Let me back the car out before you get in."

Gabriel Eisenberg opened the driver's side door and got behind the wheel. Seconds later the Fiat exploded. The blast peeled back the roof from the rest of the car's body. The engine hood totally separated landing on another parked car. The interior burst into flame as gasoline ignited everything combustible. That included the body of Gabriel Eisenberg.

Emma Nicoletti had been standing behind the car parked next to her Fiat waiting for Eisenberg to back out before getting in the passenger side. While partially shielded from the direct blast shock wave by the car parked next to the fiat, enough force still caught her to knock her off her feet.

Driven backward, Nicoletti's head struck the pavement hard. A metal fragment from the blast caught her in the left cheek and several glass fragments struck her along her left arm. Blood streaming from her nose and ears caused by the concussive force of the blast along with lacerations from debris. The force also proved violent enough to dislocate her left shoulder and fracture her left clavicle leaving her arm resting at an awkward angle.

Brother Gideon's associate watching from a safe distance could see only that Nicoletti lay unmoving on the pavement. The force of the explosion proved more powerful than he expected. He moved to join a crowd gathering closer to get a better look as emergency personnel began descending to the scene. Closer visual observation confirmed only that she was unconscious. Appearing badly injured, he could not determine if she was dead or alive. Police then began pushing back the spectators as paramedics arrived to attend to the victim. Firefighters worked to extinguish the burning vehicle. The watcher remained until paramedics lifted the woman onto a gurney then into an ambulance.

After the ambulance drove from the scene with sirens blaring following a police car leading the way, the surveillance agent turned from the scene and reentered the railway station. Finding a payphone, he telephoned Brother Gideon. "Subjects returned to Milano Centrale less than an hour ago. Explosion killed the male subject without question. Status of the female is uncertain. She was outside the vehicle at the time of the blast. Transported by ambulance. Appeared unconscious but cannot verify if dead or the extent of injuries."

CHAPTER 8

Milan, Italy | June 1979

Archbishop Tagliente was seated in an elegant sitting room of a 19th century villa within the town of Frascati. He arrived only an hour earlier. Dusk was already turning to night as the sun settled behind the hills. Only twenty kilometers southeast from Rome's Termini railway station, Frascati was easily assessable by local train in thirty minutes. A delightful town situated in the hills with Rome viewed from its advantageous elevation.

While Tagliente enjoyed a single malt Scotch whisky, an elegant woman walked into the room holding a glass of red wine. She wore an ankle-length designer silk robe offset by a string of pearls. A diamond bracelet adorned her wrist. With a stylish coiffure and minimal makeup, her face with its olive complexion looked years less than her sixty years.

Coming to sit next to Tagliente on their favorite loveseat, Isabella Leonardi said, "Angelina is preparing us rare Florentine steaks with risotto for dinner. This full-bodied Tuscana Rosso will pair perfectly. I missed you this weekend, Marcello. Your call mentioned something unexpected would delay you coming until today. Is everything under control?"

Quite the contrary, things were decidedly not under control. The stolen document photocopies recovered from the journalist only bought time if the woman survived. That remained highly probable from the earliest reports received from sources within the hospital. After twenty-four hours, the woman's status remained critical based largely on the unknown extent of her head trauma, but her vital signs were strong. That meant she would recover with renewed vengeance. The missing Vatican Secret Archive documents would be used to bolster allegations against Marcinkus and the Vatican Bank. It would establish a long participatory relationship with Michele Sindona then later with Roberto Calvi and the growing Banco Ambrosiano financial disaster.

Those revelations might be weathered by sacrificing Marcinkus. Yet that was not likely to happen given Pope John Paul II's support of Marcinkus. Revealing the complicity of Pope Paul VI in sordid financial crimes was a far more inflammatory matter reflecting even on the papacy of current Pope John Paul II. Coming on the heels of suspicious circumstances surrounding the unexpected death of Pope John Paul I after only several weeks following his election could only exacerbate conspiracy rhetoric with Marcinkus' dismissal claimed as a cover up or scapegoat.

Pope John Paul I's death was a totally mishandled sequence of events, largely the fault of French Cardinal Secretary of State Jean-Marie Villot. As *Camerlengo,* Villot acted as the interim administrator of the Holy See during a papal vacancy with the interregnums of 1978 following the deaths of Paul VI and John Paul I. Among Villot's several mistakes were authorizing embalming of John Paul I. This gave rise to various conspiracy theories. How did a seemingly healthy man of sixty-five die suddenly in his sleep? With the remains embalmed before examination by medical experts, speculation about poisoning abounded.

Coupled with rumor that John Paul I was about to dismiss Bishop Marcinkus as president of the Vatican Bank made Marcinkus a possible suspect in foul play. Cardinal Villot himself then died of pneumonia in March of 1979 just five months after Pope John Paul I's death. Villot's mistakes and any expectation of resolving the mysterious death of John Paul I died with him.

Tagliente's Holy alliance agents investigated the death of the pontiff. They found no credible evidence of poisoning. Possibly an accidental dose of blood thinning medication by the pontiff himself. Known only to those few close to him, Pope John Paul I suffered from chronic circulatory problems evident by severe swelling of his legs. Embalming without first taking blood samples then the internment of the remains eliminated ruling out poisoning, therefore rumors persisted.

Following Villot's death, Tagliente briefed John Paul II on everything he was able to learn. Pope John Paul I most likely died of natural causes, possibly exacerbated by accidental overdose. No evidence of foul play. The incidents feeding the rumors came from unfortunate actions taken in covering up how, when, and by whom the deceased pontiff was found along with other misleading or inaccurate information. Tagliente assured John Paul II that Marcinkus had nothing to do with his predecessor's death. Pope John Paul II was immensely relieved and thanked Tagliente profusely for his service. While Tagliente believed Marcinkus innocent, Marcinkus would undoubtedly find out that Tagliente's support with the new pope proved invaluable. Brash American Bishop Paul Marcinkus was not popular with many prelates, therefore Tagliente became an important ally given his stature with the new pope.

What concerned Tagliente was the extent to which the missing documents made the case for the Vatican's connection with the Mafia. That connection, although buried in layers of misleading transactions by Calvi's bank using offshore holding companies, the paper trail nevertheless existed. Ever the realist, Tagliente knew that the failure to remove Emma Nicoletti held dire threat. Beyond the negative implications for the Holy See, the manifest unholy alliance with organized crime was an exceedingly important source of revenue. The Vatican Bank must remain a unique offshore tax haven with broad recognition as a place of financial trust in order to exercise financial transactions in international markets.

Tagliente smiled at Isabella, "Nothing is ever completely under control within the Vatican. Undoubtedly no different than with any government. The difference being Vatican institutions function under archaic patterns of ill-defined authority. To those on the outside, it is byzantine, secretive, and accustomed to silence."

Isabella added, "And your place in this menagerie of old men is the most secretive of all. Few within Vatican City even know what you do. The fact that you even shared with me that you are the dark prince of the ultra-secretive Vatican secret service attests to your love and generosity for me. I have learned never to intrude by asking details."

Tagliente reached over and squeezed her hand. "You enrich my life beyond measure, Isabella. A woman of expansive perception. A worldliness about you. A remarkable range of intellect. Accomplished musician. Courageous enough to understand why I have forsaken the vow of celibacy because of you. Confident enough to pursue a most unusual relationship ladened with inconvenient secrecy."

They kissed. "Perhaps you can get away for a week to come to Como as the summer progresses."

Leonardi made her home in a magnificent villa on the west bank of Lake Como. Much cooler summers than Rome where Marcello could go about incognito under an assumed name. Frascati served the same refuge while being only thirty minutes by train from Rome. She purchased the Frascati villa after what began as an affair in 1963 soon transformed into a lasting relationship. A transformative relationship for both her and Marcello.

Isabella Leonardi became a widow less than a year before meeting Tagliente. While the marriage to a handsome but philandering playboy scion of a wealthy industrial family was probably doomed for failure, his unexpected death still proved emotionally jarring. The crash of his new Ferrari 330 while exercising its handling performance on the winding Les Corniche roads in the hills above Monaco occurred while she was performing at a concert in Genoa.

Her former husband held a marketing position in his family's industrial holdings. She was forty-three at the time. Well-established in her musical career as first violinist for the Milan Symphony Orchestra. Having studied at the prestigious Conservatorio Giuseppe Verdi in Milan, she began her performing career with the orchestra of the La Scala Opera in 1942. World War Two erupted only a few months earlier when Mussolini foolishly joined Hitler in declaring war on the United States. A difficult time for a professional musician to maintain proficiency. With performance venues under constant threat during the eighteen months of German occupation following invasion of the Italian mainland by American and British forces, she adapted to another period of adjustment by resuming her career in 1945 in heavily damaged Italy.

For Marcello Tagliente, the new pontiff Paul VI, formerly Cardinal Giovanni Montini, immediately elevated him from monsignor to bishop. He worked closely with then Monsignor Montini in the Vatican Secretariat of State office during the pontificate of Pius XII, then through the five years of John XXIII's reign. More importantly, Pope Paul resurrected the Holy Alliance after being held in abeyance during the pontificate of John XXIII. Paul VI had need of a trusted ally functioning beyond the control of the powerful Roman Curia. Adding further to the secrecy of the Holy Alliance, the pope let it be known unofficially that his private secretary Monsignor Pasquale Macchi would oversee its operations. Yet the pope left no doubt that operational direction of the Vatican secret service resided with the experienced Tagliente leaving Macchi to focus on his demanding role as papal secretary. Pope Paul understood that leaving the lines of authority unclear provided him greater autonomy from interference by the Curia.

It was Montini that had assisted German Bishop Alois Hudal and Croatian priest Father Krunoslav Draganović through Tagliente as intermediary in establishing the Vatican Ratlines in the post-war years. Now as pope, Montini understood the wider usefulness of the Holy Alliance and Monsignor Marcello Tagliente.

To explain the elevation of Tagliente to bishop, Tagliente was given a position within the Vatican Administration of the Patrimony of the Apostolic See, the APSA. This separate financial institution from the Vatican Bank acted as the treasury and central bank of Vatican City and the Holy See under direction of the Curia. Tagliente's academic education in economics made that assignment explainable. It also allowed Tagliente to officially continue his service within the Secretariat of State reporting to the aging Cardinal Amleto Giovanni Cicognani who additionally occupied the dual roles of cardinal secretary of state and president of the APSA. A striking example of the complexity of lines of authority within the internal workings of the Vatican.

†

Isabella Leonardi was drawn to Tagliente when first meeting him at a benefit orchestral performance hosted by the Bank of Italy at the Jesuit church Oratorio del Caravita on the Via Corso in Rome in 1968. Escorted that evening by her father, she performed as the featured soloist with the Orchestra dell'Accademia Nazionale di Santa Cecilia. Alessandro Leonardi was a respected gentleman of stature well-connected to the Roman Catholic Church and a confidant to Giovanni Montini from when Montini was Archbishop of Milan before elevation to pope.

Leonardi's father was the managing director of the investment management division of Italy's largest insurance company Assicurazioni Generali. The Leonardi family descended from old Italian banking wealth from 18th century ancestors associated with the five-hundred-year-old Banca Monte dei Paschi di Siena. In the 20th century Alessandro Leonardi had dealings with Bernardino Nogara, the architect of the modern international scope of Vatican finances and responsible for establishing the Vatican Bank in 1942 under Pope Pius XII.

At the reception following the performance, Alessandro Leonardi guided his daughter toward two church prelates. Both were dressed in black clerical ecclesiastical suits with white reverse collars and the zucchetto skull cap denoting rank within the Roman Catholic Church. Scarlet for the older cleric a cardinal, violet known as amaranth for the taller younger cleric a bishop or archbishop. The diminutive older cleric probably in his eighties seemed almost weighed down by a large gold pectoral cross. The tall handsome fit younger priest appeared in his forties.

Alessandro Leonardi said, "Your Eminence and Your Excellency, may I introduce my daughter Isabella. My dear, this

Vatican Cardinal Secretary of State Amleto Cicognani. Effectively the chief of staff for the Vatican. And this is Bishop Marcello Tagliente associated with the Section for Relations with States within the Secretariat. Something much like a foreign ministry. My congratulations on your elevation, Bishop Tagliente."

Following her father's lead, Isabella kissed the rings of the hands offered by both prelates in the Catholic custom of *baciamano*, a way of demonstrating reverence for the bishop's office and the individual being greeted. She and Tagliente locked their eyes for a moment longer than necessary. Both would later remark on that auspicious beginning of their romance.

Cicognani said, "I enjoyed your performance immensely, Signora Leonardi."

Tagliente offered, "A remarkable performance, Signora Leonardi. I particularly appreciate violin concertos. Mendelssohn's concerto in E minor is a favorite. Your interpretation conveys the true beauty of the composer's vision of the piece to the listener. Seamless transitions. You play sections slower than many soloists today, allowing us to hear nuances otherwise easily missed. Choosing Pagani's *Devil's Laughter* caprice as an encore made a perfect conclusion."

"Oh, my, you recognized it even by name! You know something about great music, Bishop Tagliente."

"Not really, Signora Leonardi. I just appreciate the art of the great composers and a musician talented enough to bring that art to life. Where do you usually perform?"

"Mostly in the north. Milan usually. Summer is more tolerable in Milan than Rome."

Both Tagliente and Leonardi were smitten. Both mature enough to understand the difficulties of such a relationship while confident enough to forge ahead.

Following that first meeting they immediately began engaging in frequent contact by spending considerable hours on the telephone over several weeks. Correspondence was out of the question. They must avoid any paper trail. Eventually their increasing desire culminated with Tagliente finding an official reason to go to Milan. Listening to violin pieces of the great masters was

Tagliente's daily routine for relaxing. Learning that Isabella owned a highly respected 150-year-old violin manufacturing firm located in Cremona, he used that as a reason to pay her a visit. From Cremona they drove to Isabella Leonardi's principal residence, a villa on the west bank of Lake Como. That first romantic weekend began their long secret relationship.

Isabella Leonardi was a wealthy aristocratic widow of the landed aristocracy with old money stretching back to the 19th century. Like Tagliente, a family heritage of the Black Nobility. His same age. No baggage such as children or former husbands. Charming. Intelligent. Artistic. Well-read. Active in Catholic charities. Both understood the restrictions of their relationship requiring well-crafted secrecy.

Early into their relationship Tagliente candidly rationalizes to Leonardi, "I do not believe our relationship to be a sin. Nor should you. To the contrary, it is a gift from God. That it goes against my vow of chastity is obvious. God may condemn my lapse of the vow of celibacy but not our intimate relationship. Chastity is an ecclesiastical law that was adopted in the Middle Ages by the Roman Catholic Church. Created by man for secular reasons rather than ordained by God. Devotion to the service of God's work is the true measure of my ordination. I stand ready to be judged accordingly by the Creator."

†

Isabella Leonardi knew little of Tagliente's professional life serving in the Vatican. When he spoke about the roles of other prelates, as an outsider it was difficult for her to understand what he did. Tagliente intentionally avoided relating anything substantive making the function of the Vatican secret service opaque. Never passing along rumor, he confessed to her that he had a reputation of being self-absorbed, even unfriendly. She detected if that reputation was accurate, it did not bother him. He was self-absorbed. In that she felt herself a special exception with what he did reveal to her. While guarded, he shared enough for her to feel his unqualified trust.

That trust best exemplified by his sharing of the important secret roles he occupied. Head of the Vatican Secret Services and the Vatican Secret Archive. Recently he acquired the added responsibility of assisting in managing the public relations crisis of involvement of the Vatican Bank in the international Italian Banking Scandal. He had served several popes from Pius XII to John XXIII, to Paul VI, then John Paul I, now John Paul II. Each of these very different pontiffs invested trust in Marcello Tagliente for his considerable skills in managing difficult situations.

Having revealed to Isabella his responsibilities for running Vatican intelligence, Tagliente educated her in its background as a way of sharing the importance of his responsibilities.

"Santa Alleanza was founded in the 16th century. The Holy See from that time until the Risorgimento, the unification of Italy a hundred years ago, was a sovereign country. The Papal States occupied a central portion of the Italian mainland. However, the Roman Catholic pope played a secular political role with the Church dominating most religious life in western Europe.

"As such, intelligence was vital for the dealings of the pontiff with international affairs of state. The pope went far beyond just meddling in the activities of Catholic nations using the power of his spiritual status. He possessed a virtual army of intelligence sources in Catholic priests and monks throughout the western world. The pope also had papal envoys now called apostolic nuncios, equivalent to ambassadors to important nations. I started my ecclesiastical career in the Vatican Secretariat of State. With my academic background in economics and international law, I began working in the Section for Relations with States, the Vatican equivalent to a foreign ministry.

"With fluency in Italian, English and German, I immediately became involved as a liaison for apostolic nuncios. By definition, the gathering and use of the natural flow of politically related information is an intelligence function. Writing reports eventually led to requests for broader interpretive editorials. Intelligence analysis. Knowledge is power. The pontiff plays a secular role in the world even today. Broad based intelligence is vital for the Holy See to effectively exercise its spiritual influence."

While she knew his areas of responsibility functioned separately from administrative control by the Roman Curia, she knew almost nothing related to any specifics. Marcello was careful never to divulge confidential information as a matter of ethical principle. He once told her that she had no reason to know sensitive Vatican information. He softened his comment by citing the analogy about not wanting to know how sausage is made. The details were his burden of office in service to the Church. Impossible to relate unpleasant aspects of Vatican intelligence work to an outsider that would question the necessary utility for a religious institution.

While secretive about what he did, to Isabella he was expansive in sharing his personal views on why he chose the priesthood as a chosen career. Without him stating in specific words, she believed she understood some of the underlying reasons. A conservative powerful family closely aligned with the Roman Catholic Church. A favorite uncle, a bishop, serving in the Secretariat of State office under Pope Pius X. A great uncle a retired archbishop. Tagliente must have undoubtedly gravitated to the grandeur and universal power of the Roman Catholic Church. For an Italian with family close to the apex of power within the Vatican hierarchy, it must have represented almost a family profession.

In his own words he summarized his philosophical makeup. "I believe in the biblical God and Jesus Christ. I am politically conservative and that generally applies to my religious views. However, my conservatism is more personalized. It is conditional. I am governed by logic. Realistic about changing circumstances where the Church must adapt to remain relevant. I do not feel bound by every element of dogma. For example, while not aligned with John XXIII's left-leaning populist pontificate, the Second Vatican Council was necessary to move the Church into the 20th century. The Latin mass had become anachronistic.

"So is the concept that the pope is infallible. I believe God *may* speak through him, but I do not believe in the doctrine of papal infallibility. The pope is just a man with all that represents. I do not believe the hand of God dictates the selection of a pope from a body of imperfect cardinals voting in conclave.

"Celibacy of the clergy is unnatural. Designed as a mechanism to bind priests to the Church as a means of signifying their elevated status from the faithful. Not even dogma. It was made mandatory by ecclesiastical law in the Middle Ages for practical rather than religious reasons. I find no personal fault in my disregarding its observance. God has set us together, Isabella. That cannot be deemed a sacrilege."

†

A doctor bent down to look into Emma Nicoletti's eyes as she sat propped up in the hospital bed of the *Policlinico Universitario Agostino Gemelli*. "How are the headaches?"

"Not as frequent. Less intense but that may because of the medication that helps a lot."

"Any problems with vision or hand coordination?"

"No. Worse discomfort is my shoulder."

"Well, it has only been days since the injury. No swelling of the brain so no indication of internal cranial bleeding. Still could be residual effects for some time. I will let Doctor Ferrero comment on your other injuries."

What most concerned Nicoletti was the laceration on her cheek. It ran from just under her left cheekbone for about four centimeters downward. She had not seen how bad it was or the scarring prognosis. She saw the lacerations on her left arm when the nurse changed the dressing. They made her shudder at what the implications might be for the facial laceration. Fortunately, as she approached her car to get into the passenger seat, she had fumbled with balancing the carboard tray of sandwiches and coffees. This caused her to stop behind the car parked next to hers to let Gabriel back out her car. In that process her body became turned away from much of the direct blast force. The injuries would have been significantly worse had she taken the blast force full-frontal.

Replaying events brought a twinge of guilt for worrying over scarring while Gabriel died. Made all the worse by newspaper accounts of his incineration but at least already dead from the blast effects of the explosion.

After the doctor left, two men entering her room, causing her to exclaim, "Michael! Thank you for coming. I'm so sorry!" She burst into sobs as Gabriel's brother Michael approached her bed and reached for her right hand while kissing her on the forehead.

After several minutes waiting for Nicoletti to regain her composure, Eisenberg said, "This is Frank Amatrano. A close friend going back to our college days. Gabe asked me to give him a call. Frank has a background in government security and criminal investigation. Currently works for Interpol at their headquarters outside Paris."

Nicoletti nodded to Amatrano, but the tears begin to flow again as she said to Eisenberg, "I feel so responsible bringing Gabe into this mess. Should have known what we were doing threatened a lot of bad people."

Eisenberg held tightly to her hand. "Not your fault, Emma. Like you, Gabe was a tenacious investigative journalist. Had he known he was in danger, he would have proceeded anyway."

Amatrano said in Italian, "Do you have any idea who might have done this, Signora Nicoletti?"

Somewhat surprised, she replied, "You speak Italian like a native Italian."

"I am a native. Born in Genoa. My given name is Francesco. Anglicized to Frank. I have both American and Italian citizenships. So, you do not believe this was a terrorist bombing by the *Red Brigades*?"

"No. There is no reason. I work for a financial newspaper. Not a high-profile target for Marxists."

Amatrano said, "Gabriel telephoned me. Said you were working together on a new project involving the Italian Banking Scandal. Mentioned the names of Michele Sindona, Roberto Calvi, and the Vatican Bank. Do you believe the bombing might be involved with that?"

"Possibly. No, probably."

"Why probably?"

Nicoletti lowered her head but remained silent.

"Signora. This was an assassination. Whatever you were doing is the reason. Cost Gabriel his life. You survived only by chance circumstances. I also know quite a lot about this Italian Banking Scandal. However, I'm not allowed to discuss official confidential police investigative information. By the way, I'm not a police officer. Interpol is strictly an international investigative organization assisting law enforcement agencies of its signatory member nations."

"That is not very comforting given the inability of Italian law enforcement to suppress recurring widespread acts of violence. Makes a journalist consider that corruption may be involved."

"I understand completely, Signora Nicoletti. Reason enough for trusting an investigative outsider. I work in Paris and come to Genoa occasionally to visit relatives when I travel to Italy on official business. I offered to visit you and Gabriel in Milan unofficially. Gabriel asked if I might assist with how you might expand your research with Italian law enforcement. I'm also aware there are certain compromised Italian law enforcement officials to avoid, if you understand my meaning. I have both a professional and personal connection to Gabriel Eisenberg's murder. Now perhaps I can be of assistance with navigating your interaction with Italian authorities. I have professional relationships within the *Guardia di Finanza*. Trusted senior officers I have worked with for years."

Nicoletti looked at Amatrano. Never in her life had she felt so unsettled. Uncertain how to proceed. Should she trust this Interpol official?

Amatrano continued, "You are still in danger, Signora Nicoletti. Whoever ordered your killing knows you are now of even greater threat. Gabriel said you came into possession of confidential documents implicating the Vatican Bank's involvement in money laundering. Is that what this is about?"

Nicoletti nodded, "But how did they know?"

"Who do you mean as *they*?"

"Somebody in the Vatican Secret Archive undoubtedly."

"Is that the origin of these documents?"

"Yes."

"What makes these documents so important?"

"They directly implicate the president of the Vatican Bank Bishop Paul Marcinkus as a willing participant in the financial crimes by Sindona and Calvi. Since Sindona has known connections with the Sicilian Mafia, it may lead to evidence of the Vatican Bank participating in money laundering for organized crime. That needs further investigation to integrate the Vatican documents with other known information to make a convincing case. Many of the documents have the signature of Pope Paul VI. You may not know this, but the Vatican Secret Archive is just that. Secret. Exceptionally limited access. It is not part of the Vatican Library. The secret archive is the personal repository of the current pontiff. Few areas in the already hyper-secret Vatican are as inaccessible."

"How did you come by these documents?"

Nicolette thought for a moment before answering, "I'd rather not say. I feel obligated to protect my source."

"I understand. I will return tomorrow. We can talk further. I told Gabriel I would come here to lend assistance. Seems now my mission has changed. Keeping you safe becomes the priority. Where are these documents?"

"In my apartment. Photocopies. Originals are safe in a Swiss bank vault."

"Has anyone checked your apartment since the bombing?"

Nicoletti closed her eyes. Traumatized by the shock of Gabriel Eisenberg's horrible death and her own injuries, she had not considered that. "No."

"If the documents are missing that confirms the likely reason for the assassination attempt. Certainly, dispels this as a terrorist attack by the *Red Brigades*. Would you like me to check your apartment?"

Nicoletti nodded, "Yes. I would appreciate you doing that. Not yet ready to trust Italian police. My address and apartment key are in my handbag in the closet over there. The Vatican documents are in the bottom drawer of my office file cabinet. Thank you, Signore Amatrano."

✝

As Frank Amatrano and Michael Eisenberg left Nicoletti's room, a nurse followed them out. Stopping at the reception desk for admitting visitors, the nurse asked the attending clerk, "Who were the visitors to the patient Nicoletti in room 308?"

Looking over the visitor signing in log, the clerk said, "Francesco Amatrano and Michael Eisenberg."

The nurse then went to a payphone and reported the names as instructed.

CHAPTER 9

Milan, Italy | June 1979

Leaving the hospital, Michael Eisenberg said to Amatrano, "I have an appointment at the U.S. consulate. They will help with the arrangements for returning Gabe's body to New York. Is Emma still in danger?"

"No doubt. Unless you need me, I will check her apartment for these documents. Then I'll pay a visit to the *Guardia di Finanza*. The Italian financial police. I work often with them both here in Milan and Rome. Have a close colleague that is executive commander of the *Gruppo d'Investigazione Sulla Criminalità Organizzata,* the organized crime investigation group of the Guardia known by the acronym GICO based at the headquarters in Rome. The Guardia is a separate police agency reporting to the ministry of Economy and Finance. Gabe's murder more properly falls under the jurisdiction of the Carabinieri that is part of the Italian military. But considering it involved a bombing, its jurisdiction overlapped with the GICO. Such is the confusing organization of Italian officialdom.

"If the documents are missing from Nicoletti's apartment are you going to tell the Italian police?"

Amatrano shook his head. "Not yet and not before consulting with Miss Nicoletti."

"If the documents are missing, then who does that point to for ordering Gabe's murder?"

"Someone associated with the banking scandal. This was not a leftist terror attack. Regardless of the perpetrators, Signora Nicoletti is still in danger if the documents are gone. If that's the case then it only confirms the reason behind the bombing. The original documents still exist in a Swiss bank accessible only by Emma."

Frank Amatrano knew the probable suspects. Those associated with the bankers. People with the means to contract the Mafia for murder. The bombing most likely the work of the Mafia. Amatrano already saw circumstantial evidence from the FBI that associated Michele Sindona with the Sicilian Mafia. From the Italian Guardia di Finanza and the *Servizio per le Informazioni e la Sicurezza Democratica*, the SISDE, the domestic intelligence service, suspicions existed that Roberto Calvi may also be laundering Mafia money through his web of offshore banks and holding companies.

The Vatican Bank's association in the scandal through the criminal Italian bankers had not yet risen in Amatrano's mind as having a direct link with the Sicilian Mafia. However, he knew of Vatican Bank president Bishop Marcinkus' culpability in a major counterfeit corporate bond scam in the early 1970s devised by the American Mafia. The scam was thwarted before the Vatican could take delivery of the bonds. The U.S. Justice Department never made a case implicating the IOR. Amatrano made a mental note to revisit the case history from Interpol files. Yet even with Nicoletti's documents claiming to incriminate the Vatican Bank in subsequent financial misdeeds, he doubted the Vatican would knowingly be involved in murder. His cynicism had not yet gone that far. Of course, he did not yet know about the existence of an actively functioning Vatican secret service.

†

Amatrano entered Nicoletti's apartment using her key. Making a cursory look about, he found no evidence of forced entry. No disorder. Satisfied that he was alone, he opened the bottom drawer of the file cabinet next to a desk. Empty. The other file drawer containing Nicoletti's project notes appeared to remain undisturbed.

Amatrano left the apartment then drove to the Milan headquarters of the Guardia di Finanza, acronym GdF, on Via Melchiorre Gioia. The collection of buildings stood behind a tall metal fence with armed officers controlling entry. The wave of violence directed at Italian law enforcement heighted security throughout Italy.

Amatrano passed through security and made his way to the office of Lieutenant Colonel Claudio Pagliaro second in command of the Milan division of the GdF. Amatrano met regularly with Pagliaro working on financial crimes plaguing Italy where organized crime was involved.

Colonel Pagliaro welcomed him, "Good to see you, Francesco. What brings you to Milan?"

Shaking hands and taking a seat offered by Pagliaro, "Well, it started out to be a personal visit, Claudio. Turned into something much different. Murder to be specific."

Pagliaro registered surprise, "Murder?"

"The bombing at the train station days ago. The victim killed was an American. The brother of a friend from my college days. Telephoned me after hearing of his brother's death. Asked if I could come to Milan and help sort things out."

"You knew this American journalist?'

"Not really. Met him many years ago. His younger brother Michael Eisenberg and I are close friends. Together we visited the female Italian journalist this morning recovering in the hospital. She and Gabriel Eisenberg were working together. I offered to see what the police knew about the bombing. Since I work more closely with the Guardia than the Carabinieri, I came here first. But I'm not on official Interpol business."

Pagliaro nodded, "We're working closely with the Carabinieri on this. No leads yet. Dynamite bomb set in the engine compartment. Wired to the ignition. Not remotely activated. Probably rigged after Eisenberg and Nicoletti took a train to Rome. All we know is they spent a night in a Rome hotel and returned to Milan the next morning. Unfortunately, Signora Nicoletti has not been forthcoming with much information about what she and Eisenberg were working on or what they were doing in Rome."

"Journalists zealously protect their sources. You know of course she and Eisenberg wrote a book together many years ago."

"Oh, yes. Titled *Ratlines*. About the Vatican helping war criminals escape to South America. We asked her if this might have anything to do with this ongoing banking scandal where the Vatican Bank is frequently mentioned. She said she could not comment on what she was working on."

"Your best guess, Claudio?"

"The bombing has the earmarks of the Mafia or the *Red Brigades*. Don't see Eisenberg and Nicoletti as being high enough profile to be symbolic of capitalism for Marxist terrorists. Nicoletti's newspaper is not even considered biased toward the ruling Christian Democrats. That leaves the Mafia.

"You and I both know there are trails leading back to Sicilian Mafia involvement in this banking scandal. Especially connecting Michele Sindona going back to his early life in Sicily. Enough to suspect money laundering of organized crime drug proceeds. Neither we nor American law enforcement have yet found evidence enough to bring prosecution. Yet, I suspect the Sicilian Mafia engineered the bombing. No way to speculate who else might have been involved. But to your question, everything points to this being an attempt to silence Eisenberg and Nicoletti. Why remains unknown unless Nicoletti becomes more helpful. Maybe you can be of assistance there, Francesco."

Amatrano said, "I'll see what I can do. My thoughts lean that way also. Signora Nicoletti is expected to recover. I only met her for the first time today. However, I have the impression that the murder of her associate will not dissuade her from continuing. Before joining Interpol, I served many years in American diplomatic security. Protecting diplomats, that sort of work. Seems the least I can do is to offer her my professional advice on how to protect herself."

Pagliaro said, "Walk her through the process of obtaining a firearm license. I'll be happy to expedite the paperwork. You can recommend the best choice of a weapon and show her how to use it. Of course, even armed police officers are getting murdered by Mafia gunmen. Her best protection is to work from someplace in seclusion under an assumed identity. Perhaps from outside of Italy."

"I agree. Thanks for your help. Anything you learn that you can pass on, please telex my office. Not sure how long I'll be in Milan, but I check in daily."

†

The following morning, Amatrano arrived with Michael Eisenberg at the hospital to inform Nicoletti that the photocopies of her documents were gone. As they walked into her room, she immediately asked, "What about the documents?"

"They're gone. The file cabinet is entirely empty. Nothing else in your apartment appears disturbed. No forced entry. Assumed they picked the lock."

Nicoletti made no reply. After several moments of silence, Amatrano said, "Let me be blunt, Signora. This was not a terrorist attack. Clearly this involves the documents. However, the perpetrators know the originals still exist. My guess is the bombing was the work of the Sicilian Mafia. Quite possibly on orders by someone involved in this banking scandal that seems only to be getting worse. They meant to kill both you and Gabriel. You remain a loose end. Likely they will make another attempt to eliminate you. However, the circumstances have changed. The original documents still exist but now you are forewarned which makes you an immediate threat. That could mean possibly a kidnapping attempt to learn the whereabouts of the original documents."

Nicoletti took a deep breath and turned toward Michael. "I knew this was explosive material. I needed your brother's expertise to pursue this. I'm so sorry to have involved him, Michael."

Michael Eisenberg came closer and grasped her right hand. "Not your fault, Emma. He spoke about the underlying dangers that came with going after stories involving influential people. Even spoke of concerns when you two were working on *Ratlines*. Not that the Vatican might come after you or him when the book came out, but some deranged mental case that might see you guys as doing the work of the devil."

Amatrano interrupted. "This threat is far more specific and likely to materialize. What do you plan to do, Signora?"

"I have no choice but to continue with the project. You made it clear that no matter what I do the people that murdered Gabe cannot let me live. I will take precautions but not submit to their terror."

Amatrano nodded. "I suspected that's what you would say. I cannot promise a foolproof solution, but I can offer you my professional assistance. Make you as safe as possible. Give you time enough time to make your work public. That is the only way for ultimately ensuring your safety. I cannot protect you in my official capacity as an Interpol officer. I can however offer to remain in Milan on personal holiday for a couple of weeks."

Nicoletti looked at him with a questioning expression. "That is a most generous offer, Signore Amatrano. Without meaning to sound ungrateful, why would you do that?"

Amatrano smiled. "I have my reasons. If your claims that these documents conclusively prove the Vatican is knowingly involved in criminal activity, then it personally offends my sense of justice. Whomever is behind this must be brought down. I cannot in good conscience leave you to become another victim. The Italian police cannot be entrusted with protecting you. They cannot protect their own officers. What's it to be, Signora Nicoletti? Will you accept my help?"

It was her turn to offer a smile. "I can hardly refuse your kindness, Signore Amatrano."

"Very well. I have only one condition. You need to tell me everything you know. How you came by these documents. When you are well enough, I also need to see the originals. Agreed?"

Nicoletti nodded. "Call me Emma, Frank. Thank you. Where do we start?"

"When do the doctors say you can leave the hospital?"

"Probably in a couple of days. It's about observing the effects of the concussion. That will be one week since the ...incident."

"Once you leave here, we need to improve your security. Are you right-handed?"

"Yes."

"Good. Ever fire a handgun?"

"No."

"Then I'll teach you. I have friends in the Italian police making it easy to get you a suitable weapon with a firearms license. Then we go to Switzerland. I want to see these documents. How did you come by them?"

"A priest that worked in the Vatican Secret Archive removed them. He selected documents incriminating the Vatican in criminal activity involving the Italian banking scandal. Dying of terminal cancer, he hid the documents in a Swiss bank in Lugano. Bequeathed them to me only by getting my name as a reporter for the financial newspaper *Il Sole 24 Ore*. Assumed I would be able to recognize the value of the documents. He also knew of my book *Ratlines,* so he knew I had no qualms about going after the Vatican."

Amatrano asked. "Any idea how the documents were discovered missing? Or how that led to you?"

Nicoletti shook her head. "The priest, Monsignor Vittorio Scarpelli addressed a letter to me. Explaining why he chose me to do something with this documentary evidence. His death was approaching quickly. In that letter, he made a special point of cautioning me about a powerful Vatican prelate. Archbishop Marcello Tagliente. The letter is with the original documents in the Swiss bank vault.

"Scarpelli said that Tagliente's official role was as the Archivist of the Vatican Secret Archive but more importantly as the functional head of *Santa Alleanza,* the *Holy Alliance,* sometimes called the *Entity.* The Vatican secret service. An historical Vatican institution I thought existed only in antiquity. Whatever it is called, the Vatican secret service seems to have a current function according to Scarpelli, but he did not elaborate."

"You believe then that Archbishop Tagliente might logically have been the one to learn of the missing documents? If true about him heading the Vatican secret service, then you suspect him of possibly being behind the attack?"

Nicoletti said, "That is the most logical scenario. Who else within the Vatican would have the wherewithal to do something so extreme?"

Amatrano acknowledged her comment with a nod. "If you did not know Scarpelli, how did you receive notification of his bequest?"

"From a Swiss law firm in Lugano."

†

Frank Amatrano's offer to continue helping Nicoletti was an emotional response. Difficult to explain even to himself. He knew Gabriel Eisenberg but only as the brother of an old friend. Eisenberg and Nicoletti just more victims of the pervasive violence sweeping Italy. What he did feel was professional frustration. An angst festering for a long time. Taking the form of direct action felt satisfying.

Interpol was only an investigative body. Assisting law enforcement of its signatory members to reach across international borders to pursue criminals. The frustration came from the inability to directly go after criminals. Interpol was no better than a consultive body.

This thing with the Italian Banking Scandal that involves international financial transactions would ordinarily be where Interpol could be most effective. Particularly with the use of offshore foreign banks and corporations in tax haven countries that did not require normal reporting of movement of money or the identification of accounts or stockholders. However, Interpol had limited investigative influence with respect to the Vatican City State. The Vatican was not a signatory member to the Interpol protocol. Interpol is further limited in its investigative mandate as defined in Article 3 of the Interpol Charter that states: *It is strictly forbidden for the Organization to undertake any intervention or activities of a political, military, religious or racial character.*

Amatrano saw the effects of this limitation years earlier with the counterfeit U.S. corporate bond fraud. That fraud would benefit organized crime and the Vatican. The U.S. FBI and New York City law enforcement exchanged evidence associated with the investigation with Interpol since it involved foreign connections in Europe. Amatrano recalled seeing a photocopy of a letter that specifically acknowledged a schedule for the Vatican Bank to take delivery of the bonds. Although the signature on the letter was illegible with no typed name, other evidence implicated the Vatican Bank. Specifically, its president Bishop Paul Marcinkus. The U.S. authorities were never able to make a case against individuals or any institution of the sovereign foreign Vatican City State. Interpol recused itself from participating based on restrictions defined in their charter.

Michele Sindona was under recent indictment in U.S. federal court on various charges stemming largely from the failure of Franklin National Bank in 1974. Yet Sindona's financial empire continued to function although in serious financial difficulties. His likeminded banker associate Roberto Calvi was also now under serious criminal investigation by Italian authorities. Among this continuing serialized international scandal, the Vatican Bank and its president Bishop Marcinkus are frequently mentioned.

For years, Amatrano had seen prima facie evidence of Mafia money laundering by Italian financial institutions. Buried in layers of offshore foreign shell corporations moving money through the international monetary system. Among that evidence, the Vatican Bank occasionally appeared. Nothing conclusive but recurring enough to suggest something intentionally concealed existed. The surrounding circumstances of this bombing incident pointed directly to the Vatican. According to Nicoletti, the documents came from the Vatican Secret Archive and incriminated the Vatican Bank when placed along with other known evidence of financial criminality.

Nicoletti's revelation about the Vatican secret service headed by Archbishop Tagliente immediately added a sinister element to the assassination that took the life of Gabriel Eisenberg. Could the Vatican conceivably be behind this? Did they use Mafias as proxies to execute the bombing?

†

That morning, Amatrano assisted Michael Eisenberg with making the final arrangements for the return of his brother's remains to New York. Michael would fly back to New York with the body in two days.

In the afternoon, Amatrano paid another visit to Lt. Colonel Pagliaro. "Claudio, I need your help. Unofficially, I am staying on in Milan for a couple of weeks. I felt obligated to temporarily remain to protect Signora Nicoletti. At least I need to secure her a firearm. Can you help with issuing a permit?"

"Absolutely. What about for you also? You hold Italian citizenship? Unless that conflicts with Interpol regulations."

"It shouldn't. As long as I don't carry it for official duties. I'm in Italy on holiday. Unfortunately, Italy is a dangerous place. Makes sense if I'm to protect her."

Frank Amatrano ordinarily did not feel threatened. From 1972 he worked closely with the Israeli Mossad investigating the locations of PLO participants in the Munich Olympics Massacre. Subsequently helping target them for retribution proved satisfying. During his time spent in Israel, Amatrano was introduced to *krav maga* the combat martial arts technique taught to Israeli IDF and Mossad agents. A vicious form of various martial arts combining defensive with offensive tactics to kill or disable your opponent in a quick succession of moves. Given a commitment to protect Emma Nicoletti from the Mafia, having a firearm though made sense.

†

The day before Nicoletti's discharge from the hospital, Amatrano said, "Before taking you home, are you up to accompanying me to a gun shop?"

"I guess so. Will you show me how to use it?"

"Of course. There's some paperwork of course for a concealed weapons permit. I have a professional relationship with the Milan division executive officer of the Guardia de Finanza. He has agreed to escort us to a gun dealer. He will authorize sidestepping the normal requirements given your special circumstances. I will also obtain a weapon since I will act as your bodyguard. How are you feeling? Headaches easing?"

"Getting better. You mentioned going to Lugano to examine the original documents. Are we going to do that soon?"

"If you're up to it. Need to see what the documents reveal. It you go public with them, there is no reason for your attackers to pursue you further."

"I understand. But that means never avenging Gabe's murder. Or even identifying who was behind it. I can't back away from this, Frank."

"Didn't think you would. I admire what you're doing, Emma. This entire financial scandal infuriates me. Especially involvement of laundering Mafia money. Vatican participation in criminal activity is an obscenity. I believe that you have found compelling evidence that might expose Vatican culpability. Might be hard to achieve justice, but maybe it will serve to shut down the credibility of the Vatican Bank to engage in international financial transactions with impunity.

"On a practical note, can you take care of your personal needs once you leave the hospital?"

Nicoletti grinned for the first time. "You mean like going to the toilet and bathing with my arm in a sling."

"Something like that. But household chores like cooking and cleaning."

"I pay the teenage daughter of one of my neighbors to clean the apartment once a week. Maybe I can see if she can arrange to cook us dinner after school and help me shower. She might welcome the extra money. You and I can manage making morning coffee and sandwiches for lunch I trust."

"Fair enough. I can't cook but I can wash dishes and make sandwiches. How do you explain my presence to your friends and neighbors?"

"How about something close to the truth. A bodyguard hired by my newspaper until I can return to work. Play on the rumor that this might be a misguided symbolic attack directed against the establishment by the Marxist *Red Brigades* because I work for a capitalistic publication."

CHAPTER 10

Milan, Italy | July 1979

The failed elimination of the journalist Nicoletti was a temporary setback. Recovery of the photocopies of the stolen Vatican Secret Archive documents however allowed Archbishop Tagliente to turn immediate attention to other matters. Damage control for the revelations of Vatican complicity in Sindona's and Calvi's banking transgressions became increasing pressing. Sindona's indictment in March in U.S. federal court on 68 criminal counts would likely end in conviction. A lengthy prison sentence including financial restitution and fines would force liquidation of Sindona's assets. Along with other financial institutions, the Vatican would sustain large losses. More worrisome was further exposure of incriminating involvement of the Vatican Bank that could threaten its utility for international investment.

Central to Tagliente's strategy was to counsel Vatican Secretary of State Agostino Casaroli to steadfastly maintain that the Vatican Bank was another victim to Michele Sindona's illegal activities. Financial transactions hidden behind a complex network of offshore entities incorporated in tax havens that duped many sophisticated financial institutions. Behind the scenes, Tagliente would initiate moves to extradite the Vatican as Sindona's empire collapsed. He would then contend with the growing problem of Roberto Calvi and issues surrounding his Milanese Banco Ambrosiano.

Tagliente would help seal Sindona's fate by encouraging public comments by influential persons friendly to the Vatican portraying Sindona as nothing more than a clever financial criminal. In the background, Donaggio would surreptitiously provide information linking Sindona to related violence by the Sicilian Mafia.

The Mafia murders did indeed generate headlines not only in Italy but in the international press since the many of the victims were government officials. Since the beginning of 1979, Italy was awash in violence. A mix of terrorist attacks by the Marxist-Leninist *Red Brigades* and Italian organized crime. The public conflated all these attacks on Italian officials and institutions as an attack on Italian society.

The worst of the wave violence started the prior year. Former Italian prime minister Aldo Moro, friend of Pope Paul VI's student days, was kidnapped by the *Red Brigades* in March 1978. The kidnapping kept the world and the Pope in suspense for 55 days. On 9 May, Moro's bullet-riddled body of Aldo Moro was found in a car in Rome. Moro's murder undoubtedly dealt a terrible emotional blow to already ailing Pope Paul VI who died three months later. The pontificate of Pope John Paul I then suddenly ended with the new pontiff's death after only a month. The badly mishandled circumstances surrounding his death then resulted in overtones of possible foul play. The invocation of a second conclave of cardinals that year to elect yet another pontiff added further turmoil of this largely Catholic country.

The bombing to eliminate Eisenberg and Nicoletti in June became just another in a string of upheavals combined with unrelenting violence. However, it still remained necessary to resolve the threat presented by the missing documents conclusively.

Meeting with Donaggio, Tagliente said, "This Swiss lawyer you coopted to provide the information that led to the Nicoletti woman is our only link to the documents. Do you believe he might succumb to a far greater threat than threatening to expose his adultery?"

"Might depend on what is being asked of him. What do you have in mind, Your Excellency?"

"Recovery of the original stolen documents becomes essential. Even removing Nicoletti leaves a measure of insecurity with their existence beyond our control in the Swiss bank. Perhaps we can achieve both objectives of eliminating Nicoletti and then recovering the documents. Arrange for our Sicilian associates to perpetrate another shooting. This time Nicoletti and this Interpol agent. It may add credibility to connect this shooting with the failed bombing. Therefore, stage the shooting at the Milano Centrale station."

Donaggio raised an eyebrow, "How do we arrange for her to be at the train station? She may not be sufficiently recovered."

"Doesn't matter when, but she must return to Lugano to finish her work. She's a journalist. Not about to hand over documents illegally obtained to her Interpol bodyguard. Someone that is staying with her in an unofficial capacity?"

"Yes, Your Excellency. Agent Francesco Amatrano is personally connected to the Eisenberg family. I found that he is on personal leave from Interpol headquarters in Paris."

"All the better. When Nicoletti returns to Lugano to retrieve the documents, instruct our Sicilian associates to remove her and the bodyguard. Given Swiss banking secrecy, she must appear in person to examine the documents. My guess is she will let them remain in the bank vault rather than attempt to make another set of photocopies. She already had time to work on the original set photocopies before your people removed them from her apartment. She may choose to let them remain in Switzerland and consult them only occasionally. The train journey from Milan to Lugano takes only ninety minutes. Assessable as often as necessary while the documents remain beyond our reach.

"When she returns to Milano Centrale Lugano arrange for her and her bodyguard to be shot as they step out of the train station. Following their demise, you will then convince the Swiss lawyer to draft the necessary documents authorizing you to take possession of the documents held in her account at the bank. Armed with her death certificate by this time you can masquerade as a member of the clergy authorized by the family with power of attorney. What do you think of the plan, Ettore?"

"They might drive to Lugano by car, Your Excellency."

"Prepare for that possibility. Waylaid on the highway works as well," Tagliente said.

"I will contract with our associates in Palermo to bring people from Sicily to Milan prepared for either eventuality, Your Excellency. As to the attorney, I believe Signore Volpi will cooperate once Nicoletti is dead. He will welcome the permanent removal of the threat of blackmail."

†

The day after leaving the hospital, Amatrano made coffee and waited for Nicoletti to get up. The previous afternoon she was greeted by her neighbors and their teenage daughter Loretta. After spending a couple of hours with Nicoletti's neighbors over dinner, an exhausted Nicoletti claimed she must lay down. Time to take her medication for the headaches that made her groggy.

Having slept through the night, she opened the bedroom door and went into the bathroom. A short time later she came out. Slightly disheveled in a bathrobe, no makeup, and her hair brushed without undue care.

"God morning. Sleep well?" he asked.

"Soundly. The medication sees to that."

"Feeling well enough to venture out tomorrow or the day after?"

"I believe so. What do you have in mind?"

"We need to purchase firearms. Both of us. We are far too vulnerable. Look at the killings every day in the newspapers. We don't know who is behind this but neither of us believes it to be left-wing terrorists. That leaves the Mafia."

"Or the Vatican secret service," Nicoletti said. "Perhaps using the Mafia as proxies. There's enough information floating about their involvement in the banking scandal. The money laundering allegations along with Sindona's known connections to the Sicilian Mafia."

"Possibly. At any rate its violent people that have already tried killing you. Whatever the reason, nothing has changed. So, we arm ourselves. Agreed?"

Nicoletti nodded.

"I'll call Colonel Pagliaro and make arrangements. I'll feel better if he picks us up in a police car with two officers. Just going outside the apartment presents a risk."

Making the call, Amatrano spoke with Pagliaro for several minutes. After hanging up, he said to Nicoletti, "Tomorrow morning. Ten o'clock. He'll send a police car to take us to his office. After we do the paperwork, they'll take us to a gun dealer specializing in firearms for the Guardia. Paperwork will not be a problem. Especially for a targeted journalist amidst this wave of violence."

Nicoletti said, "Fine. Tomorrow is Saturday, Loretta doesn't have school. She can help me dress." Then she asked, "Will they take my picture?"

Shit. He had not thought about that. "I image that's required."

She looked at him. Her eyes reflected a dread that she feared might forever be present.

Amatrano came to her. "It'll be alright."

She shook her head. "No, it won't. Either my picture with an ugly bandage, or without the bandage and an ugly scar. Can't we wait until I'm healed?"

He put his left hand on her uninjured right shoulder. "We need to do this now, Emma. The healing will take time. I spoke to the head nurse. She said your surgeon did a wonderful job minimizing the scarring with the way he did the sutures. Once they're removed it will continue improving. You'll not be disfigured."

"Okay. But I'll only take a photo with the bandage in place."

Amatrano nodded, not sure of the required protocol for the photograph or for that matter, what her cheek wound would look like once healed. The best he could do was make sure of her safety.

Nicoletti said, "I meant what I said about the Vatican secret service being possibly behind this. I firmly believe that someone within the Vatican is responsible. Don't believe it could be Bishop Marcinkus who's the focus of so much attention as the president of the Vatican Bank. Must be someone higher up in the hierarchy. As the most secretive sector within the already hyper-secretive Vatican, that makes the Vatican secret service the most suspect. Let me show you something."

She went to her work area and returned with a copy of her book *Ratlines*. From inside, she extracted three folded typed pages. "Look at this. This is the letter Monsignor Scarpelli wrote to me. A sealed envelope given to me by the Swiss lawyer handling his estate. I did not keep it with the photocopied documents stolen from the apartment following the bombing. Scarpelli went out of his way to point me toward Archbishop Tagliente."

Amatrano read the letter. "I see what you mean. What do you know about Tagliente?"

"Not much. Best I could uncover was confirmation that he runs the Vatican secret service. Archbishop Luigi Poggi is officially considered the head of the Holy Alliance while Archbishop Tagliente secretly functions as operational chief using his official position as Archivist of the Vatican Secret Archive primarily as cover. That is according to a very reliable source."

"If Tagliente is behind the bombing, he could be a formidable adversary. If the Vatican secret service functions as a true intelligence service, it has the benefit of exceptional secrecy within a secretive sovereign country. On the brighter side, he does not have this letter giving him advance warning naming him specifically. Seems Scarpelli believes him also likely involved in the financial misdeeds of the Vatican Bank. Working for Tagliente in the Vatican Secret Archive, he undoubtedly knew him well."

The next morning Loretta came early to the apartment. Having slept poorly, Amatrano woke early and made a pot of coffee. Shaved and dressed, he ate a cannolo prepared by Loretta's mother as his breakfast. Loretta went to the bedroom to help Emma get ready.

Thirty minutes later Emma emerged. A transformation from her robe and unkept hair. Dressed in a cream-colored summer dress that fit her well and emphasized her olive skin tone. Her left arm remained in a sling because of her fractured clavicle. Stylish heels. Hair in place. Lipstick. A smaller fresh bandage replaced the dressing applied before leaving the hospital. Nothing detracted from a thoroughly favorable impression.

Amatrano smiled broadly, "You look outstandingly attractive, Emma."

"Thanks to Loretta. She changed the dressing on my cheek."

Loretta added, "I'm no judge but the wound doesn't look bad, Signore Amatrano. Once the sutures are removed Emma will be just fine."

Emma touched Loretta's cheek. "Thank you so much for agreeing to help me out until I recover."

"You look marvelous. Where are you off to?" Loretta asked.

Amatrano answered, "Just some necessary business involving the police. They are sending a car for us this morning."

Arriving at the Guardia's Milan building complex, they were escorted to Pagliaro's office where Pagliaro greeted Nicoletti effusively. After some small talk, Amatrano asked, "What handgun do you recommend, Colonel? For both of us."

"Why not the same as the Guardia uses?"

Pagliaro was in uniform with a sidearm in a holster at the waist. Withdrawing the weapon, he ejected the magazine and racked the slide to make sure it was free of any live rounds and handed it to Amatrano. "Berretta model 92. Came out last year. 9x19mm. Standard 15-round magazine. This is the standard-length barrel. Also comes in a shorter barrel version making it more compact. Are you going to use a shoulder holster?"

Amatrano replied, "Yes," as he hefted the weapon and extended his arm. "Been a while since I've carried a sidearm. What about for Signora Nicoletti?"

"Why not the same shorter-barrel version? Better to have the punch for protection. Still fits into a decent size handbag."

Amatrano handed Pagliaro's unloaded weapon to Nicoletti. "Not as heavy as I thought," she said.

"It'll be a bit heavier with a loaded magazine that goes into the butt of the handle. You'll manage though." Turning to

Pagliaro, Amatrano asked. "Good choice, Colonel. Where can we do some target practice?"

"In the cellar of the gun dealership they have a fifteen-meter shooting range. Let's finish the paperwork. Then I will personally drive you to the gun dealer. Make sure there are no issues. Italian bureaucracy has a deservedly poor reputation.

"I'll need your signatures on these several forms." Spreading the papers out on his desk, Pagliaro added, "Concealed handgun permits. I added comments that Signora Nicoletti was the victim of a bombing attack that took the life of her associate. On your application I sighted your background in law enforcement then sixteen years with Interpol and of course your Italian citizenship. All we need are your photographs for processing." Turning to Nicoletti, he said, "Even with your bandage, Signora, you are a very beautiful woman."

Pagliaro's comment temporarily broke through her distress over the cheek injury. She offered a smile and even blushed slightly.

They left the police building through a rear entrance and got into Pagliaro's car driven by another officer. Once at the gun dealership, after Pagliaro provided the clerk with the required permits, Amatrano told the clerk, "In addition to the two Berettas, we'll also need one concealed-carry shoulder holster, two boxes of ammunition, and a cleaning kit."

Colonel Pagliaro said, "I will leave you and Signora Nicoletti to do some practice shooting. The clerk will call my office when you are ready to leave. I'll send a car to escort you back to your residence. Too many unresolved gangland killings. I do not care to lose you two while you are in my charge. A pleasure meeting you, Signora Nicoletti. You are now in the excellent care of Signore Amatrano. Did he perhaps tell you that as a bodyguard he is lethal using only his hands? Now that he is armed, he is truly formidable."

Amatrano settled the purchase and tried on the shoulder holster harness. Slipping on his suit jacket, it was barely noticeable if not buttoning the jacket which he never did.

An hour later after firing fifty rounds between them in the cellar shooting range they returned upstairs. I didn't do very well, did I?" she commented.

"Nonsense. You did fine. Takes a great deal of practice to become proficient. Should you ever need to use the gun your target will likely be far closer. Remember what I taught you. Always fire two rounds in quick succession aimed at the torso."

Nodding, she said, "Are we now ready to go to Lugano?"

"If you're up to it. How about the day after tomorrow? That's Monday. The bank will be open."

The Guardia police car arrived at the gun dealership and returned them to Nicoletti's apartment. However, the two watchers that followed the Guardia di Finanza picking them up earlier that morning and depositing them at Guardia headquarters never saw them leave with Pagliaro from the reserved parking in the rear of the Guardia compound. Several hours later they were still waiting outside the police building.

Eventually, one watcher left to report to an unhappy Brother Gideon. Nicoletti and Amatrano meeting with the Guardia di Finanza was understandable given the ongoing investigation of the bombing. Did they spend all day inside with the police? Having lost track of them, the Mafia watchers returned to wait outside Nicoletti's apartment, reporting later with nothing more than observing the targets returning in a police car. Brother Gideon disliked relying on the Mafia. Undisciplined thugs that lacked skills even for something as simple as surveillance.

CHAPTER 11

Milan, Italy | July 1979

Amatrano and Nicoletti boarded an early train from Milano Centrale on Monday. With only a cursory check of identification papers after crossing the border into Switzerland, neither declared that they were armed. After disembarking the train, they arrived at the Societe Generale bank. Nicoletti requested to see the manager who previously assisted her in producing photocopies of the documents.

Coming out from his office he was suitably distressed looking at her. Taking her offered hand, "Signora, I read of the .... bombing. A miracle that you survived. My condolences for the death of your colleague."

"Thank you, Signore Koehne. The Italian Carabinieri believe it was leftist terrorists by the signature use of a bomb. I may have been targeted because I work for a financial newspaper. Part of the bourgeois capitalist establishment. Because of the incident, my employer insisted on providing me with a bodyguard. This is Signore Amatrano."

Koehne nodded to Amatrano, "Please come into my office, Signora."

Seated in Kohne's office, Nicoletti said, "The photocopies of the sensitive documents you are holding in your vault represent valued research I am doing for a new book. Regrettably, the photocopies used in my work were in my car and destroyed in the fire. It may be possible the bombing was not the work of terrorists but rather those that do not want me to continue researching my book project."

"Good lord! That is truly alarming. I can certainly assist by having my staff produce replacement photocopies."

"I don't believe that will be necessary, Signore Koehne. I need probably just a few documents photocopied today. However, you could be of assistance in another way."

"Certainly, Signora. How may I be of assistance?"

"I live and work in Milan. A manageable commute by train to Lugano. If I could have use of a small workspace to occasionally spend a day working here in the safety of the bank, I would feel more secure."

"I am more than glad to offer you such a small service, Signora. Do you wish to do some work today?"

"Yes, I would. Signore Amatrano can assist me if that is acceptable."

"Absolutely. Please follow me. I have a comfortable small conference room you can use."

As they all stood up, Amatrano said, "Signor Koehne. Considering the attempt on Signora Nicoletti's life, I am armed. I doubt you would welcome firearms within your bank. May I leave my weapon with you until we leave?"

Koehne's eyes opened in surprise as Amatrano extracted the Berretta from inside his jacket, ejected the magazine and racked the slide to ensure no rounds remained. Koehne held the disarmed weapon with an expression of discomfort. "Thank you. I will place this in my desk drawer."

Escorted to a conference room, a bank staffer wheeled in the steel vault box on a cart. "I will need your signature here, Signora. Herr Koehne is sending in some coffee. If you need anything, just lift the telephone receiver and you will be connected to a staff member."

After the door closed, Nicoletti said, "Signore Koehne was aghast when you handed over your gun."

"Couldn't very well risk someone detecting I was armed inside a bank. Served though to emphasis the seriousness of your situation to reinforce his extending special consideration. What's your plan for today?"

"Besides making a few photocopies from work that Gabriel and I did, I want to walk you through the most telling of the documents. By telling, I mean those reflecting information bearing on Vatican involvement in illicit financial transactions. Money laundering, currency manipulation, tax evasion, and various criminal acts of bank fraud. Indirect involvement with the Sicilian Mafia tied to a maze of offshore shell companies owned by Sindona, Calvi, or the Vatican Bank.

Let me start by explaining that the Vatican Bank was deeply involved in supporting Michele Sindona's efforts to expand his financial empire. They became integral for masking his illegal activities by appearing as unconnected entities disguised behind foreign shell companies. They then continued the same practice with Roberto Calvi's mad pursuit to expand Banco Ambrosiano into the foundation for his own financial empire. Both Sindona and Calvi used vast sums available from Mafia money as a means of short-term funding without having to seek conventional loans. Concealed in a labyrinth of connected transactions between foreign shell companies, the Vatican Bank made that possible without Calvi having to report anything internally on his books."

Amatrano asked, "Concealed in what manner?"

"Trade-based and service-based money laundering mechanisms mostly. Amongst the transactions, the Vatican Bank played an instrumental role by using its special status of implied trust and conservatism. Nothing in writing links the Vatican Bank directly to Mafia money laundering. However, certain documents taken as pieces of a puzzle can be used to make a compelling indictment of the Vatican Bank's criminal activity. That's what I want to focus on to build a case. That becomes the exceptional newsworthy element to the continuing banking scandal. The Holy See, the governing body of Roman Catholic Church sinking to the depths of profiting from illegal activities of organized crime. Not just duped by criminal bankers, but willing accessories for its own financial gain.

"I have identified eight foreign shell companies either directly or indirectly controlled by the Vatican Bank connected with Calvi's own foreign subsidiary Banco Ambrosiano Andino S.A. of Lima, Peru. This offshore bank originated when Calvi began a series of moving funds around in recent years. He started by centralizing his foreign banking beginning with Cisalpine Overseas in Nassau, Bahamas. I suspect he was worried about Ambrosiano's accounting firm becoming uncomfortable about the massive lending to two offshore entities under shareholder ownership by the Vatican Bank, Manic S.A. in Luxembourg and United Trading in Panama. Therefore, Calvi relocated much of Cisalpine's holdings in 1977 to a new creation in more remote Managua, Nicaragua named Ambrosiano Group Banco Commercial. The Nicaraguan entity itself was a subsidiary of Ambrosiano Luxembourg."

Amatrano shook his head. "A bewildering collection of entities all hidden in secretive tax havens. Back to the issue of Mafia money laundering. You think you have enough to make a compelling case incriminating the Vatican Bank?"

"Journalistically, yes. Depends on gathering further information from other sources. More accessible sources. Acquire enough evidence even circumstantial to make an informed reasonable public case. The question is not so much about how illicit cash enters into the international financial world as dirty money but how it returns to the Mafia in the form of legitimate assets. The key is identifying the end of that process with strong evidence. With that, the Vatican Bank's participation in the sequence of financial transactions explains how the Vatican Bank profits."

"That's a tall order, Emma. While I understand your principal interest is tying the Vatican into indirectly colluding with the Mafia, do these documents accomplish that? According to what you are explaining, the documents largely just reveal the Vatican Bank's association with these criminal bankers. That's undoubtedly how the Vatican Bank became drawn into this cesspool."

"I think so. Maybe not officially in a legal sense, but the Vatican Bank will never face a judicial accounting. As a sovereign country, the worse they face is possible sanctions by various countries in moving money through international channels. Central banks could deny transactions in important financial centers severing a vital revenue stream for the Vatican. If the international financial community finds the Vatican Bank suspected of illegal activities it loses its stature as a uniquely trusted tax haven. Legitimate banks in most countries refuse to participate in wire transactions involving suspect entities operating without oversight. That becomes a big deal. Shutting down the ability to move funds through the banking systems of western countries effectively cripples not only money laundering but normal legitimate investment."

"How's that important to Vatican finances?"

"Starting with Bernardino Nogara's efforts decades earlier, the Vatican Bank operates in the world of international finance the same as any international corporation. Vatican Incorporated is an exceptionally profitable corporation by any estimation. All that becomes jeopardized if conclusive evidence ties the Vatican to the criminality of Sindona and Calvi who have ties with the Sicilian Mafia. Hiding behind a cloak of sovereignty will not be enough. Current publicity already has them terrified."

"That means you remain a threat."

"I understand. The risk of being an investigative reporter."

†

Amatrano and Nicoletti left the bank in the middle of the afternoon. When arriving, they took a taxi from the train station to the bank. It turned out to be only one mile. A fifteen-minute walk. Amatrano took the opportunity to try spotting any surveillance. "Such a nice day let's walk to the train station," he said.

Outside a car waited a block away. During Amatrano's tenure with the U.S. Department of State Diplomatic Security, he received training in surveillance tradecraft. Amatrano took a more indirect route using several turns making covert surveillance more difficult. However, Monsignor Donaggio's S.P. agents were very experienced. One agent exited the car to proceed on foot, while the other drove the car past the targets and proceeded to the train station.

That Amatrano did not detect any surveillance he knew that did not mean they were not out there. As they walked Amatrano reflected on the problem of how to protect Nicoletti indefinitely. Yet he could not simply walk away. With Italian police and magistrates targeted for killings, supplying police protection to conceivable targets was impossible. Retreating into hiding, preferably outside Italy, appeared to be the best way for ensuring Nicoletti's safety. She already rejected that option.

They took adjoining seats at the very end of a train carriage. He could observe other passengers in the carriage and anyone entering from the far end. Seated directly next to the right of the sliding door at the other end, he could thwart any surprise attack with quick access to his Berretta under his left arm.

Ninety minutes after boarding they disembarked the train at Milano Centrale station. As they stepped outside the vast building toward the taxi queue, Nicoletti stopped unexpectedly. Amatrano instantly became alert. "What's wrong?"

She sighed and shook her head. "Nothing. Sorry. Just a flood of memories going back to that day. Gabe and I stopped to buy sandwiches and coffee. Gabe said he would take our bags, and I was to carry the food. Standing right here, that's when I gave him my car keys. I'm fine now. Let's go."

Amatrano scanned the area looking for possible threats before telling the taxi driver standing on the opposite side of the taxi the address. He then opened the rear door allowing Nicoletti to get inside. He closed the taxi door and took a step toward the rear of the taxi to go around and enter the taxi from the other side. In the next instant he heard the pronounced sound of a car engine loudly accelerating accompanied by a slight squeal of tires. Instinctively he withdrew the Berretta.

The first shots came as a burst from a submachine gun. Rounds hit the trunk of the taxi causing Amatrano to step taking cover back behind the taxi. Simultaneously he took a step to the left while crouching next to another taxi parked behind their taxi. Rising to a standing position, he leveled his weapon at the attacking vehicle when it braked suddenly to a stop next to their taxi. From the rear window of the vehicle protruded a Thompson submachine gun.

As the shooter unleased another burst raking the driver side of the taxi, Amatrano from between the two taxis unleashed several rounds from his Berretta. Only ten feet from the shooter, he took a step closer then fired a volley of sustained rounds. Rounds struck the shooter with the Thompson while two of the rounds struck the driver in the head. The vehicle then rolled forward, coming to a gentle stop against the curb.

Reloading the Berretta with a fresh magazine from his pocket, Amatrano ran to the vehicle to ensure the threat had been neutralized. Inside the driver slumped forward over the steering wheel. Opening the rear door, the shooter lay across the back seat with his right cheek and neck ripped open by multiple wounds. Satisfied, Amatrano immediately turned and rushed back to the taxi. The taxi driver lay collapsed on the pavement badly wounded with blood beginning to pool. Amatrano pulled open the rear door. Nicoletti was trying to raise herself off the seat using her good right arm by reaching for the back of the front seat.

"Are you wounded, Emma!"

Without responding she raised herself to a sitting position and looked at Amatrano with eyes wide in shock. He shouldered his Berretta and cleared away larger pieces of glass to help her exit. No obvious indication of having suffered any wounds. However, clearly going into shock, she might soon be overcome from the sudden release of adrenaline.

Helping her to a safe spot sitting her on the curb, he leaned down to her with his hand on her right shoulder, "Emma. You're alright. No wounds. Help is on the way. You're safe. Put your head down and breathe slowly. I won't leave you."

Within a minute, several *Polizia Ferroviaria* railway police officers from the train station arrived on the run. Amatrano extracted his Interpol credentials. As the officers approached with drawn weapons, he said in Italian, "I am with Interpol. The situation is stable. Two attackers are dead. I shot them. The taxi driver and this woman passenger in the taxi are victims requiring medical attention."

One officer pointed his weapon at Amatrano, "You shot the attackers?"

"Yes." Amatrano opened his jacket with his left hand to expose his sidearm in the holster."

A second officer disarmed him then took his offered Interpol identification. He remained holding his weapon pointed at Amatrano while his colleague went to assess the carnage. Within moments the wail of sirens followed with several police cars coming to a stop close by with more converging on the area.

†

Amatrano and Nicoletti were seated in a police holding room at Milano Centrale's police headquarters. Emergency medical personnel had examined Nicoletti finding no new injuries. After contacting Guardia di Finanza Lt. Colonel Claudio Pagliaro, the captain commanding the Polizia Ferroviaria at Centrale afforded Amatrano the professional courtesy of personally supervising their statements.

Pagliaro arrived at the train station within an hour of the incident. He allowed the captain to continue his questioning without interruption. Asked why they were in Lugano for only the day, Nicoletti said only that it involved pursuing a lead but declined to elaborate. At the conclusion, the captain said he must keep Amatrano's Berretta for forensic ballistic evidence.

A non-too-happy Pagliaro said, "Not sure what this is about but whoever is behind this is still a threat. You are fortunate that Signore Amatrano chooses to protect you and had the foresight to go armed. A bold move for an Interpol officer who is not armed in the course of official duties."

Pagliaro paused and shook his head in frustration. "Italian law enforcement cannot protect you. Those two dead assassins outside I believe to be organized criminals. Professional hitmen. Haven't identified them yet but I'm certain they are not left-wing terrorists. You are not politically important enough to be a target. Especially as the victim of a second attempt. I understand your reasons as a journalist for keeping your work confidential.

"I'm sure Signore Amatrano has told you this, but I must also warn you. This will not end. I don't want to read about your death, Signora. My advice is to leave Italy until you complete your work. Listen to my friend Francesco. He just risked his life while saving yours." Turning to Amatrano, "If you're going to stay involved in protecting Signora Nicoletti, Francesco, obtain a replacement weapon. Your permit is still valid."

Nicoletti stood up and extended her hand to Pagliaro. "I appreciate everything you have done to help us, Colonel. I know I represent a problem for you. Yet I believe what I'm doing is important. More than that, I can't abide letting the intimidation of professional criminals rule my life. I'm sure you harbor the same feelings."

Pagliaro grasped her hand and smiled. "Take good care, Signora Nicoletti. And listen to Francesco."

†

Within a few days, Colonel Pagliaro called, "As I thought, Francesco. The two hitmen you killed were Sicilian Mafia. Connected to the Santa Maria di Gesù Family in Palermo. You know these nasty characters as well as I do. Not sure what Signora Nicoletti is into, but you need to help her find a solution for preserving her safety."

The incident convinced Amatrano this was about the stolen documents from the Vatican Secret Archive. With Archbishop Tagliente the official archivist and the operational head of the Vatican secret services, he becomes the likely suspect behind this. Unrestricted access to the secret archive afforded him knowledge of the content of the missing documents. Undoubtedly the first to be notified of documents missing. Monsignor Scarpelli knew Tagliente. Vatican intelligence had the operational capability to use Mafia gunmen as expendable proxies deflecting suspicion away from the Vatican Bank.

While the attacks on Emma might be on orders from Sindona, or Calvi, Amatrano knew enough of the Italian Banking Scandal to discount their abilities to engineer these attacks. Bishop Marcinkus didn't fit the profile of a criminal mastermind. It was his financial incompetence that helped get the Vatican Bank involved in this mess. Unlikely the Mafia could be doing this unilaterally. That left Archbishop Tagliente. Even if he was working with higher ranking cardinals, he must be involved at the operational level. Given Amatrano's disdain for believing in conspiracies, odds pointed to Tagliente acting as a rogue prelate to protect the Vatican?

CHAPTER 12

Milan, Italy & Paris, France | July 1979

Frank Amatrano telephoned his immediate superior at Interpol headquarters outside Paris from Pagliaro's private office before he and Nicoletti left. He dreaded the likely blowback when explaining his circumstances to the executive director of Interpol's Organized Crime Unit. Although his salary was paid by the United States government, Amatrano with his dual citizenship was currently the operations manager for Italy. That close involvement with working with Italian law enforcement did not extend to involvement with the shooting in Milan.

Monsieur Henri Étienne already knew of the incident at Milano Centrale train station by a telex bulletin before taking Amatrano's call. After learning details through a conversation with a senior Guardia official, his displeasure came from Amatrano's breaking of protocol. By engaging in unofficial activities outside the prescribed norms of a strictly investigative body, Étienne faced uncomfortable questioning from Interpol President Carl Persson. For the typically reserved Frenchman, Étienne did not hide his anger when Amatrano came on the line.

In good French, Amatrano tried to give a brief explanation. Étienne was in no frame of mind to listen. "I expect you back here in my office the day after tomorrow. No excuses. Where did you get a gun?"

"From the Italian GdF, *Monsieur Directeur*."

"*Mon Dieu*!"

Before returning to Nicoletti, Amatrano huddled with Colonel Pagliaro. "I need a favor, Claudio. I must return to Paris for maybe a couple of days. I need to place an around-the-clock armed guard on Signora Nicoletti. Do you have a couple of officers willing to do that while off duty? I know you don't have the budget. I'll personally pay them well for their time."

Pagliaro nodded. "I'll compromise and put a couple of officers on overtime for several hours. You can compensate them for working additional off duty hours to make up the difference. Are you going to arrange to return to Milan? Do you have a plan for keeping Signora Nicoletti safe from these gangsters?"

"Haven't worked that out yet. Playing it one day at a time. All I know is I can't leave her unprotected. Maybe this will convince her to temporarily relocate."

Nicoletti appeared emotionally recovered but physically exhausted as they rode in the back seat of a police car. She needed rest. Her head rested on Amatrano's shoulder in the back seat of the police car. Her deep breathing indicated she had dozed off until they arrived at her apartment. The officers helped them through the gate then to the building entrance. They told Amatrano they had orders to stay outside the gate until they were relieved by another team.

Inside he helped Emma into the bedroom and laid her gently on the bed. He took off her shoes and found a blanket to cover her. Her eyes closed as she dozed off again. Turning off the light, he started to leave when she sat up abruptly turning on the lamp next to the bed.

Her eyes were wide with fear. Tears streamed down her cheeks uncontrollably.

"Didn't know where I was for a moment."

"You dozed off. Coming down from what happened today. You're safe now. Police are standing guard outside. All night and during the day. I must return to Paris tomorrow if only for a day.

I have been recalled to headquarters to give a report of what happened. I'll return the day after tomorrow. I arranged with Colonel Pagliaro to provide you with around-the-clock police protection until I return."

"She threw her feet off the bed onto the floor. No! Please don't leave me, Frank!"

"Emma, I have no choice. You'll be safe with police officers always outside."

She shook her head vigorously as she stood up and wrapped her arms around him holding him in a tight embrace. Suddenly pulling away, she said with her eyes wide and pleading, "Can I instead go with you to Paris? That way I'll be safe while take care of what you have to do."

Amatrano realized that was actually a much better solution. Maybe convince her to take a leave from her newspaper and work on her project from Paris. "Okay. That works. Are you up to it?"

"I'll make myself up to it. Go next door and ask Loretta if she can come over early and help me get bathed and dressed. Don't tell her what happened. They'll learn about it soon enough in the news. Her family might feel safer with me away. Tell Loretta you suggested a short vacation in Paris since you have demands at your office."

†

Loretta knocked on the door early the next morning. Having slept little, Amatrano was already shaved and dressed having coffee. Loretta knew nothing about the events of yesterday, or their arrival back at the apartment in a police car.

"Good morning, Loretta. Time to wake up Emma. Her headache medication makes her sleep soundly. We have tickets for a nine o'clock train. Emma needs clothes for several days."

"I'll get her ready. So glad you are getting her away for a few days to relax. I've never been to Paris. That will do her good."

The train trip to Paris took nine hours including a train change and hour layover in Zurich. Flying would have been quicker, but Amatrano was not anxious for what probably awaited his return to headquarters. Interpol did not like publicity. Emma looked recovered and the train ride was relaxing with interesting scenery. He took the opportunity to divert their conversation away from the overwhelming weight of having escaped another murder attempt. Circumstances in which he found himself emotionally involved.

"How is it you speak excellent English?' he asked.

"From my parents. Both academics prior to World War Two. Anti-fascists, but not communists. We became partisans. That included me as a teenager. My father was killed by the retreating Nazis in late 1944. Mother survived the war and returned to teaching at the University of Bologna.

"Mother worked with the American occupying forces as a liaison to what remained of Italian civilian authority. Using her influence with the American command, she somehow arranged for me to go to New York to attend Columbia University. Italy was destroyed. Mother wanted to ensure I had a future. My university years in New York became a blessing. That's where I received a degree in journalism in 1950. Where I met Patricia, Gabriel Eisenberg's future wife. Total immersion in English. How about you?"

"Born in Genoa. I'm a naturalized U.S. citizen yet I still hold Italian citizenship. My family emigrated to New York when I was only two years old. Father was a lawyer specializing in international trade agreements and was fluent in English. I grew up in Brooklyn. At home we spoke both English and Italian daily. Mother mostly Italian even to this day."

After taking lunch in the dining car Emma asked, "Are you in any difficulty with what happened yesterday?"

"Not with Italian authorities. Not certain how Interpol will view this. Interpol agents are not law enforcement. Just investigators. We don't officially carry sidearms or make arrests. That is left solely to law enforcement of our member countries. I was not acting in my official capacity when I shot those assassins. However, there may be more to it. My boss sounded very unhappy when I spoke to him."

She pursed her lips and sighed. "Sorry to have dragged you into this, but I'm thankful you saved my life."

"Nothing to be sorry about. Within Interpol I work in the organized crimes unit. My function is to uncover evidence for use in prosecuting those monsters. More often than not I am disappointed. The Mafia intimidate witnesses or kill them when necessary. The Sicilian Mafia is the worst. They even came to America. Having the opportunity to remove two of their gunmen by lethal force felt immensely satisfying."

"What do you suggest I do, Frank? Is there no way I can continue doing my work without constantly fearing another attempt on my life?"

"We'll find a way to get through this. Spend a few days in Paris thinking this through."

"Where do you live?"

"In Paris in the 15th arrondissement. The Central Paris district south of the Eiffel Tower. Just a short drive from Interpol headquarters in the suburb of Saint Cloud."

"Do you have a nice apartment?"

"I'll let you be the judge. That's where you'll be staying. Good size. Two bedrooms, modernized bathroom, adequate kitchen, large living area. A wall of bookshelves. I have a weakness for books."

Silent for a moment she asked, "Does bringing me to Paris complicate your personal life?"

He looked at her and smiled, "Coming to Milan did more than just complicate my life. But if you mean am I involved in a relationship, the answer is no."

"Thank you for not leaving me, Frank. I could not imagine staying alone in my apartment even with police protection. Not sure how I can ever feel safe again. At least for the moment, I'm in a much better place."

"Coming to Paris was the perfect immediate solution. Didn't like leaving your protection to the Italian police. Gives us some time to work out what to do next."

The train arrived at Paris Gare Lyon train station at six o'clock in the evening. Amatrano hailed a porter to get a cart for their suitcases and Emma's portable typewriter. At the taxi queue, Amatrano opened the back door of the taxi. Emma suddenly started looking quickly left and right. The image of the same circumstances of what happened in Milan flashed in her mind..

"It's alright, Emma. You are safe here in Paris."

He was sure of that but did his own scanning of the area. Instinctively he reached inside his jacket to feel the butt of what was actually Emma's Berretta as he went to get into the other side of the taxi. Even with a police escort leaving her apartment in Milan, he was not about to go unarmed. His own Berretta held as police evidence in the death of the Mafiosi he killed.

"Only a short drive. We'll cross over the River Seine. The drive along Boulevard Saint-Germain will give you a feel of the *Rive Gauche*, the Left Bank of the Seine. Get you settled into the apartment then we'll take a short walk to have dinner at a small restaurant I often frequent. It's a nice warm evening for a stroll in Paris."

Amatrano's apartment building was much the same as Nicoletti's in Milan. You enter through a gate into an interior parking area off a one-way street. His apartment was on the top floor serviced by a lift. A corner unit in an upscale building with a view to the north with the Eiffel tower represented a major financial investment when purchased more than ten years earlier. No regrets when relocating from his small apartment in Bern, Switzerland after first joining Interpol in 1963.

Entering the apartment, Emma was pleasantly surprised. "Oh my. This is wonderful, Frank!" she said walking immediately to the large adjacent corner windows looking out over rooftops with the Eiffel Tower in the background.

"Let me show you to the guest bedroom. Doesn't get much use. My parents are getting up in age and don't come to Paris often. No siblings. It's yours for as long as necessary. Been thinking today that staying in Paris might be the best short-term solution. Staying outside of Italy. Maybe you could continue working for your newspaper remotely as a temporary arrangement."

After entering the large bathroom, she remarked, "This is like a five-star hotel."

"Since it was so large, I splurged years ago with a remodeling."

Touring the spacious living room with a far corner arranged as a small study with bookshelves and a comfortable reading chair, she remarked. "Beautifully decorated, Frank. All your doing?"

She detected the slightest change in his eyes when he replied, "Not entirely. Someone from my past. Her name was Iska. She had excellent tastes. I met Dr. Iska Weiss soon after coming to work in Paris. We never married but lived together for many years."

Emma forced herself not to ask the obvious question about what happened.

In a moment, he said, "Regrettably, Iska died in March 1975."

Emma touched her hand to her mouth. "Oh no. That is so sad, Frank."

"She died in Tel Aviv, Israel. At the hands of PLO terrorists. Killed along with her mother and others."

"Why was she in Tel Aviv?"

"Visiting her mother. Her mother was also a physician. The family was Polish. Jewish. Iska escaped Poland in 1939 along with her parents and older brother after the Nazis invaded. Two weeks later the Soviets invaded Poland from the east. Poland fell within weeks. The family managed to escape to England.

"Her father was a Polish army officer. Fought in the British RAF as a pilot. Died in combat. Her brother fought in the British Army. He still lives in England. Mother eventually emigrated to Israel. Iska was in Tel Aviv visiting her mother and staying at the Savoy Hotel. A handful of PLO terrorists arrived by small boats. Spotted by Israeli police they took refuge in the Savoy Hotel taking hostages. Eight civilians died in the attack."

Emma just stood there. Nothing she could say while imagining the same death by gunfire she just narrowly avoided.

"Enough about the past, Emma. You are out of danger, and I am immensely relieved. We must take the time to breathe. Appreciate life for what it is. No better place than my beloved Paris. Please sit down. Care for a drink?"

"I'll have a glass of wine."

"Wonderful. Along with books French and Italian wines are another weakness. I'll open a Barolo to make you feel at home. I believe I'll have a Scotch."

After an hour relaxing, "Ready for dinner, Emma. Hungry?"

"As a matter of fact, I am. Could you please help me remove this sling? I don't think it is necessary any longer. It was only for securing my broken collar bone."

"You sure it's okay to remove?"

"Slept without it last night. I can feel the lump where the bone has healed. Shoulder is still somewhat stiff but improving."

Amatrano helped lift the sling from around her neck and off her arm. A bandage still wrapped her upper left arm.

"The arm is healing fine. I keep the bandage on mostly for appearance. Hope my cheek eventually does as well. Can you help me with this light sweater? I see you are not going armed. Does that mean we really are safe?"

"I believe so. At least from Mafiosi with machineguns. Not licensed to carry a firearm in France. Okay to have in the apartment though where you will always keep it close by. Shall we go?"

The bistro was only a few blocks away and the night was still warm.

Walking back to the apartment after dinner, Emma hooked her arm in his. Amatrano felt a pleasant sensation not experienced for a very long time.

†

The following morning, Amatrano left the apartment early to purchase food. He wanted a good breakfast before facing the unknowns of what he expected to be a difficult day. He left a note on the floor in front of her bedroom door that he would return soon after buying food from the nearby shops. Coffee is ready in the kitchen.

When he returned, she was seated in the living room having coffee while watching television.

Opening the door, "Good morning. Needed to restock the kitchen. I'll fix breakfast. Got some time before I must leave for the office."

Following a simple breakfast of scrambled eggs and toast, "Time for me to leave. I'm only twenty minutes away. The Beretta stays with you. Next to the phone I wrote a number where I can be reached. No one knows you are here. Let's keep it that way. Don't answer the telephone. If I want to reach you, I will let it ring three times then hang up and redial immediately."

She said, "I've been watching the news on television. Don't understand much French but I recognized my name and heard the Italian police officer speaking Italian to a reporter. Graphic pictures. Bullet holes along the side of the taxi. A miracle I survived. A distant image showed the car with the dead Mafia gunmen you killed laying covered on the ground."

"Put it out of your mind. Relax or do some work on your project. Must leave now."

She stood up and kissed him on the cheek. "Thank you, Frank. Hope you're not in too much trouble over this."

Arriving at the office, Henri Étienne's secretary immediately knocked on the closed door and ushered him inside without waiting for a reply then closed the door behind him.

"Sit down, Monsieur Amatrano. Please give me your version of the story. Start by explaining why you were protecting this woman journalist after a previous attempt on her life? And how is it you were armed?"

Having rehearsed describing the sequence of events, Amatrano delivered a concise narrative. Omitting any reference about stolen documents from the Vatican, he explained his going to Milan as a favor to an old friend that just lost his brother to a terrorist attack. Help him to navigate the complex arrangements in a foreign country to have his brother's remains returned to the United States. The weakness in his story was assuming the role of armed bodyguard to the woman journalist.

His boss jumped on that, "You said you did not know her. Met her for the first time when you and your friend visited her in the hospital. Why not leave her protection to Italian law enforcement?"

"Two reasons. Italian law enforcement is overwhelmed by killings. Including assassinations of their own senior officers and magistrates. They could not keep her safe. That point clearly made with a second attempt to kill her. Secondly, I believed this to be the work of Sicilian Mafia not terrorists either on the left, or right?"

"Why is that?"

"Cannot say other than she has no political connection. Works for a financial publication. Madame Nicoletti is an investigative journalist. She has not confided to me the target of her current project, but enough for me to infer it likely involves organized crime."

"Therefore, you take a personal leave, get yourself a weapon and become an Italian policeman. You are an investigator of organized crime, not law enforcement. That responsibility falls to our member countries. Instead, you publicly embarrass Interpol."

That comment hit a nerve. Something festering for a very long time. "Embarrassed? How is that? Interpol agent guns down Sicilian Mafia assassins that murdered a taxi driver while failing to assassinate a newspaper reporter?"

An angry Étienne raised his hand to halt Amatrano's verbal attack. It had no effect. Amatrano continued, "Interpol is an acronym for the International Criminal Police Organization. Note the words *criminal police*. But that's really bullshit. We're not police. We're just consultants. The police in a good many of our member countries are too incompetent or corrupt to deal with organized crime."

Étienne stood up from behind his desk. "Enough, Amatrano. You are hereby officially on administrative suspension pending a disciplinary review panel hearing."

"Perhaps I'll save you the bother and simply resign. Shooting those Mafia gunmen was the most satisfying thing I accomplished in a long time."

"Don't do something rash. You have been with Interpol for such a long time."

"Maybe too long." With that Amatrano stood and left Étienne's office slamming the door startling his secretary enough to make her jump. Once seated in his car the anger subsided but only slightly. Everything he expressed to Étienne articulated his fundamental frustrations. Did he want to continue doing this for at least five more years for a full pension? The simple answer was no. However, he had no clear idea what to do for the rest of his professional life.

†

When he unlocked and opened his front door there was Nicoletti standing with the Berretta in her hand. Gone was the robe and bare feet. Dressed now in slacks and heels with a stylish white long-sleeved blouse, the ensemble complimenting her figure. No arm sling. Hair fixed. Makeup. The bandage running down her left cheek did not detract from a picture of a most attractive woman. "I didn't expect you back so soon. Guess I'm a little paranoid," she said placing the gun gently on an end table.

"Not at all. Two attempts on your life make a lasting impression. Take nothing for granted."

"How did things go?"

"As I expected. Actually, worse than I anticipated. Not sure I'll be going back to Interpol."

"Oh no. Because of me?"

"Absolutely not. Because of me. What I've been doing for years has become frustrating. I work in the organized crime division at Interpol but rarely see results. Putting down those two Mafia gunmen was far more satisfying than presenting evidence than watching local law enforcement squander the opportunity to bring criminals to justice."

Emma remained quiet. She felt responsible for causing so much harm to others in pursuit of this Vatican documents project. A layer of guilt adding to so much uncertainty beyond her control left her dispirited.

Sensing how she must feel, he abruptly said, "How about we take a drive around central Paris. We both need a pleasant diversion. Ever been to Paris before?"

"Not really. Just passed through the airport a couple of times years ago to change planes traveling between New York and Milan."

"Well good. Then we'll make a day of it. Both of us need that. Lunch outside somewhere along Boulevard Saint Germani. Dinner this evening someplace interesting across the Seine on the right bank."

"Sounds wonderful, Frank." No idea if that's what she wished to do but seemed a better diversion than sitting around the apartment trying to force solutions to her lingering questions. Returning to work on the project? Her job at *Il Sole 24 Ore*? Her safety if and when returning to Italy?

†

The afternoon did prove wonderful. A sunny day filled with some smiles while people watching on the Left Bank, An excellent dinner at a high-end restaurant on the Right Bank.

As they prepared to retire, Amatrano came to her. Standing close he leaned forward and kissed her on the lips. "I enjoyed being with you today, Emma. I'm becoming very fond of you."

She smiled. Her eyes moistened and tears flowed down both cheeks. "Good night, Frank." She touched his face tenderly with her hand then opened the bedroom door closing it gently behind her.

Disappointed, Amatrano chastised himself for pushing things. Clearly feeling something far greater than fondness, he should have been more considerate. Sensing she felt something more than just gratitude for him, he ignored the fact she must still be in a fragile emotional state. Falling into a romantic relationship perhaps too much right now. Give it some time.

Sleep escaped him as a full moon bathed his bedroom in a low soft light with the window curtains parted and the window partly opened for the cool night air. After an hour lying in bed, he heard the flushing of the toilet. She was still awake too.

Several minutes passed before his bedroom door opened gently. Enough moonlight filtered from behind to see Emma standing there. She whispered, "Awake?"

He replied softly, "Yes."

Taking several steps to come next to his bed, "Can I join you?" With that she undid the belt of her robe. Tugging it off her shoulders, it fell to the floor.

The moonlight was sufficient for him to appreciate her naked body. Bending down, she touched her hand to his bare chest then slid it under the sheet. As she touched his growing erection, he reached up and caressed her breasts. Their mutual attentions drew pleasurable responses.

Emma placed a knee on the bed and climbed up to kneel beside him. "Don't want to reinjure my shoulder." With that she pulled back the sheet and through her left leg over his pelvis. She then guided him inside her. The sensation brought a gasp of pleasure from both of them. Rocking back and forth, her breathing became heavier as her rhythm increased. He let her guide the lovemaking while holding her firm by the hips with his hands. Sensing his impending release, she contracted her vaginal muscles bringing them both to orgasm.

Easing herself off, she laid down next to him. Facing him, the moonlight defined the length of her body. "Are we falling in love?" she said looking into his eyes.

"I think I already have. Started from the first time I saw you in the hospital."

"Even bandaged and helpless?"

"Bandaged, hair undone, but never helpless."

He reached over drawing his finger under the bandage on her cheek. "I want to take a look. May I?"

With a slight flicker of apprehension in her eyes, she nodded.

Removing the dressing, he could see clearly the nearly healed wound in the pale moonlight. Her eyes never left him while awaiting his reaction.

With a genuine smile, he said, "Not at all bad. The surgeon did a magnificent job. Used a technique that apparently minimizes the effects of the sutures. It's still healing but it looks like just a subtle crease. Can't tell in the moonlight, but it should be easily covered with makeup. You should not fear being seen. Look at how well the wounds have healed on your arm. No suture puckering there either. You're not self-conscious about that. Same holds for your cheek, Emma."

"You're just being kind. Love makes you blind."

"No, I'm not. I'm being honest. You will be totally fine. Takes nothing away from your beauty."

"That's because you are looking at me naked bathed in moonlight," she said but with a genuine smile.

CHAPTER 13

Paris, France | Autumn 1979

The next morning brought a new beginning for Frank Amatrano and Emma Nicoletti. Their personal lives had been devoid of a sustained relationship with a romantic partner for a long time. Amatrano retreated inward after losing Iska Weiss. Nicoletti's last serious relationship lasted only a few months. A successful business attorney found life with an obsessive investigative reporter incompatible. In their later forties, both were set in their respective lifestyles that did not satisfactorily mesh. Before that, infrequent romantic affairs came and went. She attributed most of those failures to her difficult personality. She fervently hoped what she felt for Frank Amatrano would prove different.

When he woke in the morning and left the bed to close the curtains as daylight streamed across the bed, Emma turned over and said, "Good morning."

He came around and sat on the bed next to her. "Sleep well?"

"Yes. Felt good with you next to me. That was wonderful last night."

He smiled. "Very special. Ready for coffee or do you want to go back to sleep for a while."

"Actually, I need to pee. Then take a shower. We both smell like lovemaking."

"Maybe we should both shower. The shower's big enough for the both of us."

"She pulled herself up letting the sheet fall away from her breasts then wrapped her arms around him. I'd like that."

In the bathroom she was uninhibited as she sat on the toilet to urinate while he turned on the shower. It pleased him that she did not go to the mirror to look at her cheek with the bandage removed. Once he entered the shower they lathered each with the purpose of arousal. Returning to bed, the lovemaking was more protracted with foreplay intended to please the other.

Over coffee, the telephone rang. "*Bonjour*," Amatrano answered.

"This is Antonio Ferrazza, Frank. Glad I finally caught you. I spoke to Colonel Pagliaro in Milan once the bulletin came over the telex. I tried all day yesterday to reach you. Pagliaro also gave me the number for the journalist involved in the incident. No answer there. Don't suppose you know where she might be?"

Amatrano replied in Italian, "Safe in Paris, Antonio. That was the second attempt on her life. Someone badly wants her dead."

"Pagliaro told me the whole story. I imagine Interpol headquarters wanted more than an explanation. How's that going?"

"Not well. That's where I was yesterday. My boss pissed me off. Pushed too far. Made my frustrations much more immediate. I'm just an investigative consultant. It felt immensely satisfying putting down those two Mafiosi in Milan. Only wish I could go after who's ordering the hit on Signora Nicoletti. Yet my boss rewarded me with an administrative suspension pending a hearing. Told the sonofabitch to expect my resignation."

"Are you serious? You've been with Interpol for a lot of years."

"Not all of them good years, though, Antonio. About time to redirect my career. Something where I can see my efforts produce results."

Like Pagliaro, Lieutenant Colonel Ferrazza was also a senior *Guardia di Finanza* officer. Pagliaro worked in the Milan regional command whereas Ferrazza was chief of staff at the Rome headquarters of the *Gruppo d'Investigazione Sulla Criminalità Organizzata,* the organized crime investigation group, known by the acronym GICO. Ferrazza worked closely with Frank Amatrano for years since they shared the same focus of organized crime. They also developed a personal friendship transcending their professional association.

"Got anything in mind, Frank? Thinking about going back to the United States? With your background shouldn't be difficult to find a suitable position in one of their many national law enforcement agencies."

"Haven't got that far, Antonio. Wasn't planning on making a career change so abruptly. Circumstances now dictate otherwise. Been working in Europe for the last twenty-five years. Missed all the chaos of the civil rights riots and the anti-Vietnam War years in the United States. Feel almost like a stranger to my home country."

"Italy is also your home country, Frank. Pagliaro reminded me you still hold Italian citizenship."

"That's true. Born in Genoa. Came to America when I was only two. Grew up in Brooklyn, New York. My English still has a distinctive New York accent."

"Yes, I remember you telling me. What about working in Italy, Frank?"

Amatrano did not respond immediately. Looking over at Nicoletti drinking coffee wearing only his shirt and nothing else became a momentary distraction. Why not Italy? Because Paris was his home was his first thought. "Are you offering me a job, Antonio?" he answered with a hint of humor thinking that unlikely.

"Well, there is an opening. A vacancy opened with someone leaving to take a position with the Carabinieri. I'm speaking of the position as head of intelligence of GICO. Your background makes you exceptionally qualified. Not totally up to me but I carry some weight with GICO commander Brigadier General Enrico Giacchetto. Confirmation of his candidate is then required from the Guardia di Finanza chief of staff. The fellow that left the intelligence position held the rank of major. With your qualifications they might even entice you by offering a lieutenant colonelcy rank. Would you be interested enough for me to talk to General Giacchetto?"

"I'd want to hear more about the responsibilities, but that's an intriguing idea, Antonio. Based in Rome I presume?"

"Right down the hall from my office, old friend. What do you think?"

"Not anxious about relocating from Paris, but I like Rome. Go ahead and offer my name for consideration. Feel free to tell the general that this incident made my decision to leave Interpol. Frustrated by the inability to directly combat organized crime by making arrests. No shortage of opportunities to make a difference as part of Italian law enforcement."

"Excellent! How can I reach you?"

"I'll give you my pager number."

Nicoletti asked after he hung up the call, "What was that all about?"

"A possible job offer with the Guardia di Finanza. That's what happens if you kill Mafiosi."

"Really. Are you seriously considering leaving Interpol?"

Returning to sit down next to her at the table, "Been unhappy there for some time. My contributions at Interpol are too limited. Politics dealing with member country law enforcement adds further frustration."

"You would move to Italy?"

"Well, I'm Italian. Besides that's where you live."

"Where in Italy would you work?"

"Guardia headquarters in Rome."

While intrigued by the possibility of joining the Guardia di Finanza, Amatrano knew only that his colleague Antonio Ferrazza was seizing on the opportunity to help him. He would wait and see if anything came of it. In the meantime, he would keep his options open. Don't rush to submit a formal resignation to Interpol. He was on paid administrative leave. Time enough to pull the plug when a formal review hearing became scheduled.

For now, enjoy the surprise discovery of a promising romantic relationship with Emma. Figure out how to keep her safe while still pursuing her investigative project. Could she make a compelling case to publicly accuse the Vatican Bank of participating in the laundering of Sicilian Mafia money? He now had time to devote his efforts to assisting Nicoletti. Possessing knowledge of Italian organized criminal activities and methods could add greatly to piecing together Emma's new evidence into the known details of the Italian Banking Scandal. That and identifying those behind the murder of Gabriel Eisenberg and a taxi driver in the second attempt on Emma's life. Justice needed to be served by delivering retribution.

Emma said, "What's next?"

"You mean with us?"

"No. I think we settled that last night and this morning. Seems more than just an affair for both of us."

"Couldn't agree more. Since I'm on administrative leave, I have time to devote to your project. With all that's happened, it's our project now. We're both skilled investigators. I believe we are safe here in France, but we still need to take precautions. We have your Berretta, but that is illegal in France. It stays in the apartment as a last line of defense."

"Those gunmen in Milan were Sicilian Mafia you said. Might they not operate in France?" Emma asked.

"Possibly. Or perhaps using surrogates. France also has organized crime. My greater concern is that someone outside the Sicilian Mafia is directing their attacks on you."

"Like the Vatican secret service?"

"Maybe. Your safety is inexorably connected to the existence of the stolen Vatican archival documents. If the Vatican secret service is involved they undoubtedly have followed the trail of Monsignor Scarpelli. They know the original documents still exist. Considering their value, they would conclude that probably means a Swiss bank vault rather than a law office. Returning to Lugano therefore becomes dangerous for us. We will deal with that when necessary."

"Speaking of my safety, I recall Colonel Pagliaro making a strange comment when I was in the hospital. Some reference to you being a bodyguard with lethal hands. What did he mean?"

"Pagliaro was speaking about my proficiency in a martial arts technique called *krav maga*. Developed in Israel in the late forties for use by Israeli Defense Forces. It combines techniques of other martial arts like judo and karate, but with a singular difference. Krav maga is defensive only to the extent of providing opportunity to apply offensive techniques designed to kill or seriously disable an attacker. It's a combat technique intended to be lethal. Also teaches how to improvise by using any object as a weapon to kill your enemy."

"Good lord! You can kill someone with just your hands?"

He nodded.

"Have you?"

"Not yet."

"Where did you learn this?"

"Working with the Israeli Mossad in the early seventies. Spent a year helping them identify the locations of the PLO terrorists involved with the Munich Olympics Massacre in 1972. Krav maga additionally became a fitness regimen that also a sense of wellbeing by feeling confident should I need to defend myself from physical attack."

"Even if confronted by someone with a gun or knife?"

"A knife, most certainly. A gun if the assailant gets close enough. Krav maga doesn't make me invincible just potentially lethal to an unsuspecting attacker.

"Let's hope you don't have to test those skills. You have much more pleasurable uses for your hands.

†

Amatrano and Nicoletti begin working jointly on examining Vatican materials to determine if there existed threads to make the case for Vatican Bank participation in Mafia money laundering.

Nicoletti commented, "There is no direct incriminating documentation that connects the Vatican Bank with the Sicilian Mafia. Their participation is commingled with transactions with Sindona and Calvi. There are continual allegations going back years with Sindona's connection to laundering Mafia money. By association with Sindona, Calvi's financial troubles with Banco Ambrosiano have become even more suspect with expanded transactions involving the Vatican Bank."

Amatrano said, "Michele Sindona has disappeared while out on bail awaiting trial in New York. All over yesterday's newspaper. His family has received ransom letters."

Not reading French, Nicoletti had not looked at yesterday's copy of La Monde laying on the coffee table. Picking up the newspaper she now noticed his name in a column heading and his photograph on an inside page. "Does it attribute the kidnapping to the *Red Brigades*?"

Amatrano replied, "No."

"If he was in New York that doesn't make sense. Must be the Mafia."

"Maybe. If so, it might be the last we see of him. The Mafia wouldn't kidnap him for the money. However, it is quite possible to keep him silent. His trial in U.S. federal court scheduled for this week has been postponed indefinitely."

Emma said, "To implicate the Vatican Bank with the Mafia we must either look to the front end of the money laundering process or the final stage where they access proceeds. Money laundering involves layering transactions using offshore foreign entities in tax havens to obscure the money trail. Impossible to untangle without possessing far more detailed information."

Amatrano of course understood all that. "Perhaps I can be of help there. I have not yet officially resigned from Interpol. I have some good friends there that probably see my administrative suspension as bureaucratic nonsense. Interpol is about going after criminals. Killing a couple of them makes me more of celebrity than a pariah. They may be willing to provide me information on what our files reveal about known Italian Mafia avenues of money laundering. We're looking for names of banks or businesses at either the beginning or ending of the money laundering cycle as you correctly point out."

Emma replied, "While you work your Interpol sources, I will begin mapping the interconnections based on the identified foreign subsidiary banks and shell companies of Sindona and Calvi.

Then I'll try to integrate what is known of Vatican Bank involvement from the Archive documents. Which shell companies they control directly or indirectly is a murky question of even those entities we know of from all these players."

"If anything comes of this possible job offer with the Guardia di Finanza GICO, then I'll have immediate access to everything Italian law enforcement knows about Mafia financial connections. The Italian underworld figures most involved with financial transactions. With names we get business and banking names. With those, audit trails exist in and out of countries with more transparent banking laws. Illicit money starts in Italy and must come full circle back to Italy as legitimate assets after moving through these offshore non-transparent shell entities..

"I know of one name that might be a starting point. Ever heard of Giuseppe 'Pippo' Calò, known as the Cosa Nostra cashier? Boss of the Palermo Porta Nuova family."

"No," she said.

"Reports from the Guardia di Finanza suggest he is possibly the most important figure in Italian Mafia money laundering. Advises other allied Mafia families. I will see if I can obtain specifics that we can use to tie him into the larger picture."

✝

Amatrano made a call to a trusted subordinate at Interpol headquarters. His administrative suspension did not set well with the staff of the organized crime division. One colleague agreed to supply him with the names of all enterprises known as being Mafia controlled. To avoid leaving a paper trail, a couple of days later, Amatrano received a telephone call verbally providing him with that list. The names extended internationally beyond just those in Italy.

Amatrano already had a general familiarity with some of the names. Most of the information came from the Italian GdF. Unfortunately, most lacked sufficient supporting evidence to make criminal charges in Italy.

Explaining what he found to Emma, "My colleague at Interpol headquarters came through with some useful information. Take a look at these names. See if you recognized any of these entities. I'm familiar with the name Banca Mercantile di San Lorenzo headquartered in Palermo. Branches in Reggio Calabria, Naples, and Rome. Other than Rome, these are the principal Mafia strongholds.

"The shareholders of Banca Mercantile consist of a very long list of businessmen, mostly in Sicily and Calabria. All operating seemingly legitimate businesses. The GdF believes all or most to be cooperating with the Mafia under coercion. The GdF believes these same shareholders who also hold accounts at the bank provide the means for introducing illicit money into the financial system. Some are cash businesses, others by using trade-based or service-based money laundering schemes.

"Italian bank examiners are highly suspicious by the regular movement of funds to three foreign companies in tax havens. Italienesch Wealth Management SA, acronym IWM in Luxembourg, Mitteleuropäische Verwaltete Beteiligungen, acronym MVB in Lichtenstein, and Banco Financiero Sudamericano, acronym Bafisud, in Montevideo, Uruguay. The ownership of the two likely shell companies and the South American bank remains unknown. The trail ends there until picked up at the other end of the laundering cycle.

"Deposits regularly appear in the individual accounts at Banca Mercantile from an offshore entity called Fondo Atlantic Investments, acronym FAI. This undoubtedly represents the return of laundered funds to the original Mafiosi now disguised as legitimate investment assets of straw accounts. While obvious, neither Interpol nor the Guardia di Finanza can uncover enough evidence for bringing criminal charges."

Emma said, "If the Vatican Bank is involved with money laundering, it is hidden behind layers of intermediate offshore financial transactions involving Sindona and Calvi. Piercing that secrecy may be impossible. However, there is no obvious reason for the Vatican Bank engaging with these criminal bankers other than for its own financial reasons. With Mafia money involved I am still convinced the Vatican is behind these attacks on me. Archbishop Tagliente becomes the principal suspect."

"Since this is about the missing documents, I agree. Do any of these names I just mentioned come up in any of the Archive documents?"

"No. Although there is one document that I haven't shown you yet. Haven't connected how it fits. Yet Scarpelli thought it important enough to add to his stolen cache. Let me dig it out."

Returning with a copy made during the last foray to the Swiss bank, she said, "Ever heard of someone named Umberto Ortolani?"

"No. Who is he?"

"Not yet sure. Haven't had time to research him further. Whoever Ortolani is, he keeps a low profile out of the public domain."

ISTITUTO PER LE OPERE DI RELIGIONE
VATICANO

20 May 1972
Greetings, Your Holiness,

His Eminence, Cardinal-Priest Giacomo Lercaro has introduced me to a much-respected gentleman by the name of Umberto Ortolani, also from Bologna. Signore Ortolani is a successful lawyer, banker, and businessman with interests in Italy and South America.

Since 1963 Signore Ortolani became recognized as a Papal Gentleman by His Holiness Pope John XXIII. In 1969 he became Ambassador of the Knights Hospitalier Order of Malta in Montevideo, Uruguay. Signore Ortolani is widely recognized as a man of honor with important associations throughout Italian business and government. Our much-trusted friend Michele Sindona spoke to me on behalf of recommending the financial counsel of Signore Ortolani.

As a gesture of service to the Holy See, Signore Ortolani has presented me with an investment opportunity. A blueprint for creating what is known as a hedge fund based in a foreign sovereignty, therefore not subject to Italian tax or currency laws. A mechanism by which to add to IOR revenues through investment opportunities that legally avoid Italian taxes. It further represents the same value for diocesan investment through entrusting management to the IOR.

Once arrangements are in place, this may additionally represent investment and tax avoidance opportunities for dioceses worldwide. It affords the ability for the IOR to act as a trusted fiduciary keeping financial affairs within the orbit of Mother Church.

I shall proceed with implementing this plan as prescribed by Signore Ortolani unless Your Holiness has other thoughts.

Sincerely, Your Faithful Servant in Christ,

P.C. Marcinkus

Bishop Paul Marcinkus

Paulus PP VI

Emma said, "Something important enough to run it by the pope. A hedge fund sounds like an investment mechanism for wealthy clients. Dioceses like those in the United States qualify as wealthy."

"That they do. So does the Italian Mafia. Your benefactor Monsignor Scarpelli included this document as relevant toward implicating the Vatican in criminal wrongdoing. The importance of this letter is the introduction of Ortolani. Goes back to 1972. While it provides no details, Umberto Ortolani becomes a new thread to investigate."

†

"*Buongiorno*, Frank. How are things in Paris?" The caller was Lt. Colonel Antonio Ferrazza in Rome.

"Getting along better than I might have imagined." He looked over at Emma and smiled.

"Good for you. Have some encouraging news. Spoke with the boss. He is very much interested in considering you for the Intelligence position of the GICO. Without being specific, I told him you were somewhat disenchanted with working for Interpol. The Milan incident made the difference between your Interpol work starkly different from direct law enforcement. Can you come to Rome and interview with Brigadier General Giacchetto?"

"I can arrange that. He's actually interested in me joining the GICO?"

"Yes, he is. Your background is a perfect fit. His words. You're Italian by birth and have been working with us for many years on Italian organized crime. I did some lobbying on your behalf. Told the General it might take some convincing for you to relocate from Paris to Rome while leaving a long career with Interpol. Will also require your working a good deal of the time in the South. Italy's concentration of the Cosa Nostra and the Camorra, stretching from Campania to Palermo. Told him I doubted you would accept the intelligence position unless it held the rank of lieutenant colonel."

Amatrano added, "That and Italy becoming a dangerous place for police officers. Anyway, I'll do my best. Thanks for the good word, Antonio. The General has met me on several occasions so I'm not a total stranger. I will telephone you tomorrow. Give me some dates available for meeting next week in Rome. Do you need me to send you a resume?"

Ferrazza laughed. "The general already has your dossier, my friend."

"Well?" Emma said listening to his end of the conversation.

"Care to come with me to Rome? Antonio Farrazza is arranging an interview with Brigadier General Enrico Giacchetto, commander of the GICO."

"Of course. I feel safer being close to you. Besides, I still have my Berretta and an Italian concealed carry permit."

"No venturing back to Milan yet. Agree?"

Emma nodded. "When will that change, Frank?"

He came over and embraced her. "Been giving that considerable thought. The issue of your safety is connected with the documents Scarpelli took that remain outstanding. Even though they do not link the Vatican Bank to the Mafia directly, from what you showed me, there is enough to badly compromise the Vatican. Confidential material intentionally buried. Compromising enough to support allegations of serious wrongdoing will make it more difficult for the Vatican to explain its participation with Sindona and Calvi. Clearly not as victims but as coconspirators.

"The origin of this new incriminating material public will generate renewed interest in the financial scandal. Material citing knowledge by Pope Paul and Pope John Paul II of association questionable figures associated with the scandal will alone prove damaging. Might shake up senior Vatican churchmen. Maybe Bishop Marcinkus. Maybe Archbishop Tagliente. In charge of the Vatican Secret Archive, the theft occurred on his watch. If you suspect him of being behind Eisenberg's murder and the attempts on your life, then publishing a flood of never before released confidential documents will place him in the public spotlight. A catastrophe for someone that operates from such secrecy."

Emma sat back down at the kitchen table. "I know all that. So, what is it you are suggesting I do?"

"Make the documents public. Once that happens, eliminating you no longer matters."

She looked at him with a shocked expression. "Are you crazy! After going through all this to give up on going after the Vatican!"

"Listen. Hear me out. Not at all giving up on going after the Vatican. I agree with you that the Vatican is behind this to cover up what the documents will reveal. We just discussed that these stolen documents do not directly incriminate the Vatican with laundering Mafia money. We need more than these documents to make a compelling public case. You and Gabriel began working Scarpelli's work to tie the Vatican Bank into the larger Italian Banking Scandal."

She interrupted, "And it does. At least enough to explain the Vatican as a participant not a victim. Now every journalist would have the same information. I'm not about to do that."

"Emma, with all that's happened, that is no longer the story. The story is about *Gabriel's murder and the attempts on your life*. Start by writing a book of the account of what happened from when these documents came into your possession. Make it read like a suspense novel taken from the headlines. Might be the only way to inflict revenge against those behind this violence."

"So, I am to admit that I came into possession of these documents knowingly stolen from the Vatican?"

"Of course. But that only becomes public in the opening chapter of your book after its released."

"You're crazy! I'm a journalist. Admitting to using stolen materials?"

"You did not participate in the theft. You are not bound ethically to withhold the contents. Monsignor Scarpelli is deceased. Journalists get material from questionable sources all the time. Police do it as a necessary part of uncovering crimes. You are doing the same."

"The Vatican will raise holy hell," she replied. "They may even take legal action to recover the documents or prohibit their use."

"Where? In Italian court? The theft is not an Italian matter. The Vatican is a sovereign state. I'm not suggesting you just hand over the documents at a press conference. Until this book is published, you will not be publicly connected with any stolen Vatican documents. After that, it becomes irrelevant."

She shook her head bewildered with his entire idea. "Then how are the documents made public?"

"We go to the Swiss bank. Make any further photocopies you might need then have the bank ship the originals to the *New York Times* anonymously. Excluding of course, Monsignor Scarpelli's letter to you. By law, the secretive Swiss bank will not divulge your identity as the account holder."

Dumbfounded by the breadth of the idea, she said nothing for almost a minute. Taking a deep breath, she stood and embraced him. "That is remarkably creative. I like the idea of feeling safe enough to begin living again. Give me until we leave next week for Rome to consider your idea. If I agree, can we stop off in Lugano to deal with the Vatican Secret Archive documents before returning to Paris?"

He kissed her. "Absolutely. Giving up the documents is the best way to remove yourself as a target. Releasing them through Gabriel's newspaper the *New York Times*, makes for a certain poetic justice."

CHAPTER 14

Paris, France | October 1979

Amatrano and Nicoletti enjoyed a leisurely Sunday. A marvelous sunny autumn day. Late breakfast, a walk in the great expanse of Bois de Boulogne Park. Over dinner at a fashionable upscale restaurant in the 16th arrondissement they discussed leaving the following morning for Rome. A two-hour flight from Orly would put them into Rome at midday. Time enough to get Emma settled into a hotel then lunch together before making his scheduled interview with GICO commander General Giacchetto at Guardia di Finanza headquarters.

Seated enjoying cocktails before dinner, Emma said, "If you get a good offer to join the Guardia, are you ready to leave Interpol after all these years?"

"Yes. Not without doubts about what I'm getting into in Italy, but definitely the decision to leave Interpol. The work there no longer engages my interest. I am bitter about this administrative suspension. Reflects the overwhelming bureaucracy of Interpol. Too much meddling by the member nations. Totalitarian member nations weaponizing law enforcement by misusing *Red Notices,* international arrest warrants, obligating other member countries to cooperate. Since walking out of Étienne's office I have received no word concerning my status. If this move to the Guardia doesn't happen, I will likely still resign from Interpol assuming I find something better suited to my interests."

"Does that mean looking for a position in the United States?"

"Not necessarily. Not my intention. I've been working and living in Europe for so long, it has become my home. I speak four languages so I'm comfortable in Europe. Besides, that's where you are." Smiling, he placed his hand over hers resting on the table.

She acknowledged him by covering his hand with her other hand. "I like that too, Frank."

"Even if it means moving from Milan to Rome?"

She smiled and nodded. "Yes. I've reached a decision too. About the Vatican Archive documents. About giving them up to remove me from being a target by unknown assassins. Once you are done meeting with the Guardia, can we train to Lugano and arrange for shipping off the documents to the *New York Times*?"

"That works. From there we'll train back to Paris."

"Good. I want to begin writing that book you suggested. First-person account of my ordeal. Set against the banking scandal. Even if I'm wrong about the Vatican being behind Gabriel's murder, the Vatican Bank is complicit in criminal activity with Sindona and Calvi. Those responsible for the violence are among that group when you include the Sicilian Mafia. The Vatican deserves the bad press. No holds barred."

†

Amatrano splurged and reserved a room for two nights at the Intercontinental Rome Ambasciatori Palace Hotel. A turn-of-the-century five-star hotel on the fashionable Via Vittorio Veneto not far from the Rome Termini train station.

After getting Emma settled into a room, they went downstairs and enjoyed a leisurely lunch before leaving for his interview appointment.

Guardia di Finanza headquarters on Viale XXI Aprile was only a ten-minute taxi ride from the hotel. Ushered into the office of the commander of the Guardia di Finanza organized crime division the GICO, Brigadier General Enrico Giacchetto greeted him warmly, "Welcome to Rome, Signore Amatrano. So good of you to come. Please take a seat."

After shaking hands, Amatrano sat across the desk from Giacchetto, "Quite an ordeal you experienced. Colonel Ferrazza told me the story of what brought you to Milan. That you chose to remain unofficially to protect the journalist Signora Nicoletti proved fortuitous. Both Colonel Farrazza and Colonel Pagliaro speak very highly of you. Your extensive background in investigating organized crime and financial crimes certainly qualifies you for the intelligence position with GICO. That you hold Italian citizenship makes that possible."

Jokingly, Amatrano replied, "Colonel Farrazza said you may know more about my background than even I recall."

Giacchetto nodded, "We are thorough. A most impressive background. The recent violent engagement with Mafiosi leaves no question as to your qualifications as a law enforcement officer. My questions are more about your interest in moving to that of operational law enforcement rather than just investigative work. Colonel Farrazza intimated that your superiors at Interpol did not look favorably on one of their senior staff engaging in a gunfight. Is that part of your interest in joining the Guardia?"

"Not really. Interpol's displeasure is a symptom of its bureaucracy. The incident in Milan was emotionally satisfying. Enforcing the law by directly serving public safety. Much different than just providing consultive investigative support without any authority to act. Something I have been thinking about for some time. In retrospect, my earlier duties in the United States Bureau of Diplomatic Security were more rewarding."

"I don't need to tell you that Italian law enforcement service has become particularly dangerous. The Carabinieri, the Guardia, and prosecuting magistrates, have all become targets by terrorist extremists or organized crime. How do you feel about that?"

"Goes with job. I am prepared for that. The situation in Italy only emphasizes the pressing need for civil society to take back the initiative from the criminal elements."

"Well, eliminating two Mafiosi hitmen demonstrates your abilities. Which brings me to a personal question that I must ask. It concerns Signora Nicoletti. Naturally, considering you as a candidate for this position with GICO, we have been investigating your current circumstances. Farrazza and Pagliaro both advise me that you and Nicoletti are in a personal relationship. That is none of our affair, except if it should compromise your duties."

"I understand your concern, General. I take no offense. Yes, we have found ourselves in a personal relationship. She even came to Rome with me. Should you choose me for the intelligence position, we will relocate to Rome together."

"I am sure you have tried to determine why Signora Nicoletti has been targeted by the Mafia. The two gunmen you killed were from the Palermo Gesù Mafia family."

"I have spent considerable time independently investigating that question, Sir. Emma Nicoletti and *New York Times* journalist Gabriel Eisenberg who died in the initial bombing attack were collaborating on writing a new book about the Italian Banking Scandal. They coauthored a book fifteen years ago entitled *Ratlines* exposing the Vatican's participating in assisting World War Two war criminals to escape to South America. As to who is behind the attacks, it remains unclear. However, I believe it concerns the banking scandal. That includes the Vatican Bank and of course the Sicilian Mafia.

"According to Signora Nicoletti, nothing either she or Eisenberg has published anything that would rise to the level of someone wanting to silence them by assassination. The bombing that killed Eisenberg and injured Nicoletti was not a terrorist attack. I believe it must be connected to the financial scandal in some way. The Mafia might be doing this on their own, but I think it is more complicated than that. They have been identified as having involvement with both Michele Sindona and Roberto Calvi. Sindona is Sicilian with a background of association with the Mafia going back the war years.

"Then again, these two violent attacks might have something to do with work these journalists published back to the 1960s with their expose of the Vatican ratlines. Could be someone mentally unbalanced that harbors some obsession to retaliate. Mafiosi profess to be Catholic. For the right amount of money, they could be persuaded to kill enemies of the Church."

Amatrano concealed the existence of the stolen Vatican Archive documents. Let that play out in the future since that would become soon public through the *New York Times* making the obvious connection that the documents originated through some association with Gabriel Eisenberg.

For the better part of an hour, Giacchetto questioned Amatrano's familiarity with Italian organized crime ranging from the Costa Nostra, the Camorra, and the 'Ndrangheta. Amatrano worked as the senior official for Western Europe at Interpol's organized crime division. Italian organized crime dominated Interpol's focus in Western Europe.

Giacchetto concluded by saying, "You are as familiar with Italian organized crime as any officer in the GICO. No question about your qualifications. Not like we are bringing in someone from the outside. You also bring a network of international personal contacts to GICO. You are Italian. Your other language skills in English, French, and German are invaluable. The incident in Milan proves you are not just a desk-bound investigator. I want you on my team, Francesco."

"Thank you, General."

"Colonel Farrazza lobbied me that it would take an offer that included the rank of lieutenant colonel to entice you to leave Interpol for the Guardia. Is that correct?"

"Somewhat. That rank reasonably equates to my level of authority at Interpol. However, the more important consideration is to use my position as head of GICO intelligence with operational parity with regional GICO commanders like Lieutenant Pagliaro in Milan. Like any large organization, hierarchy rank becomes important. Parity of rank with regional commanders will make for a more collegial working relationship."

Giacchetto nodded. "I understand. That should not be a problem. To bring you on board at this level requires the approval of Lieutenant General Angelo Moretti, executive commander of the Guardia di Finanza. If General Moretti agrees, are you ready to join us and head up intelligence? With the rank of lieutenant colonel of course."

"Yes, General. I came here today with that decision already made."

"Excellent! How long will you be in Rome?"

"I was planning on returning to Paris the day after tomorrow."

Giacchetto replied, "Perhaps I can have you an official decision as early as tomorrow. If so, you might need another day to go through all the hiring particulars. Your background check has already been validated so all that remains are administrative details."

"I can change my travel plans as necessary, General."

†

Returning to the hotel room, Amatrano knocked. "It's me." He made sure Nicoletti brought her Berretta on the trip. The threat to her life still existed. That would not end until the missing Vatican documents became public.

Opening the door, he was gratified to see she held the Berretta in her hand correctly pointed to the floor. "How did the interview go?"

He kissed her before answering. "Couldn't have gone better. My friend Colonel Ferrazza already sold me as the candidate. General Giacchetto offered me the job. Pending approval by the executive commander of the entire Guardia di Finanza. With the rank of lieutenant colonel, no less. Might know officially as soon as tomorrow. Ferrazza said they already have a dossier on me, so they already knew details of my background. Even up to date. They even know of our relationship."

"Did you tell them about the stolen Vatican Archive documents?"

"Of course not. Not without clearing that with you first. That would just complicate matters now anyway. Best to profess no knowledge if asked for comment. Let the obvious implication become somehow Gabriel Eisenberg's doing. You were just collaborating with him. He was the target of the bombing, not you. The release of the documents by the *New York Times* makes that sufficiently plausible and untraceable directly back to you. Second attempt on your life was to remove a loose end since you knew too much having studied the documents."

She nodded and embraced him. Looking into his eyes, "Shall we celebrate."

"Have something in mind?"

"Yes, I do." She took his hand and led him to the bed.

†

Both Nicoletti and Amatrano had been to Rome often. General Giacchetto already extended an offer requiring only confirmation from the chief of staff of the entire Guardia di Finanza. The following morning, they decided to explore possibilities for a residence in close proximity to central Rome. Coincidentally, both thought of the Trastevere district. The quaint residential area reminiscent of a bygone era in Rome. The other option was the peaceful residential Aventine district just across the River Tiber from Trastevere.

The hotel concierge located a real estate agency familiar with the area. They spent the morning with the agent driving them about both quarters and visiting several prospective apartments for lease. After a leisurely lunch in a tucked away part of Trastevere, they returned to the hotel.

Getting their key at the desk, the clerk said, "You have a message, Signore Amatrano."

Amatrano opened the envelope. "It's from General Giacchetto," he said to Emma as they read the message delivered by messenger. *Please return to my office this afternoon. Great news. Welcome to GICO, Lieutenant Colonel Amatrano. Signed Giacchetto.* She looked at him and smiled.

Leaving Emma at the hotel, he returned to GdF headquarters. Greeted effusively by General Giacchetto and Lieutenant Colonel Ferrazza, they took seats in Giacchetto's office.

"Welcome aboard, Francesco," Giacchetto said. "Wanted you to come in so I can personally make your appointment official. Colonel Ferrazza will help you with the employment paperwork, credentials, procedural protocols, and so forth. Get you squared away with ordering uniforms, issuing of weapons so you can hit the ground running. Only question remaining is when can you start?"

"Just need a few weeks to settle affairs in Paris. I could begin mid-November if that is satisfactory?"

Giacchetto nodded, "Yes. What do you think, Antonio?" turning to Colonel Ferrazza.

"Yes, Sir. After we finish all the paperwork, what about we introduce him to his headquarters staff. If you can stay in Rome for another day, Frank, I'd like the staff to also prepare an informal briefing. Identify for Frank the most important immediate areas of concern then spend the day after tomorrow in discussion with the staff. Something to get you thinking before you officially start."

"Makes sense. I can stay on another day. Good opportunity to meet everyone and for them to assess me."

"Excellent," Giacchetto said. "Before getting down to business, Antonio, General Moretti would like to welcome Francesco personally."

Returning to the hotel hours later, Amatrano announced to Emma, "Well it's done. Officially I'm now a lieutenant colonel with the GICO division of the Guardia di Finanza. I'm to report for duty on 12 November. Need to attend a briefing the day after tomorrow."

"That's what you wanted. We should spend tomorrow morning with the real estate leasing agent and see if we can settle on a suitable apartment. If not, we can always stay at a hotel until we find what we want. Can we stop in Lugano on our way back to Paris to arrange for shipping the documents to New York?"

"Absolutely."

"What about stopping in Milan on the way?"

Amatrano had thought about that. "I'd rather not. We must assume that your apartment might be under surveillance. Let returning to Milan wait. Preferably after the *New York Times* releases the documents."

Sighing, she said. "Fine. If I need more clothing it's a good excuse to go shopping."

†

The next day, they settled on an apartment in Trastevere. Recently remodeled with upgraded bathrooms and kitchen, with a living area overlooking a green area on the back side of the building opposite a quiet street. A personal garage space afforded some measure of added security. They leased the Rome flat for only a year. Both of them wanted to leave all options open with so much uncertainty in their lives. Emotionally, he was not yet willing to part with the Paris apartment. Keeping his home of so many years meant not severing connection with his beloved Paris. An excellent investment that could always be sublet.

The following day proved busy. A contract tailor measured him for ordering an initial compliment of uniforms. He was issued a new Berretta with a standard-length barrel of the same model as the shorter-barrel version still in police custody in Milan. The staff briefing gave him a good introduction to his team. His second in command was newly promoted from captain to major therefore did not harbor resentment for not getting the top intelligence post. The staff seemed suitably impressed with Amatrano's background. Killing two Mafia hitmen in a gunfight dramatically established his credentials. The well-constructed briefing proved especially informative. Impressed by his small headquarters staff. He could start interacting with daily telephone reports before officially starting duty.

The following day Amatrano and Nicoletti took an early train north. A six-hour journey with a train change at Milano Centrale station to reach Lugano. Arriving at the Societe Generale bank in the afternoon, the manager came out to greet Nicoletti learning of her arrival by the vault clerk.

"Signora Nicoletti, I am delighted to see you. You look so much better from the last time you were here. Then I read of a second attempt on your life when returning to Milan. An unimaginable ordeal. Are you fully recovered?"

"Yes, thank you, Signore Koehne."

Koehne turned and shook Amatrano's hand. "The newspapers said you saved Signora Nicoletti's life by killing the assassins. An extraordinary story." Turning to Nicoletti, he said, "How may I be of service today, Signora?"

"I appreciate your assistance in the past. I am here today to empty the contents of the deposit box. Could I prevail upon you to seal these documents from anyone looking at them then ship them to the United States? I shall pay for those charges."

"Most definitely, Signora. Let me help with the paperwork and you can supervise how you wish these papers packaged for shipment. It will be the bank's pleasure to handle those arrangements without charge."

Wrapped and sealed securely in a cardboard box, two hours later an Emery Air Freight van delivered the shipment to Lugano's regional airport. Addressed to Gabriel Eisenberg at the address of the *New York Times Building* on Eighth Avenue in New York. Inside a typed note simply read, *Confidential material directly removed from the Vatican Secret Archive. Use it wisely*. The anonymous submission would leave Nicoletti free to spin the story of Gabriel Eisenberg as the original recipient from an anonymous priest in the Vatican Archive.

From the Lugano bank they taxied to the train station in time to make a late afternoon train to Paris with a change in Basel before arriving at midnight at Paris Gare Lyon. A long day but Amatrano felt safer back in Paris for the next several weeks. Once the *New York Times* published the documents, Emma should be safer when they returned to Rome. Provided they were correct in believing the Vatican documents were behind the Mafia attacks.

†

The stolen Vatican Archive documents remained a threat for Archbishop Tagliente. Orders to his subordinate Monsignor Ettore Donaggio since the failed assassination attempt on Nicoletti included continued observation of Society Generale. He was to be advised should either Nicoletti or Amatrano be observed entering the bank. Should that happen, the observer was to follow them.

Brother Gideon received a telephone call from the Lugano train station. "Nicoletti and Amatrano just boarded a train to Basel."

†

"Michael, this is Frank. Lots to tell you since we spoke after the shooting in Milan. Seems like a long time ago but only a matter of weeks. First of all, good news. Emma and I are together."

"What do you mean together?"

"More than just as her bodyguard. I mean together as in a romantic relationship. I took her to Paris after the shooting in Milan. Needed to get her out of Italy. Things took a natural course. She's an extraordinary woman.

"Anyway, back at Interpol, the shooting incident did not set well with my superiors. Placed me on suspension while they investigated my participation. Have heard nothing from headquarters for weeks. Just returned from Rome and sent off my official resignation to Interpol Been thinking about resigning for some time. I was in Rome to accept a position with the Italian financial police, the Guardia di Finanza. I'm now a lieutenant colonel. Specifically, I'll be heading up intelligence for their organized crime division. Going to move to Rome where headquarters are located."

"Jesus, Frank. You ready to jump into the violence going on in Italy?"

"Already got a taste of that. It's where I can make a difference. That's been my dissatisfaction with working at Interpol. Consulting is no longer satisfying. This better suits me."

"Okay, old friend. I hear you. Glad you called. I was worrying about what was happening after we last spoke. How is Emma doing?"

"Very well. Recovered from the bombing injuries. Physically and emotionally as much as that is possible. Still sensitive about the scarring on her cheek. Not that bad at all. Correctible with plastic surgery. A future consideration. There is another reason for my call. The *New York Times* will soon receive a package of documents from a bank in Switzerland. This is what led to Gabe's murder and the second attempt to kill Emma."

"What kind of documents?"

"Confidential documents stolen by a priest from the Vatican Secret Archive. Material providing evidence of the Vatican Bank's complicity in the international financial scandal centered in Italy. I've been familiar with the scandal for several years working at Interpol. Questions frequently arise about money laundering for the Mafia. That's why Gabe had you contact me. I agreed to come to Milan and meet with him and Emma to offer professional advice. Didn't make it to Milan before the bombing."

Michael Eisenberg was silent for several moments digesting the information. "So, the bombing was not the work of terrorists. The work of the Mafia?"

"The bombing probably, the attempted assassination of Emma, definitely. Although maybe someone other than the Mafia is behind it. Once I join the Guardia, I might have better opportunities for look into things in more detail.

"I'm telling you because you have a right to know the truth why Gabe was murdered. The *Times* will eventually publish a story around these documents. Makes the Vatican look very bad. You know nothing about the source. This was your brother working on a story. The *Times* is very familiar with the scandal going back to 1974 starting with the failure of Franklin National Bank. They will integrate this information with what is already known. I've seen this material. Makes for major international headline news. Casts a dark shadow by exposing the involvement of the Vatican Bank and Pope Paul VI and the current pontiff Pope John Paul II with involvement in financial misdeeds."

"Holy shit!"

"Couldn't have thought of a more appropriate term. Remember. Keep your identity out of this, Michael. The attacks on Gabe and Emma were undoubtedly about these documents. Their release should get Emma off the hook as a target."

"Got it. Where can I reach you?"

"For the time being call my Paris telephone number. I'll be moving to Rome probably sometime in November. I'll call as soon as I have other phone numbers to give you."

"Okay. Glad to see you and Emma got together. You need a woman in your life," Michael Eisenberg said. "Both of you stay safe."

†

With their lives readjusted to a new normality Emma said, "It's time for me to get my face fixed."

Frank replied, "Don't put it that way. If you want to undergo plastic surgery, I'm fine with that. I understand completely. For me it's not a matter of fixing. Never once has it ever bothered me."

She kissed him. "I know. It's for me, darling. Partly for physical appearance, but emotionally necessary. I want to undergo the procedure before we move to Rome."

CHAPTER 15

Rome, Italy | January 1980

Italian banker Michele Sindona's kidnapping was perpetrated neither by terrorists nor the Italian Mafia. Sindona engineered his own fake kidnapping. While the New York Sicilian-connected Gambino Mafia played a part in helping Sindona, it was Sindona idea. Unrealistically he hoped he could raise enough money if he returned to Europe to help with his legal and financial difficulties. An implausible desperate effort that proved a total failure. Returning to New York in October, Sindona was found in a telephone booth with a gunshot wound to his leg. While in Palermo, Sindona had a Mafia associate inflict a bullet wound in his leg by carefully avoiding serious injury to bolster the fake kidnapping claim.

That too failed leading to additional criminal charges at his rescheduled federal trial on over sixty counts of criminal charges including fraud, perjury, making false bank statements, and embezzlement. The U.S. trial began at the end of November 1979. The well-documented evidence predicted Sindona was likely facing conviction and a significant prison sentence.

The continuing Italian Banking Scandal now shifted focus to Roberto Calvi and his troubled Banco Ambrosiano financial empire. The Bank of Italy, the Italian central bank, began increasing regulatory pressure on Banco Ambrosiano headquartered in Milan. That took the form of restricting further borrowing for expansion. Calvi determined continued growth was the best way out of his financial problem. This forced Calvi to seek funding by borrowing for expansion while attempting to plug holes from mounting losses through his principal foreign banks. Banco Ambrosiano Holding of Luxembourg, Banco Ambrosiano Andino in Lima, Peru, Ambrosiano Overseas in Nassau, Bahamas, and Banco Ambrosiano de America del Sud in Buenos Aires were already burdened with excessive debt. To create a financial network beyond oversight by the Bank of Italy and Italian financial police, Calvi created additional foreign shell companies. Starting in 1979, Calvi began creating several new foreign companies, capitalized with only $10,000 each. Nothing more than shell companies in tax haven countries to facilitate moving money about to conceal liquidity shortfalls. A creative but misguided Ponzi-like scheme of increasing debt to resolve an immediate debt crisis by moving funds one step ahead of repayment maturity deadlines among already insolvent foreign banks and corporations.

Calvi's Machiavellian instincts aligned with his skills for using complex financial transactions. Making use of the Vatican Bank as a partner in the subterfuge became a key element in his desperate effort to escape the same fate as his predecessor Michele Sindona.

Why should the Vatican Bank participate? The simple answer was because they were already so deeply invested in the criminality of Michele Sindona and Roberto Calvi that they had no other choice. It started with Pope Paul VI bringing in Sindona when faced with the crisis of losing the Vatican tax waiver on dividends from Italian holdings. The financial structure of the Holy See created by Bernardino Nogara created in 1930 and lasting for over thirty years brought the Vatican City State into modern finance. The mechanisms employed were no different than those used by any nation or large corporation. All within the bounds of lawful activity.

However, in 1942, Pope Pius XII created the *Istituto per le Opere di Religione,* the IOR. Ostensibly for management of church property for religious and charitable works. Critics would say that the conspiratorial Pope Pius did this to conceal financial transactions with Nazi Germany and Fascist Italy while remaining officially neutral. He knew the Allied powers monitored international transactions involving Western banks. The absolute secrecy of the IOR even inside the secretive Vatican, became an instrument solely of papal authority. This allowed Nogara to pursue Vatican investments in ventures benefiting the Axis powers while preserving the semblance of wartime neutrality.

When Pope Paul VI ascended the papacy in 1963, circumstances changed throughout his fifteen years as pontiff. Elimination of the Vatican's tax waiver on Italian investments by the Italian parliament laid the foundation for seeking alternative foreign investment opportunities. A cast of unscrupulous lay people close to the Roman Catholic Church found Pope Paul exceptionally trusting and receptive to financial advice. Unschooled in finance he fell prey to the engaging Michele Sindona. Adopting Sindona as a respected financier to advise the IOR on financial investment, the pope then appointed the likeable American bishop by the name of Paul Marcinkus to the presidency of the IOR. Thus began the era when the inherent secrecy of foreign tax havens proved the perfect channel for concealing financial crimes.

Marcinkus had no financial background or education to support such an important role. He became close to Pope Paul by acting as interpreter and unofficial bodyguard during the foreign visits of the heavily travelled pope. Nicknamed 'the gorilla' for his height of six feet, four inches with a muscular build and assertive manner, Marcinkus got the appointment because Pope Paul liked and trusted him. That began the IOR's involvement in financial transactions designed to obscure activities that violated Italian law. Michele Sindona then followed by Roberto Calvi proved uncommonly creative high-finance criminals devoid of scruples. Both realized the unique opportunity of using the religious prestige of the Vatican Bank as a tax haven by playing on the financial inexperience of Bishop Marcinkus. In this mix were a supporting cast of sordid secondary characters including involvement of the Sicilian Mafia awash in illicit money in need of *laundering*. By the late 1970s, the complex internationally interconnected house of cards constructed by Michele Sindona and Roberto Calvi was beginning to come undone.

The first week of the new year of 1980, the *New York Times* released the story about newly discovered Vatican documents. The front-page headline read: VATICAN FINANCIAL MISDEEDS EXPOSED. The column headline read: INCRIMINATING EVIDENCE REVEALED.

> New York, NY
> James Collingwood reporting
> Weeks ago, a package containing hundreds of documents arrived at *New York Times* headquarters from a bank in Switzerland. Other than that fact, the source is anonymous. The Swiss bank declines to provide further information citing Swiss banking confidential laws. While the documents appear to be original, the *NYT* has sought forensic assistance to determine authenticity. The conclusion of experts leaves no doubt as to the authenticity based on analysis of the signatures. Those signatures are those of various high-level prelates of the Roman Catholic Church holding positions at the Vatican in Rome. While none of the documents are authored by popes, there are counter signatures on various documents from three of the last popes. Pope Paul VI, Pope John Paul I, and the current pontiff Pope John Paul II. Because of the sensitivity of these documents, the *NYT* believes these documents originated from within the Vatican Secret Archive. Separate from the Vatican Library, the material held within the Vatican Secret Archive is considered the personal property of the pontiff, thereby excluded from administrative authority by the Roman Curia.
>
> The *NYT* believes the documents to have been removed without authorization by someone equivalent to a whistleblower. Assuming that to be the case, it is the ethical

obligation of the *NYT* to publish information related to a matter of great public importance. The Vatican may be expected to protest the means by which this information was obtained and undoubtedly will criticize the *NYT* for publishing the content. However, that ethical issue was addressed when the *New York Times* and the *Washington Post* published the *Pentagon Papers* in 1971.

These documents all have dates ranging from 1971 to 1978. All relate in some manner to what has been described as the Italian Banking Scandal. Some make reference to Italian banker Michele Sindona currently on trial in U.S. federal court in New York on dozens of criminal financial charges. Each document in some manner provides evidence of the Vatican's participation or at least knowledge in certain criminal financial activities. Criminal in the sense of violating laws either of various countries or international protocols or treaties. Readers should remember that the Vatican officially known as the Holy See, is a sovereign country under international law. What may not generally be known is what commonly is called the Vatican Bank, is officially in Italian the *Istituto per le Opere di Religione*, in Latin the *Institutum pro Operibus Religionis*, abbreviated IOR. It operates much like banks in tax haven counties like the Bahamas, Cayman Islands, Panama, etc. We shall expand on that significance in subsequent articles in what will become a series of probing the Vatican's relationship in the unresolved financial scandal. Suffice it say, the IOR as an institution in a sovereign state is not bound by any laws beyond the walls of the 108 acres constituting Vatican City in Rome. Neither the laws of Italy nor the United States apply.

Initial study of the significance of the documents has already yielded highly incriminating material based upon opinions of outside experts in financial crimes. Yet, it will not be courts that are likely to make use of this material given the Vatican's status of sovereignty. What is at risk for the Vatican Bank are potential sanctions resulting in restrictions on its use of international financial transactions that inevitably involve the world's principal central banks. Trust from within the international financial community therefore becomes paramount. Questionable activity risks denial of essential movement of funds essential to the function of any major financial entity such as the Vatican Bank.

As the *NYT* continues investigating this new information it will publish various documents and explain how it relates to the wider scandal. Many of these documents include names which may already be familiar to most readers following the international scandal.

It is worth noting that the package containing the Vatican documents was addressed to Gabriel Eisenberg at the offices of the New York Times. Mr. Eisenberg was a veteran NYT journalist. He was killed in a car bomb explosion in Milan, Italy six months ago. Speculation at the time centered on the bombing as being the work of Marxist terrorists. Following that bombing there was another attempt on the life of Italian journalist Emma Nicoletti who survived the car bombing that killed Eisenberg. That incident resulted in the police shooting deaths of two assailants identified as known Sicilian Mafia gunmen. Receipt of these Vatican documents all relate in some way to the larger financial scandal originating with named Italian bankers with connections to the Sicilian Mafia, at least as the actual perpetrators. Both the Sicilian Mafia and the Vatican Bank have been repeatedly connected with the Italian Banking Scandal.

Archbishop Tagliente arrived at his Vatican office on Monday morning. On his desk was the usual stack of international newspapers *Times of London, Le Monde, Corriere della Sera,* and *New York Times* on the top of the stack. His small intelligence staff working out of the Secret Archive reviewed the international print media early each morning to identify articles of importance to the Vatican.

Tagliente already heard the breaking news on Italian morning radio and television reports before leaving his residence. Another unexpected development of disastrous proportion. This changed the dynamic for containing damage to the image of the Vatican in the continuing banking scandal. Having never revealed the theft of the documents to either Cardinal Secretary of State Casaroli or Pope John Paul II dictated informing them immediately. Not to confess his foreknowledge of the theft but to assure them he was taking appropriate action. *A preliminary investigation by agents of the secret service believe it was a former priest, now deceased. Archive staff were now working to determine the extent of the document theft.*

Placing a call to Cardinal Casaroli, Tagliente offered his explanation to the number two prelate in the Vatican who already knew of the media headlines. "Your Eminence, I began investigating the origin of this leak early this morning. Doubtful this is the work of any current archive staff. The best guess at the moment is this could be the work of Monsignor Vittorio Scarpelli. Father Scarpelli left our service in 1978 suffering from cancer in an advanced stage. He died soon after retiring."

Casaroli knowing Tagliente's true role as unofficial head of the Vatican Secret Service asked, "Why do you suspect Scarpelli?"

"Immediate inquiries to other staff reveal that Scarpelli was deeply troubled. What might have been considered stress from his impending medical condition could have a different meaning. Some staff recall him making frequent comments about the financial scandal involving Michele Sindona and Roberto Calvi. In his supervisory position, Monsignor Scarpelli would also have had the means of covering up the theft from other staff. My people will pursue his movements after leaving the Vatican. Somehow these confidential documents reached this Swiss bank identified in the American newspaper. We should jointly inform His Holiness."

Casaroli replied, "Very well. I will arrange an audience with His Holiness immediately. This never-ending scandal now becomes an even more dire threat to the integrity of the Holy See."

"Nonetheless, while troubling, it is manageable, Your Eminence. Bishop Marcinkus' name regrettably features prominently in these documents. Regardless of our feelings about his mismanagement of the IOR, he remains a favorite of His Holiness. Both as a person as well as instrumental in working with American intelligence to funnel funds to the Polish Solidarity Movement. Something of special importance to His Holiness.

"Furthermore, Pope Paul installed Marcinkus to head the IOR, and it was Pope Paul that introduced Michele Sindona to advise the IOR in investments. Unfortunately, those investments involved Sindona's self-serving interests not those of the Holy See. To contain damage to the Holy See we must close ranks. We should counsel His Holiness to retain Bishop Marcinkus in his current role. Removing him would be seen as acknowledging credibility to the allegations. Since installing Monsignor Auerbach in the IOR, I believe you and I can forestall any further questionable financial maneuvering associated with Banco Ambrosiano..

"While Sindona is no longer in the picture, his protégé Roberto Calvi with his Banco Ambrosiano under pressure from the Bank of Italy remains a problem because of extensive financial transactional involvement with the IOR. That too shall eventually pass. However, it requires careful management. We must ensure that the financial foundation created by Bernardino Nogara decades ago continues to provide international investment opportunities providing important revenue for the Holy See."

Casaroli replied, "Very well, Archbishop. Not sure I agree totally with your advice concerning Bishop Marcinkus but support your broader strategy. How do you suggest we manage the renewed backlash from public exposure of these sensitive Vatican sensitive documents?"

Tagliente answered, "With obfuscation. Largely by avoiding attempts to defend allegations. By never engaging in discussion of specific details."

Lying to Cardinal Casaroli, "Archive staff are attempting to identity what documents are missing. However, I can assure you that as Archivist throughout the pontificate of Pope Paul VI and since then, I reviewed every document designated for repository within the Secret Archive. I cannot recall any document speaking directly about complicity in financial crimes. While many may unfortunately connect the IOR and pontifical awareness of associations with those named in the scandal, these materials do not rise to the level of evidence even in the court of public opinion. In short, we must steadfastly maintain deniability of wrongdoing by the IOR while avoiding any comments helpful to investigative journalists."

Casaroli said, "What about the Curia?"

"The same posture should apply to the Curia," Tagliente replied. "The IOR is subject only to the pontiff's authority. We must rely on the integrity of the Curia to not openly challenge that authority."

Although Cardinal Casaroli felt Tagliente was underestimating the damage of these revelations, he allowed Tagliente to make his case to the pope. John Paul took the distressing news in stride. "I will keep aloof from the controversy deferring any questions to your office, Agustino." Addressing Tagliente, he said, "Please keep His Eminence adequately informed of further developments so he may deal with the public as well as the Curia, Archbishop Tagliente."

†

Settled into their new apartment In Rome, Nicoletti began her new book project. Narrowed from the original project with Gabriel Eisenberg to expand on the Italian Banking Scandal using new materials incriminating the Vatican Bank. Her revised book project would now read more as a journalist's pursuit of how and why the Vatican Bank became involved with criminal bankers with indirect ties to the Sicilian Mafia. A first-person account of her violent ordeal should distinguish her book from other expected books on the same subject..

In his second month with the Italian Guardia di Finanza, Amatrano was now fully integrated in his new position. His presence is already being felt by his regional command counterparts as the head of intelligence by his aggressive operational perspective. From the first day, he felt energized. This was law enforcement. Finding evidence and building a case for prosecution. Active policing rather advisory consulting. The Guardia organized crime division, the GICO, became a natural extension of the same specialty of his last several years at Interpol. His first breakthrough came with the discovery of a remarkable shadowy figure. A malevolent individual that appears as if a figment of a novelist's imagination. His name was Licio Gelli.

Known with Guardia files as the former worshipful master of the Propaganda Due, or P2, masonic lodge. In 1971, the Grand Master of the Grand Orient of Italy, the masonic governing body in Italy, tasked Gelli with reorganizing the Propaganda Due lodge. Gelli did something far more radical by transforming Propaganda Due into his personal criminal enterprise.

Gelli began by taking a list of inactive members, members no longer participating in Masonic rituals because of close scrutiny by the Italian government that outlawed secret societies then converting P2 into something far outside fundamental freemasonry. The initiation of a former member of Italian military intelligence presented Gelli with 157,000 secret dossiers of influential or strategically positioned individuals in the public and private sector, including a broad cross section of governmental departments. By 1976, the Propaganda Due Lodge had evolved into something alien to conventional freemasonry causing the Grand Orient of Italy to dissolve its charter. P2 went underground. Within a few years Gelli transformed it into a criminal organization of exceptional effectiveness. For Licio Gelli, the confidential files presented endless opportunities of exercising power. Entice members by sharing in financial gain, or by simple coercion using an implicit threat of blackmail.

The Guardia file on Licio Gelli made for interesting reading. A real villain with a remarkably repugnant background. Gelli connections also extended Italian organized crime and South American right-wing dictatorships. His orbit included those of the highest level of Italian government and business. For Amatrano, Gelli became of interest through his connection to Michele Sindona and Roberto Calv. It was Gelli that connected with the name Umberto Ortolani that Amatrano recalled appearing in one of Emma's documents. Gelli's Guardia dossier made repeated references to Giuseppe "Pippo" Calò the boss of the Palermo Porta Nuova family of the Cosa Nostra thereby making connections like a spider's web.

Through interaction with the Guardia di Finanza for years, Amatrano knew of Giuseppe Calò. Knew Calò relocated to Rome in the early 1970s. Referred to as the *cassiere di Cosa Nostra,* or the cashier of Cosa Nostra, suggested Calò was suspected of occupying a larger role within Italian organized crime. Calò currently lived under the cover as a dealer in antiques using an assumed identity. Residing far from his power base in Palermo, the Guardia and Interpol suspected Calò of brokering money laundering services to other organized criminal organizations throughout Italy. Compared with Mafia dominated Sicily, centralized Rome and Milan to the north represented the power centers of legitimate Italian economic life.

For Amatrano, Calò's money laundering activities across a range of Italian organized criminals made him a likely player in connection with the Vatican Bank. Calò also offered another link to the powerful Neapolitan Camorra mob boss Lorenzo Nuvoletta. With these and other names from Guardia records, Amatrano could collaborate with Emma in searching for links connecting to the Vatican Bank. Likely that would come from links to Sindona or Calvi banks and foreign subsidiary shell companies. Information that he could pass to her without compromising his access to confidential police files.

Officially as law enforcement of an Interpol member state, Amatrano could call on Interpol resources to search for known information among the world of tax haven legal entities.

Although tax havens did not provide corporate shareholder information or require any form of financial reporting, they could not exist by remaining totally opaque. Administration of these foreign subsidiaries was almost always conducted from outside the tax haven country of record. Possible paper trails therefore might exist since offshore banks and corporations must transact business with the more visible international financial community to conduct business. That was where he and Emma must attempt to make the case for participation by the Vatican Bank in money laundering for criminal enterprises.

The Italian Banking Scandal involved violations of banking and Italian currency laws, and associated laws such as fraud, embezzlement, conspiracy, and so forth. The task was providing compelling evidence of willful participation by the Vatican Bank to counter any attempt to argue victimization. If successful, proving the Vatican Bank knowingly engaged with laundering Mafia money would raise the public outcry to an entirely greater level of venality for a religious institution. If the outcry proved intense enough, restrictions to Vatican Bank international movements of money could hurt the Vatican financially. Perhaps exerting enough pressure to force the pope to speak publicly making a sign of contrition and offering a convincing remedy.

†

An Italian court previously tried and convicted Sindona in 1976 for unlawfully taking 180 billion lire, about $225 million USD, from an Italian bank, Banca Privata Italiana, created by the merger of Banca Unione and Banca Privata Finanziaria. Buried in debt, the merger of these two modestly sized banks did nothing more than create a larger insolvent bank in Banca Privata. Tried and convicted in absentia receiving only a three- and one-half year sentence, Sindona still faced extradition to the plodding Italian justice system. In March 1980, that became largely irrelevant. After a nine-week trial the U.S. District Court for the Southern District of New York found Sindona guilty on 68 financial felony counts and sentenced him to 25 years in U.S. federal prison. By this time, Sindona's financial banking empire had completely collapsed.

The financial losses incurred by Sindona's banking empire have never been accurately estimated. If considering the losses of independent banks and the associated losses to enterprises outside his control, it undoubtedly amounted to hundreds of millions of dollars, perhaps much higher. Some estimates placed losses of the Vatican Bank alone in the hundreds of million dollars because of its significant shareholdings in Sindona offshore banks and corporations. That leaves a massive unaccounted-for hole. Many believe a significant portion of those funds involved Mafia money. The major portion of such funds could be assumed as untraceable laundered money returned to the Mafia in various legitimized forms. Yet the Mafia would have also incurred large losses as did everyone connected with Sindona.

CHAPTER 16

Rome, Italy | Spring 1980

Michele Sindona and Roberto Calvi caused the Italian Banking Scandal. Both were cleverly brilliant yet rapacious in their pursuit of power and profit. Both possessed knowingly criminal intent to subvert any laws that impeded opportunities for making money. Their means of growth involved engaging in moving funds in excessively complex transactions to conceal from financial scrutiny by using foreign tax haven-incorporated businesses and banks. These offshore foreign entities operated without government oversight allowing circumvention of laws in Italy and other countries when funds were moved abroad then returned to the onshore headquartered enterprises. Both Sindona and Calvi pursued grandiose plans for rapid expansion of their holdings as the means of wealth. The larger the operating base, the more opportunities developed and the magnitude of funds in play became ever larger.

Michele Sindona grew up in the shadow government of the Mafia in Sicily. Engaging in black market activities following the Allied invasion of Sicily in 1943, he doubled his personal wealth within a few months. Sindona possessed an Italian law degree, but it was his born genius with financial mathematics that drove his success. In the early 1950s he relocated to Milan in Northern Italy. There he became a successful tax lawyer by creating mechanisms for tax avoidance for wealthy clients using foreign subsidiary shell companies. Founding his own company, Fasco AG, he began moving money to Switzerland and Liechtenstein to avoid taxes. The Sicilian Mafia took notice.

As a Sicilian, Sindona grew up in the backwater cash-economy of Sicily. As an advisor in Italy's largest financial center, he came to understand the importance of liquid assets for providing flexibility for responding immediately to opportunities. Nothing is more liquid than cash. Approached by former contacts in the Sicilian Mafia, a symbiotic relationship developed. The Mafia had need of improved methods for laundering great sums of cash into legitimate assets. Sindona could use that cash as short-term capital for investment while simultaneously providing a lucrative profit stream in commissions for turning illicit funds into legitimate assets.

Those early beginnings in the late 1950s would expand by the early 1970s to include more complex and sophisticated mechanisms to expand the growing Mafia money laundering business. Not only for processing bulk quantities of cash into the financial system, but through other creative means to offer organized crime profits through trade-based and service-based money laundering schemes. Simply described, these payment schemes for goods or services that were never physically transacted provided a corresponding beneficial paper trail for both colluding parties. By 1960, Sindona was using money laundering profits from heroin sales for a criminal network consisting of the Sicilian Bontade, Spatola, and Inzerillo Mafia families in association with the New York Gambino family handling distribution in the large American market.

Sindon's earliest foray into laundering Sicilian Mafia money advanced to new levels of sophistication when through a priest, he met Massimo Spada. An Italian aristocrat and Vatican nobleman with the Vatican-bestowed title of prince following induction as a Knight of Malta in 1944. More importantly, Spada served as a layman in the position of Administrative Secretary of the

Vatican Bank, the IOR, in the late 1960s. Sindona already possessed a relationship with Pope Paul VI from when Giovanni Montini served as archbishop of Milan. Sindona's personal relationship with Spada and Pope Paul made his presence at the IOR a frequent occurrence. Sindona's special relationship with the Vatican during the pontificate of Pope Paul proved the beginning of the Vatican Bank's involvement in questionable financial activities. Years later the Holy See faced a financial crisis when Italy eliminated its tax waivers on dividends from its vast holdings in Italian real estate accorded the Holy See since 1929. This new tax liability precipitated the change to move Vatican shareholding assets outside Italy. With Pope Paul's sponsorship, Sindona seized on the opportunity by establishing a relationship with Bishop Paul Marcinkus following Marcinkus's unusual appointment as President of the IOR in 1971. The financially creative Sindona then oversaw the strategic shift in investments by dominating the financially inexperienced Marcinkus with his inventive but high-risk international financing schemes.

Men with flawed character like Michele Sindona gravitate to others with the same amoral tendencies. That included another person close to the Vatican, a Roman lawyer by the name of Umberto Ortolani, a fellow banker with business interests in South America that also included a bank in Montevideo, Uruguay, Banco Finananceiro. A cardinal in Bologna first introduced Ortolani to important Vatican prelates. With influential relations in Italian business and government, Ortolani added ecclesiastical sources to his impressive personal relationship network. The personable low-key Ortolani became known for his discretion. Referred to as *Mr. Nobody*, his trait for remaining in the background served to create lucrative business interests both legitimate and legally questionable.

It was Ortolani that brought Licio Gelli into this conspiracy. Of entirely different disposition from the pleasant Ortolani, Gelli was a menacing creature. Fascist, criminal, terrorist, suspected murderer, and head of a shadowy secret criminal organization. Gelli became known as *Il Maestro* for wielding power through threat of exposing secrets documented in dossiers of important

Italians. Gelli's sphere of influence extended throughout Italian government and business to the criminal underworld of the Mafia and Camorra. Extortion through blackmail provided the means for manipulating business opportunities involving millions, a fixer for securing difficult financing circumstances, suppressing prosecutions, and ordering violence using Mafia operatives.

The scope of Gelli's influence became apparent when Umberto Ortolani negotiated his assistance in arranging loan financing to salvage the disastrous purchase of the newspaper *Corriere* by powerful publisher Angelo Rizzoli in 1974. Denied financing by major Italian banks, Gelli stepped in arranging access to unlimited funding. Albeit with dire consequences for Rizzoli since the funding came from Roberto Calv's Banco Ambrosiano. Emma Nicoletti left *Corriere* the following year but did not learn until years later about this financial blunder that would eventually cost Rizzoli ownership of the newspaper.

The initial importance for Michele Sindona to laundering money for the Sicilian Mafia was to provide a continuous revenue stream from which to exercise immediate opportunities. While extracting lucrative laundering fees, Mafia money became less important to Sindona's growing financial empire. However, that changed in 1970 with the Mafia turning to trafficking heavily in heroin. Illicit money requiring laundering increased more than tenfold. Law enforcement intensified. Mafia violence began increasing with competition. Mechanisms for transforming illicit profits indistinguishable from legitimate assets demanded more sophistication for concealment behind opaque international financial transactions.

An integral part of modernizing the money laundering process was concealing the movement of money using offshore foreign subsidiaries in tax haven countries. So named because of the almost absolute secrecy from government oversight or reporting outside the sovereignty of the tax haven country. While major corporations around the world used foreign subsidiaries for legitimate purposes, tax havens' inherent secrecy became an obvious means for concealing illicit financial activity. To bolster the guise of legitimacy, the conspirators recognized the significance of the

Vatican Bank, especially within Catholic Italy. That the Vatican Bank was an ultra-secret sovereign tax haven gave its participation in the money laundering an element of legitimacy bolstered by its worldwide religious stature. That same implied trust imparted to the financial activities of Sindona and Calvi using the Vatican Bank also provided sufficient reason for the Mafia to entrust large sums for conversion into the appearance of legitimate assets.

†

By 1971, Michele Sindona, Umberto Ortolani, Licio Gelli, Massimo Spada, and Bishop Paul Marcinkus recognized the financial opportunity of laundering Mafia money. The increase in drug trafficking was now generating staggering amounts of money. Mafia money was not only useful for investment manipulations but the laundering service fee of 30% also represented lucrative profits.

Law enforcement was improving. Integrating illicit money with legitimate assets into the international financial system demanded new methods of concealment. This group of conspirators possessed extraordinary ingenuity built on a deep understanding of international finance. Seemingly operating from a different stratum of society compared to the vicious thuggery of the Sicilian Mafia, all the central players were nonetheless sociopaths. Totally disregarding ethical or moral constraints in pursuit of power through wealth.

The plan as it came into being in 1971 began with the fundamental problem of how to introduce great quantities of illicit cash into the financial system to avoid scrutiny by legal authorities. The end of the laundering cycle then requires a method of returning laundered funds to the Mafia as legitimate assets.

Michele Sindona teamed with new Mafia boss Giuseppe 'Pippo' Calò. In 1969, Calò became head of the Palermo Porta Nuova Crime family. Sindona was a friend of the younger Calò's father from the old days following the war. While Calò was thoroughly Mafia, he possessed a brilliant mind. Street-smart, likeable, and exceptional with numbers much like Sindona. Together they created the merchant bank *Banca Mercantile di San Lorenzo* based in Palermo. Within a year Banca Mercantile expanded with branches in Reggio Calabria, Naples, and Rome.

Banca Mercantile was Mafia controlled. Italian law enforcement might suspicion that but was unable to prove. Ownership consisted of large numbers of shareholders, all of which also held accounts. None had a shareholding of more than one percent. These business-owner-shareholder account holders moved their business accounts to *Banca Mercantile* under coercion. Threats of bombing their businesses or physical harm to family forced cooperation. In Sicily, the Mafia was stronger than any agency of the Italian government. No one refused to cooperate. No one talked. The Mafia reputation for extreme brutality went back generations to the prior century.

The money laundering process began by disguising normal banking transactions. Mafia cash regularly deposited among the hundreds of accounts raised no accounting records suspicions. Money came into *Banca Mercantile* as a natural flow from commerce, pooled with illicit Mafia money. It then left through interbank transactions on a circuitous international route. First to Sindona-owned bank *La Centrale Finanziaria* in Milan in the form of payments on fake loans. From there money went to Sindona-owned *Fasco International Holdings* in Lichtenstein. The fake loans to Banca Mercantile from La Centrale, both Italian banks, further supported by back-to-back loans between *La Centrale* and *Fasco* to satisfy Italian currency laws prohibiting the flight of Italian currency.

The money then underwent further laundering through transaction to the Vatican *Istituto per le Opere di Religione,* commonly called the Vatican Bank. From there the funds returned to Italy by way of *La Centrale,* now indistinguishable from legitimate funds.

The last element in the chain is to return the laundered funds to the Mafia, minus the laundering fee. Some of the funds return to *Banca Mercantile* booked as repayment credits to balance the original fake loans. Other funds take different routes.

The Mafia had long infiltrated various businesses engaged in public services. Construction, infrastructure maintenance, and trash disposal being principal examples. That is where Signore Gelli entered the picture. Using his many connections, Gelli created trade-based and service-based money laundering schemes to conceal illicit assets as seemingly legitimate trade on paper. The arrangements required only cooperation by both parties by creating corresponding records of commercial transactions that never took place.

Calò was also a visionary by looking beyond the provincial horizons of his immediate Palermo crime family to the collective Sicilian Cosa Nostra and the Camorra organization operating in the Naples region. In 1971, Calò relocated to Rome to be closer to the financial centers of power of Rome and Milan to the north. From Rome, Calò took on the role of *consigliere finanziario,* financial counselor to organized crime across Italy. The Italian Carabinieri and the Guardia di Finanza referred to him as *cassiere di Cosa Nostra,* or the cashier of Cosa Nostra.

The facilitators of the laundering scheme realize a collective commission of 30%. An important revenue stream on hundreds of millions of dollars of illicit money annually. All that became threatened when the financial empire of Michele Sindona began coming apart in 1974. Enter another Italian banker.

Although unlike Michele Sindona in personality, Roberto Calvi was equally clever and ambitious in building his financial empire. By 1975, Calvi was chairman of the Banco Ambrosiano, the *bank of priests,* a large private bank headquartered in Milan. By 1978, Calvi's financial empire rivalled that of Sindona. The foundation became Banco Ambrosiano founded in 1896, augmented by the acquisition of another Catholic bank of Venice, Banca Cattolica de Veneto, founded in 1892. Combined, Calvi's venerable and successful Catholic-centric banks inherently brought him close to the Vatican as a replacement to Sindona. In addition, Calvi had previously purchased La Centrale from Sindona years earlier, therefore was already participating in money laundering for the Mafia.

Yet Calvi began facing financial difficulties from his overly aggressive growth strategy through debt. His strategy to overcome financial reversals was to further accelerate growth. That incurred increased liquidity pressure from the Italian central bank. This forced Calvi to expand his offshore foreign subsidiaries for accessing loans from outside of Italy, hidden from Italian regulatory oversight. Mafia money served as short-term financing with money laundering fees an important revenue stream for Calvi.

Although Calvi was in serious financial difficulties, by early 1979, Sindona was in greater straits facing imminent indictment in U.S. federal court. The conspirators began reorganizing the Mafia money laundering process by adding more complexity for concealment and replacing Sondona with Calvi's network of offshore shell companies and banks.

For Archbishop Tagliente, his strategic objective was to extricate the Vatican from continued public controversy while reenforcing necessary Vatican revenue streams through investments. Mafia money laundering with increasing drug trafficking would be an important revenue component with the Vatican Bank seizing greater control. With Tagliente secretly directing control from behind the scenes, he intended to eliminate reliance on old guard outsiders. Tagliente's strategy dictated severing connection with Michele Sindona. Calvi was also a liability but temporarily necessary.

The altered money laundering channel for the Sicilian Mafia started with the same foundation of the Mafia-controlled Banca Mercantile headquarters in Palermo. Funds then moved at the direction of Ortolani's consulting firm to Calvi-owned shell companies in Luxembourg and Lichtenstein, ostensibly as wealth management offshore funds. Money then passed through Ortolani's bank in Montevideo, Uruguay. From there it passed to the Vatican bank.

The step involved a new wrinkle devised by Monsignor Auerbach, Tagliente's plant within the Vatican Bank. A Vatican Bank-controlled hedge fund incorporated in the Bahamas, Fondo Atlantic, operated like any investment fund except in this situation exclusively for Mafia accounts. Money flowed back to the

Mafia disguised as regular dividends. The Mafia could also choose to leave some funds invested to earn returns to offset laundering fees. Alternatively, the Mafia could move funds from the Vatican bank to a Calvi-owned Panamanian bank that could participate in trade-based laundering schemes with Mafia-controlled Italian businesses. Ortolani also created individual offshore accounts for the Mafia to further obscure transactional identities.

These intentionally complex routings made following the money trail impossible for law enforcement by using the secrecy of foreign subsidiaries in tax havens. The point of entry of illicit money into the financial system and reentry as legitimate assets remained the only transactional exposure available for investigators.

†

Nicoletti's Vatican documents did not identify any thread to link the Vatican Bank with Mafia other than the mention of names of those prominent in the banking scandal. Amatrano had somewhat more to begin with by access to Guardia records. Dossiers existed on Umberto Ortolani, Licio Gelli, and of course the Mafioso Giuseppe "Pippo" Calò.

Ortolani's information was sparse given his avoidance of public attention. Gelli was better known, but other than a colorful background, his current activities remained obscure. As the worship master of the Propaganda Due Masonic Lodge, officially dissolved in 1976, his subsequent activities came largely from rumor often related to his involvement with Argentina and right-wing political organizations.

On the other hand, Giuseppe Calò was well known to the Guardia and especially the GICO division. A Sicilian Mafioso residing now in Rome under a known alias suspected of involvement in money laundering but clever enough to avoid leaving any evidentiary fingerprints. Known as *cassiere di Cosa Nostra,* they could not make a case against Calò. Although Banca Mercantile di San Lorenzo headquartered in Palermo operated branches in

Rome, Naples, and Reggio Calabria, Calò conducted business through cutouts while never leaving a paper trail.

The GICO did know that Banca Mercantile shareholders were just straw men. Stand-ins that also held accounts in the bank to act as fronts for the Mafia. Italian authorities could never build a legal case. No one cooperating with Italian law enforcement lived long enough to testify in court.

After spending a couple months in GICO intelligence, Amatrano began formulating a plan. Not so much as a way of gathering evidence for prosecution, but something more insidious. Not outside Italian law but vicious in its implications. The Mafia treated society with no regard to any rules. Why not apply the same tactics toward the Mafia?

Amatrano needed time to broadly implement his strategy that required cooperation among GICO field commands and perhaps even the Carabinieri. For the moment, he would focus attention on disrupting the flow of illicit Mafia cash at the source of entry into the legitimate financial system. Banca Mercantile di San Lorenzo in Palermo.

†

While Emma Nicoletti worked on integrating the Vatican Archive documents into the larger financial scandal, the question of the possible role of Archbishop Tagliente in Gabriel Eisenberg's murder and the attempts on her life remained. She recalled their visit to Rome before the bombing to meet with her former colleague for the express purpose of learning more about the Vatican Secret service. Monsignor Scarpelli's letter went to some lengths to point a finger at Archbishop Tagliente. She decided to pay another visit to Carlo Langella the Rome editor of Nicoletti's former newspaper *Corriere della Sera.*

"My God, Emma! So good to see you. After the bombing I tried to contact you through *Il Sole 24 Ore.* Spoke with your editor. I was told you were recovering but under protection. Best he could do was pass on a message that I called. Next thing I heard was the second attempt on your life. After that you disappeared. Understandable given the circumstances. Fully recovered now?"

"Somewhat. Have this as a reminder," she said pointing to her cheek. "Was a lot worse before the plastic surgery in Paris. Almost healed."

Langella took a closer look. "Oh my, that doesn't look bad at all, Emma. The makeup covers it well unless someone is looking very closely."

"Thank you, Carlo. That's what the surgeon said. But I'll always see it as a scar."

"It in no way detracts from your beauty, Emma. I mean that sincerely."

She smiled and nodded. "I've relocated to Rome, Carlo. I'm still working for *Il Sole 24 Ore* out of the Rome bureau office now. Working on a new project. Involves the same reason Gabriel Eisenberg and I came to Rome previously to meet with you. The Vatican Holy Alliance or whatever it is called, and Archbishop Tagliente. More personal now of course."

"Not sure I have anything further I can offer then what I told you. Does this have anything to do with the attempts on your life?"

"That I don't know. It involves another line of inquiry possibly associated with the banking scandal involving new information connecting the Vatican Bank."

They continued conversing for another twenty minutes ending by Langella saying, "Wish I could be of more help, Emma. Let me make some inquiries. See if I can at least point you to someone that might know someone else and so forth. Give me your phone number. Considering what you've been through, I promise to do everything I can, Emma."

Three days later, Langella telephoned. "Good news, Emma. I have someone who has agreed to speak with you. A source I have used for many years. An insider that may have useful information."

"Oh my! That's great, Carlo. What's this person's connection to the Vatican?"

Silent for a moment, Langella replied, "A former member of the Vatican secret service in the years following the war until resigning from service at the Vatican in 1974. A priest."

"He knows about Tagliente?"

"Oh yes. Worked for him. I have promised never to reveal his identity as a source for anything I published. You must do the same. I would have approached him after our earlier meeting .... but the assassination attempts intervened. Only because of what happened to you has Monsignor Guido Orsini agreed to meet with you. Just you and me. No one else. I am to make the arrangements."

"Thank you, Carlo. I'm available anytime."

"I have of course followed the headline news released by the *New York Times*. Unauthorized removal of documents from the Vatican Secret Archive. Causing quite an uproar at the Vatican. Casts Pope Paul VI in a very bad light. Even the current pontiff is not immune. Are you involved in some way with how that came about, Emma?"

Nicoletti smiled. "I'd rather not say, Carlo."

"I understand. Is Archbishop Tagliente connected in some way?"

"Possibly. I truly don't know. Let's just say he is a person of interest given his unique stature within the Vatican. Head of both the Vatican Secret Archive from where the documents went missing and the unofficial head of the rarely acknowledged Vatican Secret Service."

CHAPTER 17

Rome, Italy | Spring 1980

Carlo Langella called Nicoletti and informed her of the arrangements for meeting Father Orsini. Outside of Rome in Tivoli, the pretty town famous for the magnificent gardens of the Villa d'Este. Ninety minutes east of Rome by train. Amatrano was not keen on the idea. Admittedly, the public release of the Vatican Archive documents should have eliminated reason for her assassination, but that was speculation. With the Sicilian Mafia party to the attacks, retribution to serve as a warning might be justification enough. Yet Emma was insistent. He agreed yet insisted that he must come along while remaining out of sight in civilian clothing Langella did not know him. He would provide surveillance from a distance. Armed of course, he also insisted Emma kept her Berretta in her handbag.

After boarding the train from Rome's Tiburtina station Amatrano took a seat in the train carriage behind the carriage where Emma and Langella were seated. All Emma knew was that Father Orsini would meet them at the Tivoli station. Amatrano assumed as a former intelligence operative, Orsini was employing tradecraft to ensure his visitors came alone. Amatrano must be careful to avoid being detected by a skilled intelligence operative.

At the train station Amatrano walked briskly from the train to the small station then out to the street to a small queue of taxis. Careful to stay out of sight at a distance, he watched as Emma, Langella and a man in a black clerical suit got into a taxi. The trick now was to follow in another taxi without being detected. That proved easy since the street in front of the train station ran for a distance along the river before crossing over into the town. A route that most taxis took when departing the train station. He explained to the taxi driver he was following his wife in the taxi ahead. If it stopped and let her out, drive past dropping him off where he indicated at a distance to avoid being seen. Handing the driver enough lire forestalled his asking questions.

The taxi moved away from the tourist area surrounding the Villa d'Este, stopping at a small café with outdoor seating on this warm spring day. Amatrano had his driver continue several blocks until out of sight from where Emma disembarked. Should this be a ploy to lose a tail, the backup plan was to rendezvous with Emma back at the train station.

Emma, Langella and Orsini took an outdoor table. Orsini ordered a bottle of wine.

Orsini said, "Have you recovered from the bombing and the second attempt on your life, Signora Nicoletti?'

"Physically. Emotionally, not entirely," pointing to her cheek. "Have this as a constant reminder. That and not being able to identify those behind this."

"Yet you know the reason you were targeted I assume?"

Nicoletti looked puzzled. "Not sure what you mean, Father."

Orsini said, "Because Monsignor Scarpelli must have sent them to you. Perhaps following his death. I believe it was you that sent the Vatican documents to the *New York Times*."

Nicoletti looked at Langella, who appeared equally surprised.

Orsini explained, "Carlo did not even speculate about that to me. You see I knew Monsignor Scarpelli very well. We both grew up in Umbria. He worked in the secret archive and I in *Sodalitium Pianum,* Vatican counterintelligence. We both worked for Marcello Tagliente in different capacities. Both of us had reason to distrust Tagliente's motives. A person that craved power. The most non-ecclesiastical prelate I ever encountered during my career.

"I read of the *New York Times* acquiring obviously stolen documents from the Vatican Secret Archive. I immediately suspected my friend Vittorio. He had the means and motivation. The theft of those documents required Vittorio to break a particularly sacred oath of obedience to the Holy Father. God's voice on earth. Or so believed by most Catholics. That must have been an agonizing decision likely made easier by his impending death.

"As with the famous fictional forensic genius Sherlock Holmes, I deduced from the facts that your interest in Archbishop Tagliente and *Santa Alleanza* might be connected to the stolen Archive documents. You write for a financial publication. The victim of two violent attempts on your life."

Nicoletti nodded. "That is correct. I came here to meet you in hopes of learning more about Archbishop Tagliente and the Vatican secret service. Since you also knew Monsignor Scarpelli, you are entitled to hear more about the story I am pursuing. It centers around exposing Vatican involvement in the banking scandal. Specifically, I believe the Vatican Bank had knowledge of money laundering buried among the complex transactions using offshore shell companies that brought down the banker Sindona and will probably become the same fate of Roberto Calvi's Banco Ambrosiano."

Orsini's expression instantly communicated distinct discomfort.

"Have no fear, Father Orsini. Neither you nor Carlo will be mentioned in anything I publish. Monsignor Scarpelli bequeathed his cache of stolen documents to me to continue what he started. Here is a photocopy of the letter he wrote to me through a Swiss law firm managing his estate. The *New York Times* does not have this. This explains my interest in Archbishop Tagliente and therefore the possible involvement of not only the Vatican Bank but possibly the Vatican secret service."

After reading Scarpelli's letter, Orsini handed it to Langella.

Turning to Nicoletti, Orsini said, "Father Scarpelli was correct in directing your attention to Archbishop Tagliente. He could even be behind the attacks to silence you and your American colleague."

"Are you saying this could be the work of the Vatican secret service?"

"Quite possibly. Especially since it has been dominated by Tagliente's leadership for two decades. He has not hesitated in the use of violence. I know of instances but prefer not to go into detail. Employing such extremes may have seemed necessary during the world war and the chaotic years that followed but not today. Totally out of place for a religious institution. One of the reasons I left Vatican service.

"Following my ordination, I spent my earliest years of service in *Santa Alleanza,* I prefer that reference to the innocuous term the *Entity* sometimes used for an organization never publicly mentioned. I became aware of a legendary agent of *Sodalitium Pianum.* Father Niccolo Estorzi earned the label as the *messenger.* Why I could not say. Rumor had it that he was from a secret order within Santa Alleanza known as the *Black Order.* An organization never spoken of within the Vatican so designated because of its historical use of violence. Created by a woman, Olimpia Maidalchini in the 17th century to root out spies within the Vatican. Her authority originated as sister-in-law to Pope Innocent X. I will leave it to you to research her tantalizing history. Forgive me for digressing.

"Maidalchini was brilliant and deviously clever. Truly Machiavellian. The same traits I ascribe to Archbishop Tagliente. My point is that I knew of Father Estorzi committing at least two murders. A German SD agent in 1939 before my coming to the Vatican. Another in 1948 with which I became directly aware. A French woman by the name Marga d'Andurain. An adventurist with a bizarre background including the probable murder of two husbands and engaging in espionage. Killed for reasons I never discovered, but it was Tagliente that ordered her death. Internal rumors suggested possible collusion with the new state of Israel. Possibly for something involving d'Andurain's involvement in Syria and Egypt when Estorzi and I both worked for Tagliente during and after the war. My point being that Archbishop Tagliente is no stranger to using murder for achieving his aims."

"Thank you for sharing your insights, Monsignor. Makes me feel even more uncomfortable, however."

Orsini nodded. "At least with the stolen archive documents made public, eliminating you no longer resolves the Vatican's public relations problem. Tagliente is too pragmatic to seek revenge for no other reason. Nevertheless, if Mafia money laundering is involved as Carlo told me is a subject of your project, the Mafia operates emotionally as violent thugs. Murder is their principal tactic to evoke terror. You must remain vigilant."

"I am. There is a licensed revolver in my handbag."

Orsini smiled, "A wise precaution. Whether Tagliente or the Mafia, these are dangerous adversaries. That brings me to speak of another person that operates in the shadows like Tagliente and his agents. Are you familiar with the name Licio Gelli?"

"Sounds familiar. Who is he?"

"That is a good question. I know only fragmented pieces of information myself. While still at the Vatican, I learned that Tagliente knew Gelli very well. I was aware a Vatican dossier existed on Gelli, but I did not have that kind of access to examine it. Among my associates, rumor has it that Gelli has influence among a vast network of important individuals throughout government and business. Even perhaps senior churchmen. Some believe he also has connections with undesirable organizations."

"Such as?"

"As in organized crime. Right-wing political groups. Strong ties with the military junta dictatorship of Argentina currently waging a brutal war against their populace. Gelli holds dual Italian and Argentinian citizenships. No one understands Gelli's basis for his extraordinary reputation for exerting influence."

"Do you have any information about Gelli's involvement in the financial scandal or money laundering for the Sicilian Mafia?"

Orsini shook his head, "Unfortunately, I do not. Tagliente runs a tight operation. Everything departmentalized on a need-to-know basis. I left the Vatican secret service in 1974. Disheartened by Tagliente's creation of dossiers on prominent prelates by

S.P. after installing a new head of counterintelligence. No reason for princes of the church to harbor subversive agendas. I suspected Tagliente of targeting those with views at odds with his own. I only mention Gelli's name because if he is involved in the Italian banking scandal, it is likely for financial gain.

"Yet Tagliente's close association with Licio Gelli undoubtedly yields other benefits. It extends Tagliente's intelligence reach into every corner of Italian society. Gelli is a dangerous criminal subversive to the Italian state. Gelli should become a persona of interest in your pursuit of your story dealing with the Vatican Bank's role in the banking scandal."

After ninety minutes, Father Orsini concluded the meeting. "I left the Vatican secret service with feelings of profound guilt for participating in what I feel is a sacrilege against my vows as a priest. Since then, I have been serving penance by devoting myself to ministering to a congregation of the faithful. I shall pray for you, Emma Nicoletti. Pray for you to discover the truth you are seeking. Stay safe and go with God." He made the sign of the cross, stood up and abruptly walked away.

Nicoletti looked around. She assumed Frank was nearby watching over her. However, she had promised Carlo Langella to come alone. No need to reveal to him that she was not about to trust a former agent of Vatican counterintelligence with all that she had been through. She and Langella would leave on the next train. Frank would take the same train back to Rome but remain unseen by Langella. They would meet back at their apartment.

†

After relating the details of her meeting, Frank said, "I was watching all the time from a distance. Concealed behind a large tree using binoculars. Mostly looking for signs of anyone else observing the three of you. As a former operative of Vatican intelligence, Father Orsini did not make me feel comfortable."

She smiled, "I knew you were out there watching over me. Kept my revolver within easy access in my handbag though. You taught me well."

Frank said, "You say that Orsini made it clear that Tagliente was not above using murder to achieve his objectives?"

"That's right. Through the meeting Carlo learned more than he ever knew about the Vatican secret service's current functions. Both he and Father Orsini are now allies. What about this Licio Gelli?"

"I've seen Gelli's dossier. A checkered background to say the least. Early fascist. Fought in Spain with Mussolini's *Blackshirts* expeditionary forces supporting Franco. Suspected of all sorts of nefarious activities. No actionable evidence of criminal activity. What is striking is the breadth of Gelli's expected involvement. An interesting dossier comment though gives some idea as to Gelli's influence. I quote: *Caution is to be exercised in the extreme for taking direct any action against Licio Gelli. Senior command level Guardia authority is to be apprised of any serious developments. Gelli numbers many government officials and prominent private sector individuals of influence among his circle of acquaintances.*

"Is there anything in the Guardia files that points to Gelli's involvement with the Mafia or the banking scandal?" Emma asked.

"Not that I've seen. However, given Gelli's breadth of influence and his close association with Tagliente, Gelli would at least know the characters involved. What is revealed in the Guardia dossier scope of influence exercised by this underground masonic lodge Propaganda Due headed by Licio Gelli."

Emma said, "If we are to make a connection between the Vatican and money laundering for the Mafia it must be through the principals involved in the scandal. As damning as they are for the Vatican, there is nothing in the archive documents that links specifically to the Mafia. That connection runs through Sindona and Calvi along with these others like Ortolani and Gelli. We must find that connection that bridges the Vatican Bank unequivocally to the Mafia. This Gelli character is a good start. Father Orsini portrays him as capable of most anything."

Frank added, "The other is Giuseppe Calò, the cashier of Cosa Nostra. Sicilian Mafia. He must be involved. I will concentrate my efforts on identifying others within Calò's orbit. Someone more vulnerable that could be turned if coerced by a credible threat of legal consequences."

†

The backlash of the release of the stolen documents resulted in a broad attack directed at the Vatican from many quarters. It provided circumstantially damning evidence of involvement with Sindona's illegal activities and Calvi's questionable financial dealings. Evidence confirming the Vatican's intimate association with a individuals named publicly in the banking scandal. Those associations known by Pope Paul VI and Pope John Paul II. Pope Paul comes under the most damaging allegations for his introduction of these criminals into positions of trust within the Holy See. Already a controversial personality on many levels, the documents exposed new criticisms of Pope Paul ranging from naiveite, to incompetence, to outright collusion in criminal activity.

Pope Paul's pontificate ending only two years previously made that still newsworthy. It also renewed speculations about the unresolved circumstances surrounding the death of Pope John Paul I after only 33 days from his elevation to pontiff. Speculation that his death might be homicide came from questions of public revelations of intense displeasure after learning of the sale by the Vatican Bank's controlling interest in Banca Cattolica del Veneto to Calv's Banco Ambrosiano. At the time Pope John Paul I, Albino Luciani, was Cardinal Archbishop of Venice. Banca Cattolica, like Banco Ambrosiano, was known as *the priest's bank*, and was close to Luciani's heart. He blamed Bishop Paul Marcinkus for relinquishing Vatican Bank controlling share holdings. No explanation has ever been forthcoming from the Vatican on benefits of that questionable transaction. Luciani's ascendancy to the throne of Saint Peter could reasonably be seen as a threat to Marcinkus and perhaps others.

Current Pope John Paul II now faced renewed mounting pressure for transparency on various uncomfortable issues. It fell to Cardinal Secretary of State Agostino Casaroli and Archbishop

Marcello Tagliente to provide counsel in managing the Vatican's public position with these new damaging developments.

†

Upon release of the documents by the *New York Times*, the pope summoned Cardinal-Secretary of State Casaroli and Tagliente for a private audience. Speaking without preamble to Tagliente, the pope asked, "Your excellency, have you discovered how these highly confidential documents went missing from the Secret Archive?"

"Yes, Your Holiness. Regrettably the most senior of the Archive staff, Monsignor Vittorio Scarpelli, removed them. He died two years ago after decades of service. Before his death he secured the documents in a Swiss bank. Instructions upon his death arranged through a Swiss law firm apparently directed them sent to be sent to the New York newspaper. It is believed that Monsignor Scarpelli removed this large cache of documents over many years. Likely one or two at time. Security has now been heightened."

"Do these missing documents all relate in some way to this never-ending financial scandal?"

"It appears that way, Your Holiness. Most damaging are those documents connecting the IOR to Michele Sindona years ago who now figures prominently in this ongoing international banking scandal."

"The doings of my predecessor Giovanni Montini."

"It appears as such, Your Holiness."

Turning toward Cardinal Casaroli, the pope asked, "Agostino, what is your counsel as to how we should respond?"

"Avoid making public comment. It is the lesser of two bad outcomes. Making comments requires becoming entangled with explaining details leading to endless material for the media to seize upon. Unfortunately, we are at the mercy of the activities of these outside bankers. We must maintain the position of victimization of the IOR. Avoiding making substantive comments obviously invites its own criticism. As painful as that is, Archbishop Tagliente and I agree it is the best course."

Turning to Tagliente, the pope asked, "And what is to be done with Bishop Marcinkus, Archbishop?"

"Bishop Marcinkus appears as a victim. It was Pope Paul that brought Michele Sindona into intimate involvement with management advice to the IOR. Further supported by respected gentlemen of the Church, Umberto Ortolani and Massimo Spada. Those relationships regrettably continued the problem by involvement with Roberto Calvi and the venerable Banco Ambrosiano in Milan. Admittedly, Bishop Marcinkus lacks a background in finance, yet he is a much-trusted churchman to not only yourself, Holy Father, but several of your predecessors. Pope Paul rightfully wanted to place a trusted prelate in the position of directing the IOR. Yet he placed Marcinkus in a most awkward position. Even Pope John Paul I did not harbor ill-will toward Bishop Marcinkus as many expected from his displeasure over Marcinkus relinquishing control of Banca Cattolica in Venice."

"Are you recommending we remove Bishop Marcinkus from his post?"

Tagliente looked at Casaroli. They discussed this beforehand with Casaroli feeling he should be removed, but Tagliente arguing against such a move. "No, Holy Father. That would invite criticism as tacit admission of wrongdoing. As we discussed some time ago, the addition of Monsignor Auerbach to the IOR staff provides the immediate means of oversight to avoid the IOR from engaging in questionable financial transactions with individuals publicly alleged in financial wrongdoing. Bishop Marcinkus should remain as president of the IOR."

Pope John Paul nodded in approval. He liked Marcinkus.

"Bishop Marcinkus is also a vital link in passing funds from the American Central Intelligence Agency to the Solidarity Movement in Poland. He assures me that none of the IOR staff knows the true identity of the source of these funds. He has advised trusted senior staff necessary in executing the transactions that the funds are those of the Holy See. Even that detail must be kept absolutely secret. A personal mission of Your Holiness directed toward destabilizing the Polish Communist puppet regime under the thumb of the Soviet Union."

The pope again nodded, "Very good. The Polish people have suffered terribly under the evil of godless communism."

Tagliente then added, "I shall offer my services to remain close to IOR management decisions during this period of crisis. I recommended the appointment of Monsignor Auerbach who keeps me regularly informed. Bishop Marcinkus and I also enjoy a very congenial relationship. As you know I possess an academic background in economics and international law, therefore I possess a good grounding in finance.

"The overriding objective is to maintain IOR investment revenue levels. Restore what Bernardino Nogara created and his successor Henri Maillardoz carried forward successfully for decades. The self-serving criminal corruption introduced by the bankers Michele Sindona and Roberto Calvi is close to coming to an end. Signore Sindona is no longer a problem. Only residual fallout remains. Bishop Marcinkus has wisely severed association with Signore Calvi. Banco Ambrosiano is unlikely to survive. The scandal will soon exhaust itself. We must take the long view and stay the course, Your Holiness."

Casaroli had not expected such a power grab by Tagliente. Yet he too understood Vatican politics. Tagliente was not a prince of the church that any prelate wanted as an enemy. Tagliente continued to be seen as a necessary fixture in the function of the Vatican successive popes going back to Pius XII. Tagliente's brilliance, while working covertly from the shadows without interference from the Roman Curia, proved a useful tool for pontiffs. Tagliente's various roles afford the pontiff plausible deniability from within the Vatican to exercise his will without the need for explanation.

CHAPTER 18

Rome, Italy | January 1981

Frank Amatrano and Emma Nicoletti both left places they called home for decades with a sense of dislocation. The aftermath of the traumatic encounters remained vivid. Yet having found each other meant a different future for devoted workaholics now in their early fifties. While danger had not passed, they felt more in command with their changed circumstances.

For Amatrano, his circumstances now came with personal danger. Moving from pure investigative work at Interpol to active law enforcement was a conscious choice. Doing so in arguably the most violent country in Western Europe energized him by the challenge of doing meaningful work. After several months in his new position heading the intelligence section for the organized crime division of the Italian Guardia di Finanza, his period of acclimation was over. Time to advance his aggressive idea for going after the Sicilian Mafia.

The intelligence sector of the *Gruppo d'Investigazione Sulla Criminalità Organizzata,* the Organized Crime Investigative Group, the GICO had stagnated. Bureaucratic compiling of data fell short of vigorous creative analysis. Overwhelmed by events of the past decade, the *Guardia di Finanza* was waging war from a defensive posture. The economic effects of the pervasive Italian Banking Scandal, terrorist violence from both the left and right, and an emboldened Mafia inflicting violence had seemingly overwhelmed Italian law enforcement. Amatrano had joined the right organization for challenging work that could make a difference.

Italian organized crime existed predominantly in the South. The loosely structured 'Ndrangheta of Calabria at the toe of the Italian peninsula. The Camorra of Campania surrounding the city of Naples. Then the worst of the criminal scourge, the Mafia, or Cosa Nostra of the island of Sicily. All originating from the 18th century or earlier. All engaged in similar illicit activities. However, it was the use of violence that distinguished the Sicilian Mafia.

It was the Sicilian Mafia that exported its brand of criminality to the United States in the early 20th century. Taking root with Prohibition in the 1920s than turning to trafficking in drugs during the decades following World War Two. That entrenched foundation now provided the Sicilians the opportunity to develop the means of internationally trafficking in heroin and cocaine to the American market. That in turn bred competitive violence in Sicily. Origination of modern tax haven countries offering transactional secrecy in the last two decades offered the perfect mechanism to transform great amounts of illicit money into the legitimate financial mainstream. The Sicilian Mafia understandably dominated the attention of GICO.

Amatrano instituted methods developed at Interpol and elsewhere. Extensive lists of those involved in organized crime with cross references made understanding organization difficult. Instead, Amatrano insisted on creating large boards surrounding the walls of the conference room of the headquarters intelligence section. These visual representations focused on the command hierarchy and interconnections outside of each organization.

These boards dealt with the principal Sicilian families. Staff meetings therefore were surrounded by visualizations of the enemy. Amatrano then began a rigorous plan of prioritization. A dynamic list of objectives divided into three groups of importance that changed as dictated by new information. In just the last few months, it began to pay off. Part of that came from enhanced enthusiasm among staff. Not only among the headquarters analytical staff but the intelligence officers in the field that saw the usefulness of their work. The Palermo command had three field intelligence officers. Sharing higher quality information with the intelligence sector of the other national law enforcement agency the Carabinieri produced further results.

Explaining to chief of staff Colonel Ferrazza, Amatrano said, "The key is not to wage war against the Sicilian Mafia on a broad front, but to proactively target vulnerabilities, Antonio. The intelligence staff must not only be looking for information that comes in on targeted individuals, but to focus particularly on antagonisms. Internally within a family and between rival families. That offers opportunities for us to exploit differences. Identify those with ambitions. Rivalries. Vendettas. Who are the most unstable? Who are the thinkers? Who are the most violent?"

Ferrazza asked, "Exploit how?"

"Through subversion. Spreading false rumors. Make arrests for the sole purpose of setting up individuals. Use various techniques to fit opportunities. For example, telling a detainee if he does not give up certain information, we spread the word through our sources that this individual gave us information in return for avoiding arrest. All manner of variations to suit the circumstances."

Ferrazza smiled, "People get killed if suspected of helping the police."

"A very real possibility. An incentive to perhaps actually cooperate. The Sicilians in and around Palermo are already on edge. Something in the wind tells me there is a storm developing. If we create internal chaos then we weaken the Mafia from within."

"Innocent people could get hurt, Frank."

"Not any more than already suffer at the hand of the Mafia in Sicily. I've spent a good deal of time there in the past months. Been working against these bastards for years when with Interpol. Life in Palermo is nothing like Rome or any of the large cities of the North. Even Naples with the Camorra does not suffer anything like life under Mafia-ruled Palermo. Competition between families is increasing. Incidents of low-level inter-family violence are on the increase. The Corleonesi seem to be the most aggressive.

"I've been working all year on identifying where best to alert commands to work sources. We must take the offensive to produce results. Make our opportunities. Become as ruthless as the Mafia Antonio."

"Very well, Frank. I will arrange a meeting with the General."

"I appreciate that. Now here's a bit of good news. One of our officers in Palermo has been working his sources with some success. Managed to identify the intermediary of the Mafia-controlled Banca Mercantile di San Lorenzo with the world of international finance."

Ferrazza commented, "The bank was Giuseppe Calò's creation years ago. The *cashier of the Cosa Nostra*. Boss of the Porta Nuova family."

Amatrano said, "Yeah. Pippo Calò now works out of Rome. The guy we found is an intermediary that makes the arrangements for moving money assisted by a slippery businessman Umberto Ortolani. Ortolani operates a consulting business, *Bologna Investimenti S.R.L.* here in Rome. We haven't been able to discover any direct links between Ortolani and Calò. We believe this Palermo lawyer serves as the cutout between the Mafia and Ortolani to move money from Banca Mercantile into to foreign shell companies connected with Roberto Calvi's Banco Ambrosiano empire."

"Who is this Palermo lawyer?" Ferrazza asked.

"His name is Paolo Falcone."

"Background?"

"Comes from old time Mafia royalty. Grandson of the venerated Mafioso Calogero Vizzini. Falcone is closely associated with the three most powerful of the Palermo Mafia families. Stefano Bontade the boss of the Santa Maria di Gesù Family, Salvatore Inzerillo of the Passo di Rigano family, and Gaetano Badalamenti of the Cinisi Mafia family. However, his services extend to all the Palermo Mafia families involved with moving money through Banca Mercantile. Officially, Falcone is the bank's general counsel.

"We've been keeping a close eye on Falcone for months. He makes frequent trips to Rome. Observed meeting with Ortolani on numerous occasions. There's something else we've discovered about Falcone."

"Something useful?"

"Depends on how we play it. A couple of weeks ago Falcone made his regular trip to Rome. This time with a woman. Not his wife. Spent a couple of nights at the Excelsior on Via Vittorio Veneto. We have photographs."

"So, he's fooling around. Blackmail doesn't sound like enough leverage to accomplish anything of value."

"Perhaps in this case it has deeper implications. You see the woman is a niece of Bernardo Provenzano, underboss to psychopathic Salvatore Riina boss of the Corleonesi Mafia clan still running things from undercover as a fugitive. Her name is Olivia Zangheri. Falcone cannot possibly know who he is screwing unless he is suicidal. On the other hand, Zangheri must know of Falcone's affiliation with the rival Palermo clans. A rivalry increasing turning violent."

The Corleonesi clan made their base in the environs of the provincial town of Corleone, forty miles south of the city of Palermo.

Ferrazza said, "Therefore, this is an infiltration scheme of the Corleonesis?"

"Appears that way unless it's just a stupid sexual relationship. Regardless, it presents us with an opportunity to turn Falcone."

"How exactly? You threaten him and he dumps the woman."

Amatrano shook his head. "Wouldn't be that simple. He then becomes suspect to both the various Palermo clans who control money laundering through Banca Mercantile. Intimately consorting with the Corleonesi means a death sentence. Barring that, the Corleonesi kill him as a matter of honor. Either way, Signore Falcone is in deep shit. The sooner we move on him the better. This could fall apart anytime then we lose the opportunity."

"What's your plan, Frank?"

"Snatch Falcone and bring him to a safe location where I will interrogate him. As they say in the American movie *The Godfather*, I'll make him an offer he can't refuse. Either he becomes an informant which I believe is a death sentence, or he gives us everything he knows. We then give him a new identity. In the United States, there's a justice department program called Witness Protection where they do just that."

"And if he denies knowing what you are talking about and refuses either option?"

"Then I tell him that is not one of his choices. Should he not cooperate, then we spread the word about his dalliance with the enemy. Possibly even infer that he might be working with the Guardia. He will know that means a very bad death."

Ferrazza nodded. "You are a ruthless bastard, Frank. I like it though. About time we took the battle to the Mafia. I'll run it by the boss. Keep your people on Falcone."

Ferrazza and his wife became good friends with Amatrano and Nicoletti. When together as couples they avoided discussing police business although each knew that much of what they did was known by each woman. Nicoletti told Ferrazza and his wife about the stolen Vatican archive documents being the source of Eisenberg's murder and the attempts on her life. Admitted it was her that sent them to the *New York Times*. She would reveal the whole story and more in the new book she is writing. Ferrazza came to consider Nicoletti as something of an intelligence source.

About to leave Amatrano's office, he said, "Are you and Emma still convinced that the Vatican is more connected with the Mafia then just as victimization by the Italian bankers."

Amatrano answered, "Yes. The Mafia never knew about missing church documents when they went after her and Eisenberg. The hitmen I killed were known Mafia. The bombing that killed the American journalist Eisenberg was Mafia-styled. Undoubtedly acting at the time as hired assassins. Could have been those connected with Sindona or Clavi, but again, they could not have knowledge of incriminating documents except from someone within the Vatican. The documents do not add greater weight to the financial scandal other than to incriminate the Vatican with more direct knowledge of suspect financial dealings. The question is more about who within the Vatican is behind this."

"You and Emma still believe it might be Archbishop Tagliente?"

Without revealing Scarpelli's letter to Ferrazza, Amatrano answered, "Emma is convinced. I believe he is the most likely suspect because of his special status apart from Curia oversight. I'd prefer to find more concrete evidence before fully supporting that conclusion though."

†

General Giacchetto readily agreed with Amatrano's proposal for going after Falcone. He told Amatrano to work out the details with Ferrazza. A week later Amatrano was in Palermo. Dressed in a civilian suit rather than his Guardia uniform, Amatrano registered at a hotel under an assumed name.

The plan was simple. Stage a minor automobile accident with Falcone using only his three local intelligence officers. Take Falcone to a Guardia-controlled location. Amatrano would conduct the interrogation.

Amatrano's agents toured him throughout Palermo pointing out Falcone's residence, his office, and several locations he frequents the first day after arriving in Palermo.

"Where do we take the target after the collision?" Amatrano asked his senior agent in charge.

"A Guardia warehouse near the port. Used for keeping gear for our patrol boats. There's an office, toilets, and a small lunch area for maintenance staff. I secured a set of keys. Once we detain the target, I will call by radio for any staff to vacate the warehouse immediately."

"Good. How about concealing your identities?"

"The agent smiled. Ski masks as you suggested. We say nothing to the target except issuing instructions. Make him believe we are Mafia. Bring him to the warehouse with a hood over his head. Secure him to a chair with nylon marine lines."

"I want him to sit there alone for at least thirty minutes. Scare the hell out of him. Let him try to imagine what this is about. Let his imagination start building his fear. Working for the Mafia, he will conjure all sorts of terror. By the time I come in, he will be in the right frame of mind for the interrogation I have planned."

That night they began the surveillance. Two unmarked vehicles. One a van with his agents, the other a car driven by Amatrano. They gave up surveillance that night when the lights of Falcone's house went out close to midnight. The plan called for seizing Falcone while driving after dark. That opportunity arrived two nights later.

Falcone spent the evening at dinner with two men Amatrano's agents identified as *caporegimes*, mid-ranking members of the Santa Maria di Gesù Mafia. It was nine o'clock when Falcone left. Somewhat unsteady after drinking too much wine he drove away in the direction toward his residence. After turning onto a quiet street, the van sped up and cut off Falcone's sedan, clipping the left front quarter panel bringing it to a stop.

Pushing open his car door, Falcone had barely stepped out when two agents emerged from the van with ski masks pulled over their faces. His eyes opened wide with fear knowing what this represented as he said something in protest. The agents grabbed him while the third agent came up behind and pulled a hood over his head. Quickly handcuffed, they bundled Falcone roughly into the rear of the van. The van drove off with Amatrano following.

An hour transpired from the time of seizing Falcone then traveling north through the Palermo arriving at the warehouse in the port area. Amatrano sat with his agents sharing a thermos of coffee before making his appearance with Falcone. Still handcuffed, he was bound to a chair around the torso and legs with nylon ropes. The hood was still in place. Hearing Amatrano open the door to the area alerted Falcone. His head turned to the sound. Amatrano could hear his rapid breathing causing the hood to suck inward with each intake of breath.

Amatrano pulled up a chair in front of Falcone. After removing his suit jacket to reveal his shoulder holster, Amatrano pulled off the hood. Falcone looked at him with terrified eyes.

"Who are you?" Falcone said.

"Well. I could be Mafia. Then again, that could mean either Palermo Mafia or Corleonesi Mafia. Big difference considering your situation. I might also be the police. Whoever I am, Paolo, you are in some very deep shit. Life as you have known it is over. What happens next depends entirely on the choices you make to-night."

Falcone sat in silence, confused and terrified.

Amatrano said, "Let me lay out what I know. Then I'm going to ask you questions. Answer truthfully and you might survive with all your body parts intact. First of all, I am the police. The Guardia di Finanza. You are a bagman for the Palermo Mafia consortium. Officially legal counsel for Banca Mercantile di San Lorenzo. The Mafia-controlled bank created by Giuseppe "Pippo" Calò, boss of the Porta Nuova family. Calò is known as the *cassiere di Cosa Nostra*. Banca Mercantile is the principal conduit for Sicilian Mafia money laundering.

"Now you may ask, why do I need you since I know so much? The answer is I want more evidence. Details. Names and connections. I intend to prosecute every Mafiosi and those connected in high places among the Italian banking and finance. You will get me the evidence I need."

"Why should I? I would be dead before you ever brought me into court as a witness. I will take my chances with whatever charges you can make against me. Following the code of *omerta* is much safer."

Amatrano smiled. "That will not work in your situation, Paolo. That all changed once you took up with Olivia Zangheri. We have all sorts of photographs of your recent holiday in Rome. Hope she was worth all the trouble she brings down on you."

"She has nothing to do with my law practice. Leave her out of this."

"Who do you believe she is, Paolo?"

"She is just a nurse. Lost her husband a year ago to cancer. He was a doctor. They worked at the same hospital in Marsala. She came to Palermo to be close to her mother who suffers from advanced cancer."

Amatrano grinned and shook his head. "For a Mafia lawyer you are either gullible or just plain stupid. Olivia is of course a nurse. Just not from Marsala. She grew up in Corleone. You know of the town of Corleone of course. She did have a husband that died. Not from cancer but from potassium cyanide poisoning."

Falcone's expression registered shock.

"You see, Paulo, Olivi Zangheri is the niece of Bernardo Provenzano, underboss of the Corleonesi. The number two boss to Don Totò Riina. Olivia's husband beat her once too often. Didn't matter to Uncle Bernie that his niece invited spousal abuse for sleeping around with other doctors at the hospital. Couldn't allow a mere Mafia soldier to show such disrespect to a person of his stature. Undoubtedly, your darling Olivia administered the potassium cyanide to free herself. Uncle Bernie made sure the husband's death was ruled from *natural causes*. Niece or not, Olivia owes her uncle a debt of gratitude.

"Now you see the situation you are in, don't you, Paolo? You are either screwing the enemy of the Palermo families you work for, or worse, your Olivia is probably a plant by her uncle Provenzano. Maybe an attempt of infiltration ordered by Don Riina. Do you now see the predicament you are in, Paolo?"

Paolo Falcone closed his eyes and lowered his head.

"Listen to me, Paolo. You are going to spend the next few hours telling me everything you know. Depending on the importance of the information you provide, we will take care of you. Under security living elsewhere under an assumed name. No lies, no making up material. Everything you tell us will be corroborated. Lie to us and we simply release you. Hard to say which Mafia faction will kill you first. Whichever, it is certain to be unpleasant. You are a dead man walking unless you choose to cooperate."

Amatrano removed the handcuffs and ropes. Falcone massaged his wrists. Switching on a tape recorder, "Shall we begin, Paolo?"

After several hours, Falcone was exhausted.

"Doing good, Paolo. Now let's talk about how you interface with those that move the money into the mainstream for laundering. Who is your principal connection?"

"Umberto Ortolani. He maintains an office here in Palermo. Most communications are by mail. Instructions for bank transactions that I pass to the Banca Mercantile president. No names are used in any written instructions."

"What about Licio Gelli?"

"I know the name. Mentioned sometime by the family bosses. I have no dealings with him."

"What about the Vatican?"

"Yes. The Roman Catholic Church."

"Well, I attend mass occasionally."

Amatrano's expression turned dark. "You've been doing well up to now, Paolo. Don't be a smartass. Do you have business dealings with anyone from the Vatican?"

Falcone swallowed and took a deep breath. "Yes."

"Who?"

"A priest by the name of Father Esposito at the Church of the Gesù. Located in the Piazza Casa Professa."

"Who is Esposito's connection to the Vatican?"

"I do not know. I was only told by Banca Mercantile president Signore Giordano that the Vatican Bank has a financial interest in Banca Mercantile. No specifics given. That was never to be spoken of. Therefore, Father Esposito is to be my only contact. Esposito passes information to me that I pass on to Giordano. Vatican."

"What sort of information?"

"I have no idea. Esposito just hands me a sealed envelope."

"How does your arrangement with Esposito work?"

"He notifies me by telephone. We transact our business in the confessional. Esposito hands me the sealed envelope with no name on it. Tells me who I am to deliver the envelope, usually the Giordano. Never anything more."

"Are there sometimes other recipients?"

"Usually Giordano, or sometimes Stefano Bontade.

"Ever open any of these envelopes?"

Falcone registered surprise. "Never."

"Are you ever called upon by your bank president or Bontade to pass information back to the Vatican?"

"Occasionally. Same arrangement in reverse. I contact Father Esposito and pass an envelope to him in the confessional."

Amatrano's expectation was that once having debriefed Falcone, his agents would drive him well away from Palermo. Cross to the mainland then take a train to Rome to a secure location. His thoughts changed when unexpectedly presented with the opportunity of establishing a link with the Vatican.

"You've been very helpful, Paolo. Time to cut ties with your criminal past. I promised you protection from a bad ending. Just one more thing you must do before we leave Palmero. We drop you off back home. You tell your wife that you were drunk. A minor traffic accident with a truck. Fell asleep after a truck ran into you then drove off. Your car is only a mile from your house. In the morning you go to your office. Place a call to Father Esposito. Tell him you have some information that needs to be sent off to the Vatican immediately."

"What information?"

"Information about the Corleonesi. Possible threats to stockholders of Banca Mercantile. Too dangerous to put on paper."

Falcone shook his head, "No! You must get me away from Palermo immediately! I've done everything you have asked."

"Not quite, Paolo. This last thing task is required." Amatrano couldn't help thinking how ironic what he was about to have Falcone do. "You will also tell Father Esposito about your relationship with Olivia. Make an actual confession, Paolo. Say you just discovered the family connection of Olivia Zangheri by accident. A niece to the Corleonesi clan underboss, Bernardo Provenzano. Tell Esposito you believe she was sent to infiltrate someone at the bank.. Having sex with you only to get information. Information you will also confess you passed to her. Someone last night warned you about who she was. That's why you got drunk and spent a bad night. Needed to pass on what you discovered immediately if something should happen to you. You fear retribution from your Mafia associates."

"Christ, I can't do that!"

"Yes you can, Paolo. You have no choice. Once you deliver your message to Father Esposito, we wait until he telephones you confirming a meeting at the church with someone from the Vatican. A meeting you will agree to attend. However, I will not require you to go that far. Once Father Esposito confirms that a meeting is on, my agents will get you out of Palermo to a safe location out of reach of the Sicilian Mafia."

CHAPTER 19

Rome, Italy | January 1981

Paolo Falcone did as Amatrano instructed the following day. Although suffering from fatigue after spending a sleepless night undergoing interrogation, then facing his irate wife, fear-induced adrenalin kept him going. After arranging a meeting with Father Esposito for that afternoon, he tried to rest and calm his fears.

Arriving at the Church of the Gesù, Falcone entered the magnificently decorated nave. Taking a seat in the last row, Father Esposito joined him at the appointed time. Exchanging no words, they walked together and entered an ornate confessional.

Without preamble, Falcone said, "A matter of urgency has arisen, Father. It involves a serious threat to the bank I work for. Something with which the Vatican Bank has a vested interest of great importance."

Father Esposito replied, "The usual procedure requires providing me with an envelope. I am only an intermediary. I am not empowered with access to any privileged information."

"In my situation you must make an exception." Pausing for a moment, Falcone began, "Forgive me, Father for I have sinned. The sin of adultery. Regrettably, that transgression becomes even worse. I have just discovered the woman comes from the town of

Corleone to the south of Palermo. Her family is a rival to the interests of my employer and therefore the Vatican. It requires communicating details of what I have learned. The Vatican representative will have undoubtedly many questions for me. I will call you tomorrow, Father."

Without saying anything further, Paolo Falcone left the confessional. A car waited for the Guardia officers to drive him somewhere beyond the reach of Mafia retribution. He was never returning to his home or family. The last thing he said to his wife when leaving to meet with Father Esposito after calling a taxi was, "Have to see about getting the car towed to a garage. Not sure when I'll be back."

✝

The following day, Falcone called Father Esposito at the rectory. He was sitting in a cheap hotel in Messina on the other side of Sicily under guard by Amatrano's agents. Esposito said, "Tomorrow at noon. Last pew. I shall collect you and escort you to a confessional. Your visitor prefers to remain anonymous."

Amatrano assigned two of his local agents to transport Falcone by car from Palermo to Messina on the eastern side of Sicily the morning of the scheduled meeting at the church. From there they would board a train to cross the strait to the Italian mainland on a ferry then proceed to Rome. Amatrano arranged to secure Falcone at a safe location under guard to remain available for further extended consultation.

Using additional undercover Guardia agents from Palermo, Amatrano arranged surveillance on Father Esposito. The morning of the day of meeting with Falcone, surveillance included two agents randomly moving through the church with cameras ostensibly appearing as tourists. The magnificent appointments inside the church made photography commonplace.

As the church bells tolled at noon, Father Esposito entered the nave. Walking briskly to the rear he did not find Falcone seated in the last pew as expected. Anxious after waiting ten minutes, he walked over to the confessional where the Vatican visitor waited.

Monsignor Ettore Donaggio sat inside waiting for Falcone to appear with growing annoyance. An uncomfortable Father Esposito did not know the Vatican priest's name. Obviously, the visitor represented someone important at the Vatican. "I apologize, Father, Signore Falcone has not arrived as scheduled."

Donaggio replied, "I shall wait another fifteen minutes."

The minutes passed. Falcone and his GICO bodyguards had already left Sicily by the time a disgusted Donaggio exited the confessional. "Take me to your office, Father. Failure of Signore Falcone to appear for his own requested meeting is troubling. I need to make a phone call."

Tagliente took Donaggio's call. Ever mindful that the Italian telephone system was not secure from Italian law enforcement eavesdropping, they spoke without using names or giving away information.

Donaggio said, "My party never made our meeting. Will immediately investigate with the assistance of my local associate and advise you when I have further information."

Tagliente made no response then disconnected the call.

To Father Esposito, Donaggio said, "Call Falcone's office."

Esposito looked up the number on his rolodex. Falcone's secretary said her boss had not been in the office all day. Falcone's wife answered the call to his home. Esposito said, "Your husband's secretary said he had not been in the office all day. I wished to discuss a church financial matter of some importance with him. Might you know where I can reach him?"

Sounding annoyed, she said, "If he's not at the office I have no idea where he might be. He got home late the night before last. Business dinner he said. Returned in the early morning hours. Said his car broke down. Walked home. He didn't look all that well when he woke me. I suspected the effects of too much wine. After a couple of hours, he called for a taxi saying he needed to see to recovering the car and getting it fixed. He never returned home. Do you have any idea what is going on, Father."

Esposito replied, "No, I don't, Signora Falcone. I'm sure your husband will explain when you see him. Please have him call me immediately. *Arrivederci*."

Donaggio said, "I need to make another telephone call, Father."

"Of course, Father," Esposito said then left as Donaggio closed the office door.

When Tagliente answered, Donaggio said, "My party is missing. Not at his office or home. Left his home two days ago in the morning according to his wife. She said he did not return home until the early hours of the next morning. Then left his home later that morning by taxi telling her he must attend to his car that broke down the previous night. He never returned. Something is wrong. I shall remain here to investigate."

"Very well, keep me informed. Be mindful of not unduly arousing concerns until we learn more," Tagliente said.

Donaggio maintained infrequent contact with Falcone at Banca Mercantile using Father Esposito as a cutout to receive information of interest to the Vatican Bank. For more direct contact with certain *caporegimes*, crew bosses of mafia soldiers for the Bontade and Inzerillo Palermo Mafia families, Donaggio used his principal operational resource Brother Gideon in Rome. It was through Brother Gideon that Monsignor Donaggio had a small army of violent proxies at his disposal. Those proxies additionally provided cover by camouflaging the use of violence as just part of the wave of widespread murder by organized crime.

✝

Before Donaggio even entered the confessional, Amatrano's agents had taken many photos. His exit from the confessional confirmed he was the Vatican representative. Within hours, Guardia headquarters in Palermo developed the film and telexed Donaggio's image to Rome. An hour later Amatrano received a call from Colonel Ferrazza.

"The Vatican priest is Monsignor Ettore Donaggio. Born 1938. Currently holds a position within the department for Italian affairs of the Section for Relations with States in the Vatican Secretariate of State. That position however is believed only a cover for Donaggio's actual role as head of *Sodalitium Pianum,* Vatican counterintelligence. Donaggio was a former secretary to Archbishop Tagliente. If Tagliente is in fact the operational head of the Vatican secret service as rumored, rather than the acknowledged prelate Archbishop Luigi Poggi, then Donaggio still works for Tagliente."

Amatrano responded, "Well, that is interesting. Clearly confirms more than a Vatican passing interest in Mafia-controlled Banca Mercantile."

Ferrazza replied, "Also ties the Vatican secret service into involvement with the Vatican Bank. Adds to your and Emma's theory of broader involvement than just mismanagement by Bishop Marcinkus. Think this is another indication of the Corleonesi becoming more aggressive towards muscling the Palermo families for control?"

Amatrano said, "Probably. Riina and Provenzano are ambitious after taking over the reins of the Corleonesi unified clan following Luciano Leggio's murder conviction in 1975. The Corleonesi are tightly organized against what amounts to a loose confederation of various Palermo families. The Falcone situation might be an attempt to exploit differences among the Palermo gangs. Or maybe the Corleonesi have designs on Banca Mercantile.

"Our exploitation of Falcone's romantic carelessness gives me another idea. With the escalating rivalry between the Palermo families and the Corleonesi there should be opportunities for us do damage through subversion."

"How's that?" Ferrazza asked.

"Spreading false rumors. Backed up with circumstantial situations to provide credibility. Set Sicily a blaze among the criminal elements by causing disruptive internal violence. Already a place on the edge of all-out war."

"Could also prove dangerous for civilians and police."

"I'm mindful of the risks, Antonio. The Mafia has had the upper hand in Sicily for far too long. Time we take risks to break the back of their hold over Western Sicily. Damaging Mafia money laundering operations takes on greater importance as a tactical objective. If the Corleonesi are targeting Banca Mercantile, opportunity exists for striking at both Mafia factions and those moving the money within international systems."

✝

Falcone went through further debriefing in Rome with a prosecuting magistrate. After spending a couple of uncomfortable nights in Guardia detention they transported him north to a more agreeable location for extended seclusion. Much remained to build a case to shut down Banca Mercantile. Falcone's information opened new avenues of investigation. To do real damage, the GICO needed evidence against the principal individuals. These included Mafiosi in control of the bank. Perhaps even Giuseppe Calò, the cashier of the Costa Nostra. Possibly evidence incriminating Umberto Ortolani.

Undoubtedly, the Sicilian Mafia considered Falcone a fugitive already placing a price on his head. He knew enough to destroy their lucrative money laundering conduit. The Guardia selected a safe house in the medieval town of Viterbo, 50 miles north of Rome. A two-bedroom apartment on a narrow street, walkable to restaurants. As a safe house, it had alternate exits to two different streets. With a population of 50,000, strangers did not stand out in Viterbo.

Two Guardia officers dressed in civilian clothing stayed with Falcone in the apartment and accompanied him on excursions about the city. Although a pleasant enough city, Viterbo was still a prison for Falcone. Not any of the trappings of the good life experienced in Palermo. Amatrano knew Falcone must be kept as comfortable as possible. Likely to be a lengthy time before his required testimony in court. Those watching over him were chosen for their congeniality.

After a week, Falcone was already descending into depression. Every aspect of his life altered left him disoriented. His future entirely uncertain. Resuming any sort of career as a lawyer now impossible even under an assumed name. Could he ever feel secure beyond the reach of the Mafia? His thoughts drifted to Olivia. That she was related to a Corleonesi boss did not necessarily make her a plant as suggested by the interrogating Guardia officer. The thought of never touching her again was difficult to bear.

†

Falcone's information provided enough detail to legally dismantle Banca Mercantile. Yet in practice, that was not that easy. For the most part, the stockholder-account holders must be assumed as victims rather than part of a conspiracy. Legitimate business owners forced to commingle their accounts with Mafia money under threat. Western Sicily was dominated by the Mafia as a shadow institution. Mafia threats carried the very real risk of loss of livelihood or physical harm to family. A way must be found to close the bank while protecting those victimized strawmen stockholders.

To accomplish that, the Guardia needed the assistance of the central bank, the Bank of Italy. Their reputation for protracted investigation leading nowhere a frustration for Italy's financial police. The most obvious example was the Bank's inability to make progress against Roberto Calvi and Banco Ambrosiano. It took years for Italy to ultimately convict Michele Sindona in absentia in 1976. He then received only three and a half years for 25 counts of banking law violations stemming from unaccounted transfers of $1.6 billion dollars from his Banca Privata Italiana to his own offshore shell companies. The United States did much better by finding Sindona guilty of 68 financial criminal counts and sentencing him to 25 years. Everything involving the Italian legal system moved at a crawl then frequently ended with unsatisfactory results.

Amatrano wanted to find a much quicker solution to put Banca Mercantile of Palermo out of business. With so many channels feeding illicit money into the bank, a better strategy seemed to focus on the outflow of funds from Banca Mercantile into the international environment of offshore shell companies. Paolo Falcone identified Umberto Ortolani as the key player in that next link in the process. Since Falcone even knew of Licio Gelli's name suggested Gelli's involvement. Somewhere along the laundering process the Vatican Bank also played a role.

Identifying Monsignor Donaggio connection meant Archbishop Tagliente was playing a role. In terms of involvement in murder, no one else within the Vatican possessed the means. This went beyond the incompetence of Bishop Paul Marcinkus. If Tagliente was manipulating the strings, who were his marionettes? Did Monsignor Donaggio act as his agent to broker services of Mafia hitmen?

From Father Orsini, Amatrano learned enough about Donaggio to consider that a very real possibility. Carlo Langella provided Emma with particulars gathered from Monsignor Orsini. "Ettore Donaggio was born in Naples in 1938. Father was an army officer killed during WWII. Mother's family were connected with the Camorra. His oldest uncle was a Camorra family underboss who took him and his sister with her three children under his protection. The uncle respected Donaggio's mother's wishes that her only son not become involved with the Camorra. Honoring his sister's wishes, the uncle arranged for Donaggio to enter a catholic seminary.

"Ordained a priest in 1962, he came to the Vatican in 1964 to a position in the Secretariate of State office. It was there that Bishop Tagliente recruited him. By this time, Tagliente was unofficially acting as the head of Vatican intelligence. Tagliente installed Donaggio in Sodalitium Pianum, Vatican counterintelligence. Donaggio excelled. All too well according to Father Orsini.

"Orsini ascribes Donaggio's fierce devotion to Tagliente as if to a Mafia don. Suspected violent acts attributed to organized crime that became convenient for Vatican interests might have origins in Vatican intelligence. While a part of S.P., Orsini never engaged in anything other than intelligence gathering. He does not claim to have specific knowledge of violence instigated by Tagliente or Donaggio. Anyway, Tagliente recognized Donaggio's services by nominating him for elevation to monsignor by Pope Paul in 1974. Monsignor being an honorary title bestowed by the pope."

Nicoletti asked Langella, "Does Father Orsini believe Donaggio could be our Vatican *black knight*?"

"Probably. Orsini has his own reasons for detesting Donaggio When Donaggio was elevated to monsignor and made head of S.P., Orsini said that was the reason he left the Vatican."

Relating all this to Frank, he said to her, "Excellent intel, Emma. You would make a good intelligence control officer running agents. Quite a network you've developed. Monsignor Scarpelli, Gabriel, your journalist associate Carlo, and especially the former Vatican intelligence agent Father Orsini."

She added, "And then of course I'm sleeping with a ranking officer in the Guardia di Finanza."

Frank kissed her. "Incentive enough to keep up your sexual attentions to maintain your high-value source."

She replied, "You should have no reason to complain. Speaking of information, I am getting close to concluding the first draft of my book. I intend to publicly expose Tagliente and his henchman Donaggio. Expose Vatican intelligence from its place of secrecy. The crowning revelation would be the exposure of Banca Mercantile as a Mafia conduit for moving illicit money. Including this latest development directly implicates the Vatican with the Mafia. Obviously, I can't do that until that information becomes public. What is happening there?"

"Working on it. Falcone gave us enough information to assemble a case. If not to a prosecuting magistrate for criminal charges at least enough to pressure the Bank of Italy to find sufficient irregularities to close it down. That will force Ortolani and Calò to create a new conduit to launder Mafia money."

"If the Bank of Italy closes down Banca Mercantile, does that become public information?"

"Oh yes. Free to use it in your book. Careful of course not to introduce any confidential information I provided."

†

It took Brother Gideon's contacts within the Bontade and Inzerillo Palermo Mafia families a week in which to uncover that

Paolo Falcone was engaged in an affair with a nurse at a Palermo hospital. From that information, Donaggio contacted a confidential source within the records department of Carabinieri headquarters in Rome.

The database returned an unexpected record for Olivia Zangheri. Investigated for the suspicious death of her husband in 1972, no criminal charges were ever brought. That happened in Corleone. Further background information led to Zangheri's relationship with Bernardo Provenzano, her maternal uncle and underboss of the unified Corleonesi clan. Whether Paolo Falcone knew his girlfriend was Corleonesi or not was irrelevant. Donaggio needed to establish if Falcone was dead, took flight for some reason, or in Italian police custody?

The answer to that took another several days to determine. If being held incognito by either the Carabinieri or the Guardia di Finanza, Donaggio needed higher access than available to his police informants. Tagliente contacted Licio Gelli for assistance. Gelli's extensive network of individuals willing to engage in trading information included access to certain senior police officials. Gelli also had a vested financial interest in Mafia money laundering.

Gelli replied in a matter of hours on Tagliente's secure Vatican telephone line from a public telephone. "Paolo Falcone is in GdF custody by the GICO division. Being held incognito outside of Rome. A most regrettable complication, Archbishop."

Already dismayed by the setback, Tagliente ignored Gelli's comment. "Since the woman is related to the Corleonesi, how do they fit into this?"

Gelli replied, "Before contacting my police sources, I took the liberty of calling Bernado Provenzano. When I reported that Falcone was seeing his niece and now in police custody, he became angry. Said Falcone knows too much. Must be eliminated."

"Did Provenzano know of his niece and Falcone?"

"I got the impression that learning of the relationship did not come as a surprise. Maybe he even put his niece up to it. At any rate, he said he would personally see to the elimination of Falcone.

I gave him the particulars of Falcone's location in the town of Viterbo north of Rome."

Tagliente would prefer to have retained operational control. However, if Provenzano wanted to do the dirty work, it deflected potential allegations against the Vatican should the killing prove messy. "Give me those details of Falcone's location, Licio. Best if I have my people monitor Provenzano's operation being so far away from Sicily."

Disconnecting the call, he considered this latest development. He did not trust the Corleonesis. Salvatore Riina was an overly violent psychopath. Bernado Provenzano is not much better. Yet they might be taking over the Western Sicilian Mafia. With Falcone giving up everything about Banca Mercantile, the Palermo families would soon become cut off from accessing international financial systems to launder money. The Vatican Bank needed Mafia revenue. That meant quickly reconstructing a new conduit for moving Mafia funds with Banca Mercantile already compromised.

When Donaggio reported later by telephone from Palermo, Tagliente related his conversation with Gelli. Giving Donaggio the details where the GICO was holding Falcone, he said, "Send Brother Gideon to Viterbo tomorrow. If Provenzano does not act by Friday, Brother Gideon is to take care of the matter himself. If possible, without collateral damage."

CHAPTER 20

Rome, Italy | Spring & Summer 1981

After almost three weeks, Paolo Falcone was a wreck. Confined with his keepers with nothing but television as a diversion was wearing thin. Too much wine and cigarettes made matters worse. Viterbo might be an interesting medieval city, but daily outings offered little interest. Realization set in that confinement here might continue for an indeterminate duration. Eventually expecting only transition to a miserable life under an assumed name while forever looking over his shoulder induced a deepening depression.

It was an overcast day when Falcone and his two Guardia bodyguards came out of a narrow street into a small piazza at lunchtime. Few people were about, all appeared to be locals. From behind them came the distinct sound of a woman's heels clicking on the cobble stones. All three men turned.

Falcone could scarcely believe his eyes. It was Olivia Zangheri. Even with dark glasses, no question it was her. The trim figure he knew so well dressed in a knee-length wool skirt and tight sweater. He stopped and his mouth dropped as she walked past. His minders did the same. Smiling, one said as Zangheri walked past them, "Look at that ass will you!"

As Zangheri took a table outside a trattoria across the piazza, the other Guardia agent turned to Paolo and said, "How about we have some lunch while feasting our eyes on that sexy woman."

Falcone just nodded and made for the trattoria. What the hell was she doing here? How did she find him? Was she working for the police? As a spy for her uncle? All the time they were together?

Zangheri had just lit a cigarette as the three men took a table facing her. Only one other table was occupied by a couple of men drinking wine.

After the men heard Olivia ordering a glass of wine, she left her cigarette smoldering in the ashtray and stood up. She then walked inside the trattoria toward the back where a sign read *toilette.*

Falcone could barely contain himself. Turning to his minders, "Got to go to the toilet."

One Guardia agent said, "Maybe you could try asking the beautiful woman to join us for lunch. That should cheer you up, Falcone." Both Guardia agents laughed as Falcone walked into the trattoria.

Falcone turned down a short hallway at the back with two doors each marked *toilette.* Standing next to one of the doors, Olivia appeared trying to turn one of the doorknobs with her left hand as if it was locked.

Falcone whispered, "Olivia! What are you doing here?"

Olivia turned abruptly to face Falcone. Without a word, she extracted a hypodermic from her handbag with her right hand. Without uttering a word, she jammed it into his chest simultaneously depressed the plunger emptying most of the cylinder. The same way she killed her abusive husband.

Falcone reacted with confusion but within seconds began suffering the onset of symptoms of potassium cyanide. Leaving the hypodermic stuck into Falcone, Olivia pulled open the door to the toilet and pushed him inside before he collapsed.

Potassium cyanide absorbs quickly into the system. By preventing cells from using oxygen effectively, the effects become almost immediate. Falcone's heart rate began increasing rapidly while struggling for breath. A look of confusion overtook his face from lack of oxygen to the brain. As he slumped against the back wall of the toilet then sliding down to the floor, Olivia reached down and removed the hypodermic dropping it back into her handbag.

Returning to her table, she took a sip of wine while still standing. Laying money on the table, she then walked out. The Guardia officers smiled as they watched her exit.

After five minutes, one officer became concerned about Falcone's absence. He walked to the toilet area to check. Knocking on each toilet door and receiving no reply, the officer tried the first door that opened at his touch. Seeing Falcone on the floor with his chin slumped on his chest, he reached to check for a pulse at the neck. Falcone's heart had already stopped.

After confirming that Falcone was dead, he ran out of the trattoria attempting to spot the woman. However, Olivia Zangheri was already out of sight using the warren of narrow streets to make her escape.

Although not involved in the assassination, Brother Gideon stood in the piazza after following Falcone and his minders. Armed with photographs of Falcone and Zangheri, he was just a spectator. His objective was ensuring the death of Paolo Falcone. Either by Provenzano's Mafia hitmen or by his own hand. Surprised by seeing Olivia Zangheri, he allowed the scenario to play out. When she left and the police alarm sounded a short time later, he knew the woman was involved. More finesse then typical for a Mafia hit, but at least subtle enough to avoid killing the police guarding the target.

Falcone's death was confirmed when police and medical personnel descended on the piazza. Identifying both of Falcone's guards, Brother Gideon knew that the body under the sheet wheeled out on a gurney was that of Paolo Falcone.

†

Amatrano was dismayed by the death of Paolo Falcone. While Falcone gave up all the useful information on the operation of Banca Mercantile, his death still deprived the state of using him as a witness in a trial. Yet the most troubling aspect of Falcone's murder was identifying where he was being held. How did Monsignor Donaggio obtain that information? That could only have come from a source within the Guardia. Did Vatican intelligence have that breadth of reach?

What about the manner in which Falcone was killed? Likely by the hand of Olivia Zangheri after the Guardia officers identified her from photographs. Without physical evidence the Guardia would not be able to get an indictment, much less a conviction. Was this nothing more than a Mafia hit? Not by using their usual crude methods. Obviously not by the Palermo families. Was Olivia Zangheri part of a Corleonesi strategy to take over Western Sicily?

The only bright spot was unexpected progress with the Bank of Italy. Guardia experts did outstanding work in assembling sufficient evidence to raise questions about the stockholders. That proved the weakness of the organization of Banca Mercantile because of its commingling with stockholder legitimate business. Targeted Guardia di Finanza audits of these firms uncovered widespread evidence of fraudulent accounting.

The Guardia additionally presented evidence to a prosecuting magistrate to suspend Ortolani's operating license for his consulting firm Bologna Investimenti S.R.L. for currency violations. This cut off the outflow of funds into international financial systems. The Guardia produced enough evidence for the Bank of Italy to suspend Banca Mercantile from engaging in any international financial transactions. Domestically any inter-financial institutional transactions became subject to oversight. Effectively, Banca Mercantile ceased to be a channel for Mafia money laundering. The financial interests of the Mafia and those benefiting from access to such sums of money that also provided lucrative commissions became the latest crisis for the financial conspirators. This included the Vatican Bank, Umberto Ortolani, Licio Gelli, and most of all Roberto Calvi.

Roberto Calvi was most affected by his growing debt exposure aggravated by continually mounting losses of his Banco Ambrosiano banking empire. Calvi was surviving only by using his foreign subsidiaries in a never-ending shell game of moving money around. Filling a hole from a loss by creating another hole elsewhere. A gigantic Ponzi scheme falling suddenly under additional pressure with the inability to put Mafia funds into play.

The Vatican Bank was so deeply intertwined with Calvi's network of foreign subsidiaries, they remained his only potential lifeline. Bishop Marcinkus continued receiving intense pressure from the Bank of Italy stemming from growing questions of financial irregularities of Banco Ambrosiano. The publication by the *New York Times* of the stolen Vatican Secret Archive documents, many signed by Marcinkus, added to mounting pressure. Marcinkus held off the Bank of Italy only through claiming the sovereignty of the Holy See. With internal pressure from Archbishop Tagliente, Marcinkus held Calvi at arm's length as Calvi's appeals intensified for requesting a Vatican bailout loan of staggering proportion.

So far, Pope John Paul stood aloof and silent following recommendations from Archbishop Tagliente and Cardinal-Secretary of State Casaroli. Tagliente's strategy of holding fast by supporting Marcinkus, stonewalling Calvi, and not engaging in public debate, placed Tagliente under increased pressure with his overseeing of Vatican Bank operations. Now Tagliente faced the added problem of the loss of important Vatican revenue from money laundering fees.

Tagliente soon faced another disaster that would complicate efforts at reshaping the lucrative laundering channel for the massive sums of Mafia money from international drug trafficking. Armed with search warrants, the Italian Carabinieri raided Licio Gelli's residence and office in Arezzo in March. A compulsive keeper of records, Gelli inexplicably left a treasure trove of incriminating documents unsecured at his office. Among the papers were records of membership of 953 members of the Propaganda Due Masonic Lodge of which Gelli was the worshipful master. The lodge charter dissolved by the governing Grande Oriente d'Italia Masonic organization continued operating for years outside Italian law prohibiting secret organizations. The list included individuals from every walk of public and private life in Italy.

Forty-eight members of Parliament, four cabinet ministers, the heads of the three Italian secret services magistrates, senior law enforcement, business executives, bankers, and even Roman Catholic prelates. More importantly investigators recovered thirty-two manilla folders containing photocopies of bank records and transactions illicit payments to government officials.

Exceptionally careless having kept such material poorly hidden, it would prove Licio Gelli's downfall. Although he received an advance tip of the raid, it proved too late. The documentation discovered by the police not only exposed official corruption, but incriminated Gelli in political conspiracy, bribery, fraud, and even espionage. Gelli fled to Switzerland to avoid arrest. From there he flew to Uruguay using an Argentine passport.

The confiscated records also included incriminating evidence of criminal activities of Umberto Ortolani. Ortolani followed Gelli into exile by fleeing to Brazil. Both Gelli and Ortolani had extensive business interests in South America along with influential political connections while out of reach for extradition by Italy.

For Archbishop Tagliente, this new setback would make reconstructing a new money laundering conduit under Vatican Bank control more difficult. Yet Ortolani and Gelli were not completely out of the picture. Both could still operate remotely from South America. Gelli in particular was necessary with his relationship with *Cosa Nostra cashier* Giuseppe Calò. Gelli also demonstrated having direct access to the Corleonesis who appeared set to move against the Palmero families in taking over lucrative Sicilian drug trafficking operations.

Another event made reconstructing a new money laundering network more imperative. The Guardia di Finanza recently arrested Roberto Calvi at his flat on Via Frua in Milan. Within hours, Calvi was sitting in a jail cell in Lodi twenty miles south of Milan.

While in jail, a despondent Calvi tried to commit suicide, or at least made it appear as such. After two months of incarceration, an Italian court convicted Calvi of illegally exporting $26.4 million dollars to Switzerland. Sentenced to four years in prison along with a $11.7 million fine, he was released on bail pending appeal.

Restrictions from the conviction placed financial transactions of Banco Ambrosiano effectively preventing Calvi from moving money throughout his network of foreign subsidiary shell companies and banks. Borrowing hundreds of millions of dollars now became the only way to stave off financial collapse. That would make Calvi more desperate and therefore dangerous to the Vatican. The Vatican Bank remained his only hope for financial rescue. Bishop Marcinkus had already cooled to Clavi's entreaties for funds. Tagliente reinforced that position by implying that Pope John Paul had said as much to him and Cardinal Casaroli.

†

Several weeks after the Falcone incident, the Corleonesis make their move against the Palermo families. Mafia boss Stefano Bontade was driving home from celebrating his forty-second birthday on the night of 23 April. Stopped at a traffic light in his Alfa Romero on Via Aloi in Palermo, a motorcycle with two riders pulled alongside. The rider on the rear sprayed bursts from an AK-47 assault rifle leaving Bontade slumped in the front seat, his face unrecognizable.

Three weeks later, the same Corleonesi assassins shot to death Bontade's close associate Salvatore Inzerillo outside the home of his mistress. The killings of the most prominent of Palermo Mafia bosses triggered the onset of what would become known as the Second Mafia War.

†

For the Vatican, the year of 1981 continued to prove challenging. Pope John Paul II appeared among a crowd of the faithful gathered in St. Peter's square, riding in his Fiat *popemobile* in the late afternoon of Wednesday 13 May. Jumping out from the crowd to get closer, an assassin fired multiple shots from a 9mm pistol striking Pope John Paul II and two bystanders. One round struck the pontiff in the torso narrowly missing vital organs with another round struck his left index finger. Gravely wounded,

Pope John Paul was rushed to a hospital where he would survive. The attempted assassination by a Turkish terrorist shook the world. Italy continued to struggle with its never-ending paroxysms of violence.

†

Surviving his gunshot wounds allowed Pope John Paul to remain apart from the renewed public backlash about the list of P2 membership including many Catholic prelates. In fairness what Licio's records labelled as members of Propaganda Due, may not have applied for membership. All had some connection with Gelli, but none of the churchmen were implicated in Gelli's criminal activities. Still, it became another awkward allegation in view of longstanding papal denunciations of freemasonry as irreconcilable with Catholic doctrine.

Nicoletti's publisher withheld the release of her new book until July when it was clear the pope would be completely recovered from his injuries. While she was scathing in her indictment of Pope Paul VI, Pope John Paul II also came under attack. Not the least for his failure to clean up what was now becoming called the Vatican Bank Scandal. Bishop Marcinkus remained as president of the IOR. Reporting for *Il Sole 24 Or* Nicoletti routinely published articles about the IOR stonewalling investigative efforts of the Bank of Italy by hiding behind its status as a sovereign country outside Italian legal jurisdiction. A convenience for the tiny108-acre Vatican City where its handful of citizens mostly resided in Rome outside the Vatican walls.

However, when Nicoletti's book *For God & Gold* came out in both Italian and English formats, the scandal escalated to an international outcry. No longer was this solely about questionable financial dealings. Going further, she made broad allegations that the murder of Gabriel Eisenberg and attempts on her life *must* be the work of the Vatican. Who else would have known of the missing documents published by the *New York Times*? The bombing that killed Gabriel Eisenberg had the signature of the Mafia. The second attempt on her life resulted in the death of known Mafiosi with criminal records from Palermo Sicilian Mafia families left no question as to the perpetrators. Yet was the Mafia acting on orders from the Vatican? Who specifically? Motivated by what?

She went further by casting questions of participation in violence by the Vatican secret service. Falling short of making direct individual accusations, she named Archbishop Marcello Tagliente as a prelate of interest. His official position as Archivist of the Vatican Secret Archive placed him in a position to discover missing documents long before made public by the *New York Times*. Identifying Tagliente as unofficial operational head of Vatican intelligence, formerly known as the Santa Alleanza, in English *Holy Alliance*, sometimes referred to as the *Entity*, made for an explosive new revelation. What is the function of an intelligence service for the Holy See? Is there significance of the roles Archbishop Tagliente serves within the Holy See? The Vatican Secret Archive and the Vatican intelligence service report directly to the pope. The same holds true for the Vatican Bank, the IOR. The Roman Curia serving as the administrative body of the Holy See has no jurisdiction over all these institutions. Might Archbishop Tagliente play a role in the functioning of the Vatican Bank?

For God & Gold read with the pace of a suspense thriller with Nicoletti's violent experiences embellished with little known Vatican history. Promoted by advance reviews as captivating and provocative, the book immediately went to the top of international bestseller lists within days of public release.

That the Vatican even had an intelligence service was not common knowledge. Nicoletti went into detail explaining the Vatican Holy Alliance going back to its creation in the 16th century. That creation for the sordid purpose of removing Protestant Queen Elizabeth I from the English throne by assassination. Nicoletti then went on to introduce newly acquired information about the activities of Vatican intelligence since WWII. This included evidence of Vatican intelligence facilitating escape routes to South America for war criminals she previously wrote about in her 1963 book. To this she added information provided by Father Orsini identifying specific incidents of engaging in acts of murder. On the dustjacket of *For God & Gold*, a book review comment by the

New York Times read, *Emma Nicoletti makes a compelling case for Vatican intelligence possibly reverting to earlier times of secular excess.*

CHAPTER 21

Rome, Italy | Autum & Winter 1981

Few outside the Vatican knew the name of Archbishop Marcello Tagliente. The publication of Nicoletti's book changed all that. The *New York Times* even ran a specific article on the front page titled, *Who is Archbishop Tagliente?* The column went on to repeat excerpts from Nicoletti's book, adding additional material. Subsequent NYT articles dealt with explaining the little understood byzantine structure of the Vatican. Of special interest were those institutions not part of Roman Curia administrative governance. It provided clarity for explaining the Vatican Bank's ability to remain unresponsive and seemingly not held accountable for involvement in the continuing saga of the Italian Banking Scandal. The special document repository of the Vatican Secret Archive being separate from the Vatican Library proved a little-known revelation. Why the need for a special documents' repository separate to the Vatican Library? A place to bury uncomfortable classified material? Why the need for a religious institution to now have an intelligence agency? Why the need for private bank operating separately in secrecy from the Vatican central bank, the Administration of the Patrimony of the Apostolic See, the ASPA and outside the administrative governance of the Curia?

It was the existence of a Vatican intelligence service that provoked the most tantalizing public interest. For Cardinal-Secretary of State Agostino Casaroli, Nicoletti's book became yet another public relations disaster. Cloistered in his office with his close friend and ally Archbishop Luigi Poggi they discussed the more subtle problem of Archbishop Tagliente.

"Archbishop Tagliente has become a liability, Luigi. The Holy Father made a mistake by allowing him to take responsibility for the IOR."

"I agree Agostino. Far too much power vested without oversight."

"Yet the Holy Father remains a firm supporter of Marcinkus. Even with the public fallout, he inexplicably allows Marcinkus to remain at the helm of the IOR. Tagliente took that as an opportunity to expand his influence by providing the Holy Father with a way of keeping Marcinkus."

"Are you suggesting something to remedy this problem, Agostino?" Poggi asked.

Casaroli said, "It is impossible for me to answer the public uproar generated by the Nicoletti book. With the Holy Father still recuperating from his wounds, it falls to me to represent the voice of the Holy See. I must at the least consult with the Holy Father about how to proceed. Unlike his recent predecessors, he is not indecisive. I am asking a favor of you Luigi. Accompany me in a private audience with the Holy Father. I feel dutybound to press for something be done to curtail the authority of Archbishop Tagliente."

Poggi understood his presence would constitute endorsing whatever position Casaroli intended to present. "What exactly do you wish to present to the Holy Father?"

"Largely to continue avoiding any public argument by getting into any details associated with the financial scandal, but also to limit Archbishop Tagliente's functional role. Wait for the storm to subside. Provide no information that will sustain public interest. I suggest making a public statement clarifying the subject of Vatican intelligence service. Not by outright denial of its existence. While we avoid acknowledging its existence, it is a poorly protected secret. I would suggest making a declarative explanation by adding the caveat that what is sometimes referred to as Vatican intelligence or secret service is nothing more than gathering information from our apostolic nuncios who are ecclesiastical diplomats. This is the normal function of our worldwide spiritual outreach for understanding the many secular environments of the faithful."

Poggi replied, "How will that prove helpful, Agostino?"

"By denying the inaccurate assertion that Archbishop Tagliente serves in some fictionalized role as a covert head of an intelligence service. Within the confines of the Vatican, you are understood to be the official head of the Vatican secret service. For outsiders, let that remain an indistinct characterization of your position as heading the Vatican Secretariat of State Section for Relations with States. In effect, supervisor of the corps of apostolic nuncios. Foreign Minister of the Vatican"

Poggi did not like anything about Casaroli's proposal.

"I'm not convinced the Holy Father will find favor with your suggestion, Agostino. He may prefer to remain simply silent on the question of the existence of a Vatican intelligence service."

Irrespective of Poggi's reluctance, Casaroli remained his superior. Pope John Paul received them together in a private audience in his study. Although it had been four months since the wounding of the pontiff, he limited his duties to avoid fatigue and undue stress.

The pope allowed Casaroli to present his proposal before responding, "I appreciate your acceptance of this burden on your shoulders, Agostino. However, I believe proceeding no differently than before the publication of this book. It is nothing more than the latest assemblage of hearsay and unproven accusations for financial gain. Popularized fiction dressed up as exposé.

"Let us proceed as Archbishop Tagliente counselled some time ago over allegations of IOR mismanagement. This book tries to further implicate the IOR in illicit activity. This journalist is after all a reporter for a financial newspaper. We shall stay the course. Make no public pronouncements other than stating the Holy See will not engage in public debate over allegations having no basis in fact. The author has manufactured a narrative by weaving stolen confidential information into a work of fiction."

The papal audience ended abruptly. Once outside the papal apartments, Casaroli said to Poggi, "Regrettably, I believe the Holy Father is much angered by the book's association of him directly into the financial scandal by those published documents that he initialed."

Days later they learned something of the nature of Pope John Paul II.

Since his election as pontiff, Pope John Paul II held a fondness for Bishop Paul Marcinkus not unlike that exhibited by his predecessor Pope Paul VI. That even extended to ignoring advice from several senior cardinals to remove Marcinkus from the IOR.

Without fanfare just days after Casaroli's and Poggi's meeting came a press release from the Vatican Press Office. Likely the only other person with foreknowledge was John Paul's private secretary Father Stanisław Dziwisz. The release stated simply the elevation of Bishop Paul Marcinkus to President of the Pontifical Commission for the State of Vatican City, effectively making him the governor of Vatican City. The elevation also granted Marcinkus the corresponding ecclesiastical status of archbishop.

To Casaroli and Poggi this was a stark demonstration of John Paul's stubbornness and willfulness. And the fact that he held absolute authority. Marcinkus seemed an indirect way of communicating his support of Archbishop Tagliente. Casaroli took that thought further. Not necessarily the person of Tagliente, but Tagliente's role as the means of John Paul pursuing his personal agenda without interference by the Curia. This pope was no passive figurehead to be directed by Vatican bureaucrats.

John Paul II installed Luigi Poggi as head of the Section for Relations with States. In effect, supervision of the apostolic nuncios. Poggi was himself apostolic nuncio to Poland and close to Karol Wojtyła before his elevation to pope. Poggi knew the details for channeling covert United States Central Intelligence funds to the Polish trade union Solidarity, including the utility of Tagliente's covert network of agents. Tagliente and Marcinkus therefore became essential for John Paul's obsession with destabilizing the communist Soviet Union puppet government of Poland.

Luigi Poggi knew more than most other senior churchman about the workings of the Vatican secret service. With the surprise announcement of the promotion of Marcinkus, Poggi commiserated with a troubled Casaroli by saying, "While Nicoletti's book made public the name of Archbishop Tagliente, it did not touch on details of how Vatican intelligence operated. Cloaked in more secrecy than any other sector of the Holy See, Tagliente continues to be of concern. With this indirect expression of confidence by the Holy Father, Tagliente will become further emboldened."

A disheartened Casaroli replied, "I fear the depth of injury to the Holy See with these continuing public relations catastrophes. Is there no way to constrain Tagliente from making matters worse? You know more of the inner workings of Vatican intelligence than anyone, Luigi."

"Archbishop Tagliente has troubled me for some time. His reputation as someone apart from our ecclesiastical community is well-deserved. Feared by the Curia is not an exaggeration. His decades-long tenure spanning several pontificates is unprecedented. I cannot offer a clear solution. However, we are not without resources, Agostino. I have certain useful sources of information.

"Tagliente may be secretive, but he does not function in a vacuum. He demonstrated his intelligence skills following WWII. As this new book revealed, Tagliente personally participated in the logistics of Pope Pius's unfortunate efforts to allow certain misguided churchmen to assist criminals of the most horrific stripe escaping justice. A strategy of protection by plausible deniability is nothing new. If there is any truth in the accusations of Tagliente committing deeds as foul as murder, it will be through his principal lieutenant, Monsignor Ettore Donaggio."

"What do you know about Donaggio?"

"Donaggio heads the counterintelligence unit *Sodalitium Pianum*. It was Tagliente that nominated Donaggio to that position and lobbied Pope Paul to bestow recognition as monsignor *for unspecified services to the Church* says much about Tagliente's influence."

Casaroli said, "Tagliente and Donaggio are powerful adversaries as the Holy Father just demonstrated. Yet they have enemies within the Holy See. Perhaps we should consider engaging in our own counterintelligence operation, Luigi."

Poggi replied to Casaroli, "Perhaps. But counsel with the utmost caution, Agostino. Secrecy inside our cloistered world is difficult to maintain. I may however have resources outside these walls that can be called upon to monitor the activities of Monsignor Donaggio."

†

The day of the press release announcing the promotion of Marcinkus, Pope John Paul summoned Tagliente for a private audience.

"Many of those I most trust are undoubtedly surprised by my decision to elevate Bishop Marcinkus. While disturbed by the betrayal of a trusted archive priest, it is necessary to look at the larger picture. I acknowledge the professional shortcomings of Marcinkus but not his devotion to the Holy See and to my person.

"It is paramount that we weather this terrible financial storm without undue damage to Vatican revenue producing investments. As my predecessors going back to His Holiness Pius XI realized, the spiritual impact of the Roman Catholic Church rests in large part on its secular relevance. Within that secular environment we realize it is necessary to survive in the secular world to promote our ecclesiastical mission. That is your value to the Holy See, Archbishop Tagliente. And your burden. I read somewhere a quote from a seventeenth-century cardinal named Paluzzi degli Albertoni. Your predecessor as the reputed head of *Santa Alleanza* during the pontificate of Alexander VII. In substance it stated by example that if the pope ordered the killing of someone in defense of the faith, he speaks with the voice of God. I recall it as an extreme example of the burden of authority vested in those occupying the seat of Saint Peter.

"I mention this now to express my trust in you to do whatever necessary to preserve the Holy See, Archbishop. While I pray your responsibilities do not extend to extremes of violence, I shall trust in your devotion to the Faith to make the right decisions. Receive my blessing, Archbishop."

Tagliente dropped to a knee and kissed the pope's ring.

†

Dressed in a gray business suit, Tagliente took a taxi that evening to Rome Termini train station for the thirty-minute trip to Frascati. When the release of Nicoletti's book made headline news, Isabella Leonardi immediately trained down from her Lake Como residence to be with him. His name now prominently featured in the international press must prove disturbing. His efforts to keep his name concealed from public recognition shattered by the book's implicit allegations of wrongdoing. She must be at his side. Far more than just lovers, she knew she was his closest confidant. Intellectual equals. After being together for twelve years she knew much about his secretive responsibilities.

The darkest of those secrets Tagliente still withheld. Isabella possessed a strong Catholic faith that could never condone the use of murder regardless for the benefit of the Holy See. Nor could engaging in relations with organized criminal elements for financial benefit have a moral rationale. With the publication of Nicoletti's book, he must now explain more to Isabella than he wished to answer by deflecting the public accusations with reasoned explanations.

After a long embrace when he stepped into the villa, "She said. We have the villa to ourselves for the whole weekend. Regina prepared dinner for us now being kept warm in the oven before leaving a short time ago. Shall we have a drink and relax?"

"That would be nice."

"How are you doing, Marcello?"

He smiled, "Managing. Disappointed with Monsignor Scarpelli for betraying a sacred trust by removing confidential papers from the Archive belonging to the Holy Father but that scurrilous letter personally attacking me that the journalist published in her book. Nonetheless, my responsibilities are often beset with setbacks. The nature of what I do has recently been dominated by damage control. Reacting to circumstances does not always follow a plan."

Settling next to each other on a sofa with their drinks, Tagliente said, "I already feel the stress melting away just being here with you, Isabella. Admittedly the last several months have been trying. I see you have a copy of the book."

The book with its unmistakable dustjacket lay on the coffee table in front of them. "Got it at Milano Centrale when I changed trains. Once on the train, I read the beginning where the author recited the assassination attempts on her life there at the train station. Been reading the book all day. Accusing the Vatican of murder and the second assassination is bad enough without supporting evidence. Very displeasing with how she wove your name into her larger narrative, leaving the impression you might be responsible."

"To be expected by journalists. Sensationalism is lucrative."

"Is your position threatened by the publicity from Nicoletti's book?"

"I do not believe so. I am too valuable to the pope, especially with my added responsibilities for the Vatican Bank. The banking scandal remains a grave concern for the pontiff. Nicoletti's book is really about that larger issue. She just sensationalized the narrative by recounting the violent attacks she regrettably suffered. The day after the press release announcing the promotion of Bishop Marcinkus IOR, the Holy Father summoned me for a private audience. Emphasized the importance of my areas of responsibilities. Expressed his full confidence in my duties and gave me his blessing."

Isabella said. "Who do you believe was responsible for the attacks on her that led to the death of her American colleague?"

"Obviously the Sicilian Mafiosi executed the bombing and the attempted shooting. They left two of their dead as evidence. Nicoletti makes much out the stolen Vatican documents pointing to Vatican involvement. That ignores the larger body of evidence of

Sindona and Calvi having been directly connected with the Mafia. Sindona is even Sicilian with an early history of working with the Mafia. Then there are others connected with these notorious bankers. I believe it was someone from this collective group of conspirators that somehow learned of the missing documents. Their Mafia partners simply acted in their violently crude style."

Isabella asked, "Yet if the Vatican Bank has been victimized, how is that Marcinkus remains in charge? And why did the pope seemingly reward him by elevating him to archbishop with increased responsibilities?"

"Ah, those are good questions of which I do not have answers. Everything within the Holy See moves to its own logic. None more so than the thinking of the pontiff. Cloaked with absolute authority as if speaking for God, his pronouncements are above question for those of us serving in the Vatican..

"I can only speculate. Pope John Paul is fiercely loyal toward those he feels a particular affection. Paul Marcinkus is among those. Cardinal-Secretary of State Casaroli is also among those. The pope's kind words spoken to me in reassurance make me believe I too enjoy his affection as well as trust in the services I render."

Isabella knew that he was the operational head of the Vatican secret service. However, Tagliente's sanitized version left out elaborating on details of activities necessary to the function of a two-thousand-year-old spiritual institution. She knew of the existence of *Sodalitium Pianum* and Monsignor Ettore Donaggio. The need for a Vatican counterintelligence service seemed even more obscure, but she avoided confrontive questions. Tagliente explained the reason for the pope's reliance on him was managing circumstances through covert means to ameliorate crises that invariably arose. While unsatisfactory, she left it at that.

"Operating unofficially allows me to work my network of agents and sources as necessary to achieve results. The accepted head is Archbishop Poggi with the logic of intelligence gathering coming under his role as head of the Section for Relations with States. In effect, Poggi is the supervising prelate of the diplomatic corps of apostolic nuncios. An obvious organization for gathering foreign intelligence useful to the Holy See."

"What about Monsignor Donaggio? Why the need for counterintelligence?"

"For the reason that the influence of the Holy See has incalculable importance. Agents of every foreign and domestic association have an interest in knowing and affecting pontifical policy. Unfortunately, churchmen are human beings with many of the same undesirable proclivities. The function of *Sodalitium Pianum* is internal security to guard against unwarranted intrusion. Originated in the early part of the 20th century to protect against infiltration with the rise of intelligence services in Europe.

"The value of resources under my direction is acquiring information. Without revealing methods, this entire attack on the Vatican Bank stems from ill-advised associations with outsiders. Clever outsiders, but not properly vetted. Vatican intelligence was prohibited from interfering with Pope Paul VI's personal decisions placing these individuals in positions of trust. Positions which allowed for manipulating the devoted but financially unqualified Bishop Marcinkus into making massive loans involving complex transactions using foreign subsidiaries in tax haven countries.

"It is my covert group that burrowed into understanding the methods and players associated with this extraordinary financial labyrinth. Given time, that information will allow the Vatican Bank to extricate itself from this quagmire and continue its vital contribution to funding the Holy See. That is why I offered to assume oversight of the Vatican Bank. All my duties are shielded by exceptional secrecy within a body known for its secrecy. Allows me freedom of action but comes with the drawback of becoming a target of attack.

"As to your question about by trusted subordinate Monsignor Donaggio, his people have been instrumental in uncovering information otherwise hidden from us. That's what they do best."

CHAPTER 22

Palermo, Sicily | Spring 1982

The Second Mafia War began its second year of sustained violence in northwestern Sicily. In Italian called the *Mattanza* meaning slaughter, it altered every aspect of life in western Sicily. It began with the murder of Palermo Mafia boss Stefano Bontade. The instigator was Corleonesi Mafia Don Salvatore 'Totò' Riina. Riina representing the unified Mafia clan from the outlaying area of Corleone was part of the three-member Sicilian Mafia Commission established in 1970 to maintain order among the Sicilian families. The other two were Palermo bosses Stefano Bontade and Gaetano Badalamenti. Bontade's murder was an act of unexpected betrayal by Riina.

The explosion of Mafia internecine violence afforded an unprecedented opportunity for Amatrano to begin his subversive campaign against the Mafia. The plan was simple. Arrest known Mafiosi on charges however weak and unlikely for successfully prosecute. Prosecution, not being the objective, the intention was solely intended to sow dissent. Creating sufficient distrust to cause the violence to turn inward. Threaten the arrestee with either turning informer or risk the police floating rumors of their cooperation. Insidious but effective. In the climate of paranoia among the Mafia, even if suspected as deliberate police misinformation, it became safer for the Mafia to act than risk an informer within their midst. With open warfare between rival factions, the climate for using disinformation became perfect.

While the GICO division of the Guardia di Finanza focused on going after Mafia finances, the Italian Carabinieri shifted resources to combat the violent lawlessness consuming western Sicily. Carabinieri General Carlo Alberto dalla Chiesa arrived in Palermo the first of May to assume command as prefect for Palermo.

GICO chief of staff Lt. Colonel Antonio Ferrazza said to Amatrano, "Since you want to attack the Mafia from within, Frank, how about coordinating your efforts with the Carabinieri? Perhaps they might want to join forces. Sending General Carlo dalla Chiesa to Palermo signals our sister police force means business. He is a division general no less. Experienced working against the Mafia in Sicily ten years ago and against the *Red Brigades* in the north since then."

"I will do just that, Antonio. I will be in Palermo next week."

"Yes, I know. Starting your subversive efforts by getting close to the source."

"That's what you hired me to do."

Ferrazza smiled. "Attempting to turn Olivia Zangheri is a bold move. She might not survive your offer that she cannot refuse."

Amatrano shrugged. "Well, this is war. Must expect casualties."

"Are you taking along just those two officers that lost Falcone?"

"Yes. A smaller team is easier for disguising our presence in enemy territory. They're good men. Motivated to make restitution for what they see as their failure to properly protect Falcone."

"This is truly a war, Frank. You take care. Would hate to lose you."

†

Making advance preparations in Rome, Amatrano's two officers secured a suitable vehicle to disguise as an ambulance. They chose a Fiat Daily light utility van recently delivered to the

Guardia. Not yet painted with Guardia colors and fitted for border duty, it was already fitted with a bubble emergency light and siren with seats for four people including the driver. They took the basic vehicle painted white then applied specifically printed vinyl decals converting its appearance to an ambulance.

Before leaving Rome for the long drive to Palermo, Amatrano rehearsed the plan with his team by defining the mission emphasizing the critical points while allowing improvisation to adapt to unforeseen circumstances. He personally took photographs of the local hospital where Olivia Zangheri worked. Part of the planning involved their clothing. The two officers wore uniforms of the fictitious ambulance service displayed on the side of the van. "Starting now, we do not use our real names." Pointing to each he said, "You are Abel and you are Baker."

"And you, Sir?"

"Doctor, of course. Just like my nametag reads. *Doctore Mors. Mors* is Latin for death. *Doctor Death* seemed appropriate."

They left Rome for the twelve-hour drive to Palermo on the east side of Sicily. They would spend the night in Villabate on the eastern outskirts of Metropolitan Palermo. Villabate was located at the junction of the highway running thirty miles south to Corleone and the main east-west coastal highway between Palermo and Messina on the northeast corner of Sicily. Their van displayed the logo *Servizi Medici Messina.* The name identified them as from eastern Sicily but still provided a reason for their presence in remote Corleone. Should explanation be needed, they were here to transport an elderly terminally ill patient to Messina to be closer to her family.

After a good night's rest, they rehearsed how they would seize the woman. Amatrano used the same team of local Guardia agents that participated with the seizure of Paolo Falcone for maintaining surveillance on Zangheri. They established her work schedule as the second shift at the hospital from 5pm to 2am. She drove her own car. Lived in an apartment two miles from the hospital. At 5pm, Amatrano received a two-way radio transmission. "Target arrived at location in her work uniform."

The local officers would continue maintaining surveillance and report in each hour. They were carefully concealed in a stand of trees using binoculars. The exterior lighting around the hospital provided a well-lit field of vision that included the staff entrance and Zangheri's car in the parking lot.

The ambulance pulled near to the emergency room entrance at 1:30AM. Amatrano and his two officers all exited. It was a warm spring night. The plan called for Amatrano to loiter outside while his two officers took up strategic positions in the parking lot within immediate reach of Zangheri's car. The two undercover surveillance officers were to remain concealed. They would only serve as backup if something went wrong.

Once Zangheri exited, Amatrano would fall in behind her as she walked toward her car. The unknown was how many other staff might be in the parking lot with the change of shift. If the opportunity presented itself, Amatrano would apply a technique he learned as part of his krav maga training called vascular neck restraint. A widely known police method of restraining combative individuals. Applied correctly, the subject loses consciousness within five to ten seconds. Recovery time offered sufficient opportunity to handcuff Zangheri and apply duct tape over her mouth to prevent screaming.

Hospital staff for the third shift began arriving before 2AM. Departing personnel from Zangheri's shift began exiting on the hour. Amatrano seemed in luck. Zangheri was not among the first group leaving. However, she exited the building talking to another nurse as they proceeded walking together across the parking lot.

Amatrano followed from behind appearing as if he too was leaving. If Zangheri reached her car first it might not allow for an opportunity to subdue her unseen. Zangheri and her companion then stopped to bid each other good night. The other nurse went off to the left. Amatrano seized chance. "Excuse me. Did you or the other nurse perhaps drop these keys?" he said to Zangheri.

Zangheri turned. Twenty feet away dressed in a doctor's white coat with a stethoscope visible hanging from his pocket, he aroused no suspicion as he walked closer. Holding her car keys, she replied, "Not mine, doctor."

Stepping next to her, he said, "I will take them back inside. My first night here. Who should I give them to?"

"Just hand them to the …." as she began replying, Amatrano sprung quickly using a krav maga takedown move that dropped her to the ground between her car and the next parked car. In the process of taking her down, he placed her neck in the crook of his right arm applying the vascular neck constraint. Correctly applied pressure compresses the carotid arteries, decreasing cerebral blood flow to the brain. With his left hand clasp over her mouth to muffle any scream, Zangheri lapsed into unconsciousness within seconds. By then Amatrano's officers stepped out from concealment.

The encounter went unnoticed. Departing hospital staff drove off leaving no one in the parking lot within a few minutes. Handcuffed and with her mouth taped, Zangheri remained unconscious. One officer positioned the fake ambulance behind the parked cars, while Amatrano and the other officer bundled Zangheri inside placing her on an air mattress on the floor of the van.

Before departing, Amatrano extracted Zangheri's car keys from her handbag, opened her car door and dropped the keys on the driver's seat. From inside the ambulance, he radioed his surveillance agents, "Keys are on the front seat. Return the car to subject's place of residence."

The ambulance then drove off. Amatrano sat in one of two folding canvas director chairs positioned in the rear of the van next to the air mattress. A box with sandwiches and water would sustain them through what might be a long night. Zangheri's eyes eventually fluttered open. Amatrano reached down and ripped the duct tape from her mouth.

Her eyes now wide with terror, "Who are you? Do you know who I am?"

"I am your worst nightmare. Note my nametag. Latin for doctor death. And you are Olivia Zangheri. Your mother's name is

Maria. Maiden name Provenzano. Sister to Corleonesi Mafia underboss Bernardo Provenzano."

Amatrano's pronouncement only increased her fear. "Are you with those from Palermo?"

"Do you mean perhaps the Mafia family of Santa Maria di Gesù? Or perhaps Passo di Rigano? Those at war against your Corleonesi clan? Worried your kidnapping might be in reprisal for the murders of the heads of these families ordered by your uncle and Totò Riina?"

Zangheri struggled to sit up with her wrists handcuffed behind her back. Breathing heavy from both fear and shaking off the effects from passing out, she asked with resignation, "Are you?"

"No. We are with the police, Signora Zangheri. You are under arrest for the murder of Paolo Falcone. At a restaurant in the town of Viterbo north of Rome. Death by a lethal injection of potassium cyanide. Coincidently probably the same way you killed your husband years ago. Officially ruled a suicide. Also by potassium cyanide poisoning. Very unpleasant. Not the way most people would choose to kill themselves. Obviously, your uncle spread enough money around to cover up what you did. Circumstances this time are different, Olivia."

"What do you want?" she defiantly.

"Everything, Olivia. Ever see the American movie, *The Godfather*? About a Sicilian Mafia family in the United States having originated right here in Corleone. Anyway, there is a line delivered by one of the characters about how he was going to get someone to do something they refused to do. He simply made the person an offer they could not refuse. I shall make you such an offer."

Zangheri sat in silence.

"You are going to become my informer. A *pentito* as you Mafiosi say. An inside source to everything your uncle and Riina are doing."

Fearing the alternative counterpoint, she asked, "Why would I do that?"

"Because you will otherwise die. Reprisal from your own people. Your blood family even. We shall simply hold you in custody pending trial for murder."

She blurted, "You can't prove I killed Paolo!"

"I think we can. However, it does not really matter. We will just let out the word that you are cooperating with the police. At that point it no longer becomes about Paolo's murder. You must know too much to remain alive. If I am wrong and you know very little of value that becomes worse for you, Olivia. Means the police don't need you. You become expendable. Totò Riina is a psychopathic murderer. Being related to your uncle will mean nothing.

"You will not be safe in any prison. You killed Falcone while held secretly under police protection. Even your killing of Paolo Falcone will be reason enough for the Palermo Mafias to put out a contract on you as a spy for the Corleonesi. Therefore, you will become my inside source for information or one Mafia faction or the other will kill you while in jail. I do not need to paint you a picture of how brutal such a death might be."

"You can't do that!" she screamed.

"I just did. If you do not agree to cooperate I will formally arrest you for murder. That alone will place you in danger with all that is going on in Sicily. Then I announce your arrest publicly. Release information of your affair with Paolo Falcone and your family relationship with a rival Mafia clan looking to take over Palermo."

Olivia Zangheri broke down in heaving sobs. The extent of the impossible predicament settling end. The ambulance continued driving toward the town of Marineo twenty miles north of Corlene. Amatrano had reconnoitered the area previously when planning the mission to seize Zangheri. Zangheri withdrew into silence.

Arriving in Marineo, Amatrano provided directions for exiting the main highway and venturing a couple of miles down a little used dirt road. Here they would stop. Amatrano hoped to sell Olivia Zangheri to cooperate as an informer. If unsuccessful, arresting her for the murder of Paolo Falcone was not an idle threat. They would then drive to Messena and place her in custody. At that point she no longer would be of value. A cruel tactic, however, Amatrano regarded her as nothing more than a Mafia murderer.

Pulling off the dirt road into an area surrounded by trees, Amatrano removed Zangheri's handcuffs. Handing her a bottle of mineral water he said, "Are you hungry? We have sandwiches."

She looked at him with undisguised hatred, making no reply. He nevertheless reached into the box and handed her a ham and cheese sandwich on a baguette. She did not refuse.

After Amatrano handed sandwiches and water to his officers seated up in front, they stepped outside into the warm night leaving Amatrano and Zangheri alone.

"Time to make your decision, Olivia. What you decide determines if you live or risk an almost ensured bad death. What's it to be?"

"I'll tell you whatever you want to know if you'll leave me alone."

Amatrano grabbed her wrist roughly. "You don't seem to understand, Olivia. You will tell me tonight everything you know. But that will not be enough. You will be my eyes and ears inside the Corleonesi Mafia. That means going out of your way to gather useful information."

She pulled her arm from his grasp. "But I'm not close enough to know the kinds of things you want."

"You are lying, Olivia. Tell me why you murdered Paolo Falcone. I have seen pictures of you making love with Paolo in a Rome hotel. Was that real affection or are you just a Mafia whore?"

Amatrano waited without saying anything further.

A minute passed when she said, "I had no choice. Don Riina personally ordered me to kill Paolo."

"Really? Then you knew Paolo worked for the Palermo families that operated Banca Mercantile?"

"Yes."

"Before or after you met him and became lovers?"

Exhausted and not thinking clearly, she answered, "After. When it became too late."

"You are lying, but it doesn't matter. You still must decide to be an informant or be jailed on murder charges. Which is it to be?"

"How do I pass information without risking being discovered?"

"A very simple process. When you have information of value you will place a call to a telephone number I give you. Only call from a public telephone. Your call will be answered with a recording saying *state your name and start your message. Reply using the code name Vedova Nera.* Disconnect the call when finished. If you need to speak to me, give me the number of a public pay phone and a time to call you. Only you and I shall know of this arrangement.

"Make no mistake, Olivia. I expect results. Bullshit information of no value will not keep you safe. I expect a call at least every week. Do not fail in this, Olivia or I will assume you have gone over to the other side. That will prove fatal. You may try to think of some way out of this, but any mistake ends in death. So long as I receive useful information you will not be arrested for Paolo's murder. Your fate rests entirely in your hands. Do we have an understanding?"

She nodded and said, "Yes."

"Here is the telephone number to call. Memorize it and then destroy it."

Taking the piece of paper with the telephone number, she said, "Now what?"

"Begin telling me everything you know. About the Corleonesi and what you learned from screwing Paolo Falcone. How your uncle learned that the Guardia was holding him, and where? How you became his assassin? Do not pretend that you are just a bystander. Even if that were to be true, I won't believe you. I simply don't care. Answer my questions without hesitation or I will assume you are holding something back."

From a briefcase, Amatrano removed a tape recorder. Switching the machine to record he said into the microphone, "Interview with Olivia Zangheri, 25 March 1982. State your full name, date and place of birth, and your affiliation with Sicilian organized crime."

After two hours, Zangheri was exhausted. Amatrano was surprised by how much confidential information she possessed.

Bernardo Provenzano was not just her uncle. They were particularly close, apparently his favorite niece. She admitted that her uncle had coerced her to begin an affair with Paolo Falcone to learn details about the operation of Banca Mercantile. Pressed hard by Amatrano, she broke down with racking sobs when admitting to reluctantly committing the murder. Her seemingly genuine distress failed to move Amatrano.

From her infiltration of the Palermo Mafias with her relationship to Falcone, she related specific details about Mafia-corrupted Palermo mayor Vito Ciancimino. That along with detailed information on Banca Mercantile's money laundering operations produced information of vital importance to Corleonesi takeover plans.

Switching off the tape recorder, "A good start, Olivia. We will drive you back to your apartment. One of my officers already drove your car there from the hospital. The keys are under the driver's seat. We will let you out of this fake ambulance a couple of blocks from your apartment where no one will see you before daybreak. You have had a difficult night. Get some rest. Make your first call within a week. Bring me something of value."

Amatrano gave only even odds that Olivia Zangheri would come through with important information. More likely she would try to figure another way out of her predicament. A careless mistake and they would find her bullet-ridden body on the side of the road. Totò Riina used his killings to communicate terror.

Having returned Zangheri to Corleone, Amatrano rendezvoused with his local agents to return with them to Palermo while the two Rome officers headed back to Rome. He had further work to do in Palermo. Olivia Zangheri was only the first Mafiosi to fall victim to his subversive tactics of disrupting the Mafia from within. The circumstances in this bloody struggle for territory offered endless opportunities to set the Mafia against each other. Find compromising information on an individual or simply invent something. Easy enough to then introduce rumors to play on paranoid suspicions.

CHAPTER 23

Palermo, Sicily | Spring 1982

The new year of 1982 promised no respite from Mafia violence. The conflict spilled out into everyday life. Palermo became a warzone. Much of the indiscriminate killings were driven by Corleonesi boss Salvatore Riina. It was not hyperbole to characterize Riina clinically as a homicidal psychopath. Since taking over the top spot in 1974, Riina held command of the rural Corleonesi clan. Even though forced underground as a fugitive following indictment on a murder charge since 1969, that did not diminish Riina's tight control. It was Riina's ambition to appropriate all organized criminal activity in Western Sicily under his control by removing the rival Palermo families' leadership.

Among all Mafiosi, Salvatore Riina was a fearsome specter. He resorted to violence as his preferred means of achieving results. The death count from the Sicilian underworld war often came from attacks instigated by Riina. However, Riina also exhibited a megalomaniacal complex. That exhibited itself with an irrational act of violence that would have far-reaching implications eventually proving disastrous for all Italian organized crime.

On Friday 30 April, Pio La Torre, a Communist Party member of the Chamber of Deputies, the lower house of Italian parliament, was shot to death in Palermo. Traveling on a one-way street near Communist Party's headquarters in Palermo, a stopped car blocked La Torre car's driven by his driver Rosario Di Salvo. Five Corleonesi Mafia hit men then riddled La Torre's car with Thompson .45 submachine gun rounds killing him and his driver. The hit ordered by Salvatore Riina was in reaction to a pending anti-Mafia parliamentary bill introduced by La Torre.

Among the wave of Mafia violence centered in western Sicily, La Torre's murder struck a collective nerve all over Italy. The following day the Italian Carabinieri reacted by appointing General Carlo Alberto Dalla Chiesa as prefect for Palermo. Dalla Cheisa was Deputy General Commander of the Italian Carabinieri. The appointment of such a senior police official signaled the will of the Italian government to put an end to the violence of the Second Mafia War. Dalla Cheisa came to Palermo with a successful record of going after leftist terrorists in northern Italy. His mandate was to put an end to the Second Mafia war.

A week after La Torre's murder, General dalla Cheisa arrived in Palermo with additional police resources. Following orders, Amatrano immediately offered his services to directly share Guardia di Finanza intelligence with the Carabinieri in Palermo. Olivia Zangheri had begun delivering regular information to Amatrano. Following the assassination of Pio La Torre, she provided the names of the five Corleonesi hitmen. Amatrano presented the names to General Dalla Cheisa in their first meeting.

"Excellent work, Colonel Amatrano. How did you come by this information?"

"A well-placed source. Not a willing source. Someone I gave little choice to either cooperate or I would leak disinformation that would result in a terrible death ordered by Totò Riina."

Dalla Cheisa replied, "I see you extend your intelligence gathering duties into operational areas. Those same tactics did not end well for that Palermo lawyer Falcone."

"His death revealed the extent of organized crime infiltration into our police forces, General. Falcone became a casualty. He gave up everything he knew before his murder, making him of limited further value except as a witness. Emphasized the importance of holding the identity of sources more tightly. I took that to heart with the source providing the names of the perpetrators of La Torre's murder."

"A hard line, Colonel, but I agree with your tactics as necessary to prevail against an enemy that observes no civilized constraint."

Amatrano replied, "It's time that we took the offensive against the Mafia, General. Finding evidence to bring prosecutions is the strategy for the long term. We should also employee the same kind of rough tactics the Mafia uses to enforce silence that prevents our ability to gain support from the populace and get convictions. The Guardia, especially my organized criminal division, the GICO, and the Carabinieri need to get down and dirty.

"Create internal chaos from within the Mafia. The Corleonesis started this war. We use that to our advantage by using subversive tactics to play on their distrust to cause internecine chaos. Create intelligence opportunities in the process."

†

The collapse of Banca Mercantile, engineered by the Guardia di Finanza, accelerated Archbishop Tagliente's efforts to create a new money laundering channel. Roberto Calvi's Ambrosiano financial empire no longer was functional. Its imminent collapse now possessed only a threat for the Vatican Bank. The Sicilian Mafia War held the opportunity to replace the Sindona-Calvi channel. Whereas that channel existed to benefit the bankers, Tagliente envisioned a new conduit under control of the Vatican Bank with a greater commission return. The Corleonesis having damaged the control of the various Palermo families with the failure of Banca Mercantile would make a new money laundering channel essential.

Tagliente would take command of the financial restructuring to benefit of the Vatican. Although Umberto Ortolani and Licio Gelli were in exile in South America, they might still be useful but in a lesser role. Through his chief lieutenant Monsignor Donaggio, Tagliente had direct access to the Mafia. That included leadership remnants of the Palermo Mafia families, the Corleonesi, and particularly Giuseppe Calò. Calò maintained close ties to both warring Sicilian Mafia factions. Working out of Rome, he also became a readily assessable figure for Tagliente's Vatican Bank inside staffer Monsignor Auerbach.

Repeated failures of Roberto Calvi to make any inroads with financial relief from the Vatican Bank prompted Calvi to unwisely make thinly disguised threats to Archbishop Marcinkus. Calvi and Banco Ambrosiano now became a dangerous liability to the Vatican. Tagliente knew the Mafia had even less tolerance for the disastrous circumstances brought about by Calvi. The house of cards that was Banco Ambrosiano now held captive tens of millions of dollars belonging to the Mafia that would likely be lost.

"Roberto Calvi has become a direct threat to Vatican interests," Tagliente said to Monsignor Donaggio. "Calvi's financial empire has no chance of survival. The Sicilian investors will suffer extensive losses. For that matter so will the IOR. Yet we will recover financially. However, Calvi has imprudently threatened to drag the IOR further into this disaster of his own making. I will not have the Holy See suffer further public condemnation. Calvi must be sent a strong message. I need you to communicate with our associate here in Rome, Signore Calò."

"Do you have something specific in mind, Your Excellency?"

"Removal of the vice chairman of Banco Ambrosiano, Roberto Rosone. The Mafia to take the blame. A clear warning to Calvi to keep silent. Tell Calò that Calvi is desperate. Threatening to make information public that is not in the interest of Calò's Sicilian associates, or the Vatican. Tell Calò I am personally exploring possibilities for recovering some portion of Sicilian *investments*."

Four days later, Rosone left his apartment on Via Ercole Oldofredi not far from Milano Centrale train station. Only a short walk since his flat was above a branch office of Banco Ambrosiano on the ground floor of the same building. The building concierge warned Rosone of two suspicious men loitering outside. Ignoring the warning, Rosone walked outside.

One of the men pulled on a balaclava and aimed a semi-automatic pistol at Rosone. The pistol jammed, allowing Rosone to run away down the sidewalk. Freeing the jammed weapon, the shooter then fired at the fleeing Rosone, hitting him in the leg. The other assassin jumped on a Vespa with the shooter climbing behind. Armed guards typically protected banks during this era of terrorist violence. A bank guard shot at the fleeing Vespa killing the assassin.

Surprisingly, the assassin was identified as an important Rome gangster named Danillo Abbruciati rather than just a low-ranking thug. Someone of convenience being in Rome that Giuseppe Calò turned to. The Rosone incident proved a repeat of the failed Mafia attempt to gun down Emma Nicoletti.

†

Amatrano made his next overture of using disinformation to sow dissention within the ranks of the Sicilian Mafia. His target the Corleonesis. Salvatore Riina with his proclivity for extreme violence created the perfect climate for attempting to turn his clan against one another. Olivia Zangheri would provide him with suitable names for targets.

Using the prearranged communications protocol, he spoke with Zangheri calling from a public payphone. "You have been doing well, Olivia. Bearing up okay?"

None too happy, she replied, "As well as expected."

He replied, "I have a specific assignment. It concerns the whereabouts of Salvatore Riina?"

Responding with evident fear in her voice, "I have no idea where he is. If I did, I would have already told you."

"I understand, Olivia. What I want are the names of those that regularly meet with Riina. Those that protect him. You can exclude your uncle who undoubtedly knows."

"How am I to do that? Nothing about how Riina remains hidden is ever spoken of."

"You must then be creative. Your Uncle Bernie knows how Riina manages to hide in Sicily. That requires the help of many others. I want some of those names, Olivia."

A couple of weeks later, Zangheri came through. "The crew of a capo by the name of Angelo Giancola acts as Riina's bodyguard. Riina moves all over among safe locations mostly to the south of Corleone. Giancola keeps an apartment with his mistress in Corleone. Communicates regularly with my uncle. One of Giancola's soldiers is named Mario Venanzio. Giancola's driver."

From that information Amatrano began an intense background check of the names. Both were known to the Guardia GICO and the Carabinieri. Records of arrest but no convictions or even prosecutions. Typical dead ends that lacked sufficient evidence. Testimony of witnesses against Mafiosi in Sicily was virtually unheard of out of fear of retribution. Even more so in the rural environments that represented Corleonesi-controlled areas. In spite of that Amatrano with a team of select Guardia officers and Carabinieri officers manufactured enough creditable circumstantial evidence to obtain arrest warrants. The fake evidence would eventually break down and never pass scrutiny for prosecution, but it would never come to that.

Amatrano and his intelligence counterpart of the Carabinieri in Palermo would lead the interrogations of these two individuals. Each would conduct simultaneous interrogations of the two Mafiosi in separate locations.

The mission began with several days of round-the-clock surveillance of Giancola's Corleone apartment to understand the movements of their target. Following Giancola into the rural areas was not possible. He would never go directly near any location where Riina was hiding. Amatrano just wanted to catch him and his driver at night away from any witnesses.

The Carabinieri supplied the manpower. Amatrano and his counterpart would show up at dusk. If Giancola was not there or did not leave, they would wait several hours before returning the following night. On the third night Giancola's driver arrived close to midnight. A short time later, Giancola left the residence and got into the car. A few miles out of town Carabinieri stationed cars at probable locations should Giancola head south. Having established the route, a Carabinieri car blocked the highway three miles away. Two additional police vehicles then followed.

The arrests went without incident. Giancola made a few defiant remarks while being handcuffed but seemed reconciled to suffering through the ritual that would never go anywhere. General Dalla Cheisa was already aggressively applying pressure in Palermo and the surrounding rural areas including Corleone. Yet a showing of strength from the police meant nothing to the Corleonesi.

Each of the detainees were placed in a different police vehicle. Amatrano went in one car with Giancola and two officers. The Carabinieri intelligence officer in another vehicle with Giancola's driver.

Expecting to be returned to the police station in Corleone, Giancola's expression reflected some concern as the police car wound down a dirt farm road. Amatrano pulled Giancola roughly out of the back seat causing him to fall out to the ground losing his balance from being handcuffed behind his back. Uttering an expletive, Amatrano pulled him up by the arm then drove his fist hard into Giancola's belly.

"You are under arrest, Angelo, as an accessory to murder. We have witnesses. This time witnesses that will testify against you."

"Who was the victim?"

"You know who, Angelo. Stefano Bontade and Salvatore Inzerillo. A year ago. Ordered by Don Riina. The killings that started this war with the Palermo families."

"You can't pin that on me. You've got the wrong person."

"Don't think so. Got people that say you planned the hit on Bontade by Giuseppe Lucchese and Giuseppe Greco. Then three weeks later you hit Salvatore Inzerillo."

Giancola grinned and shook his head. "Blow it up your ass, cop. I'm not going to tell you anything. That why you brought me way out here? Beat information out of me? I want to call my lawyer."

Amatrano's turn to grin. "Not going to beat you, Angelo. No way to call a lawyer out here. Just going to have a conversation with you, Angelo. You're an important fellow to Riina and Provenzano. You know all the secrets. You pass the information between them. Riina was stupid enough to get himself charged with murder now he's been a fugitive for years forced into hiding like a rat. You're now in the same fix, Angelo."

"Fuck you," Giancola said.

"Care for a cigarette? Hungry? We have sandwiches, wine and beer in the trunk. We're going to eat and relax for a couple of hours. You can join us. I'll even take off your handcuffs."

Giancola looked at Amatrano with a quizzical expression. "What's all this shit about?"

"It's very simple, Angelo. You're going to stand trial for murder which means no bail. Months at least in jail. Or you can bleed your soul out by giving me enough evidence to make protecting you worthwhile."

The very idea shocked Giancola. "Are you crazy? Why would I do somethin' that stupid? You can't make a case for murder against me."

"Maybe not. But while you are sitting in jail, what if word gets out that you are cooperating with the prosecuting magistrate? Giving up evidence. Jailed in Palermo along with other Mafiosi, what do you think your chances of surviving might be? You have only tonight to make your decision, Angelo. Start talking and convince me you are worth protecting at a safe location far from Sicily. You know Totò Riina better than anyone. He's a psychopath. Prefers eliminating people rather than rely on trust."

Sitting in the moonlight, Giancola's expression registered understanding of his dire circumstances, yet he said nothing. Amatrano assumed he was frantically trying to calculate his alternatives to this unexpected scenario.

"There's another wrinkle to this scenario, Angelo. Your driver is also undergoing interrogation in Corleone. We don't have murder charges we can make stick against him, but enough other charges to keep him locked up for a time. Even if released on bail, we are giving him the same deal. Cooperate or we float a rumor of cooperating to get released. All sorts of ways to do that.

"Is Riina going to believe your story of us keeping you out all night until the next morning before booking you in Palermo just to make you look guilty? Now he gets the same story from your driver booked earlier in Corleone. Does Riina buy that nonsense and do nothing? That's not Riina's way, is it?"

Amatrano shouted to one of the officers, "Time we had something to eat."

Turning to Giancola, "We've been watching your mistress' apartment for hours, Angelo. We're tired and hungry. Unless you cooperate, we are then taking you to Carabinieri headquarters in Palermo. Your new home for a while unless you convince me tonight you're worth the trouble of keep you alive in some safer place outside Sicily. "Are you sure you wouldn't like some food or drink while you consider the problem?"

Amatrano did not expect Giancola or his driver to even consider cooperating by giving information against the Mafia. Giancola probably had nothing to do with murdering Bontade and knew the police evidence therefore would not stand up. That was not the point. Giancola's situation was not the same as Olivia Zangheri who did face conviction of murder. The offer to these Mafiosi was only meant for them to sound less believable when trying to explain what happened.

Amatrano gave Giancola an hour to change his mind. "Decision time, Angelo. Not going to waste more time out here tonight unless you make it worthwhile. What's it to be?"

"Fuck you!"

"Suite yourself, Angelo. Let's get you situated in lockup in Palermo."

Riina and Provenzano would find it difficult to ignore Amatrano's contrived circumstances along with loose comments made to the local police when booking Giancola and his driver. Odds favored their meet a very unpleasant end.

CHAPTER 24

Rome, Italy| Spring 1982

In the wake of Roberto Calvi's worsening financial problems, Archbishop Tagliente was prepared to construct a new money laundering channel for Mafia funds. Those funds offered too lucrative a source of revenue for the Vatican to abandon. Although forced to flee Italy to avoid criminal arrest, Umberto Ortolani and Licio Gelli they remained safe from extradition in South America. Both still possessed influence in Italy and were therefore still useful.

In simplest terms, Tagliente's revised money laundering scheme involved creating new offshore banks and shell companies controlled by the Vatican Bank. Replacing the former Sindona and Calvi offshore entities in the money laundering channel entitled the Vatican bank to double its fee to 20%. Ortolani and Gelli could still participate in reduced roles at correspondingly reduced fees. For the Mafia, the total cost remained the same percentage. However, it would remain for the Mafia to find their own methods of introducing great quantities of bulk cash to take advantage of this new routing to transform the funds that become recognizable from legitimate financial assets.

Tagliente's plan was to use Ortolani's Banco Financiero in Montevideo, Uruguay as the repository of illicit Mafia money. With the closure of Banca Mercantile in Palermo, the Mafia must now smuggle large quantities of cash out of Italy into Uruguay. Ortolani had a vested interest in assisting. Gelli in exile in neighboring Buenos Aires, Argentina had strong ties to the ruling military dictatorship and his extensive connections in Italy might also be able to offer smuggling solutions.

To put this together Tagliente would direct the plan from afar and only from the top level. Separate secure overseas calls to Ortolani and Gelli received a positive response. Both men were eager to continue receiving payments from Mafia money laundering. They were in no position to negotiate their reduced commissions.

Tagliente instructed his subordinate in the IOR, Monsignor Auerbach to create required new foreign subsidiaries in tax havens countries. A bank in Panama and another in Luxembourg with shell companies in the Caribbean, Luxembourg, and Lichtenstein. He then counselled Marcinkus that it was part of his larger strategy to move the IOR investments away from outside bankers.

Monsignor Donaggio dealt with the criminal underworld. There could never be any direct link for Tagliente personally. Should Donaggio's association ever become exposed, Tagliente would sacrifice him by claiming deniability for a trusted subordinate becoming corrupted for personal gain.

"It is necessary for the Holy See to retain our revenues from offering financial services to the Italian criminal underworld. An evil that unfortunately is useful on many fronts as you know better than anyone, Ettore," Tagliente said to Donaggio as they shared wine in Tagliente's study at his residence. "Make contact with Pippo Calò. Tell him it is in his hands to reconstruct the means of moving illicit cash in bulk into legitimate financial systems.. That must now be done in South America. How they accomplish that becomes their problem.

"They should consult with Umberto Ortolani and Licio Gelli operating now from South America. I assume they will know how to make contact."

"Calò is going to want to know details. Calò understands finance and the Mafia bosses."

"Not so many bosses I should think now. Start with Salvatore Riina and Bernardo Provenzano. They seemed poised to take over Western Sicily. Tell Calò only that the new arrangement is going to be under total control of the Vatican Bank. Not some outside bankers with their own investment agenda. The reason why the former arrangement came undone. Sindona and Clavi have cost the Mafia and the Vatican Bank heavy losses. That will not happen under this new arrangement. Same total cost in commissions for the Mafia as before. The whole operation can restart within sixty days after the Sicilians figure out how to get their money to Ortolani's bank in Montevideo, Uruguay. I have spoken with both Ortolani and Gelli. They are anxious to move forward. Both believe the Corleonesis will prevail in this territorial war. Regardless, the Mafia will survive. Great amounts of illicit money must find creative means for blending with legitimate funds."

Donaggio replied, "I know Calò has a close association with the Corleonesis. He's the Mafia's moneyman no matter what the clan. Banco Mercantile was his creation. I will contact Calò immediately, Your Excellency."

†

Within days of being seized by Amatrano, trusted Mafia caporegime Angelo Giancola was visited in the Palermo jail by a Mafia attorney. He was being held in custody in the facility managed by the Carabinieri on murder charges filed by the Guardia di Finanza. True to Amatrano's threat, Giancola was not placed in a segregated cell away from the general inmate population.

In a secure room reserved for inmates and their counsel, Giancola related the threat delivered by Amatrano. "The sonofabitch thinks he can make this murder charge stick. That's bullshit. I didn't have anything to do with hitting Bontade and Inzerillo. The Guardia cannot have evidence. Anybody says different gets wacked."

The lawyer said, "You said this Guardia officer was not in uniform? Nor the other two with him? Said only they were Guardia. Did he show you his badge?"

"No. Didn't have to. I knew they were cops. What difference does that make?"

"I'm looking to identify this person is all, Angelo. Take a look at these photographs."

Giancola took the stack of photographs of Guardia midlevel-rank officers and began thumbing through them. Coming to Amatrano, he blurted, "This one!" Turning the photo over, it read *Lt. Col. Francesco Amatrano, Gruppo di Investigazione Criminalità Organizzata.*

"The fucker is a dead man! Tell Bernardo I want to do him myself. Can you get me out of here on bail?"

"Going to try. You are locked up here on a high-profile murder charge, though. That's up to the prosecuting magistrate."

"Shit. Do what you can counselor but do it quickly."

"I will. I don't need to tell you to keep your mouth shut. No discussing any sort of deal proposed for an offer of bail."

Incensed, Giancola responded, "Think I'm stupid. Tell Bernardo and Don Totò they have nothing to worry about."

The lawyer immediately reported his conversation with Giancola to Corleonesi Underboss Bernardo Provenzano.

Provenzano said, "So this is the Guardia policeman that wants to play dirty. First they send General dalla Chiesa and more police. Now we have this GICO *stronzo*. How was, Angelo?

"Furious. Claims the police cannot make a murder case against him."

"Can they?"

"Haven't seen the evidence yet. Probably will take some time before the assignment of a prosecuting magistrate who will make that determination. Giancola expects to get released on bail. That depends on the strength of the evidence."

"How long might that process take?"

"Hard to say. Could be weeks."

Two days later, Angelo Giancola lay dead in the prison exercise yard. Bled out from multiple stab wounds before any possibility of medical help. The murder was witnessed by several inmates, but no one identified the assailant. To do so meant certain death.

The following morning, the body of Giancola's driver, Mario Venanzio, was found on a Palermo backstreet. Regardless of years of trust, Don Totò Riina took no chances.

†

Olivia Zangheri took the news of Giancola's death badly. Reading it the newspaper, she nearly fainted. She gave up Angelo Giancola's name to the Guardia officer. A particularly trusted capo that acted as intermediary between her uncle and people outside the Mafia. Killed while in jail? Another newspaper column commenting on the increasing gangland violence that cited the death of Mario Venanzio, his body dumped on a Palermo street. She knew Venanzio was Giancola's driver.

Since her uncle would expect a reaction when she learned of Giancola's death, she must play the role. Showing up at her uncle's residence before going to work at the hospital, "I just read of Angelo's death in jail? I liked Angelo. Why was he in jail, Uncle Bernie?"

"Police charged him with multiple murders. Some new Guardia police officer out to make a name for himself. The police grabbed Angelo and his driver Mario Venanzio. Tried to strong arm them with arrest charges. Venanzio makes bail but Angelo's murder charges prevented his release."

She did not ask her uncle the obvious question of who killed Giancola or Venanzio.

"Angelo identified this new cop from a stack of photos his lawyer showed him. His name is Francesco Amatrano. Came to Sicily along with this Carabinieri general." He handed Olivia the photo. "Learned just this morning the name of this *poliziotto*."

Olivia looked at Amatrano's official photo in Guardia uniform and felt faint. This all began because her uncle convinced her to seduce Paolo Falcone. Paolo was good looking, indirectly part of the Mafia. Educated, managing tens of millions of lire. Working in international finance rather than the crude workings of ordinary crime. She styled herself as some sort of seductive spy as portrayed in the movies. That fantasy now turned into a deadly reality.

Real life intruded into Olivia's fantasy when told by her uncle she must kill Paolo. That she committed murder before by killing her abusive husband did not make sticking a needle into Paolo any easier. Then giving Angelo's name to police causing his death. There seemed no end to this cycle. Her own survival hung only by a thread.

Provenzano said, "I've got people in Rome looking into Amatrano's background. Need to see what he is up to. Trying to threaten our people with facing criminal charges unless they cooperate with the police will accomplish nothing."

Olivia thought, not exactly nothing. It accomplished the killing of an important Mafiosi by his own clan. In her situation, Amatrano's threat of facing murder charges or cooperation worked all too effectively.

The *people* in Rome Provenzano made reference to was Giuseppe "Pippo" Calò, cashier to the Cosa Nostra. Instrumental in the creation of the now defunct Banca Mercantile. Calò possessed secret contacts with access to the Vatican Bank, essential to a new channel for money laundering. Amatrano represented the Italian financial police making his aggressive efforts even more a threat.

Calò connected with Licio Gelli in Buenos Aires. Gelli's list of well-placed individuals willing to trade in information ran into the hundreds. Among these contacts were police officials in the Guardia di Finanza, the Carabinieri, and the various Italian intelligence services. A member of Gelli's outlawed secret masonic lodge Propaganda Due was also a member of *Servizio per le Informazioni e la Sicurezza Democratica,* the Italian domestic intelligence agency. Calò had photocopies of Amatrano's official dossier within a day. By courier, Bernardo Provenzano received a set the following day.

Seated in a large well-appointed room in a 16th century monastery in a remote rural location Provenzano recited Amatrano's background to Salvatore Riina. "Here is the most interesting piece of information, Totò. Amatrano is living with this woman that just published that book using stolen Vatican documents."

"Sonofabitch!" Riina barked, setting down his glass of wine hard. "Yes, I know of this book. It accuses the Vatican of being involved in money laundering and behind the murder of her American associate. Another attempt trying to kill her. Bungled by Bontade's family leaving two of their dead behind as evidence. We will not make that mistake. Get some of our people on watching this Colonel Amatrano. For that matter, do the same for that bigshot Carabinieri general they sent to Palermo. Understand their regular movements, their vulnerabilities."

"We must be careful, Totò. The blood is running like never before. No telling what might happen if we push too far."

"Too far? The Italian government is run by old women. This police business is all for show to the public. We run Sicily. As long as we confine our efforts to the South, Rome will do nothing. What can they do? If they knew what to do, they would have already tried."

CHAPTER 25

Rome, Italy| Summer 1982

Archbishop Tagliente ran Vatican intelligence since the final years of the long pontificate of Pope Pius XII in the late 1950s. Pope John XXIII suspended its function during the five years of his pontificate, before its resurrection by Pope Paul VI. Pope John Paul II instantly saw the utility of a secret intelligence service in this time of Cold War with the evil incarnate of Communism.

Preserving the subterfuge of appointing an official head of Vatican intelligence, John Paul appointed Archbishop Luigi Poggi. They became friendly when Poggi was papal nuncio to Poland in 1973. About this same time Ettore Donaggio was elevated to monsignor and appointed head of *Sodalitium Pianum*, Vatican counterintelligence. Effectively Donaggio become Monsignor Guido Orsini's new boss. If Orsini distrusted Tagliente, he harbored an undisguised dislike for Donaggio. Orsini promptly resigned, accepting a pastoral position at the Jesuit church Chiesa di Sant'Ignazio di Loyola in Campo Marzio in Rome.

The deteriorating public situation of the multi-year continuing Italian Banking Scandal had worsened for the Vatican. The crisis further inflamed with the embarrassing documents removed from the Vatican Secret Archive and published by the *New York*

Times. The convictions of Michele Sindona in Italy and United States placed him behind bars. The recent arrest and conviction of Roberto Calvi in Italy, now released on bail pending appeal, foretold the imminent collapse of Banco Ambrosiano. Yet Calvi's demise only heightened the bad press directed at allegations of complicity by the Vatican Bank.

The bestselling book by the journalist Emma Nicoletti became the latest disastrous development making international headlines. Tying together threads of the financial scandal with added weight of the confidential archive documents, she went further by directly accusing the Vatican of violent criminal activities. Not only money laundering for organized crime, but murder and attempted murder to cover up its involvement. Her firsthand accounts implied that the shadowy Vatican intelligence service might be involved.

With all this, Pope John Paul refused to take action by at least changing management of the IOR. Not only elevating Paul Marcinkus to archbishop and awarding him governorship of Vatican City but also expanding Archbishop Tagliente's responsibilities to include the IOR. Casaroli and Poggi believed this staunch denial of the worsening crisis by remaining defiantly silent would irreparably damage the Holy See's spiritual influence in the world.

Although Archbishop Poggi was only officially the head of the Vatican secret service, he knew of the covert use of the IOR to funnel U.S. CIA funds to the Polish labor movement Solidarity. Yet Poggi knew little about covert intelligence tradecraft. He knew of Monsignor Guido Orsini's former role in Vatican counterintelligence. Internal rumors spread after the long-serving Orsini's abrupt departure. General suspicion shifted to Archbishop Tagliente consolidating power using his longevity directing the most secret areas of the Vatican. Senior prelates fostered distrust of Tagliente with his unique authority falling outside control of the Curia.

A disheartened Archbishop Poggi would now turn to Monsignor Orsini. Someone experienced in the ways of covert activities yet someone outside the Vatican. Perhaps Orsini would provide a better understanding of the possibility of the truth of accusations directed at Tagliente by Nicoletti's book.

On a Sunday afternoon, Archbishop Poggi entered the Jesuit Church of St. Ignatius of Loyola on Via del Caravita in Rome, two miles east of the Vatican. He was dressed in a black suit with clerical collar, an amaranth-colored zucchetto with matching waist sash, and a gold pectoral cross studded with a ruby at each station of the cross. With the last mass of the morning concluded, the pews in the nave quickly emptied of parishioners.

Poggi walked toward the altar where a priest was making preparation for the late afternoon mass. Making the sign of the cross, Poggi steeped onto the altar, "Excuse me, Father. Can you tell me where I might find Monsignor Orsini?"

The priest turned making a slight bow of the head acknowledging the senior churchman. "Welcome to Sant'Ignazio, Your Excellency. I believe he should be in the rectory. I will take you there."

"Thank you, Father. Perhaps you might ask the Monsignor if he would be so kind as to join me here. I believe I would just like to sit and admire your magnificent ceiling. So grand and peaceful in the quiet of this magnificent sanctuary. The Monsignor knows me from his years serving in the Vatican. I am Archbishop Luigi Poggi."

"Yes, Your Excellency. I will inform him immediately of your presence."

Minutes later Monsignor Orsini walked in from a side door. Distinguished looking in his early sixties with a full head of gray hair he walked with a brisk stride. Seated in the front pew, Poggi stood to greet him.

"Your Excellency. What brings you to Sant'Ignazio?" Orsini leaned forward to accept Poggi's offered hand to kiss his ring.

"A matter of grave importance. Likewise, particularly sensitive demanding absolute confidentiality. Is there somewhere just the two of us can speak privately?"

"Perhaps right here. Masses are over until later this afternoon. A pew toward the middle of the nave will be entirely private this time of day."

Once seated, Poggi said, "The matter about which I wish to speak must remain only between us. Only one other person knows why I am here. That is Cardinal-Secretary of State Casaroli. Do I have your solemn word of not speaking of this?"

With a look of concern Orsini nodded, "Yes, Your Excellency. I swear to hold your words in absolute confidentiality."

"Thank you. I must apologize in advance for asking you personal questions that you may find uncomfortable or even objectionable. If answering any question should violate a previous oath, please do not hesitate to say so."

Orsini nodded his agreement.

"Have you followed this financial scandal that continues to raise uncomfortable allegations directed at the Vatican Bank?"

"Of course, Your Excellency. Publications that paint the Holy See as accomplices to criminal bankers is most distressing."

"Are you familiar with this new book just published by a journalist working for *Il Sole 24 Ore?"*

"I have read Signora Nicoletti's book with a very heavy heart. She adds much more troubling accusations directed toward the Vatican than just financial fraud. Murder specifically. Her firsthand account of surviving a bombing that took the life of her American colleague. Then a second attempt on her life by Mafia gunmen is exceptionally chilling."

Orsini wondered where this was going. He was not yet ready to reveal his meeting with Emma Nicoletti. He broke ties with Vatican intelligence and had no reason to trust Poggi.

"As you may or may not know, I am nominally the official head of Vatican Holy Alliance. That of course is just cover for Archbishop Marcello Tagliente remaining as the actual operational chief as he was when you served in that service. Can you tell me why you abruptly left the Vatican?"

"Before answering that question, can you enlighten me further as to the reasons that might involve me, Your Excellency?"

"Fair enough. I shall be candid, Monsignor. Both His Eminence Cardinal Casaroli and I believe there is reason to believe that some of these public accusations of criminal behavior by certain persons within the Vatican may have substance. Signora

Nicoletti leaves little doubt that she suspects Archbishop Tagliente. We cannot fix what is broken without understanding the cause."

"Very well. I left the Vatican intelligence service because of Archbishop Tagliente. I believed he used his secret offices to further his personal ambitions. In the process of gaining power, I believe he was interacting with those outside the clergy that were pursuing unethical and even criminal activities."

"What lead you to become suspicious enough to leave?"

"Ettore Donaggio. I worked in *Sodalitium Pianum* the same as Donaggio. However, it was to Donaggio that Tagliente seemed to assign missions that remained secret even to others within S.P. Counterintelligence is a necessary function in this time of the Cold War. Foreign agents, both friend and foe to the Vatican, provide reasons for engaging on counterintelligence. However, I had reason to suspect dark activities by Donaggio and certain agents under his authority. I prefer not to go into detail since I have no conclusive proof. By dark, I mean criminal, including violence. Our function had no reason to ever employ violence. When Tagliente convinced Pope Paul to elevate Donaggio to monsignor and place him in charge of S.P., I could not continue serving under someone I felt this strongly about."

"Are these accusations that Nicoletti makes about Vatican collusion with the Sicilian Mafia credible?"

"Entirely possible. Might simply be the Sicilian Mafia since they are rumored to be involved with Banco Ambrosiano. Insufficient reason for the Mafia to act unilaterally. Someone else is likely behind this. If someone at the Vatican is involved, it could not be Marcinkus at the IOR. It would then point to Tagliente and Donaggio using the resources of the Vatican secret services. Agents of *Sodalitium Pianum* possess covert operational capabilities. Our function was not just the gathering of intelligence but conducting operations to thwart outside infiltrations. Those same skills are easily redirected to clandestine operations for any purpose."

Poggi digested Orsini's comments with dread. Remaining silent for a moment, he finally said, "Should I call on your services once again if it be to protect the Holy See, would you consider accepting a commission to act on our behalf, Monsignor Orsini?"

It was Orsini's turn to pause for a moment for reflection. "Yes. Conditionally. As long as I clearly understand that it serves the Church without compromising my devotion to God as a priest. You do understand do you not, Your Excellency, that removing cancerous tumors like Tagliente and Donaggio may require radical surgery?"

Taken back by Orsini's frank statement, Poggi nodded with a sigh. That in fact was what he was suggesting. "We shall trust in God to guide us. And for Him to provide us with the resources of faithful churchmen like yourself, Monsignor. Are there others you know that might join us?"

"Perhaps a couple. When I left the Vatican, others followed me. Should you need my services, do not hesitate to contact me. In keeping with intelligence protocols, use the code name Father Estorzi, a name from the past when contacting me. If we need to meet, best to come dressed as a priest rather than a prince of the church, Your Excellency."

Both men stood. Poggi said, "Bless you, Monsignor Orsini. Go with God."

†

Orsini watched Poggi leave. Undoubtedly to converse with Cardinal-Secretary of State Casaroli or whomever else he is conspiring with before moving forward. A remarkable undertaking might perhaps be unfolding. Orsini kept in close contact with sources inside the Vatican. Reading the tea leaves of rumor and conjecture seeping outside the walls of the Vatican, Orsini sensed the turmoil within. The pope could obviously just remove Tagliente. Or could he? It was not the Vatican way to admit wrongdoing. Obfuscate, sidestep, and ultimately remain silent. Let uncomfortable events pass unresolved into history. The Holy See being eternal would survive. Therefore, what Archbishop Poggi was about might involve Pope John Paul II.

Nevertheless, Guido Orsini felt dutybound to serve the Holy See in this hour of need. Marcello Tagliente was a cancer. He had learned enough from past personal experience. Enough facts have emerged about IOR misdeeds participating with criminal bankers. No question that Sindona and Calvi had ties to the Sicilian Mafia. Money laundering would be a compelling reason.

Then there was Signora Nicoletti. She favorably impressed him with her character and the telling of her story when they met. The beginning of her violent ordeal caused by the removal of Vatican Secret Archive documents. She made a compelling case for the Vatican being behind the violent attempts to silence her. Who else would know of the missing documents? Her making the obvious case for motivation to conceal IOR complicity with financial crimes. The chilling experiences of the bombing killing her associate and injuring her. Then a second attempt to kill her. If she is correct, the only prelate capable of directing this is Archbishop Tagliente. That in turn meant the covert efforts of Monsignor Donaggio and agents of *Sodalitium Pianum,* even if nothing more than subcontracting the violence to the Sicilian Mafia.

†

Guido Orsini took his sacred vows as a priest as the center of his life. He reflected constantly on his decades of service in the Vatican intelligence as a test from God. The years spent after leaving the Vatican in reexamining how he measured up. So many actions tested the boundaries of his ecclesiastical training. Rationalized as serving the Holy See in a capacity necessary to its secular areas of concern. Many of those activities were morally troubling at the time. More so in reflection. Castigating himself for his many sins of omission for simply remaining in the Vatican intelligence service while having knowledge of actions he could never morally condone.

Perhaps God was still testing him? A more substantial form of atonement for past sins never fully acknowledged in the confessional. As a Jesuit he was given to endless intellectual debate. Thirty-five years in counterintelligence also left Orsini skilled in clandestine tradecraft. Applying logic, might not God expect him to use those skills productively as the appropriate means of atonement?

Regardless of his intellectual musings, Archbishop Tagliente was a clear and present danger to the Holy See if the most senior Vatican churchmen felt the same. Orsini felt morally obligated to act. As an experienced intelligence professional, he realized that the necessary remedy to remove the threat would likely involve further moral compromises. He made up his mind. Time for planning was at hand accompanied by endless prayers for divine guidance.

The following day after his meeting with Archbishop Poggi, Orsini reached out to certain trusted friends. Likeminded priests that also saw their service in Vatican intelligence morally compromising. Too often, completely irreconcilable with their training as priests.

Like Orsini, Father Alberto Salerno and Father Lorenzo Rossi were also Romans. Leaving Vatican service, they took up positions among the many Catholic churches of Rome. From their shared unusual background, the three priests developed a close friendship. Working and living in close proximity, they saw each other frequently. Orsini telephoned each inviting them to dinner at his favorite restaurant. It was late May with the weather warm enough to enjoy outside seating. What Orsini wished to disgust required a quiet and confidential setting.

Orsini ordered wine and appetizers as if settling into a typical multi-course Italian dinner. With glasses of a good wine, Orsini said, "So glad to have such good friends with whom I can share so much. Both pleasant events as well as difficult circumstances. I have need now of your friendship and good counsel on something truly disturbing."

Both his friends set down their glasses waiting for Orsini to continue.

"We are not only friends but have a shared background that included many unpleasant happenings. Yet as priests we responded to the calling from those we vowed to obey. For fundamentally very similar reasons, we all chose to leave our service in

Vatican intelligence. Regrettably, the same circumstances that lead us to seek more spiritual roles have only worsened within the Holy See."

Father Alberto Salerno's face darken, "Does this concern the circumstances we read in the newspapers every day? The IOR being mixed up in financial wrongdoing? Money laundering? Accused of murder by this new book? Accusations against Archbishop Tagliente?"

Orsini nodded. "All that and more. Let me share with you certain personal events I experienced these last months. After I relate details of an unexpected and most extraordinary visit yesterday, you will understand why I need both of you. Your thoughts both spiritual as well as professional."

Orsini proceeded to summarize the background events. He started by relating his confidential sharing of information on Vatican affairs with Rome journalist Carlo Langella. That relationship eventually led to a meeting with the journalist and author Emma Nicoletti. Her telling of the events surrounding the stolen Vatican archive documents. The traumatic events leading her to accuse the Vatican as behind the attempts to silence her resulting in the murder of her associate. The extensive detail included in her book to implicate Vatican associations with prominent criminal figures named in the financial scandal. Scarpelli's posthumous letter to her. His express warnings about Archbishop Tagliente and possible role of Vatican intelligence in all this.

"Now you know the background. Please consider what I am about to tell you as equivalent to the secrecy of the confessional. It must remain only between us three. Yesterday, I was visited at Sant'Ignazio by Archbishop Luigi Poggi. Unannounced. Our conversation conducted in the empty nave after the last morning mass. Perhaps Poggi is just a figurehead in Vatican however His Excellency understands basic intelligence tradecraft."

Father Rossi said, "Isn't Poggi the acknowledged head of Vatican intelligence?"

Orsini nodded. "While Archbishop Tagliente continues as the operational chief just as he has done for so many years going back to Pius XII. Archbishop Poggi came to me to discuss Tagliente.

Poggi stated in direct language that Archbishop Tagliente must be removed."

Father Salerno said, "Removed in what manner?"

Orsini replied, "His Excellency chose not to be that specific. Yet it is only reasonable to assume it must involve, shall we say unpleasant circumstances? Why else would he come to me? The Holy Father could just remove Tagliente. That undoubtedly might result in a crisis of its own making with unintended consequences."

Both priests crossed themselves.

Salerno asked, "Who did Poggi say would sanction such an extreme act?"

"Poggi stated he was here on behalf of Cardinal-Secretary of State Casaroli. Beyond that, he remained vague. I did not press the point."

"Would not such an act require specific authorization of the Holy Father?" Father Rossi asked.

Orsini replied, "Without question. My guess is that it is premature to take something like this to His Holiness without absolute proof of the most damning offenses that could not otherwise be addressed by less harsh means.

"That is why I believe Poggi came to me. To feel me out. If this goes further Poggi will want to know how such an operation could be mounted. That in fact is why I came to you two. Should Poggi return to me, I want to know more about the comings and goings of Tagliente and Donaggio to give him a more qualified answer."

"You want us to gather intelligence on Tagliente and Donaggio?" Salerno asked.

"Precisely. Think about it before committing. Let me know in the next couple of days. Now let's get another bottle of wine and try to enjoy dinner."

Orsini looked at his two friends. Their initial shock somewhat worn off now replaced by questioning interest. Did Orsini see a hint of excitement in their expressions? Younger than Orsini, they were skilled professionals reflecting on their past experiences. Possibly an opportunity to serve justice against two despised priests that renouncing fundamental principles of their spiritual calling? Like Orsini, did they feel in this the hand of God delivering retribution?

Both priests looked at each other before responding.

Salerno said, "I do not need to further consider what you ask, Quido. I believe this is necessary. However offensive to my sensibilities, I see this as a righteous act for my personal atonement."

Rossi nodded in agreement. "I also agree. What do you want us to do, Guido?"

"With only the three of us, we do not have the resources do a proper surveillance. However, we at least need a better understanding of the habits of Tagliente and Donaggio. For the time being, I shall take on Tagliente. Having served in the Vatican for over so many years, I still have friends inside the walls. About time I renewed old acquaintances as reason to visit. Easy enough to pick up the latest gossip on the secretive archbishop given that his name is suddenly in the public sector portrayed in such a bad light.

"Both of you can then focus on Monsignor Donaggio. His movements may involve much more activity outside the Vatican than Tagliente. You can take turns for the thankless boring task of surveillance. If Archbishop Poggi moves this matter forward, it will require additional resources. Do you still have people outside the clergy that you might call on to do surveillance or basic logistics?"

Both priests nodded.

Orsini smiled. "Enough unpleasant business for tonight. We may have a difficult journey ahead. Let us enjoy this pleasant evening in fellowship."

CHAPTER 26

Rome, Italy| Summer 1982

With continued crushing losses while free on bail pending his appeal on conviction of financial crimes, Roberto Calvi continued desperately searching for a way to forestall disaster. He believed a loan could salvage disaster, but the required magnitude was staggering. The only possible source was the Vatican Bank. Although the IOR participated in Calvi's complex international transactions, he unrealistically believed he could somehow convince the pontiff of the IOR's complicity in his financial reversals. On 5 June 1982, Calvi sent a letter addressed to Pope John Paul II.

In the letter, Calvi warned of the imminent collapse of Banco Ambrosiano unless the IOR could provide relief with a massive loan. He cited IOR obligations in what he termed joint responsibility for the losses. However, he went further by putting in writing threats better left undocumented. Calvi cited the Banco Ambrosiano's participation in laundering $700M from the ruling Argentine military junta to purchase French-manufactured Exocet anti-ship missiles. Labelled *Operation Flying Fish,* the IOR received $11M. Worse however, the Exocets were then used against British warships in the Falkland Islands War beginning in April. A conflict now seemingly in its final phase with assured British victory.

Calvi used direct threatening language stating the collapse of Banco Ambrosiano would provoke a '*catastrophe of unimaginable proportions in which the Church will suffer the gravest damage.*'

On Monday 7 June, Calvi finally got a meeting with Archbishop Marcinkus. Calvi presented Marcinkus a copy of the letter to the pope that Marcinkus claimed he had never seen. Nonetheless, Marcinkus held firm following instructions telling Calvi that there was nothing the IOR could do. A loan close to a billion dollars was out of the question. Marcinkus reminded Calvi of his letter stating that none of the debts of his subsidiary companies that technically reflected shareholder Vatican Bank control, would never incur financial obligations for the Vatican Bank. Calvi manipulated stock ownership in those companies to suit his own interests over the years. Calvi at the end of his tether unwisely made even further disturbing verbal threats to Marcinkus.

Marcinkus had seen the letter. Shown to him by Tagliente who intercepted it but did not say if Pope John Paul had read it. Marcinkus accepted the meeting with Calvi on instructions from Tagliente. Secretly recorded, Tagliente played back the Marcinkus-Calvi exchange, replaying Calvi's threats.

Calvi's irrational state of mind made him dangerous to all those involved in his failed expansionist greed. He must be eliminated. To appear as a suicide, but foremost, it must be done soon.

The following morning, Monsignor Donaggio sat in Tagliente's office. "Another crisis Ettore. It involves Roberto Calvi. His financial empire is doomed. Although a disaster of his own making, he threatens to take down the reputation of the Vatican Bank as well. Suicide is preferred but we cannot be overly discriminating if such an arrangement is not possible. At the least it must appear the work of our associates in Sicily. They are going to lose a lot of money when Banco Ambrosiano goes under making for an obvious revenge motivation.

"Another job for Brother Gideon," Donaggio replied.

"Is the good friar sustaining his faith with our frequent requests for his dreadful skills?"

"I believe so, Your Excellency. Gideon sees himself as some holy warrior from the Old Testament. He came to the Church to save himself from a violent past. Undoubtedly, violence remains in his nature. We provide an outlet allowing him to exercise his natural proclivities while serving a righteous cause that reenforces his faith."

"Tell him to do his best but it must be done quickly. Within a matter of a few days.

A couple of days later it was too late. Roberto Calvi's driver arrived at his home on Thursday morning. Calvi had disappeared having taken an early train to Venice. From Venice, he flew via Zurich to London's Gatwick Airport on a private jet. The arrangements were made by Calvi's close confident Flavio Carboni a Sardinian entrepreneur and fixer. Carboni was also closely connected to Licio Gelli as well having direct Mafia connections. Through Carboni, Calvi obtained a false passport necessary for travel since his actual passport was held by the court pending his conviction appeal. Obtaining the false passport through Mafia financial organizer Giuseppe Calò, Carboni revealed Calvi's plans to flee Italy for London. Calò immediately passed those details to Monsignor Donaggio. The Mafia and Vatican Bank shared a common interest in Roberto Calvi's elimination.

Calvi registered at the Chelsea Cloisters Hotel in West London as Gian Roberto Calvini.

The following Monday, with Calvi declared a fugitive for violating his terms of bail, the Bank of Italy dispatched inspectors to Ambrosiano headquarters in Milan. Armed with court orders to access all bank records, Ambrosiano stock immediately fell twelve percent. That same day back-to-back loans amounting to $250M dollars became due. For Roberto Calvi, the end was imminent.

At 7:30 on the morning of Friday 18 June, a postal employee walking to work across the River Thames on Blackfriars's Bridge on the Thames River saw Roberto Calvi hanging by the neck from a makeshift noose tied to construction scaffolding under the bridge. In Calvi's pockets, police found five bricks weighing twelve pounds and the equivalent of $14,000 in three different currencies.

On the same day of Roberto Calvi's death sometime on Thursday 17 June, the Milan financial newspaper *Il Sole 24* Ore under Emma Nicoletti's byline published the text of the Bank of Italy's declarative letter of 31 May to Calvi as Ambrosiano chairman. The letter stated Banco Ambrosiano and its many offshore foreign subsidiaries under its control had an unaccounted balance sheet deficit hole of between $700M and $1.5B U.S. dollars equivalent. It further disclosed that Ambrosiano's largest debtor was the Vatican Bank.

The following day, Calvi's private secretary committed suicide by jumping from an upper window of Banco Ambrosiano headquarters in Milan. She left behind a handwritten note that rebuked Calvi for destroying the bank and so many lives among its employees.

The same day as Graziella Corrocher's suicide, Bank of Italy regulators seized control of Banco Ambrosiano Group. At the time, it was the largest private bank in Italy with 39,000 depositors and 4,200 employees.

†

For Archbishop Tagliente, Calvi's demise paved the way for the Vatican Bank to begin recovering from the 1970s financial scandal onslaught. Yet the crude circumstances of Clavi's death raised new conspiracy theories. Getting out onto the scaffold, then precariously climbing up to rig a noose using orange nylon rope while ladened with bricks in his pockets seemed absurd. He was dressed in a gray suit, waist coat, and striped shirt. Wearing shoes and socks, he wore no belt. An expensive wristwatch and wads of cash in different currencies. Unmistakenly the clumsy work of the Mafia. Learning of Calvi's fleeing Italy, Giuseppe Calò immediately dispatched a hit team to London then informed Monsignor Donaggio. Brother Gideon was ordered to stand down.

By the end of summer 1982, further complications arose for Archbishop Tagliente. The death of Roberto Calvi continued making news with the London coroner's initial verdict of suicide. The inconsistences so evident that it fueled a continuing story that kept the financial scandal and the Vatican Bank prominently in the news.

The curious death of Calvi's private secretary further added to conspiracy theories. Her suicide note made no personal comments to relatives, or even a sense of her own personal distress sufficient for taking her own life.

In September, the mysterious Licio Gelli was charged with espionage, political conspiracy, criminal association, and fraud. Gelli was arrested in Geneva, Switzerland on 13 September while attempting to access money held in a Swiss bank account. Without access to his vast network of influence, Gelli could no longer participate in a new money laundering channel controlled by the Vatican Bank. The subject of two international arrest warrants, Umberto Ortolani was forced to find sanctuary in São Paulo, Brazil. Undoubtedly that limited his utility.

Dealing directly with the Mafia held far too many risks for Tagliente given his recent public notoriety. Tagliente functioned in the shadows. His power came from clandestine activities with the cloak of plausible deniability. He felt the lucrative source of important revenues from access to illicit Mafia funds slipping away.

"A final threat also remained from the Vatican Banks' association with Roberto Calvi. The deputy director of Banco Ambrosiano's Milan headquarters Giuseppe Della Cha. Tagliente's questioning of Marcinkus at some length about what Della Cha knew made him uneasy. Della Cha was the designated messenger between Calvi and Marcinkus. It was Della Cha that verbally transmitted information of such sensitivity that no record trail existed within the Vatican Bank or Banco Ambrosiano. Giuseppe Della Cha knew everything. With Banco Ambrosiano undergoing a complete restructuring dictated by the Bank of Itay that meant replacing all former executive level management.

Della Cha suffered a nervous breakdown around the time everything began unraveling at Banco Ambrosiano. Donaggio's sources inside Ambrosiano headquarters reported Della Cha was scheduled to return to his office on the first Monday in October after several months of sick leave absence for depressive anxiety syndrome. He was 54 years old. Damaged professionally by association with the long running scandal of Banco Ambrosiano under Calvi's tenure, then suffered a protracted mental collapse. Undoubtedly circumstances make it difficult for someone his age to find new employment in banking. Tagliente also feared that Della Cha perhaps faced a long investigative process to answer unresolved questions related to the most spectacular banking failure ever in Italy.

Once again Archbishop Tagliente turned to Donaggio. Giuseppe Della Cha was the last loose end. "Another assignment for Brother Gideon, Ettore. Hopefully the last in this unfortunate financial scandal saga. Your discovery of the date of his return to work fixes the date of his demise. Unlike the removal of Calvi, Della Cha's death must clearly appear as suicide. In the same manner from the same building as Calvi's secretary. Jumping from a window from the Banco Ambrosiano building. Is that possible to stage?"

"A most difficult operation with so many people in a highly secured building. I shall have to consult with Brother Gideon."

"Again, time is short. We have only a week. Once he returns to his office there is no telling what might happen. Committing suicide on his first day back fits with someone having suffered a mental breakdown. A fresh shock triggering a spontaneous act of self-destruction."

†

After a couple of days of research, Brother Gideon devised a plan. The problem was not in how to commit the act of dumping the victim out his office window but rather gaining entry into the bank building protected by armed security. Even once inside, he must find the means of gaining entry unseen to Della Cha's office on the fifth floor.

Gideon's plan centered on the building's elevator. Researching the Banco Ambrosiano building plans on file in the Milan building department authority for the issuing of public permits provided a solution. Architectural plans detailed the make and model of the elevator system as an *Astor* elevator, the trademark of Italian manufacturer Alberto Sassi S.p.A. Gideon then obtained a full set of elevator drawings and schematics.

As with any intelligence service, the ability to manufacture credible fake documents is essential. Vatican intelligence was no exception. Brother Gideon created a fictious identity as an elevator service company. This included identification credentials using a disguised photograph, a work uniform with company logo to match a decal on a rental van, a work order for annual inspection certification, and a fake Banco Ambrosiano purchase order. Rounding out his disguise was a toolbox with suitable mechanical tools, electrical meter, and a systems service manual for the Astor elevator.

Theatrical clear-lens glasses and fake mustache while wearing a cap altered his appearance. Added years to his appearance. The loose-fitting overalls concealed his muscular build.

A former senior sergeant of the Italian Army's special forces 9th Paratroopers Assault Regiment with sixteen years of service made Brother Gideon a lethal weapon.

Born Gideon Daviti, his parents were devoted Catholics that delighted in their biblical-origin surname, give their youngest son an ancient biblical companion name. Daviti left military service in 1972. Looking to satisfy a spiritual need, he joined the Jesuit Institute of the Brothers of the Christian Schools in Rome as a lay brother at age 37. Monsignor Donaggio recruited him into Sodalitium Pianum in 1974. In Vatican intelligence, Daviti found a perfect place of devoting himself to the Church in a capacity that made use of his former military skills. Violent acts now justified as sanctioned by the Holy Father speaking as if from God. A necessity to maintain the Church's stature in the secular world. Brother Gideon's devotion to his singular holy crusade to protect the Church made him Donaggio's most trusted agent for the most unholy types of missions.

Dressed in a maintenance uniform with an embroidered logo, Brother Gideon entered Banco Ambrosiano headquarters located on Largo Bortolo Belotti, a three-minute walk from the La Scala Opera House in Milan. With the abundance of terrorism threats banks and government buildings maintained armed security. An attempt on the life of Ambrosiano vice chairman Roberto Rosone just months earlier attested to the threat climate. Brother Gideon came prepared with fake paperwork and convincing identification. After examination of his toolbox and search of his person, security personnel escorted him to a desk where he received a visitor badge. From there he took the elevator to the top floor. Walking down the hallway he came to a glass door marked stenciled *Giuseppe Della Cha, Vice Direttore.* He stepped inside and approached a secretary seated behind a desk.

"Excuse me, Signora. Could you direct me to the stairway to the roof? I am here to inspect the elevator."

"The other end of this hallway beyond the elevator door marked *maintenance, authorized personnel only.* Here is the key."

"*Grazie.*"

Inside the secretary's outer office he observed that he must have passed by Della Cha's inner office. Walking back toward the end of the hallway he came to a door marked *private* that must be another entrance to Della Cha's private office. He turned the doorknob slowly, discovering it was locked. With no one visible in the hallway, he extracted a lock pick case from his pocket and unlocked the door within less than thirty seconds.

Listening for any sound coming from inside, he opened the door. Della Cha was not inside. The inner door to the secretary's outer office area was closed. Quickly surveying the office layout, he then left closing the door to the hallway leaving it unlocked. To maintain his cover, he would go to the roof where the elevator control panel and mechanical apparatus were housed before returning to check again for Della Cha.

An hour later he descended from the roof. If Della Cha was still not in his office, he would linger by the elevator with the doors open as if checking on functional performance. However, listening at the door to the hallway, he heard someone speaking on the telephone. He stood there looking at his clipboard as if filling out paperwork. Hearing the conversation ended, he made his move.

Seated behind his desk with window and door leading out to a balcony overlooking a courtyard at the rear of the building behind him, Della Cha looked up in surprise.

Seeing the interior door to the secretary's area closed, Brother Gideon also feigning an expression of surprise. "Ah! Excuse me, Signore. I was looking for the door to the stairs to the roof." Taking a couple of quick steps toward the side of the desk, he thrust the clipboard out toward Della Cha as evidence of who he was. Within a couple of seconds, Gideon wrapped the crook of his right arm around Della Cha's neck preventing any outcry while reducing blood flow to the brain. Within ten seconds, Della Cha lapsed into unconsciousness. Gideon then eased Della Cha from his chair to the floor. Quickly he locked the office doors to prevent unwanted entry.

From an inside pocket Gideon extracted a handwritten suicide letter and placed it on Della Cha's desk. The letter written on duplicated Banco Ambrosiano stationary was drafted by Donaggio and written in longhand by a skilled forger using samples of Della Cha's handwriting. Addressed to his wife and two daughters the brief note read, *It is my fault. Kisses to Milena, Susi, and Gabriella. Papa.*

Unlocking and opening the door to the balcony, Gideon dragged the unconscious Della Cha outside. Lifting the victim from under his arms, he rested the body on the balcony railing. There appeared to be a few windows from other buildings that had line of sight but that could not be avoided.

Grabbing the body over his shoulder, Gideon let it slip over the railing to the courtyard below. The resounding thud of the body striking the ground from this height confirmed fatality.

Immediately, Brother Gideon left by the hallway door locking it first from inside then walked the elevator taking it to the ground floor. Exiting the elevator, there appeared no indication that the body of Giuseppe Della Cha had yet been discovered. After wiping his fingerprints from the visitor badge with a rag, he deposited it on the appropriate desk in the bank lobby. As he stepped outside, he heard the first panicked exclamations coming from inside. Walking briskly away to the van parked out of sight around a corner, he left unobserved before the arrival of the police.

CHAPTER 27

Palermo, Sicily | Autumn 1982

At 9:15pm on the evening of 3 September, 1982, Carabinieri Palermo Prefect General Carlo Dalla Chiesa was headed for dinner in the suburb of Montello. His wife Emanuela Carraro was driving a small Autobianchi A112 mini-coupe. Following was a larger unmarked Alfa Romeo Alfetta driven by police officer Domenico Russo.

Passing along Via Isidoro Carini, a Honda CB motorcycle pulled alongside the Alfetta. Driving the motorcycle was driven by Giuseppe Lucchese with Giuseppe Greco seated behind him. Both were experienced Mafia hitmen and favorite assassins of Corleonesi Don Salvatore Riina. Greco fatally shot Officer Russo with an AK-47 assault rifle causing his vehicle to crash.

Simultaneously, a BMW driven by Calogero Ganci pulled alongside Della Cheisa's car. Seated in the passenger seat, Antonio Madonia fired thirty rounds from an AK-47, instantly killing Carabinieri General Carlo Della Cheisa and his wife.

Frank Amatrano arrived at the scene within twenty minutes after receiving the news over the police radio as he was having dinner with other GICO officers. The following day, newspapers across Italy ran headlines of the *VIA CARINI MASSACRE.*

All of Italy was outraged. The assassination of a popular senior officer of the Carabinieri, following not long after the assassination of the member of parliament and anti-Mafia crusader Pio La Torre in April, crossed an unseen boundary. No longer would the Italian populace accept the unrestrained rampage of organized crime violence in the Southern Italian peninsula, especially the horrors of enveloping Western Sicily. Popular wrath now even turned against local Sicilian politicians that previously allowed the Mafia to operate illicit enterprises provided it did not spill over to killing civilians and police.

Just ten days after the assassination of General Della Cheisa, the Italian Parliament in emergency session passed the Rognoni-La Torre Law, Article 416 of the Italian Penal Code enacted on 13 Sep 1982. It included a unified version of proposed legislation by Christian Democrat minister Virginio Rognoni and draft legislation proposed by the Communist Party delegate Pio La Torre before his assassination.

The new Rognoni-La Torre Law, known also as *416-bis*, introduced swiping police and judicial powers into the Italian criminal code. It was patterned after the United States Racketeer Influenced and Corrupt Organizations Act, acronym RICO, enacted in 1970. The American example was proving an invaluable tool against combating organized crime.

The principal features of the law designated participation in a recognized organized criminal enterprise as a new category of criminal conspiracy. The courts could now confiscate assets of those actively involved in conspiratory as well as those acting as fronts and accessories. It made any association with organized crime a criminal offense. The language of Article 416 drew on the definition of organized crime as defined in 1930 under Mussolini's fascist rule that drove the Mafia underground until after World War Two.

For Frank Amatrano, the new law allowed him a rich list of Mafia targets from which to choose for arrest. Making a case no longer relied heavily on witness testimony or conclusive forensic evidence. The Mafia threat of violating the *omertà code* no longer became an impossible obstacle. Information already amassed in police dossiers of a lengthy list of known Mafia figures would prove enough to obtain arrest warrants. For Amatrano, vast new opportunities opened for turning Mafiosi against themselves by spreading misinformation.

†

Olivia Zangheri sat next to her uncle Bernado Provenzano at his home outside of Corleone. A large table set under shade trees on a sunny day with lunch being served to friends and family by several women. Early autumn was a particularly pleasant time of year this far south. Warm yet without the extremes of summer heat. Two smaller houses set off to one side of her uncle's grand house. Three agricultural production buildings of a working olive oil producing operation occupied half of the compound area surrounded entirely by a three-meter-high stone wall. Seventy-five hectares of olive trees surrounded the walled compound.

Bernado Provenzano, the underboss of the unified Corleonesi clan, lived on a grand scale. Unlike the don of the Corleonesi Mafia clan, Salvatore Totò Riina who remained a fugitive under an old murder charge, Provenzano remained free. Provenzano was more careful than the more impulsive Riina. A good working arrangement that allowed Riina to exercise his authority through Provenzano, who could operate more freely.

Yet Bernado Provenzano could be just as ruthless as Riina. He had come by information of a most disturbing nature. Something involving his favorite niece. A close family member that had killed on his orders. The information came from an informant within the Palermo Carabinieri headquarters. A civilian clerical staffer. Overheard comments suggested the police had a highly placed informer within the Corleonesis. Information pointed to the Guardia di Finanza intelligence officer from Rome working with General Della Cheisa, Colonel Amatrano.

Provenzano knew this was the same policeman that got Angelo Giancola killed after trying to turn him into an informer. The same policeman he learned responsible for arresting Paolo Falcone. The Palermo banker his niece was sleeping with to gain information for the Corleonesis. His favorite niece that killed the banker on his orders. Could this policeman have somehow gotten to Olivia? Threatened a charge of murder perhaps? Provenzano did not want to think that likely, but in his business you did not take unnecessary risks. A skilled covert entry technician placed a listening device on her apartment telephone. He assigned other people to monitor Olivia's movements.

After several weeks he received troubling information. On multiple occasions his watchers observed Olivia making calls from public telephones in the evening. Given the paranoia of Don Riina and the uncertainty of this new anti-Mafia law, Provenzano must determine if his niece is an informer. Her mother was Provenzano's sister, but Olivia's deceased father had never been involved with the Mafia. Could he be sure of her allegiance? Did she kill Paolo Falcone only because she had no choice? Did this policeman turn her? Don Riina would simply cut bait and eliminate her with question. Yet she was his blood family. That deserved certainty.

With the table being cleared of the afternoon feast, Olivia started to leave along with the others. Her uncle placed a hand on hers. "Stay a moment, Olivia."

Provenzano poured wine into Olivia's glass, saying "How have you been, my dear?"

Surprised, she answered, "I'm doing well, Uncle. Why do you ask?"

"No special reason. Just that we don't seem to talk like we used to. I feel bad for involving you with Paolo Falcone. Never could have expected the necessity of having to use you to *resolve the problem.* Yet you performed admirably. We live in a difficult world full of unpleasant tasks. You have a life ahead of you, Olivia. Remember, I am always here for you."

"Thank you, Uncle." She had no idea what prompted his comments.

A younger man approached, "I have some information for you, Boss." The man hesitated as he looked at Olivia.

"It's okay to speak, Tommaso. Olivia is family."

Still uncertain, the man said, "Greco and Madonia want to leave Palermo. Too many police patrols have been canvasing the area since the attack on the Carabinieri general."

"Where are they holed up?"

"An apartment above the Bar Villa Grazia on Via Falsomiele."

"Very well. Get word to them. We'll arrange to get them out of Sicily within two days."

An hour later, Provenzano embraced Olivia as she prepared to leave. With a look of sadness, even the appearance of tearing in his eyes, he kissed her on the cheek and forced a weak smile. "Goodbye, Olivia. Thank you for driving out here today."

Once Olivia drove away from the estate, Provenzano stood next to Tommaso. "You played your part well, Tommaso. Do we have people watching the Bar Villa Grazia?"

"Yes, Boss. They will call should the police show."

Provenzano acknowledged only by a nod accompanied by a heavy sigh.

†

Olivia Zangheri placed the call to Amatrano that night from a public telephone before reporting for her shift at the hospital. The call went to voice message. "I have information on the location of the possible assassins that killed the police general and his wife. Giuseppe Greco, nicknamed *Scarpuzzedda,* and Antonio Madonia. Greco is a favored Corleonesi assassin. Killed lots of people. Worked with Madonia on other jobs. For something this big, Greco must be involved. I overhead a conversation. Greco and Madonia are hiding in an apartment above the Bar Villa Grazia on Via Falsomiele. Some urgency to get them out of Sicily within two days because of increased police activity." She disconnected the call.

†

Within hours of receiving Olivia Zangheri's message, Amatrano mounted an assault force with joint GICO and Carabinieri officers. All the officers were armed with Berretta model 93R machine pistols fitted with 30-round extended magazines. Amatrano carried the same weapon within immediate reach as he led the assault in an unmarked Guardia car with a driver. The Model 93R was developed from the standard model 92 with the ability to select a three-round automatic burst mode, stabilized with a ported barrel. For urban close-range work a lethally effective weapon.

The assault force descended on the poor neighborhood of southern Palermo in unmarked vehicles and a couple of motorcycles with officers in plain clothes. Assuming the targets might be protected, Amatrano brought enough manpower to hit the bar while surrounding the building.

Two officers ascended the stairs leading to the upstairs apartment protected by a ballistic shield held in front. Reaching the top landing, they kicked down the door. Nothing happened. Moving quickly within the apartment with two additional officers coming in behind, they found no occupants.

Amatrano joined the search. A sterile location with no clothing in the closets. His guess, a Mafia safe house. Used sporadically. A place to bunk down. Food, drink, and protection provided from the bar below.

A few nights later, Amatrano discovered what happened. A call came from the Palermo Carabinieri commander. "Dispatch received an anonymous telephone. Caller said there was a dead body a hundred meters from our headquarters. The body of a woman in her late thirties. Wearing a nurse's uniform. Corleone Hospital. Badge identifies her as Olivia Zangheri. Wrists bound behind her back. Bullet to the back of the head. Was she known to the GICO, Colonel?"

Amatrano replied, "Yes. She was a niece of Bernado Provenzano. Maybe a victim of a Palermo Mafia family retaliating against Corleonesis. Another victim of this Mafia War."

Although he knew this could happen, Zangheri's violent end still troubled Amatrano. Although she had committed murder, she did not fit the mold of Mafia thug. Somehow her death felt different than the deaths of Angelo Giancola and his driver. A dirty business against an enemy that did not value life. However, Olivia Zangheri was not that much different.

†

For Bernado Provenzano, the necessary death of his niece was profoundly different than any other killing he ever committed. Personal family. She performed as well as any *made* soldier by infiltering the enemy then carrying out a necessary killing of someone with whom she was sleeping with.

Olivia's mother, Provenzano's sister, was distraught. His tale that this was the work of rival Palermo Mafia did nothing to alleviate her anger and grief. She railed against Provenzano for not protecting her.

For Bernado Provenzano, Olivia's death provoked the Sicilian cultural imperative for revenge. He was not to blame. This was the work of Colonel Francesco Amatrano. Olivia gave up that name when shown photographs before Provenzano personally delivered the fatal shot as she sat bound to a chair. Therefore, he must find the means of satisfying that revenge.

Killing this policeman might now become more difficult after the killing of General Della Chiesa. This unexpected new law added operational difficulties. After consulting with Don Riina, Provenzano placed a call to Giuseppe Calò.

†

The likely repercussions of Olivia Zangheri's death at the hands of her own family were not lost on Frank Amatrano. Might Emma now come under a new threat? For a Sicilian Mafia strongman like Bernardo Provenzano causing him to spill family blood warranted vendetta. Emma therefore became a likely target to get to him indirectly. With that in mind, Amatrano returned to Rome.

Explaining the circumstances to Emma, he said it was safer if she left Italy for a time. The apartment he never sold or rented was still vacant. "You could supervise remodeling. Been thinking we should never rent it. We need to spend more time there. We can afford to keep it while living in Rome."

"I'm not going to Paris while you remain here. Bad enough you must spend time in Sicily while I remain here in Rome. Sicily is a warzone. We've had this discussion before. I carry my Beretta."

"That's not good enough, Emma. Don't need to tell you the Mafia has a wide reach. This is no longer related to the financial scandal and the Vatican Bank. I am inflicting damage on these murderers. Causing internal distrust so they kill their own. Going to get worse with the new anti-Mafia racketeering law. Since I caused Provenzano to execute his niece, this undoubtedly becomes a Sicilian vendetta. You therefore become an obvious target as the means of getting to me."

She came and embraced him. "How much longer will this go on? I want us to live together in some in peace like normal people."

"This war will not go on indefinitely. Can't say how much longer, but I too want a life with you free from constant fear of a bullet. Returning to Paris together is something I think about often."

"You worry about my safety, yet you are the one on the front line. How do you protect yourself? If they can assassinate a Carabinieri general and his wife, how do we protect ourselves?"

"I have taken measures for myself. Always conducting my movements accompanied by other police officers. By avoiding maintaining consistent habit patterns. Staying in a secure police barracks when working in Palermo. If you are adamant about remaining in Rome, we need to elevate your security here in a similar manner."

"What does that mean?"

"The apartment is fairly secure. We are on the third floor. Only direct entry is the door to the hallway. It's a solid wood door. I'll add another deadbolt lock and have a carpenter fit a cross beam internally tying it to the door frame. Prevents forced entry from anyone trying to kick down the door. You cannot drive about yourself, though. I'll arrange for the police to drive you to and from your newspaper office. I will personally determine if the newspaper building is adequately secure. Lastly, while at home alone, you need to be better armed."

"You think all that is necessary?"

"I do. And I need the peace of mind."

As for firepower, he provided Emma with a Berretta 93R machine pistol with spare magazines. At the police firing range, while hesitant at first, she quickly became confident after firing hundreds of rounds.

"I see what you mean. Having this does provide a feeling of security," she admitted. Doesn't feel like a machine gun with these short three-round bursts."

"That's the point. Keeps the weapon on target. Keep it handy at all times when home. Remember outside the apartment to remain vigilant. That's where you are most vulnerable."

"I will. I always carry my regular Berretta in my handbag while holding it in my hand out of sight. You taught me well."

CHAPTER 28

Rome, Italy | Autumn 1982

Amatrano did not realize the stress he had been operating under since the death of General Della Cheisa. They had become friends. Dinner together with his wife. His personal security proved entirely inadequate. Underestimated the enemy. Amatrano would not make the same mistake.

Over dinner, Amatrano said to Emma, "Here is some news you will appreciate. I am placing Monsignor Donaggio under surveillance. Under the new Rognoni-La Torre Law, I have ample documented evidence providing probable cause of his association with organized crime. He might be a citizen of the Vatican, but that does not provide immunity outside its walls. Considering his ecclesiastical status, I still need something more incriminating to criminally charge him."

"Is it possible to monitor telephone calls from the Vatican?" Emma asked.

"Technically speaking yes. Politically, no. The Holy See has special status as a sovereign country embedded within Italy. No different than any foreign embassy."

"Someone else you should be interested in. You have heard me mention the name the name Giuseppe Calò. He's Sicilian

Mafia from Porta Nuova in Palermo. Known as *cassiere di Cosa Nostra* because of his financial expertise. Instrumental in creating the now defunct Banca Mercantile in Palermo as a Mafia-controlled back for money laundering. Calò also has historical connections with the Neapolitan Camorra. We believe Calò is key to Italian organized criminal money laundering.

"Calò lives in Rome. Goes by the alias Mario Agliarolo, an antique dealer. Been under surveillance by the Guardia and Carabinieri for years yet without success in gathering sufficient evidence for prosecution. That might change now with the new anti-racketeering law. Calò will undoubtedly be connected with restructuring Mafia money laundering with so many of the former principals out of the picture. Sindona, Calvi, Banco Ambrosiano, Ortolani, Gelli. The Vatican Bank remains the only entity still in play. If you are correct in your assertion that the Vatican Bank is deeply involved in trafficking illicit money, where will the lines intersect?"

Emma said, "Not likely that would be with Archbishop Marcinkus directly. He is under too much public scrutiny already. Doesn't have the required financial expertise. That leaves Archbishop Tagliente. Ultra secretive. With the brains and background. Has covert intelligence resources at his disposal."

"And Tagliente is suddenly thrust into the spotlight thanks to your publications," Amatrano said.

"Which means Tagliente must work through his covert operatives. Monsignor Donaggio in the forefront," she added.

"My thoughts exactly."

"With the new law, I have been successful in enlisting the Italian SISDE domestic intelligence service in monitoring electronic communications of Tagliente, Donaggio, and Calò. They already elevated their surveillance of known Mafiosi like Bernardo Provenzano some time ago. Crippling their communication makes doing business harder, especially with Salvatore Riina giving orders while still sought as a fugitive. More chances for making mistakes."

†

Although the Corleonesis increasingly became successful in taking territorial control of western Sicily Mafia operations, they began feeling the pressure of the Rognoni-La Torre Law. Arrests were on the rise. Witness testimony became less a factor for conviction thereby eliminating witness intimidation as the Mafia's most effective legal defensive tactic. Prosecuting magistrates could now make criminal indictments stick based on more easily obtainable evidence of criminal association. By ordering the murders of parliamentarian Pio La Torre and Carabinieri General Della Cheisa, Salvatore Riina pushed civilized Italy too far.

Among larger issues of war with rival Palermo Mafia families and increased police threat, pursuing a personal vendetta compromised the attention of Corleonesis Underboss Bernardo Provenzano. Killing Colonel Amatrano and his paramour the troublesome journalist became a matter of honor.

Summoning his most productive killer, Giuseppe Greco to his home, Provenzano issued him simple instructions. Using the common abbreviation of Giuseppe, "Pino, I have a mission for my most trusted assassin. An honor killing. I want to get at this Guardia Colonel Francesco Amatrano. A difficult target. He foiled a previous attack and killed both hitmen. Yet he possesses a weakness. A woman. This one also needs killing. But that must wait until she becomes bait to lure the policeman to his death.

"The mission is simple. You are to select two others to help you kidnap a woman named Emma Nicoletti. She is Amatrano's lover. You will seize her then transport her back to me here in Corleone. A suitable van with provisions will be provided for the journey. You should take her when she is alone at her place of residence. Best if you can do that without raising an alarm from other residents. You are not to harm her. She will die but not until her usefulness comes to an end with the death of Colonel Amatrano by my own hand."

Provenzano handed Greco a quantity of cash. "This should be sufficient to pay your team and expenses. Everything you need will be provided by people in Rome. Your contact is known only as *Il Cassiere*. Call this number from a public telephone. Give the person that answers the number you are calling from. You will receive a callback within ten minutes. The caller will provide all the information you will need and answer any questions."

"Are you ready to do this service, Pino?

"Yes, Boss."

"Then prepare to leave for Rome by train tomorrow. Air travel is too risky. Use false identifications. Take no weapons. Those will be provided once you reach Rome. I understand you will want to survey the location and make your plan. Do what is necessary but I want this done as soon as possible."

†

Pino Greco and two other Mafiosi soldiers watched the apartment in Trastevere for three days. They observed Amatrano leaving each morning and returning in the evening. Nicoletti left briefly only one time to walk a short distance to buy food. Greco took the opportunity to walk to the apartment door to determine how best to make quick entry. Two deadbolt locks plus the door handle lock made picking multiple locks impractical. That left kicking down the door. That risked alerting neighbors. This must be done quickly enough to grab the woman and make their escape. Another day, Nicoletti was escorted by two police officers then driven away in a Guardia di Finanza car.

Better to grab her outside the apartment, but that left it to only a chance opportunity of her going out within the neighbor for food. Provenzano counseled against that. Too many witnesses to raise the alarm. Waiting for such an opportunity might also take days. Provenzano wanted this done immediately. That meant making entry into the apartment soon after Amatrano left the apartment the next morning.

Kicking open the door could be difficult. The extra locks would delay making entry. Once back at the safehouse Greco went over the plan for the next morning with his two colleagues. He said, "To break through the door quickly, get a heavy short-handle sledgehammer at a hardware for breaking the locks. Noisy but quick. Park the van where I showed you. We then steal a car and drive it to the apartment building. Before dawn. Early enough to observe Colonel Amatrano leaving. After ten minutes we make our move. Any witnesses will see us leave in the stolen car that we abandon within minutes.

"Make sure everything is ready in the van for the long trip to Sicily. The Boss promised healthy bonus for pulling this off. Tonight, we will eat well with a little wine, but no hard liquor. Long day ahead tomorrow."

†

The next morning, Amatrano dressed in uniform and strapped on his sidearm. Emma was dressed in a sweater and slacks. "What's on your agenda today, darling?" he asked.

"Work, same as you. A few phone calls but mostly sitting in front of the typewriter."

"Not going anywhere?"

"No. We have pasta from yesterday. Stop and get a baguette and some wine when you come home. Maybe after dinner we can share each other for dessert."

He smiled broadly. "That's a deal." Before leaving they embraced with a lingering kiss.

Touching his cheek with her hand as she pulled back, "Now leave before I make you late."

"Is the machine pistol close at hand?"

"Of course. Once you leave, I keep it always within reach."

He unlocked the door then checked the hallway. After waiting to hear Emma set the locks he made his way down the stairs. Always with the flap on his holster undone with his hand on the Berretta, he carefully stepped outside scanning the area. Nothing stood out. His driver was sitting at the curb with the unmarked Guardia vehicle idling. "Good morning, Enzo. Anything look out of the ordinary?"

"No, Sir." Amatrano noticed with satisfaction that his driver had a Berretta 93R machine pistol sitting within reach on the passenger seat.

Pino Greco sat in the front passenger seat of the stolen car watching the apartment building with binoculars from a safe distance. Allowing several minutes for Amatrano to leave, they repositioned the car in front of the apartment building entrance.

All three Mafiosi exited leaving the car running in idle. The street was clear of pedestrians at this early hour. No traffic on this residential street in one of the quietest sectors of Rome.

The lock to the outer door of the building was quickly picked open. They proceeded up the stairway. Stopping at the landing before proceeding up to the top floor, the building remained quiet at this early hour.

Arriving at the apartment, Greco put his ear against the door. He could hear the faint sound of a typewriter. Turning toward his colleagues, he nodded while pointing to each of the three locks in turn indicating where to use the sledgehammer. Greco then backed away with one of the men to allow the other with the short-handle sledgehammer room to take full swings.

The top deadbolt lock dislodged on the first blow but held in place. A second blow tore the bolt away from the door jam. The next deadbolt took three blows to separate from the door jam. The man then stepped back attempting to kick the door open with only the door handle lock holding.

Unknown to the assailants, more than just the visible lock held the door in place. A steel pipe rested across the inside of the door fixed in cradles to each side of the door jam. Old fashion security, but effective.

Once the man stepped back to deliver a kick with his foot, a burst of three 9mm rounds pierced through the door. An instant later another three-round burst, followed in seconds by a third burst. The man wielding the sledgehammer took two rounds to the torso and a third to the head. The second man who had moved in closer when his colleague was about to release his kick, took a round in the lower abdomen and another to a knee.

Pino Greco could not believe the catastrophe. He dared what might be his fate if he returned to Palermo without the woman. Better to shoot her and claim one of his team disobeyed his orders.

Greco picked up the sledgehammer and gave a blow to the door handle lock expecting to open the door. It did not budge. Stepping quickly to the side, more rounds pierced through the door narrowly missing him.

Another blow with the sledgehammer failed to break through the door. In return more rounds came from inside.

Bewildered and fearing failure, no choice but to leave. The man with the head wound looked dead. The other might die from loss of blood from the gut wound. Regardless, he could not haul him down two flights of stairs with his knee disabled. Sirens in the distance told him he had little time to make his own escape and get out of Rome.

Inside the apartment Emma remained kneeling from behind a sofa. Her machine pistol poised in position over the back of the sofa refitted with a new magazine. The telephone pulled to the floor at her side. After several minutes of no further sounds from outside the door, she called Amatrano's private line.

†

By the time Amatrano arrived at the apartment, police were swarming the area. The dead man was laying in the hallway covered with a sheet. Emma was seated at the kitchen table drinking coffee with a female Rome Municipal police officer. She was composed but seething with anger. This had happened too many times to her. What had Italy become? Some third world country where civil society could no longer function?

After comforting her, Amatrano said, "Pack some things for a few days stay at a secure location. When you gather everything needed, have the police deliver you to my office. I will meet you there as soon as I can. I need to pay a visit to the wounded assailant at the hospital. You going to be alright?"

"Yes. Going to write up everything that happened. It will be in my newspaper tomorrow and out for syndication within hours. The police officer in charge already told me they identified these guys as Sicilian Mafia. Specifically, as Corleonesi Mafia."

At the hospital, Amatrano entered the police ward. At the side of the bed of the surviving wounded Mafia man fitted with all sorts of tubes, he said, "How you feeling, Santino?" The man looked away making no reply.

"You know of course Magnini didn't make it. Must have been a nasty surprise for both of you getting all shot up. Doctors say you'll live but fucked up. Never going to walk right with that knee. Lost some of your small intestines undergoing surgery. Might affect your eating or ability to shit right.

"Can't do anything about your physical problems. But you will be going away to prison for many years. How you get through that might have to do with where you serve time. Here's the situation. Witnesses say there were three of you. I want the name of the third guy and who ordered the hit."

"Fuck off, *poliziotto*."

"Thought you might feel that way Santino. Here's the deal I'm offering. You tell me what I want to know and give me a video deposition. If you do, I will see you serve your sentence in a prison far way to the north where few Sicilian Mafia serve time. Keep silent, then I comment to the newspapers that you are cooperating with the police. I will say the hit was ordered to get at me by Don Riina leaving the impression you confirmed that. Then I will see that you serve your time somewhere in southern Italy. Prisons full of Sicilian Mafia. How do you think Totò Riina will react?"

Santino Lanza said nothing for several moments, clearly digesting Amatrano's comments.

Amatrano stood silently waiting for Lanza's response.

"The guy in charge was Giuseppe Greco."

Amatrano said, "The same guy involved in the Via Carini Massacre."

Lanza looked surprised. "You know that?"

"Yes. Getting hard for you assholes to keep secrets. Things are coming apart, Santino."

"Who ordered the hit?"

"Provenzano. No comments about me to the newspapers then? You'll find me a safe prison to serve whatever sentence I receive?"

"The deal stands if you deliver your video deposition."

†

Emma Nicoletti released a blistering denunciation in print against the Mafia for targeting her a third time. She used the opportunity to link the Mafia to the financial scandals that she reported on regularly. In this latest article, she delved into the circumstances of the death of Roberto Calvi ruled initially as suicide in London. *Many articles have appeared in publications challenging the findings based on the reported forensic details. The overwhelming consensus among a host of experts contends that the finding of suicide is totally inconsistent with the evidence leaving the obvious conclusion as homicide.*

Could this conceivably again be solely the work of the Sicilian Mafia? The recent death of Banco Ambrosiano deputy director Giuseppe Della Cha in Milan makes the third death attributed to suicide of people associated with the scandal ridden bank. Add to this the remarkable coincidence of the death of Della Cha occurring in the same manner at Banco Ambrosiano headquarters by falling from a window as did Roberto Calvi's private secretary Graziella Corrocher in June. All these findings of suicide are currently called into question. I further suggest it makes compelling evidence that someone other than the Sicilian Mafia is behind multiple attempts on my life.

CHAPTER 29

Rome, Italy | Autumn 1982

Cardinal-Secretary of State Augustino Casaroli sat in his ornate office with Archbishop Luigi Poggi. "What do you make of this news of yet another attack by the Mafia on this journalist Emma Nicoletti, Luigi? She is widely known as a harsh critic of the Vatican. Could that involve the Vatican in some way?"

"Possibly, Augustino. Anything concerning Signora Nicoletti will undoubtedly resurrect her allegations of Vatican involvement and therefore accusations directed at Archbishop Tagliente. These latest assailants were Sicilian Mafia like those involved in previous attacks on her life. Yet her personal relationship with a colonel in the Guardia di Finanza might have other implications.

Casaroli replied, "Yet I still feel uneasy. Perhaps I am becoming paranoid about our colleague that lives in the shadows. These repeated attacks on Nicoletti all seem connected with the Archive documents. If her allegations of Vatican intelligence are credible, could the Mafia again just be acting under instructions from Tagliente? Perhaps it is time you have another discussion with this priest, Monsignor Orsini. We need his assistance in determining if Archbishop Tagliente or Monsignor Donaggio might be complicit in acts of violence. There can be no justification for ordained churchman engaging in such deeds of sacrilege."

"I share your unease, Augustino. I will consult with Monsignor Orsini immediately."

"You told me Orsini dislikes Tagliente. The reason for his leaving the Vatican secret service. Can his objectivity be trusted?"

"I believe so. Orsini strikes me as a good man. A devote priest. Skilled in the ways of covert intelligence functions. I also trust his motivation to render service to the Holy See. He explained leaving the Vatican because of Tagliente and Donaggio for the very reason he disagreed with their concept of what it meant to serve the Church. Using unholy methods contrary to the vows of the priesthood."

"Very, well. Enlist Orsini in doing what he can to find out more about Tagliente and Donaggio. If we are to counsel the Holy Father into removing Tagliente, we must present a convincing body of evidence."

"I understand, Augustino. I shall keep you informed." Luigi Poggi recalled Monsignor Orsini's reference that *removing cancerous tumors like Tagliente and Donaggio may require radical surgery.* For the pope to sanction such extreme action would require presenting truly compelling evidence that left no other less extreme remedy. That might prove impossible.

Poggi left Casaroli's office and made several telephone calls. Although without operational control over the Vatican secret service, he possessed tacit recognition as its official head. While never publicly acknowledged, the existence of a Vatican secret service was known among Italian law enforcement.

Poggi was also known as one of the most influential Vatican prelates within Pope John Paul II's intimate circle of advisors. A long-serving member of the Vatican Secretariat of State office, and personally close to Cardinal-Secretary of State Casaroli. Poggi therefore had access to influential senior Italian law enforcement officials. Yet he must be cautious. What he was going to ask could expose the serious drama playing out within the secretive Vatican closed community.

Poggi placed a telephone call to Lieutenant General Angelo Moretti, executive commander of the Guardia di Finanza. "General, I have a favor to ask of you. As one professional to another in our roles with dealing with matters of intelligence, this favor is particularly sensitive."

"I understand perfectly, Your Excellency. How may I be of assistance?"

"Within the Vatican secret service is a priest by the name of Monsignor Ettore Donaggio. Does the GdF have any reason to believe that this priest has connections with organized criminal elements?"

Moretti assumed Poggi might be pursuing allegations made by the journalist Nicoletti. Moretti also knew of Nicoletti's intimate relationship with Lt. Colonel Amatrano, one of his most productive senior officers.

Moretti replied, "Let me check and get back to you, Archbishop. I understand the sensitivity of your inquiry.

"One other question, General. The deaths of Roberto Calvi in London and the deaths of his private secretary at Banco Ambrosiano in Milan followed by the recent death of the deputy director of the bank have been reported as suicides. In the case of Calvi, there is much dispute over that finding. What is the opinion of the GdF?"

"Ah, that is an interesting question, Your Excellency. Is this somehow connected with the question about this priest?"

"Possibly, General. Like you, General, I am reaching into murky waters attempting to discover truth in the pursuit of justice."

"Very well, Your Excellency, I understand. You will hear back from me soon."

"God bless you, General."

Poggi placed the same request to General Moretti's counterpart in the Carabinieri, the other Italian national law enforcement agency.

Poggi's final call was to the Sant'Ignazio rectory. "Would Monsignor Orsini be available?"

"I believe he is in his office. Who might say is calling?"

"This is Father Estorzi. He knows me."

Orsini came on the line. "Good afternoon, Your Excellency. Been thinking about you and wondering if you might call on me again."

"Circumstances have progressed, Monsignor Orsini. Not for the better. I believe it is time that we meet again. Would this evening be a good time. Perhaps over dinner?"

"Absolutely. Since our last meeting, I have uncovered information you will find of interest. Do you have a place in mind?'

"Would the Hostaria Farnese on Via Dei Baullari, just off the Piazza Farnese, at 8:30 be satisfactory? Quiet location. Outside tables where we can speak privately."

"I will see you there, Your Excellency."

†

It was a comfortably warm October evening. Poggi arrived promptly at 8:30 and took a seat at an outside table. Ever the wary intelligence officer, Monsignor Orsini had been watching from a short distance away ensuring Poggi was alone. Approaching the table, Orsini noticed no indication of Poggi's elevated status as a prince of the Church. "Good evening, Father Estorzi," he said with a smile.

Poggi stood up and shook hands. "Thank you for joining me, Monsignor."

As they sat down, a waiter approached. "Might you have a good bottle of Barolo this evening?" Poggi asked.

"*Certamente, Padre,*" the waiter said and left.

"His Eminence Cardinal Casaroli has empowered me to seek your special assistance in the matter we discussed previously. We feel recent disturbing events indicate our concerns are justified. We must learn more before contemplating taking action. Will you help?"

Orsini nodded. "That two of the most respected prelates felt such a deep concern to seek my assistance in our early meeting left me profoundly troubled. I therefore set out immediately to begin taking action of my own to see if I could corroborate those concerns."

Poggi said, "God bless you. You then feel our fears are justified?"

"Regrettably, I do. I served in Santa Alleanza for thirty-five years. During my early years I know of at least two killings sanctioned by then Bishop Tagliente. The killer was a priest, the real Father Estorzi. Like me, he served in the counterintelligence *Sodalitium Pianum.* Father Niccolo Estorzi was known internally as the *messenger.* You might imagine how that reference came about. My point being that Tagliente sees his role in protecting the Holy See much differently than myself. Monsignor Donaggio is a malignancy devoted to Tagliente's Machiavellian ambitions above all else. But enough of historical background."

"Not at all, Monsignor. It confirms that I have come to the right person to lead us back into the light godliness."

Orsini replied, "A tall order. I have taken the liberty of enlisting the aid of two close friends. Both are priests. Both former agents of the Vatican secret service. Both left the Vatican for the same reasons I did. Like me, they returned to serving God in a conventional spiritual role. They are younger than me yet experienced in the tradecraft of intelligence work."

The waiter arrived. After waiting for him to remove the cork and pour wine then leaving, Orsini continued, "We have uncovered information of disturbing significance. Information confirming good reason for your concerns. Let me begin by revealing something that happened over two years ago that relates to Archbishop Tagliente. It involved a meeting I had with the journalist Emma Nicoletti who again appears as a victim of another attempt on her life."

"You met with her?"

"Yes. The meeting was at the request of a trusted journalist that I have known for some time. This journalist is a veteran Vatican watcher who is also closely associated with Signora Nicoletti. Our clandestine meeting occurred following the second attempt on Nicoletti's life. The killing of two Mafia gunmen following the prior bombing that took the life of Nicoletti's friend."

"Why did she come to you?" Poggi asked.

"Because of her belief that the attacks on her must have originated from the Vatican, not the Mafia. As she subsequently wrote in her recently published book, those attacks occurred before release of the confidential documents stolen from the Vatican Secret Archive. Signora Nicoletti is a skilled investigative journalist. If someone at the Vatican was behind these attempts on her life, then it must be the Vatican's Santa Alleanza, the historical name for the Vatican secret service I prefer to use.

"She knew that Vatican intelligence is run not by you but by Archbishop Tagliente. Since Tagliente heads the Vatican Secret Archive, he would likely have been the first to discover documents missing. Nicoletti correctly concluded the attacks were directed toward recovering the documents. The Mafia simply became the perpetrators acting on orders from someone else."

"What of this latest attempt on Nicoletti by the Mafia?" Poggi added.

"That is unknown. Might be solely Mafia retaliation as an indirect attack on her romantic partner. The former Interpol agent, now a Guardia officer with the anti-Mafia GICO division that saved her life by killing two Mafia gunmen. My information suggests Colonel Amatrano has become a serious threat to the Sicilian Mafia."

Poggi said, "You are remarkably well informed, Father."

"Old habits die hard. Trafficking in information is the way of intelligence. However, the attack might still involve Tagliente indirectly. Just reading the published accounts with added confidential information from the Vatican Archive casts credible suspicions on IOR involvement with the illicit activities of Sindona and Calvi. At best, Marcinkus has been a willing dupe. The IOR, the Archive, and the Santa Alleanza all exist outside control of the Curia. Tagliente has an academic background in finance. What other prince of the church has as much secret power secured by accountability only to His Holiness?"

"I see what you mean, Monsignor. Have you discovered anything else of interest since our first meeting?"

"Oh yes. Perhaps we should first order dinner. I see the waiter eyeing us."

After placing their orders, Orsini resumed. "If Tagliente is involved with the Mafia, he must discharge much of his clandestine activities through Monsignor Donaggio. Since you and I last met, Donaggio has twice met secretly with Giuseppe 'Pippo' Calò, boss of the Porta Nuova family from Palermo.

Poggi closed his eyes and shook his head. "That is truly dismaying. There can be no legitimate purpose for a Vatican priest meeting secretly with a notorious organized crime figure."

Orsini replied, "No there is not. Then of course Monsignor Donaggio is no ordinary priest. Calò has for years made his home in Rome. Close to the centers of power in the north. He uses an assumed name and operates under the cover of an antique dealer. He is known to the police as the *cassiere di Cosa Nostra*. They have not been able to build a case against Calò but believe he services not only the Sicilian Mafia but also the Camorra in Campania. There seems little reason for Donaggio and Calò meeting other than for something related to the financial scandal that is plaguing the Vatican with allegations of wrongdoing. The recent deaths of those connected with Banco Ambrosiano could therefore also be connected.

"And possibly the recent Mafia attack on the journalist Nicoletti?" Poggi added.

"Possibly," Orsini nodded as the waiter appeared with their dinner. "Let us enjoy our dinner before I pass along other information."

After the waiter served their food and left the table, Orsini said. "Thank you for suggesting this place, Your Excellency." After sampling his entrée, "The food and wine are excellent. Back to business. In the course of surveilling Donaggio, my associates believe someone else might also be doing the same."

"Who?"

"No way to tell. Cannot even be certain. Good operatives learn how to disappear into their surroundings. But there can be slight indicators to the trained eye. If correct, I suspect the police or possibly even Italian domestic intelligence the SISDE. The relevance being that others beside you and the cardinal secretary of state are suspicious of the activities of Santa Alleanza and therefore Archbishop Tagliente."

Poggi sighed with despair.

Orsini said, "I myself have watched Tagliente's private residence for several hours on many evenings as my surveillance contribution. He lives in a large house on the Piazza Fiammetta. On three occasions, I observed Monsignor Donaggio paying a visit. Typically staying for over an hour."

"Why is that of significance?"

"Could just be something involving matters requiring more immediate attention after Tagliente has left his Vatican office. However, it could be Tagliente observing another layer of secrecy. Not only does he operate covertly from the outside world, but also from within the Vatican itself. Whatever his involvement in a conspiracy, it must involve keeping records in a secure place from which he can conduct business. Tagliente is brilliant and highly practiced in intelligence tradecraft for more than three decades. Do not expect him to make mistakes."

"You describe a formidable adversary," Poggi remarked.

"That he is. You might also say he is a most usual prelate of the church. A throwback to a period in history before the unification of Italy. A time when the Vatican operated as a secular monarchy. When churchmen were more a part of that secular world with all that entailed. Mounting armies. Engaging in espionage. Conducting affairs of state involving all manner of unsavory activities. Churchmen acting as men with normal carnal desires."

Poggi raised an eyebrow registering surprise.

"Although it is not related to Tagliente's suspected sins representing your concerns, it is relevant to understanding the man. You see, one evening I followed Tagliente to the train station. Dressed not in clerical garb, but rather a normal business suit in gray. I took the same train. A short journey to Frascati where we both disembarked. Following discreetly, Tagliente walked to a lovely mansion where he knocked on the front door. A woman answered. A beautiful woman. They embraced and kissed then disappeared into the house. I stayed long enough to see the lights turn out after midnight. Tagliente spent the night."

"Who is this woman?"

"The following day, I learned her name. Isabella Leonardi. An aristocrat. Unrelated to Tagliente. Making further inquiries, it is clear Leonardi is Marcello Tagliente's mistress of many years."

"I understand how that adds to your broader characterization of Tagliente the man."

Orsini continued. "One final piece of information that is more relevant, Your Excellency. If Tagliente and Donaggio are involved in any activity as debased as murder, it might involve a lay Jesuit brother by the name Brother Gideon. His full name is Gideon Daviti. Attached to the Institute of the Brothers of the Christian Schools headquartered on Via Aurelia here in Rome. He is employed in an obscure position that involves a link with the Vatican. Daviti's parents are devote Catholics. In his own distorted way, so is Daviti. Delighted by having a biblical origin surname they gave their youngest son an Old Testament matching biblical name.

"Brother Gideon came to the religious life at age thirty-seven. Why that came about I do not know. Before that he served in the Italian special forces for sixteen years. Violent skills learned in the military later became available to Donaggio.

"I left Santa Alleanza in 1974 when Donaggio was elevated to monsignor and became head of Sodalitium Pianum. However, my two fellow priests assisting me served after 1974. It became common unspoken knowledge that Brother Gideon was Donaggio's most covert operative for missions that have no place within a religious body. Santa Alleanza has existed for five hundred years based solely for purposes outside the spiritual necessities of the Vatican. Therein lies its ethical divide from Roman Catholic Christian beliefs."

Poggi said, "I take your meaning to be that Archbishop Tagliente not only possesses the ambition to pursue ventures far removed from the moral teachings of the church, but that he also possesses the means."

"That is correct. The rationale for Tagliente, Donaggio, and Brother Gideon all taking vows within the Church to then embrace actions that conflict with those vows in the extreme is impossible for priests like us to comprehend. Yet for their own twisted reasons they have bonded in an unholy alliance. The cancer has advanced so far that it will require extraordinary spiritual will for devout priests to listen to their hearts and act with God's guidance. The Holy See must be saved from suffering yet another moral catastrophe."

Before parting, Poggi said, "I trust you will continue your efforts, Monsignor. Do you require funds for your special endeavors?"

"Not yet. It is just me and two fellow priests doing God's work in a different manner.

Poggi made the sign of the cross and shook Orsini's hand, "I shall convey everything you have told me to Cardinal Casaroli. I shall also pray for you and your fellow priests. God bless you, Monsignor Orsini."

"God bless you, Archbishop Poggi for having the courage of your faith."

†

After Poggi conveyed everything from his meeting with Orsini, Cardinal Casaroli said, "Our worst fears made real, Luigi. Is that overstating the problem?"

"Not at all, Augustino. Everything points to Archbishop Tagliente pursuing some sort of clandestine conspiracy that we are trying to piece together from fragments of evidence. Enough though to form a troubling picture of a senior churchman acting against everything the Church should stand for. Why and exactly what Tagliente has embarked upon can only be speculated. However, evidence of what is happening leaves little doubt as to his collusion with the Sicilian Mafia.

"That is borne out by the sequence events surrounding the stolen Vatican Archive documents. Nicoletti is correct, and Orsini agrees, that the bombing and subsequent attempts on Nicoletti's life point directly to the Vatican. Tagliente was the only senior churchman who was aware documents were missing. That meant that the bombing that killed Nicoletti's colleague and the subsequent two attempts on her life happened with Tagliente's full knowledge. Probably on his orders."

Casaroli commented. "Now Orsini has confirmed repeated contacts between Monsignor Donaggio and an influential Mafioso."

Poggi replied, "And that mafioso is likely connected with the financial scandal where money laundering for the Mafia is a repeated allegation against bankers and others with which the IOR has been connected with all manner of documented association. Then there are the questionable deaths of those associated with Banco Ambrosiano. Could be the acts of a vengeful Mafia for having suffered financial losses. I believe there is more to it than that. Regardless, the Vatican becomes tainted by its intimate connection between Archbishop Marcinkus and Roberto Calvi."

"Could it be any worse, Luigi?"

"Possibly. I am still waiting for replies to inquiries I made to senior officers of both the Guardia di Finanza and the Carabinieri. Officers with which I have a good relationship. Depends on what they know and are willing to divulge to me concerning those involved in the Italian banking scandal, their connections with the Mafia, and how any of this affects the Vatican. I expect replies very soon."

Casaroli said, "We can weather this financial scandal by continuing to claim the IOR was victimized by unscrupulous bankers. A flawed assertion with the abundance of evidence in the public domain. Yet, it will pass into history given time. However, I fear any association with the worst criminal elements of organized crime for financial gain will irreparably damage the Holy See. There can be no justification. Worse than the forgotten stain of assisting murderous war criminals following the Second World War."

Poggi added, "Tagliente was even involved in that misguided episode in our history."

†

The following day, Guardia di Finanza General Moretti telephoned Luigi Poggi. "Before I provide you with highly confidential information, I must ask who you will share it with, Your Excellency?"

"Certainly, General. I realize my inquiry is most unusual. I truly appreciate your assistance. I swear to you that I will only identify you as the source of this information to Cardinal-Secretary of State Casaroli and the Holy Father, should that even become necessary."

"Thank you, Your Excellency. Regarding your question about Monsignor Ettore Donaggio, we do have a dossier. The first entry is 1976. It began with an observed meeting with the Sicilian Mafia Don Giuseppe 'Pippo' Calò of the Palermo Porta Nuova Mafia family. Calò has been a person of interest for years. We have amassed a sizeable dossier on him. Known as the *cassiere di Cosa Nostra,* we believe he has extensive networking connections within the broader Italian organized criminal community. That means money laundering. We have never been able to assemble sufficient evidence to bring criminal charges.

"Anything beyond this connection to this Mafioso Calò?" Poggi asked.

"Yes, there is. Donaggio maintained a frequent connection with the Palermo Mafia. He used the confessional at a Palermo Catholic church to secretly meet with an individual involved with a Mafia-controlled bank. That individual was later assassinated by the Mafia while in police custody as a witness.

"As to your question about the deaths of the three individuals associated with Banco Ambrosiano officially all ruled as suicide, there is serious doubt. My people categorically disagree about Roberto Calvi's death being self-inflicted. The forensic details reported to us by London Scotland Yard clearly point to homicide. The crude preparations to appear as suicide suggest the work of the Mafia. They are never subtle.

"As to Calvi's secretary jumping from a window at the banks' headquarters in Milan, the evidence points to suicide although the suicide note is unusual for making no statement of regret to her loved ones. However, the same death by falling from a high window at the same building for the deputy director of the failed bank remains in question. We have not released further comments because an investigation is ongoing.

"If nothing else, the coincidence is troubling. Yet the handwritten suicide note appears genuine, although it is short and somewhat cryptic. More troubling is testimony from several bank employees about an elevator maintenance man visiting the bank the same morning that the deputy director fell to his death. The bank made no request for service on the elevator. With the name of the service company nonexistent, cause of death remains at best unexplained.

"Add to that uncertainty, Banco Ambrosiano Deputy Director Della Cha was known to be the messenger between Roberto Calvi head of Banco Ambrosiano and Archbishop Paul Marcinkus of the Vatican Bank. The last person of interest that might have further information on the relationship between Ambrosiano and the Vatican."

"Are you saying someone other than the Mafia might be involved in these questionable deaths?" Poggi asked.

"Let me be candid about the financial scandal surrounding Banco Ambrosiano, Your Excellency. You of course must be familiar with allegations raised by the journalist Emma Nicoletti in her financial newspaper and recent book."

"I am painfully aware of her allegations directed toward the Vatican."

"Not the Vatican as a whole but specifically the wrongdoings of the Vatican Bank. She has also brought forth from the shadows the existence of Vatican intelligence. In the process she makes thinly veiled allegations against Archbishop Marcello Tagliente. The Guardia di Finanza believes much of Nicoletti's information is accurate. We cannot say that Archbishop Tagliente is guilty of any wrongdoing, however associations with criminal figures by his chief lieutenant Monsignor Donaggio rightfully raise suspicions."

"Can you be more specific, General?"

"Certainly. First of all, there exists convincing evidence that the Vatican Bank is criminally involved with financial crimes in its association with Banco Ambrosiano. If not for the Vatican's stature as a sovereign foreign country, charges would otherwise already have been brought in Italian court.

"Secondly, we believe that Nicoletti's allegation that someone in the Vatican was behind at least two of the attempts on her life. That first attempt resulted in the murder of her associate. The assailants killed in the second attack being Mafia does not alter that assertion. Something is truly rotten within the Vatican, Your Excellency.

"Lastly, the collapse of Banco Ambrosiano has crippled Mafia money laundering. Law enforcement efforts have closed a Mafia-controlled bank in Palermo instrumental in funneling illicit drug trafficking money into the international financial environment for laundering by comingling with legitimate assets. The Mafia must be desperately looking for a means of repairing that process. Monsignor Donaggio's association with the Mafia's principal moneyman becomes of interest."

Poggi felt devastated. "Your information leaves me with a heavy heart, General. I understand that we of the Church must do something to address our own shortcomings. My sincerest appreciation for your candor. May God bless you, General."

That same day, Poggi received a call from his Carabinieri contact. He received similar information about Giuseppe Calò, but nothing specific about Monsignor Donaggio. Of more interest was a detailed description of the Mafia attack at Emma Nicoletti's residence. The Carabinieri saw this as a probable indirect attack on Guardia Colonel Amatrano for his anti-Mafia campaign in Sicily following the assassinations of La Torre and General Della Cheisa. His source did make the comment that Nicoletti's allegations that the prior two attempts on her life were initiated from within the Vatican remained a credible possibility.

CHAPTER 30

Rome, Italy | Autumn 1982

Cardinal Casaroli sat in his large office across from Archbishop Poggi. Sunlight poured into the elegantly appointed room from two large windows in the high-ceiling room. Poggi had just finished recounting the information received from his Italian law enforcement sources.

Casaroli said, "There remains no question that Archbishop Tagliente must be removed. How becomes the problem. We must first convince the Holy Father. That may not be easy. His Holiness seems to have an affinity for the ambitious Tagliente."

"Perhaps not so much for the archbishop personally but for the utility he represents," Poggi offered.

"What do you mean?"

"The Holy Father is strong willed. He has distinct views on the secular dealings of the Church. Living his life under the political strain of Communism has shaped his world views. He has placed Archbishop Tagliente in positions where he exercises absolute control. Santa Alleanza, the Secret Archive, and now the IOR. All outside the meddlesome oversight from the Curia. The challenge centers on convincing His Holiness to remove Tagliente from heading Santa Alleanza. After decades in charge, Tagliente has transformed Santa Alleanza into something far removed from information gathering. Sodalitium Pianum is nothing more than covert operational agents like the American CIA or the Soviet KGB. All responsible for engaging in disreputable missions."

Casaroli said, "Repercussions associated with simply reassigning Tagliente to some diocese far from the Vatican must also be considered. Tagliente might become vindictive. He might even leave the priesthood. Such a move could unleash a torrent of unintended consequences beyond our ability contain. Tagliente's misdeeds would undoubtedly come to light.

"Tagliente is disliked by our brother prelates. Too many outsiders in law enforcement and the Bank of Italy possess incriminating evidence of Vatican involvement with Italian organized crime. That is the singular issue that would create a scandal of catastrophic proportions. Vatican participation with the Mafia to launder money for its own economic interest. Acting like some tax haven hiding behind its sovereign state status with a self-imposed reputation for secrecy. The IOR becomes a financial pariah. To the faithful, something profoundly far more damaging. The Holy See acting against the very foundations of our Faith."

Poggi added, "The resulting scandal will also consume the pontificate of Pope John Paul II. Some of this began during Pope Paul IV's reign, but the worst excesses continued under John Paul's governance. Plausible allegations of involvement in multiple murders while in league with the Mafia, the scope of such a crisis becomes impossible to image. The stain may never be erased."

Casaroli took a deep breath to calm himself. He then asked the question to which he feared he already knew Poggi's response. "What course of action do you recommend, Luigi?"

Poggi now paused before uttering the inconceivable. "Tagliente must be physically eliminated. Monsignor Donaggio as well. Only their deaths attributed to the hands of others far removed from the Vatican can cleanse us of the problem while burying their past misdeeds."

Casaroli shook his head, "The Holy Father will never sanction something ... something so extreme. My God, he is the pope!"

Poggi said, "Then he must be kept in the dark. We must convince him with evidence of the necessity of removing Tagliente. We then convince him that you and I have agreed to find the means of accomplishing this in such a way as to protect the Holy See and his person from further damage. We offer to relieve him of the unpleasant burden while avoiding specifics. We give His Holiness plausible deniability, even to himself."

"Very well, Luigi. We have no choice. Neither of us can avoid our ecclesiastical responsibilities and vows by doing nothing. Inform Monsignor Orsini to proceed. He need not inform us of the details. Explainable deaths of Archbishop Tagliente and Monsignor Donaggio by forces unknown becomes the singular requirement. Obviously, should Orsini and his associates fail in this mission, we shall disavow any knowledge."

"I understand. I will meet with Orsini today, Augustino."

Casaroli said, "While Monsignor Orsini pursues his dark business, I need your expertise in outlining the background facts and circumstances. Then framing our recommendations to His Holiness in a manner that argues there is no other alternative. Prepare for me the principal points of what we are to counsel His Holiness as a course of action. Powerful enough to convince the Holy Father of doing something requiring what he will see as a supreme sacrifice."

Poggi nodded and stood up from his chair. "Pray for divine guidance, Augustino. The fate of the Holy See perhaps may rest on our shoulders."

†

Poggi sat with Monsignor Orsini again at the Hostaria Farnese. "I received information that corroborates the concerns you raised, Monsignor. The time has come for us to take action."

"Specifically, what course of action?" Orsini asked.

"The removal of Tagliente and Donaggio. To use Shakespear's phrasing in Hamlet, *devoutly to be wished. To die, to sleep.* However, in such a manner as to leave nothing pointing toward the Vatican. Can that be accomplished?"

"Difficult. Not without extreme risk, but I believe it to be possible. I am surprised that you have arrived at the same conclusion I suggested as your only assured option for closing off repercussions. As a former professional in covert activities, I gave the problem considerable thought."

"How can this be done?" Poggi said.

"Might you prefer not to know details, Your Excellency?" Orsini raised his eyebrow in a questioning expression.

"Perhaps you are right. Would you and your associates be willing to undertake such a mission?"

"Yes. We are only three priests but share your devotion to the Church. Like you and Cardinal Casaroli, such an unpleasant undertaking is regrettably necessary. While you need not know all the details, I will require your participation in providing a couple of critical items."

"What items?"

"A letter signed by the Holy Father. A document written to an individual stating only in unspecific terms a request for his service. It should contain the following." Handing a typewritten page to Poggi, it read: *You are needed to provide a service in absolute secrecy to the Holy See. The details of that service shall be expressed to you at a later time by His Excellency, Archbishop Poggi. By accepting this duty you are solemnly swearing to hold secret from conveying any details to anyone on pain of excommunication. We extend our blessing to you Brother Gideon. Go with God."*

"This is the same person you told me about that is suspicioned as committing violent acts for Donaggio?"

"That is correct."

"Why should he help you?"

"Because he is a fanatic. While devoted to Tagliente and Donaggio, I will count on his greater devotion to the Holy See, represented by the Holy Father. As a former soldier, we must risk playing on not only his devotion to the Church that brought him into a religious life, but to the chain of command indoctrinated in the regimentation of a soldier. The pope ranks as the commanding general. To solidify that, I shall need you to show Gideon that letter in my presence, of course. However, you shall retain the letter in your possession, and I presume then destroy it after serving its purpose.

"That is to be followed up with a blessing personally by the Holy Father."

"God lord! Are you serious?"

"Necessary to convince Brother Gideon to betray his immediate superiors by such an extreme act. This undertaking is without precedent. Brother Gideon may balk in taking such extreme action. A calculated risk. In which case he becomes expendable."

"What if he simply turns to Donaggio or Tagliente and exposes your plan."

"That is certainly a possibility. Should that happen, the obvious repercussion is providing Tagliente with knowledge of a conspiracy against him. That will undoubtedly place all our lives in jeopardy given his proclivity for resorting to violence. Perhaps using Brother Gideon or the Mafia as proxies. That becomes a risk we all must take. Part of our vows. Worse ways to die than martyrdom for our faith."

Orsini's comment stung Poggi for his timidity in this grave hour. "Why is Brother Gideon so necessary to this plan?"

"Because he understands explosives. He becomes the only resource available with proficiency in bomb making. Using a bomb is the most effective way to mask this as a Mafia assassination or terrorist attack. Removing Tagliente and Donaggio in any other manner is fraught with problems adding to unacceptable risk. Discovery of our involvement would create an even greater crisis of faith for the Holy See.

"Let me add this additional caveat. By executing Tagliente and Donaggio Brother Gideon has effectively sealed his silence. Even if discovered as the perpetrator, we all have plausible deniability. His allegations will hold little credibility for someone with his background. Portrayed as mentality unbalanced, who would believe his rantings asserting that orders to kill these churchmen came from other higher-ranking churchmen? What could be the motive?"

"What about this papal blessing?"

"Simply obtain a ticket to the papal audiences held at the Vatican most Wednesdays. His Holiness needs only to hand the parchment to Brother Gideon and give his usual blessing to that day's group of supplicants. It is not necessary for His Holiness to know anything of Brother Gideon beyond his being a lay member of a Jesuit service order."

Poggi said, "I take it your plan involves the use of explosives?"

"Probably. That might change. Explosives make this arguably the work of terrorists or the Mafia lashing out for some undefined reason. Brother Gideon will know how to disguise his bomb with the technical signature making it appear the work of others known for using explosives."

"I shall discuss your plan with Cardinal Casaroli. If he agrees, I shall deal with attempting to get this papal letter signed by His Holiness. Assuming we are successful in convincing him of removing Tagliente.."

"That will require some clever subterfuge. I don't suspect you can be candid about what you and Casaroli are up to with the Holy Father. All of us might be risking excommunication should our plotting go awry."

"May God be with us in this sacred endeavor, Monsignor Orsini. I shall be in touch."

†

Poggi returned to the Vatican immediately after meeting with Orsini. Being late in the evening he went to Cardinal Casaroli's private Vatican apartment in the San Carlo Palace. Casaroli was expecting him.

After Poggi completed reiterating the details of his meeting with Orsini, Casaroli said, "My God, Luigi. What we are about to do makes me physically ill. Does Orsini believe he can induce this Brother Gideon to kill Tagliente and Donaggio?"

"Not Orsini, me. Acting in my capacity as the official head of the Vatican Secret Service, not Tagliente. Speaking for the Holy Father evidenced by this letter we need His Holiness to sign. Regarding your question, the willingness of Brother Gideon to do this depends on Orsini's reading of Gideon's devotion to the Church and therefore the Holy Father. Does he supersede his loyalty to his immediate superiors? May depend on how well I present a convincing presentation that I am making a direct plea as if speaking for the Holy Father. I shall portray this as a calling from God as described in the Old Testament. Back it up by a personal letter signed by the Holy Father. That letter naming Brother Gideon specifically becomes the instrument to convince him this is a holy mission personally sanctioned by the pope to save the Church."

Casaroli sighed and lowered his head. "Pray with me now, Luigi. We both require the opening of our hearts to listen for divine guidance. Is what we are about to embark upon truly God's will?"

The two prelates in their sixties left their chairs then used cushions from a sofa to kneel on the hard parquet floor before a crucifix hanging on the wall. Their silent prayers lasted for ten minutes.

After struggling to their feet, they returned to their chairs and looked into each other's eyes.

Casaroli spoke first. "I see no alternative but to proceed by relying on Monsignor Orsini. Allowing Tagliente to create further harm to the very foundation of the Holy See is unconscionable given our sacred vows. What does your soul counsel in this matter, Luigi?'

"I am in agreement, Augustino. Finding Monsignor Orsini may be God's answer. Without Orsini's special assistance, there would be no recourse to end Tagliente's reign of sacrilege."

Casaroli said, "To begin, I need you to draft a working scrip of how best to proceed with the Holy Father. Do your best work, my friend, but quickly. If His Holiness cannot be convinced of removing Tagliente then we will not move forward. Agreed?"

"I fully agree. We shall take the decision of His Holiness as that of God speaking."

"Proceed then with informing Monsignor Orsini. Inform him that it becomes contingent upon the Holy Father agreeing to remove Archbishop Tagliente, albeit without knowing the drastic form of that removal. Tell Orsini to pray for all of us."

✝

Archbishop Poggi drafted a thorough reciting of the factors that dictated the removal of Archbishop Tagliente from his Vatican offices. Perhaps the most important document he ever created. The difficulty was making a strong enough case to counter Pope John Paul's obvious reliance on Tagliente. The pope reaffirming his support for Marcinkus against an onslaught from numerous Vatican prelates he trusted gave some insight into the Holy Father's managerial style. Removing Tagliente seemed an even greater hurdle.

The other challenge was presenting a compelling case that had many moving parts. The equality of the body of evidence against Tagliente required explaining the significance in detail to understand its context within a complex narrative. That narrative could fill pages just explaining the significance of a long list of associations with disreputable characters. Presentation time was limited for making a convincing case for such a momentous move. He did his best to condense the material into a persuasive executive summary.

Casaroli read Poggi's package. A working document that he carefully organized into a concise overview bullet point presentation to stay on message. He and Poggi would deliver this in a private session with the Holy Father. Casaroli as the most senior churchman, second only to the pontiff, would deliver the dramatic objective for requesting the private papal audience. Poggi was closest to understanding all the interlocking details and therefore would best be able to answer questions necessary for making their case.

Finishing studying Poggi's material and asking questions, Casaroli said, "Brilliant work, Luigi. Remarkably persuasive when taken in its entirety. Even if the Holy Father is conceptually in agreement, he may still not follow our recommendations. He might even make matters worse by doing something unexpected."

"True. That remains beyond our control. Do not lose sight of another unintended consequence should His Holiness approve our actions. Think of the aftermath if Orsini's plan is successful. Two churchmen killed in an explosion. Coincidental? The pope may legitimately conclude that we mislead him, Augustino. I know of no way around that. Martyrdom may mean the end of our ecclesiastical careers. Should that happen, I will accept that as my sacrifice.

"Let us assure ourselves through continual prayer that we are acting righteously. One last question before we proceed in requesting a private audience with the Holy Father. What becomes of Brother Gideon after executing this deadly act?"

"Orsini will promise to relocate Brother Gideon to any Jesuit organization in the world with a modest financial stipend. His activist days dealing in violence are over. He can never confess to crimes of murder without personally suffering the consequences of excommunication or murder under Italian law."

Casaroli sighed and said, "Are you ready to seek an audience with the Holy Father?"

"Yes. Although with the greatest fear I have ever experienced. May God truly help us, Augustino."

CHAPTER 31

Rome, Italy | Autumn 1982

The pope's secretary opened the door to the pontiff's study allowing Casaroli and Poggi to enter. The door closed behind them as they walked to Pope John Paul seated in a chair around a low table. After kissing his ring, John Paul shook their hands in a personalized handshake of affection using both his hands. Both churchmen were among his closest advisors as well as close friends. Augustino Casaroli, as secretary of state, met with the pontiff almost daily. Having served within the Vatican Secretariat of State office for many years, including as nuncio to Poland, Luigi Poggi worked closely with John Paul's efforts in promoting engagement with Communist countries.

John Paul said, "Be seated my dear friends. What brings us together? Stanislaw made your request for an audience sound dire by its sense of urgency, especially without revealing its nature." Father Stanisław Dziwisz was John Paul's private secretary. A fellow Pole, ordained by John Paul. "These are trying times. What is troubling you gentlemen?"

Casaroli began, "A dreadfully unpleasant matter that we believe harbors the most dire consequences for the Holy See, Your Holiness. Allow me to frame the problem with some background.

Archbishop Poggi and I have been closely following events appearing in newspapers internationally for several years. Beginning with what might be called the Italian Banking Scandal, accusations repeatedly appear speculating, even making accusations against the IOR.

"The situation changed three years ago with a car bombing outside Milano Centrale train station. An American journalist died, and his Italian associate was badly injured. Only weeks later, another attempt was made on the life of that same Italian journalist injured in the bomb blast. Her name is Emma Nicoletti. Two assailants identified as Sicilian Mafia attempting to again kill her died at the hands of an Interpol agent protecting her."

John Paul commented. "Yes. More of this unceasing violence plaguing Italy. This is the journalist that is unfriendly to the Holy See. I read excerpts from her latest book. She also authored an earlier book that resurrected an unpleasant episode following the Second World War during the pontificate of Pius XII."

"Regardless of her intentions, Your Holiness, Archbishop Poggi and I have unfortunately concluded that her allegations condemning of the Vatican for recent events are most likely correct."

John Paul looked surprised by Casaroli's comment but made no comment.

"That became the starting point for uncovering a most distressing sequence of events. Within the last several months Archbishop Poggi and I have uncovered conclusive evidence pointing to the likely commission of horrific acts of violence directed by a senior Vatican prelate. Archbishop Marcello Tagliente.

John Paul's expression instantly turned grave yet he continued remaining silent.

"As unbelievable as that sounds, Archbishop Poggi and I embarked on an intense investigation. Luigi has discreetly used certain outside sources to assemble a damning picture of conspiracy by Archbishop Tagliente. At the heart of his misdeeds lies irrefutable evidence of his direct association with known organized crime figures using his subordinate Monsignor Donaggio, the head of Vatican counterintelligence, Sodalitium Pianum.

"Corroborated circumstantial evidence convincingly implicates someone within the Vatican behind the bombing intending to kill Emma Nicoletti that caused the death of her American colleague. The reason for the attacks on Nicoletti stemmed from attempts at recovering documents stolen from the Vatican Secret Archive. The documents that later appeared in the *New York Times*. Those documents added further weight to allegations against the IOR.

"While the two attacks on Nicoletti were the work of Sicilian Mafiosi, the Mafia had no knowledge of missing Secret Archive documents, or their importance. Therefore, it had no direct interest in recovering the missing documents. Only the Vatican had such an interest. That clearly points to Archbishop Tagliente. Head of the Archive. Operational head of Vatican intelligence. His subordinate Monsignor Donaggio has regularly been making clandestine contacts with the Sicilian Mafia according to senior Italian police sources. Archbishop Tagliente is familiar with finance. Enough to understand that the bankers Michele Sindona and subsequently Roberto Calvi were actively engaged in money laundering vast sums of Mafia illicit money.

"The Guardia di Finanza believes the Mafia has been forced to seek new methods of laundering money with the collapse of the financial empires of Sindona and Calvi. They believe the IOR has now become directly involved with the Mafia in these illicit financial ventures to replace prior arrangements with Sindona and Calvi. For reasons beyond much of his control, Archbishop Marcinkus regrettably fell victim to the machinations of those criminal bankers. If the authorities are correct about Vatican involvement it points to Archbishop Tagliente. He possesses a financial background. Successfully inserting his own subordinate Monsignor Auerbach into the IOR gives him direct involvement. As covert operational head of the Vatican secret service, he has covert resources at his disposal without Curia oversight. The case against Archbishop Tagliente is compelling.

"International financial systems involve complex transactions among foreign subsidiaries located in tax haven countries. All major corporations engage in their use to legally reduce tax exposure and seek investment opportunities. Unfortunately, the system offers the perfect opportunity for organized criminal elements to introduce illicit money into the system thereby combining with legitimate financial assets. The process of money laundering. The IOR itself is a tax haven of the utmost secrecy operating autonomously in a sovereign country."

Casaroli's presentation was not lost on John Paul. He might be strong-minded and stubborn, but John Paul also possessed a sharp intellect. Notwithstanding his support for IOR president Marcinkus, John Paul understood the extent of IOR mismanagement and the origin of some of those missteps. That mismanagement continued to plague the Vatican. The confidential stolen documents further implicated him and his predecessor Pope Paul VI with having relationships with individuals later to be proven criminals. He also understood the argument that Tagliente was likely the first to learn of the missing documents. Perhaps earlier than he claimed.

"Thank you, Augustino. I understand your concerns. Those are grave accusations you make against Tagliente. I have many questions. Can you provide more details corroborating your suspicions?"

Turning to Poggi, "I will let Archbishop Poggi elaborate further."

Poggi began, "Your Holiness, at the heart of our concerns is not only the likelihood of involvement with money laundering for the Mafia, but complicity in acts of murder that represents the foremost existential threat to the Holy See. Augustino already cited the murder of the American journalist and attempts on Nicoletti's life. Add to that the murder of a witness in police custody by the Mafia. The victim was a lawyer involved with a Mafia-controlled Palermo bank cooperating with the Guardia di Finanza. The lawyer met regularly with Monsignor Donaggio, photographed clandestinely using a Palermo church confessional for secrecy and a priest as intermediary. The lawyer confessed to the police as being the middleman between the Mafia and the Vatican.

John Paul asked, "Could this not just be the work of Monsignor Donaggio?"

Poggi replied, "Not likely, Your Holiness. The deeds uncovered go well beyond the reach of Monsignor Donaggio. This began with the stolen Archive documents. Donaggio would have no knowledge of that. Add to that a condemning letter written by the priest that removed the documents to cite his concerns over the involvement with the IOR in criminal undertakings. He then willed the documents to the journalist Nicoletti. In his posthumous letter to Nicoletti, he went to great lengths to point her toward Archbishop Tagliente who he knew from working under him for years in the Vatican Secret Archive. Nicoletti published Scarpelli's letter in her book where he makes allegations against Archbishop Tagliente. If nothing else, the letter publicly exposes the existence of the Vatican secret services. Regrettably Monsignor Scarpelli even connected Your Holiness, by speculating that Tagliente's covert actions might serve your purpose. Nicoletti's book therefore eliminates any utility afforded by Tagliente's continued service in his present secretive capacity.

John Paul absorbed Poggi's comments in several moments of silence before turning to Casaroli, "What are you recommending be done, Augustino?"

"Archbishop Tagliente must be removed from his offices. Timing is critical before subsequent events provide further evidence of Vatican collusion with organized crime in money laundering of great sums of money coming from drug trafficking. The Sicilian Mafia represents the principal conduit for smuggling drugs into the United States and Western Europe. Should such evidence become public it would constitute a crisis for the Vatican without precedent. This will go far beyond the damage we have suffered from the years of the continuing financial scandal. The Vatican cannot survive being proven as a participant of such a morally debased conspiracy. The outrage of the faithful cannot be overestimated.

Poggi added, "This can be accomplished without undue fallout. Archbishop Tagliente's responsibilities fall entirely under your direct authority. No other prelate will openly question your decision. To the outside world, this will appear as an organizational change of no earthshaking effect. You shall remain silent from commenting. Like all storms it will eventually spend itself and pass.

"Cardinal Casaroli and I also counsel reorganization of Vatican intelligence. Disband the counterintelligence unit Sodalitium Pianum. The operational excesses of covet S.P. agents have no place within the Holy See. It is anachronism. That means removing Monsignor Donaggio. We shall rely on intelligence gathering solely through our papal nuncios. No secular operational adventurisms. I shall assume control. The move will receive no fanfare since I officially occupy that role currently."

"By removing Archbishop Tagliente and Monsignor Donaggio, how is that to be accomplished?" John Paul asked.

"Reassignment to other church duties outside the Vatican. Assignments where they can do no further harm."

"The reason given?" John Paul asked.

Poggi responded, "None given. Cardinal Casaroli will execute the unpleasant task. We all remain silent."

Poggi detected an almost imperceptible mental shift in John Paul's demeanor. Expecting a forceful pushback, the pope instead appeared to be trying to process their recommendations. Maybe contemplating less extreme measures than simply Tagliente's immediate dismissal.

John Paul said, "Archbishop Tagliente possesses a forceful personality. As you point out, a man used to functioning clandestinely without oversight. What if he chooses not to go gently into retirement?"

Poggi sighed, "That would be unfortunate. Should he lash out, that itself could be harmful. In the course of my investigations, I have uncovered a personal secret that Tagliente would not wish to become public. He is practiced in living and working in the shadows. He would realize that casting himself in the harsh glare of more public scrutiny disconnected by the protection of the Vatican, that secret would undoubtedly be discovered by investigative journalists. A personal indiscretion as a priest that would harm someone close to him if exposed."

John Paul chose not to hear further details. "Is there anything further to add?"

"Just one more loose end, Your Holiness. There exists a certain individual reporting to Monsignor Donaggio. I have met with a priest formerly serving in the Vatican. Someone with thirty years of service in Vatican intelligence, specifically Sodalitium Pianum. He related to me a great deal of disturbing information. Recounting commission of murder by agents of Sodalitium Pianum. Unconscionable acts that occurred during Archbishop's tenure of operational control. This priest has identified an individual agent that has undoubtedly been responsible for recent murders.

John Paul closed his eyes processing what he was hearing. "What is to be done with this individual?"

Poggi replied, "The individual is a lay Jesuit going by the name Brother Gideon. A man with a violent background in the military. Renounced that life with religious fervor. He also is to be reassigned to some distant location away from Rome. Brother Gideon is believed to have committed acts of violence. It is important to ensure his silence. We shall relocate him outside of Rome. It becomes essential to reassure him that his many sins committed in the past have been in the service of the Holy See, however misguided by his trusted ordained superiors. He is a devout Catholic. Believes his unconscionable deeds have been in service to the Church. We provide this letter to be signed by Your Holiness that acknowledges his service and forgives his sins. His penance is observing a vow of eternal silence on penalty of excommunication."

Poggi extracted a short letter on papal stationary, handing it to John Paul. "It requires only your signature. I will personally show Brother Gideon this letter to communicate I am expressing the will of the Holy Father, implicit as speaking for God. However, I shall keep the letter in my possession and destroy it immediately after it has served its purpose."

John Paul's expression might be described as overwhelmed by emotion. Although comfortable in dealing with the challenges of the secular world before his elevation to the throne of Peter, this situation spoke to his larger sense of preserving the Holy See, the universal governing body of the Catholic Church worldwide. It was his duty to shepherd the situation beyond these frightfully damaging circumstances within the Vatican.

The pontiff had viewed Tagliente as an effective tool in dealing with the financial mess and invaluable as a source for directing operations of the Vatican secret services. All while hidden within another layer of Vatican organizational secrecy. However, things continued spinning further out of control. As a pragmatist, John Paul agreed with Cardinal Casaroli that it is time to cut losses and regroup. Tagliente has taken the Vatican far afield of its spiritual foundation by engaging debased activities. Whether by ambition or misplaced objectives becomes irrelevant. Publicly exposed he loses his importance.

The pope remained silent for a moment before acknowledging his agreement with what Casaroli and Poggi proposed by a nod of his head. In a grave soft voice, John Paul said, "Archbishop Tagliente has served us well. Let his personal sacrifice bring an end to unfortunate intrigue and error. Do as you must Agustino."

Taking the letter addressed to Brother Gideon, John Paul signed it with a flourish using a pen offered by Poggi, then handing the letter back to Poggi.

John Paul signaled the end of the audience by saying, "I thank you both for your diligence in this unpleasant matter. It cannot be easy for either of you. Go now with God's blessing, my dear friends."

Taking their dismissal, the two churchmen rose and kissed John Paul's ring. The pope remained seated and appeared deflated as they left, as they quietly closed the door behind them.

Once down the hallway of the papal apartment out of earshot, Casaroli stopped. "As detestable as all this is, we are also deceiving the Holy Father. Do you wonder how he will react when events play out differently from what he expects?"

"In all of this, that concern is ever present. Perhaps deceiving he Holy Father by our sin of omission saddens me the most."

Casaroli nodded in commiseration. "You will set things in motion with Monsignor Orsini, Luigi?"

"Immediately, Augustino."

†

Seated once again at the trattoria Hostaria Farnese with Monsignor Orsini, Poggi said, "The time has arrived for moving forward, Monsignor Orsini. Cardinal Casaroli and I met privately with Pope John Paul. We laid out the evidence. Sufficiently convincing since he agreed to removing Archbishop Tagliente and Monsignor Donaggio."

"Removal by what means?" Orsini asked.

"Something less dramatic than what we have in mind by using Brother Gideon. The Holy Father would never consent to such an extreme measure. We simply recommended removing Tagliente from his Vatican positions. All of which report directly to the pontiff. The Curia need not be involved or even told in advance. With the ability for His Holiness to stand silent, he believes this provides a way to eliminate further misdeeds by Tagliente. Cardinal Casaroli and I do not share that as a viable solution. Tagliente will not go quietly. He thrives on power and will not relinquish it without causing a catastrophic public scandal. Therefore, we stand guilty of deceiving the Holy Father."

Orsini responded, "Perhaps I might offer the more charitable view that you removed the burden of such a decision from the shoulders of the Holy Father. A selfless act for devout princes of the Church. I agree with you and Cardinal Casaroli that there is no other option if we expect to steer the Vatican on a truer course. Are you then giving me instructions to proceed as we discussed?"

"That is correct, Monsignor. Now that the decision is made, how soon can this be accomplished?"

"I have given much thought on exactly how this can be accomplished while disguised as an accident. More difficult to execute, but preferable to attributing the incident as just another violent crime. I need not trouble explaining the details to you, however, it relies on Brother Gideon's willing participation. He must determine the timing. Do you have a letter signed by the Holy Father sufficient for him to betray his current superiors?"

Reaching inside his suit jacket, Poggi extracted an envelope handing it to Orsini.

4 December 1982
Brother Gideon.

Your years of service to the Holy See have just recently come to my attention. That those services involved terribly sinful acts, I understand you were obeying instructions from a prince of the Catholic Church believing those acts necessary to protect the Church. Those instructions were entirely false. Either misguided acts of error or venal acts of personal ambition.

Yet, I and others believe you acted in accordance with your devotion to the Faith. Nonetheless, these are sins of the most abhorrent nature. I therefore call on you to make amends by making your confession of all your crimes to Archbishop Poggi. Archbishop Poggi has been elevated to officially head all Vatican secret service functions and becomes your new superior. Archbishop Poggi shall speak for me. Therefore, he indirectly speaks for God.

Confess your sins and I empower Archbishop Poggi to give you absolution for your past sins regardless of how dreadful those acts may have been, provided you make atonement according to his direction. Your penance is to forever remain silent on the penalty of excommunication should you ever speak of this to anyone.

May God bless you, my son. Go in peace finding a new life in righteous service to God.

Bishop of Rome

Joannes Paulus II

Orsini replied after reading the letter. "So, you have volunteered to directly participate in this, Your Excellency? Face Brother Gideon and command him to betray Archbishop Tagliente? You realize there is a very real personal risk if I have misread Brother Gideon's loyalties?"

"Indeed. All of us share in that risk, Monsignor. This desperate venture is fraught with nothing but unknown risks. If we are successful, it will only be because of God's intervention and the devotion of you and your fellow priests, Monsignor."

"Thank you. I suggest a meeting with Brother Gideon. The same arrangement as our first meeting. Among empty pews at a church. Just the three of us. The church I have in mind is Santo Spirito on Via dei Penitenzieri just a short walk outside the Vatican."

"I know this church. Why there?" Poggi asked.

"That is the church Brother Gideon frequents. He attends seven o'clock mass most mornings. Puts him close to the Vatican where his official duties conveniently require his regular presence. Tomorrow is a Monday, probably a lightly intended mass at that hour. Can you be there?"

"I shall be there."

"Should Brother Gideon attend, I shall approach him following the conclusion of mass by telling him to remain because an important churchman wishes to speak to him privately. Gideon should recognize me from years ago when I served in Sodalitium Pianum. Stay out of sight and watch me. After the congregants vacate the pews look for me to signal you to join me and Brother Gideon. For this meeting dress in the amaranth-colored sash and zucchetto of an archbishop with your heavy pectoral cross. Remember you are sitting in for the Holy Father. Play the part appropriately by exhibiting authority. You are here to literally scare the devil out of him, Your Excellency. Enough for him to act against his instincts of loyalty serving Tagliente."

"I shall be there tomorrow. If Brother Gideon does not show at the church, then what?"

"We then try the next day and every day until he does."

CHAPTER 32

Rome, Italy | Autumn 1982

Archbishop Poggi arrived at Santo Spirito at 6:45am Monday morning. Dressed as instructed by Monsignor Orsini in the colors of his elevated rank, he wore an overcoat to conceal his identity as a prince of the church with his amaranth zucchetto in his pocket. He stood in the toward the back of the nave. To the side aisle of the sparsely occupied pews, he observed Monsignor Orsini standing alone. Both acknowledged each other by a slight nod. Poggi then took a seat in the last pew furthest from the altar.

A few minutes before the hour Poggi observed Orsini leave his standing position in the aisle. He followed a man in his forties dressed in a cassock who took a seat in a middle pew otherwise unoccupied by congregants. As Orsini took a seat next to the man, Poggi could see a look of surprise as the man turned toward Orsini. The men exchanged words before the mass began and both fell silent throughout the mass.

Before the conclusion of the mass, by prior arrangement with Orsini, Poggi left his seat and walked to a position near three confessional booths. Shedding his overcoat, Poggi fixed the distinctive amaranth zucchetto on his head and unbuttoned his suit jacket. The pectoral cross and the colorful sash at his waist signified his lofty ecclesiastical rank.

As Orsini guided Brother Gideon to Poggi who extended his hand inviting the kissing of the bishop's ring. With a stern countenance, Poggi said, "I am Archbishop Luigi Poggi, Brother Gideon. The Holy Father has sent me to personally hear your confession."

Having just kissed Poggi's ring Brother Gideon looked up in surprise. "My confession, Your Excellency?"

"That is correct, my son. We have weighty matters that must be discussed. I shall explain everything. Following that, you will make your confession to me as directed by the Holy Father."

Brother Gideon stood speechless. His expression revealed confusion as he struggled to comprehend what was happening.

Poggi began by saying, "The Holy Father has selected me to assume responsibility for Santa Alleanza, or the term the *Entity* used by some. His Holiness has charged me with a sacred mission. It has been discovered that Archbishop Tagliente has betrayed his vows as a priest and committed great sins that threaten the Holy See. You, Brother Gideon, have been the instrument of assisting Tagliente in unholy acts of violence. Yet the Holy Father understands you have been deceived by Archbishop Tagliente and his dark emissary Monsignor Donaggio by unwittingly participating in a conspiracy. Should the details of that conspiracy become known, it would vilify the Holy See in the eyes of the faithful around the world.

"That must not be allowed to happen, Brother Gideon. The Holy Father has decried that Archbishop Tagliente and Monsignor Donaggio must be removed. Because the nature of their transgressions can never be revealed they must be eliminated in a manner that buries forever their evil conspiracy.

"The Holy Father has issued what is called a decretal letter. This letter is addressed specifically to you, Brother Gideon. Something exceptionally unusual. It shall remain secret.

"The Holy Father recognizes that you have unwittingly been misguided. However, you are not without personal guilt. Your redemption is contingent upon making atonement. Therefore, I am charging you to be the instrument in eliminating Archbishop Tagliente and Monsignor Donaggio in a manner that safeguards the Holy See.

"Quoting from my 17th century predecessor heading Santa Alleanza, Cardinal Paluzzi, *if the pope orders the elimination of someone in defense of the faith, this is carried out without question. It is God's voice and we of Santa Alleanza are his right hand*. Read the letter directed to you personally and signed by His Holiness, Brother Gideon."

Poggi handed him the letter.

After Gideon read the letter, Poggi held out his hand for its return. "Are you ready to make your confession to me, Brother Gideon?"

"Yes, Your Excellency."

"Very well. Monsignor Orsini, will you accompany us to the confessional?"

Orsini gently guided a compliant and subdued Brother Gideon by the arm toward the confessional booth where Gideon and Archbishop Poggi entered into their respective places.

Brother Gideon began with substituting the normal entreaty of *Father* with *Your Excellency* in deference to Poggi's status, "Bless me, Your Excellency, for I have sinned. It has been a very long time since making my last confession."

"Why have you avoided confession, my son?"

Gideon hesitated, "On instructions from my superior, a bishop. He declared that what I have been called on to do comes from a higher authority and must never be revealed to anyone, including even a priest in confessional."

"Why are you now willing to confess these sins to me?"

"I must obey a direct order from the Holy Father. His authority overrides all others.?"

"Do you seek absolution, Brother Gideon?"

"Yes, Your Excellency."

"Please then proceed with the confessing of your sins."

Thirty minutes later Brother Gideon's confession concluded. Poggi had asked many questions as his only opportunity to learn firsthand of the violent acts committed by Gideon. Poggi constrained his disgust after hearing the disturbing details of Gideon's confession.

Poggi said, "Now pray the act of contrition, my son."

Gideon recited the conventional prayer "O my God, I am heartily sorry for having offended Thee, and I detest all my sins because of thy just punishments, but most of all because they offend Thee, my God, who art all good and deserving of all my love. I firmly resolve, with the help of Thy grace, to sin no more and to avoid the near occasion of sin. Amen."

"You have read the declaration of the Holy Father for what must be done to receive absolution. Do you know what is now required of you?"

"Yes, Your Excellency. I am to eliminate Archbishop Tagliente and Monsignor Donaggio for the sake of the Faith as instructed by the Holy Father."

"His Holiness has vested in me the manner in which that is to be accomplished. It must appear as an accident or at the least an act by others completely unconnected with the Vatican. How that is to be done will be determined by you under the guidance of Monsignor Orsini. You will obey Monsignor Orsini's instructions to the letter as emanating from the Holy Father speaking for God. Is that understood and do you accept absolution contingent upon fulfilling this designated act of atonement?"

"I understand and accept what I must do to make atonement, Your Excellency."

Poggi responded with the Fuller prayer of absolution, "May our Lord and God, Jesus Christ, through the grace and mercies of his love for humankind, forgive you all your transgressions. And I, an unworthy priest, by his power given me, forgive and absolve you from all your sins, in the name of the Father and of the Son and of the Holy Spirit. Amen."

Pausing for a moment, Poggi added, "On Wednesday at 10:00 am, you shall receive a personal blessing from the Holy Father. A ticket with your name as part of this week's recipients shall be waiting for you. Take His Holiness' blessing and henceforth as recognition of His trust and forever serve only God though righteous acts."

After a moment's silence, Poggi continued, "We shall not see each again Brother Gideon. Please remain seated. Monsignor Orsini will take my place for you to receive instructions."

Stepping out of the confessional, Poggi turned to Orsini. "Please take my place, Monsignor. Brother Gideon will now receive your instructions. God be you and all of us in this desperate enterprise."

With that, a shaken Archbishop Poggi left the church to walk back to the Vatican and report to Cardinal Casaroli. Although sickened after listening to Brother Gideon recount his acts of violence, Poggio at least felt solace in the justification of what he and Casaroli had set in motion. What would happen next was now in the hands of Monsignor Orsini and the assassin Brother Gideon.

✝

Monsignor Orsini assumed his place within the confessional after Poggi left with Brother Gideon remaining seated on the other side of the partition. "Are you prepared to proceed with this assignment Brother Gideon?"

"I am, Father."

"To appear as an accident, calls for removing Tagliente and Donaggio together. Tagliente's residence is a large house with several levels located in the Piazza Fiammetta. Continual surveillance has shown Donaggio frequently arriving in the evening and remaining for several hours. Considering your past assignments from Donaggio, it seems only fitting their deaths result from an explosion. I will leave the technical details to your expertise. The house is heated by natural gas. Rather than explosives, is it possible to cause a natural gas explosion? Created some sort of fault that will leave forensic evidence pointing to an accidental occurrence?"

"That is possible. If I can gain entry, a gas line could be damaged or loosened to cause a leak. A sufficient volume of gas is required to accumulate sufficient to kill or render the occupants unconscious from the initial explosion. Fire will then consume the entire house. The challenge is to covertly gain entrance to create the source of the leak and to devise a means of delayed timing to allow a sufficient buildup of gas volume. To be ruled as accidental, evidence must exist after the fact to point to an explainable fault causing leaking gas along with a plausible accidental source of ignition."

"This needs to be done as soon as possible. Ideally, within days at the first opportunity when both targets are in the house together. How long before you are able to devise a technical solution?

"I need to examine the location by making a reconnaissance entry. Determine how to achieve an explainable gas leak as a reliable ignition source. Give me forty-eight hours."

"Very well, Brother Gideon. One final warning. You are fortunate being given an opportunity to atone for your crimes. Do not waste that opportunity by thinking you can escape justice. You might get to me, however I think you know that I am not alone in this holy mission. You could never escape no matter where you attempted to hide. Should you go to Tagliente or Donaggio and reveal any of this, they will also deem you expendable. They have unlimited proxy resources in the Sicilian Mafia. Unlike you, crude but effective killers. Their reach extends beyond Italy. Stay faithful to the Church and obey the Holy Father. Find salvation and you will live out your days in peace. Return here on Wednesday. I expect to hear your plan for accomplishing your mission."

†

Two days later Orsini was waiting when Brother Gideon arrived for the 7:00am mass at Santo Spirito. He watched as Gideon took communion. At the end of mass, they met next to the confessional booths. This time there were others waiting to make their confessions.

Orsini said, "We shall talk outside."

Brother Gideon dressed in cassock stood next to Orsini. Just two churchmen conversing outside a Catholic church. "I made entry into Archbishop Tagliente's home by picking the lock of a rear door. Dressed in a uniform of a gas company technician should anyone observe my presence in the piazza. Waited until the housekeeper left. Made a thorough survey. I determined how this can be done."

"Housekeeper?" Orsini said.

"She has a room on the ground level," Gideon said.

Orsini had not anticipated that the secretive Tagliente might have a live-in housekeeper. An unfortunate complication. An innocent casualty was exceedingly troubling. "How do you propose to accomplish this?"

Gideon continued. "The house is supplied with natural gas for the furnace and water heater, located in a utility room with laundry facilities off the kitchen. The rear door I used for entry accesses directly into this utility room.

"I have purchased a piece of black pipe to replace a section of the gas line as it feeds to the furnace. Loosened the existing pipe section slightly in preparation. I am treating the replacement pipe with sulfuric acid to simulate deterioration by corrosion at the threaded pipe ends. The acid at one spot will be allowed to eat completely through the metal allowing me to break out a small section enough to allow gas to freely escape..

"For the ignition source, I will install a replacement light switch with the contacts modified to generate an arc when turned on. Once the utility room fills with gas the smell will seep under the door and begin permeating throughout the house. Natural gas has only half the density of air therefore it will rise rapidly.

"Once the housekeeper or someone else smells the odor of gas, they will immediately enter the darkened utility room to investigate. The light switch inside the utility room is located next to the door. Depending on the amount of gas released, the occupants should die from the force of the explosive pressure blast, but assuredly from the resulting fire. Flames will fully engulf the house before arrival of fire fighters."

Orsini absorbed Gideon's explanation of how he planned to kill people delivered in technical terms devoid of emotion. Thinking this to be expected from a professional assassin, Orsini asked, "Will this appear as an accident?"

"It should. However, that depends on the thoroughness of the examination for the source of the fire by an expert. The weak link is the pipe section. The damage by acid to simulate failure through corrosion will not stand up to chemical analysis. The ignition source as worn contacts of light switch is a common source of accidental gas explosions."

Orsini nodded. "You are then ready once Donaggio joins Tagliente at his house some night?"

"Yes. I shall set up continual surveillance beginning before dark starting tonight. Every night thereafter until Donaggio joins Tagliente."

Orsini replied, "I shall join you in that surveillance."

†

The opportunity arrived three nights later. Orsini and Brother Gideon sat in a car among other cars parked on Via delgi Acquasparta only a hundred meters from the front of Tagliente's large house visible at the end of the street.

They observed the arrival of Monsignor Donaggio who parked his car in front of Tagliente's home and ringing the doorbell. Waiting fifteen minutes after Donaggio entered, Brother Gideon left the car. He wore his gas company uniform disguise and carried a small toolbox. Inside there were tools and the modified items necessary for creating the *accidental explosion.*

Thirty minutes later, Gideon returned to the car. "We should relocate well back down the street. Once the explosion occurs, we must leave this confined parking area before police and fire vehicles arrive and block us in.

A tense hour passed before Tagliente's house erupted in a massive explosion that rocked the car. The blast destroyed the entire house with the top floor and roof collapsing into the debris from the lower levels now consumed in flames. Windows of nearby buildings and parked cars were blown out.

The blast location just north of the popular Piazza Navona drew immediate response with police sirens descending toward the area. Convinced there could be no survivors, Orsini and Gideon drove away.

Driving a battered old sedan, Orsini headed across the river the River Tiber crossing at the Port Umberto I bridge. Pulling into a parking lot next to the river, he turned to Brother Gideon, "You must discard those tools and your uniform coveralls. Throw everything into the river. I shall walk with you so that you can make your vow of silence to me. I shall then give you my benediction and instructions. You are to leave Rome in the morning. Come to your usual morning mass at Santo Spirito. Prepare your belongings ready to leave by train. Your destination is to be a Jesuit monastery in the north of Italy. Tomorrow, I will provide you with the necessary information, documents, letter of recommendation, and sufficient money for you to live well.

They both walked down the steps to the river. Orsini then said, "Remove the coveralls and stuff them into the toolbox. Then throw it into the river."

After Gideon complied, Orsini said, "Now kneel before me to make your vow of eternal silence about the matters of tonight and receive my benediction and absolution as granted by the Holy Father."

Orsini placed his left hand on Gideon's head as he knelt on the concrete pavement under the bridge. With his right hand, Orsini extracted a .32 caliber pistol then shot Gideon in the temple. As Gideon toppled over. Orsini fired another round to the forehead delivering the coup de grâce.

With effort, Orsini dragged the body of Brother Gideon to a place allowing him to push it into the Tiber. Orsini's last act was to wipe his fingerprints from the pistol tossing it well out into the river followed by making the sign of the cross.

†

This news of the explosion resulting in the deaths of a senior Vatican archbishop and two others in the center of Rome made international headlines the following day. Cardinal Casaroli paid a visit to Pope John Paul very early in the morning.

Before uttering a greeting to John Paul, the pope said, "An extraordinary development, Augustino. The news reports a gas explosion. Most unfortunate but it certainly settles matters better left buried. Thank God."

Casaroli was surprised by John Paul's reaction. The problem was now prevented from worsening. Still a long period of recovery while remaining steadfast in denial and silence, but manageable. Hopefully, His Holiness could never conceive that his two most trusted churchmen might have engineered Tagliente's death.

Casaroli said, "Regrettable that lives were lost, especially the innocent housekeeper. Perhaps God sought to remove this problem from our inadequate hands, Holy Father. It is not for us to fathom how such events happen. That the Church was spared another crisis affecting its spiritual mission is truly a blessing."

Pope John Paul nodded. Whether he believed this to be a fortuitous accidental occurrence, he chose not to raise any awkward questions. "We shall move forward in divine guidance. More vigilant I should pray in resisting intrusion of questionable outside secular forces."

†

Frank Amatrano and Emma Nicoletti experienced mixed feelings. Some unknown hand delivered appropriate justice on Tagliente and Donaggio. Divine intervention or someone else's doing? Yet, without a public accounting of corruption in the Vatican Bank concealed by the self-serving secrecy culture within the Vatican, the episode would pass into history as yet another unresolved mystery. No reason to expect change. Like other scandals of the Roman Catholic Church, the episode would blur by the passing of time.

Emma Nicoletti felt vindicated even with the fortuitous but unsatisfying conclusion to her long ordeal. Enough to turn herself from journalism to creative writing. Intrigued by trying her hand at fiction having already made a good beginning to her first novel.

Satisfied with his accomplishments since returning to Italy, Frank Amatrano looked to the time that he could put dealing with the Sicilian Mafia behind him. Having found Emma, he wanted to live a more normal life. A return to Paris seemed like an achievable objective. They both spoke about it often. He would find a way to return to Paris. Perhaps a return to Interpol. He still had enough years ahead before retiring professionally. His baptism in violence serving in Italian law enforcement satisfied whatever motivation existed for direct involvement. On balance the Italian venture proved overwhelmingly rewarding especially with Emma becoming part of his life.

†

The removal of Archbishop Tagliente did not eliminate the Vatican secret service. For Pope John Paul II, the Vatican simply retreated further into secrecy by ignoring the allegations about illicit financial mismanagement. Vatican, Inc. would continue. The Vatican Bank was simply too valuable as a source of revenue while subject to secrecy as directed solely by the pope. Marcinkus remained president of the IOR, albeit now with oversight from a committee of cardinals. Monsignor Auerbach was reassigned outside the Vatican without explanation.

The unassailable secrecy of the Vatican Bank within an ultra-secretive sovereign state made it still one of the most secure and utilitarian tax havens in the world. The perfect institution to obscure the origin of funds and details of complex international financial transactions. The Vatican Bank offered the ultimate service for money laundering, stock manipulation, transactional price manipulation, and currency manipulation of foreign exchange rates.

The Vatican had need of sources of revenue under their direct control with worldwide diocesan contributions to the Vatican in decline. Wealth was necessary for the Holy See to oversee the world's only major religious institution that ruled from a central governing body by a single absolute authority in the form of the pope. The Holy See thereby possessed secular power with influence well beyond its stature as a religious institution spanning almost two millennia with 1.5 billion adherents. Like Rome, the Vatican was eternal.

†

The last surviving principal figure of the Italian Banking Scandal Archbishop Paul Marcinkus remained in his position as President of the Vatican Bank, officially the *Istituto per le Opere di Religione,* the IOR. Whether culpable, mislead, or lacking in financial abilities, he was intimately involved at every turn of the financial scandal as the president of the IOR since 1971.

Perhaps Pope John Paul II stood by Marcinkus for personal reasons. A presumptive attack on the pontiff in Portugal by a disaffected Spanish priest armed with a bayonet was disrupted when the six foot-four muscular Marcinkus pushed him aside. The wounding was denied yet there was evidence of blood.

An avid golfer with a five-stroke handicap, Archbishop Paul Marcinkus was a regular at Rome's Acqasanta Golf Club on Via Appia Nuova. As he left the golf club a week following the death of Tagliente, Marcinkus opened his car door. An envelope lay on the driver's seat. Inside were photographic enlargements from the morgue of the burned remains of Archbishop Tagliente and Monsignor Donaggio. An accompanying note using pasted newspaper headline cutouts to spell a message reading, *DIVINE RETRIBUTION? CAST OUT THE EVIL WITHIN THE IOR. WE ARE WATCHING.*

www.ingramcontent.com/pod-product-compliance
Lightning Source LLC
Chambersburg PA
CBHW032142010726
47494CB00002B/325

* 9 7 8 1 6 3 8 6 8 1 9 6 0 *